Stella Quinn has had a love affair with books since she first discovered the alphabet. She lives in sunny Queensland now but has lived in England, Hong Kong and Papua New Guinea. Boarding school in a Queensland country town left her with a love of small towns and heritage buildings (and a fear of chenille bedspreads and meatloaf!) and that is why she loves writing rural romance. Stella is a keen scrabble player, she's very partial to her four kids and anything with four furry feet, and she is a mediocre grower of orchids. An active member of Romance Writers of Australia, Stella has won their Emerald, Sapphire and Valerie Parv awards and was a finalist in their Romantic Book of the Year award.

You can find and follow Stella Quinn at stellaquinnauthor.com.

## Also by Stella Quinn

*The Vet From Snowy River*
*A Town Like Clarence*

# A HOME *among* THE SNOW GUMS

## STELLA QUINN

FICTION
HQ

First Published 2023
First Australian Paperback Edition 2023
ISBN 9781867255697

A HOME AMONG THE SNOW GUMS
©2023 by Stella Quinn
Australian Copyright 2023
New Zealand Copyright 2023

This is a work of fiction. Names, characters, places, and incidents are either the product of the author's imagination or are used fictitiously, and any resemblance to actual persons, living or dead, business establishments, events, or locales is entirely coincidental.

Published by
HQ Fiction
An imprint of Harlequin Enterprises (Australia) Pty Limited (ABN 47 001 180 918), a subsidiary of HarperCollins Publishers Australia Pty Limited (ABN 36 009 913 517)
Level 19, 201 Elizabeth St
SYDNEY NSW 2000
AUSTRALIA

® and TM (apart from those relating to FSC®) are trademarks of Harlequin Enterprises (Australia) Pty Limited or its corporate affiliates. Trademarks indicated with ® are registered in Australia, New Zealand and in other countries.

A catalogue record for this book is available from the National Library of Australia
www.librariesaustralia.nla.gov.au

Printed and bound in Australia by McPherson's Printing Group

MIX
Paper | Supporting responsible forestry
FSC
www.fsc.org    FSC® C001695

*For Elliot.*
*Welcome to the world, mate. I'm looking forward*
*to reading you loads of bedtime stories.*

The story of campdrafting in Australia is one that begins, like the best stories do, by the campfire. Cast your mind back more than a hundred years and you'll find cattle musters the length and breadth of this country. Picture the stockmen washing down the red dust of a long day with a swig of rum, the stars looping through the night sky above like a whip unfurled. Maybe a grizzled bloke in a leather waistcoat cracks a joke. Maybe a ragged-looking kid who joined them at Cloncurry or Windorah or Boulia—no-one can quite remember now, they've been droving so long—plays a few notes on a battered harmonica.

And then … a ringer makes an idle boast about his horse.

'No bloody way,' says his mate. 'That cross-eyed sack of bones cut a heifer from the herd? Spark a stampede, more like. My horse, on the other hand …'

The bets are laid—a coin, a kangaroo-skin pouch of tobacco, a flask (quarter full) that might have once been silver and has an inscription on it that only Andy can read on account of him having been trapped into school-ing by some slap-handed nuns when he was little—and the ringers saddle up, there and then, to test their mettle.

And so a sport is born.

Campdrafting today is a more formal event, with rules and judges, and a lot less rum. A horse and rider compete to 'cut out' and 'turn' one steer or heifer from a mob of cattle in a yard known as 'the camp'; they then continue into a larger arena in which posts are staked in the dirt. Once in the arena, the horse and rider have forty seconds to drive the beast through a series of turns to form a figure 8, then through two close-set posts, known as 'the gate'.

*Points of 100 are possible, being 70 for horsemanship, 26 for the 'cut out' and 4 for completing the course. Disqualification in the arena occurs when a rider and horse lose control of their steer (or heifer), or drive it into a fence, or when the horse turns its tail in the opposite direction of the beast.*

*Campdrafting demands grit and determination of its riders, and requires one hell of a fine horse.*

From *Legends on Horseback* by Bruno Krauss,
Ironbark Station Stockhorses,
NSW Open Champion 1986–1992, 1995, 1998
Southern District Campdrafters Newsletter Archives

# CHAPTER
# 1

'Knitting *possums*?'

Hannah Cody was on her second (okay, maybe third, but they were stingy pours) paper cup of prosecco, but surely she hadn't heard Marigold correctly.

'Knitting pouches for possums, my love. Orphaned baby ones. All knit no purl, so it's a perfect beginner's project. Craft is like honey, isn't it, Vera? Sweet for the soul, balm for a wound.'

Vera De Rossi, Hannah's soon-to-be sister-in-law, was smooshed up against Hannah's brother Josh on the weathered trunk of a fallen snow gum, a fat brown dog sprawled over her boots. She was gazing up at the stars above Lake Bogong and avoided being drawn into the conversation by pretending she hadn't heard.

Traitor.

'I'm sweet enough, thanks, Marigold,' Hannah said. A lie, and everyone on the rocky lakeside within hearing distance knew it.

Best not to think about wounds, either. Not tonight. Marigold had been in her ear all week, wittering on about New Year's Eve being ripe with change and possibilities and, somehow, like a pernicious dose of tinnitus, the town's busiest senior citizen's words had stuck.

*Change.*

The idea that change might be possible, and wounds could be left behind, was why Hannah was here at the lake, mingling like a socialite while green and gold fireworks fizzed and popped in the night sky, rather than celebrating the closure of another safe year in the traditional way: in her bathtub with a book.

A clutch of kids raced past, the sparklers in their hands jumping and weaving like star puppets long after the kids' silhouettes had dissolved into the darkness. Hannah's heart grew a little heavier in her chest.

Marigold was right.

Not about the knitting. But about her desire for her life to change.

Safe had become boring. And lonely. And very, very dull.

Hannah followed Vera's gaze up to the night sky and wondered if Josh's fiancée saw the same things she saw. Vera had made her home in the lee of the mountains only recently, but Hannah? Hanrahan had always been her home. The sand was coarse and familiar under the heels of her old boots, and the stars above burned like the porch lights of old friends, brighter even than the driftwood bonfires along the lakeshore.

And beyond the lake, the mountains.

She couldn't see the Snowies now, of course, but she knew they were there. She *felt* them. Strong, resolute, steadfast: they were the backbone that she pretended to have oh so much of.

'Pondering your resolutions, love?' said Kev, Marigold's husband. He'd dressed up for the lakeside festivities in a double-breasted plaid suit that made him look like a newsreader on the television, back before colour was invented.

'Hi, Kev,' she said, and glugged down another mouthful of the cheap prosecco she'd bought from one of the food trucks up on the grass. 'I've already picked one,' she said. 'Make sure Josh gets more of the vet clinic's middle-of-the-night callouts.'

Her brother pulled a face at her then went back to nuzzling his fiancée's neck.

Revolting. Okay, fine, it was sweet. Yay them.

'I've been giving Hannah some suggestions but she's proving to be a little stubborn,' said Marigold.

Josh snorted. 'There's a surprise.'

'Joining my craft group is not only social and fun, it's useful, too.' Marigold was on a roll. 'Dawn yoga is always an option, of course. There's nothing like saluting the sun under the watchful eye of the pied currawongs to give your day a little zhoozh. Life hacks, I believe these sorts of resolutions are called these days, by the young and the trendy.'

Hannah grinned. 'I'm not that trendy.' Then her grin slipped; she wasn't that young, either, now that she thought about it. Her birthday was only a few months away and as much as she'd been trying to not think about the age she'd be turning, her headspace was not cooperating and the words *thirty-two, thirty-two, thirty-two* had been playing in an annoying loop.

'You rode dressage when you were a youngster, as I recall,' said Kev.

That was quite the conversational segue. 'Um, yeah. Fancy you remembering. Tubby and I took it very seriously when I was about eleven or twelve. But then his owner came back from boarding school and Tubby didn't need me to exercise him anymore, so that was the end of my competitive horse-riding career.'

'Maybe not.'

'What are you getting at, Kev? I'm starting to wonder if you're going soft in the head,' said his doting wife.

'Now, now,' he said. 'I've had one of my ideas.'

'Oh,' said Marigold, delighted. 'Let's hear it.'

'That horse of yours, Hannah, that's been living in our back paddock these last coupla months ever since you had your tantrum up at Ironbark, sticking his head through the fence rails and helping himself to my apple tree … I reckon he's got some skills.'

'I do not have tantrums,' Hannah said, sinking her nose into her paper cup of warming wine in case it decided to grow an inch. How did Kev know about that, anyway? She'd spun a totally feasible story about why she'd had to move Skippy to a stable nearer to town. It hadn't been a tantrum she'd had up at Ironbark, anyway. It had been a *crisis* … um, no, that wasn't right. It had been a *shock* and *alarming* and *out of the freaking blue*, but also weirdly *thrilli—*

She kicked the back of the log Josh and Vera were snuggling up on, making the lump of a dog grunt in annoyance. Whatever The Incident had been, it was Tom Krauss's fault, and she'd spent a goodly time since instructing herself to block out the memories. She wasn't about to relive them now, right when she was on the cusp of putting all that … stuff … behind her and starting a new year.

She answered the part of Kev's statement that hadn't started her insides churning. 'Of course Skipjack has skills. He spent his youth mustering sheep at a station out past Ruffy in country Victoria. He probably knows more about sheep and kelpies and barber's pole worm than I do.'

'Han, no-one wants to hear about barber's pole worm.'

Huh. Josh could apparently listen *and* canoodle *and* be handfed morsels of some delicious-looking dessert from the tin on Vera's lap. Life was so not fair.

'This resolution you're deciding on,' said Kev, 'I reckon camp-drafting's the one you're after.'

Even Marigold was silenced by that announcement.

'Pony competitions as a kid don't really qualify me for cutting cattle from a herd on horseback, Kev. Besides, I'm not too flush with cash or time. I can't buy a horse float or spend my weekends traipsing all over New South Wales and Victoria.'

'None of that matters, pet. You can ride, can't you?'

She narrowed her eyes. 'I can ride the pants off you, old timer.'

Kev chuckled. 'Now, don't get all antsy. What I'm saying is, there's a lot of campdraft tournaments hereabouts in Tumbarumba and Adaminaby and Bombala. You've got a horse who's not so long in the tooth he won't enjoy a little excitement once in a while. And—as it happens—I used to compete myself back in the day. Be happy to teach you the timing rules when the roses at the hall aren't calling out for their Uncle Kev.'

'That's super sweet of you, but I—'

'You'll be wondering where we'll scratch up some cattle to prac-tise with, but don't you worry about that. I've got plenty of space to agist and plenty of mates to assist.'

Kev was serious about this. Learning a new sport? Doable. But competing against strangers? Complicated. Travelling out of Hanra-han, where the looming peaks of the Snowy Mountains weren't there to back her up against failure?

Yeah. That was the issue. Travelling away from home had, over the years, become somehow heart-poundingly difficult.

She must have looked as overwhelmed as she felt, because Mari-gold gave her arm a pat.

'No rush to pick,' she said. 'It's not midnight for hours yet, plenty of time to narrow down your choices.' Marigold lifted a hand and started ticking off on her fingers. 'Campdrafting, which will be outside, the wind in your hair, your horse's mane in your hand. Crafting a snuggly safe space for orphan possums, which—'

Hannah decided to stop her before one of the tantrums she'd just told the world she never had started brewing. 'If you're going to start talking about the joy to be found in preserving historical whatnots or the wonder of double triple treble crochet, you're going to have to find your own patch of Lake Bogong foreshore, Marigold.'

A massive hip bumped up against Hannah's. 'But you've bagged the good spot close to the bar.'

She chuckled. 'True.'

'And much as I love a little creativity in my craft group, I feel obliged to point out that there is no such thing as double triple treble crochet. A double treble *is* a triple. Just FYI.'

Whatever. The minutiae of craft terms was something Hannah had zero desire to master. She was only marginally more interested in the rules of campdrafting.

'Besides, pet, you won't know how wonderful a new interest can be until you try it. Saluting the sun is the best part of my day.'

'I get to salute the sun often enough. I'm usually in a paddock at the time, half frozen and covered in muck. Fancy a vino?' she said, waggling her paper cup in Marigold's direction. 'My shout.'

'I'll have what you're having. Kevvy?'

Armed with drink orders, Hannah picked her way up the foreshore to where the food trucks were serving up a storm under the party lights. As she was paying for two beers, a water and two proseccos, a border terrier with a lead trailing behind it like an angry snake tore past her.

Wait. Was that—?

It was. A new client, who she'd met last month after an escape attempt through rusty barbed wire led to an intervention involving pliers and a tetanus jab. The owner was currently on the list Sandy, the clinic receptionist, had taped to the wall above the photocopier in the back office with the heading CAUTION: HASN'T PAID VET FEES.

'Millie,' Hannah called. 'Millie! Come!'

The dog stopped. Its shaggy body was heaving and its face wore the pop-eyed look that she didn't need a vet degree to know meant it was terrified. Fireworks. The border terrier wouldn't be the only dog in town currently being sent loopy by the noise, but hopefully she was the only one who had done a runner.

Ignoring the drinks that were now lined up on the counter, Hannah took off after the dog, who had bounded past a stand selling sparklers and glow-in-the-dark bracelets and was on a trajectory to crash headlong into a woman who had a baby on her hip and a kid swinging from her hand.

'Millie!' Hannah called again and lunged forward to put her boot on the trailing lead.

Just as she landed on it, a large figure loomed in the corner of her eye from the far side of the sparklers' stand. Their boot landed smack bang on top of hers.

'Oof,' she said, fighting to recover her balance, while a hand (most definitely *not* hers) landed on her rump and set her upright.

'Sorry,' said a deep voice in her ear that was delicious and totally irritating all at the same time, and which eroded every thought in her head other than *Bloody Tom Krauss*. Even the pulverised toes in her left boot forgot they were in pain.

'It's gonna bite me! It's gonna bite me real bad!' wailed a high-pitched voice.

'I'll get the dog,' said Tom.

Bossy and dictatorial as ever. She shot a look up at his face and— yes, damn it—he hadn't grown ugly since she last saw him, which was bloody selfish of him. Uglying himself up a little was the least he could do after the way he—

Well. No need to dwell on The Incident. That was in the past, but for the love of god, why couldn't he just stay up the mountain so she didn't have to feel this weird *thing* every time she saw him? And, hang on just a darned minute, *she* was the animal professional in the vicinity.

'*I'll* get the dog,' she said. 'I'll have the owner's number back at the clini—'

Too late, Tom was hauling in the uncooperative dog like he was reeling in a marlin. Hannah turned to the mother, who was attempting to bend down to the boy. The little bloke's knee was skinned and he was sitting on the grass having himself a good noisy cry.

'You okay?' Hannah said to the mum.

'Do I look okay?' said the woman, who seemed as flustered as Hannah felt, although for different (she assumed) reasons. She was a local, Hannah knew her face, but she couldn't place her. 'Here, take Margot, will you?'

And before Hannah knew what was what, she'd been given a baby.

'Oh, I'm not sure I know how to look after your kid—' She stopped talking as the baby put up a hand the size of a cat's paw and patted her cheek with it. That was kind of sweet. She did an experimental sway from side to side, the way she did when she had a fractious pup on her hands who was objecting to being separated from its mastitis-inflamed mother. The baby gurgled, which was also sweet, and way nicer to listen to than the wails coming from the bigger kid.

She looked over at Tom. He had somehow managed to get the naughty dog to sit down beside the toddler, and he'd lowered himself onto one of the copper log barriers that demarked the carpark from the foreshore.

He wore a faded plaid shirt and well broken-in jeans and his hair had grown out since she'd last seen him. He was blonder. Thinner. Paler. He also looked annoyingly adorable, perched on the rail next to the kid and the dog.

'You need to learn to keep a hold of your dog, mate,' said the mother, who was patting the kid's bloody knee with a tissue that she had just—OMG—spat on. Really, did the general populace know nothing about germs?

'I'm not the owner,' Tom said, but he wasn't paying much attention to the mother. 'Hey, kid, what's your name?'

The kid stopped wailing like he had an on/off switch. 'Barney.'

'You want to pat the dog, Barney? She's being good now.'

'She knocked me over.'

'That's because she was scared before, like you were. Now she wants to make it all better.'

Hmm. Tom was handling the kid crisis. Well, he could handle the lost dog, too, and with a bit of luck, she'd be long gone from the beach before he returned from tracking down the owner.

'You see that man?' she said into the baby's tiny ear like she was sharing a secret—which, in fact, she was. 'The hottie with the scruffy cheeks and the blue, blue eyes? Well, him and me in the same place is bad news.'

The baby burped and it sounded like a question. Who knew babies were such excellent confidants?

'He cuts up my serenity,' she said. 'And I'm too chicken to ask myself why.'

Hannah lifted her head as Marigold swooped up beside her like a flying fox, her floaty top puffing up and out like wings. 'Came to see what was taking you so long, and here you are tripping up handsome men in carparks and pilfering babies.'

'Sorry. Runaway dog drama. I left the drinks on the counter.'

'And who's this little tacker?'

The baby gave a happy squeal then burrowed into the crevice between Hannah's shoulder and neck. Her head was warm and velvety, and sort of strong and soft all at the same time. Like a little cavalier King Charles spaniel. No, like a spring lamb. No, wait … she took a scientific sniff, and soap and milk and babyness wafted up her olfactory nerve.

Like a little *person*.

Hannah forgot about the awkwardness of bumping into Tom. She forgot about her irritation with Millie's owner for losing the dog again. That was all so silly. '*So* silly,' she whispered into the soft hair.

She'd just had an epiphany, and it had tripped her up as surely as the dog had tripped up that toddler. Her subconscious must have been working on it for months, waiting for the right opportunity to pop it out, fully formed. Fully actionable.

She'd been feeling jealous and crotchety about so many things and hadn't stopped to wonder at the root cause. Josh had been devoting himself one hundred per cent to Vera. Her bestie Kylie had taken over the town mechanic's workshop and could rarely be prised from her spanners. Her niece Poppy had started ghosting her (or studying for exams, whatever) when usually she could be relied upon for daily texts and funny memes, and even Graeme, the chattiest person in Hanrahan, had lately had the temerity to preference his partner's company to hers.

It was so obvious. She breathed in another long whiff of baby. So obvious!

She wanted a family of her own. She wanted some mess and fun and love and texting and spanners and handfed morsels of cake *of her own*. Which meant change. Action.

Personal growth.

Huh. No wonder her subconscious had waited until she was tiddly on prosecco to spring the trap.

But what was the alternative? Did she want a future that involved endless lonely hours soaking in her bathtub, looking up at the pattern of daisies and ribbons in her plaster ceiling? Did she want to be a pity project for Marigold and Kev to workshop, year in and year out?

Being alone for pretty much the whole of her adult life had been safe, so that was a factor to consider. Being alone had also given her time to build her vet practice and win back her parents' trust and claw back a little (a smidge, if she was honest) of her self-respect.

But had being alone been fulfilling? For a while, yes.

But not lately. Not since The Incident, in fact.

She closed her eyes and felt the warm, heavy head of the baby resting against her neck. *This* was what fulfilment could feel like. A family of her own that hurdled the whole messy couples' thing and leapt straight into parenthood.

It would be change, but it would be safe change. Personal growth without the drama.

'You're looking all flushed, Hannah,' said Marigold. 'Are you all right? Maybe we need to head past the paella truck on the way back to the beach and soak up some of that vino.'

Hannah was barely listening. 'It's the perfect resolution.'

'You've decided? Excellent.'

Crap, she'd said that aloud, and within Marigold's nosy orbit, too.

'So what's it to be? Yoga? Crochet? Possum pouches?'

The mother had calmed the toddler—or Tom had, but Hannah had averted her eyes from the sight of him being all cute with the dog and the kid—and was now back in front of her, plucking the baby off her chest.

'Thank you so much. Sorry about snapping at you before.'

'Sure. No worries,' Hannah said as the mother took her warm little bundle away. Before she knew what was what, Marigold had her hand under arm, and was herding her to the food trucks and gabbling on about gussets and needle eyes and the pros and cons of thimbles for the stitchers who found themselves plagued by arthritis or trigger finger or tendonitis.

She needed to think.

She needed to get away from this craft chat. No way could she allow Marigold to assume control of her non-working life; her ears would explode first, followed by what little she had of patience.

And no way she could reveal the truth of the resolution she'd just—in a moment of clarity almost as blazing as the fireworks in the sky—decided on.

She needed a whatchamacallit, though, to keep the Hanrahan locals from meddling ... a misdirection, some wool over the eyes, a diversionary tactic that was doable and that she wouldn't totally hate. Thank heavens for Kev and his bright ideas.

'Campdraft,' she announced.

Marigold stopped talking. 'Excuse me?'

'That's the resolution I'm making. I, Hannah Cody, will be taking up the sport of campdrafting in the New Year.' She was committed now.

Marigold gave her a hug. 'Oh, I am pleased, pet. Kevvy's going to be over the moon. What with me flat strap on my committees, he needs a little something more in his week, and helping you learn the ropes will tickle him pink.'

Wow. That was a lot of cliches. Maybe she wasn't the only one who needed to soak up some prosecco with paella. But—

'Wait. I thought you wanted me to join your Wednesday evening craft group?'

Marigold winked. 'And have my merry crew contaminated with your double triple trebles? Oh, please, Hannah. What kind of a fool do you think I am?'

# CHAPTER

## 2

The dumbest thing Tom Krauss had ever done was lie about why he'd returned to his boyhood home after his career in the Navy imploded. Five long months later he was still wallowing in the consequences.

He could have waffled on about his house in Kiama having a long-term tenant who wouldn't shift (sort of true), or about secrecy (very true) or Royal Australian Navy ethics and the repercussions of breaching the Crimes Act of 1914 (punishably true), but that was the sort of boastful bullshit that made people more curious, not less.

'My dad's crook and needs me,' he'd told the woman at the butcher on Henry Street the first week he was back in town, 'and I was between jobs, and Dad's got some commercial property that needs sorting, like the pub and so on, so … yeah.'

Still bullshit, but the bitter kind rather than the boastful kind. Bruno Krauss would rather crawl over broken glass than admit he needed anyone. Especially his long-lost son. The only reason Tom knew his dad was crook was because Mrs LaBrooy, the Ironbark

Station housekeeper and his unofficial second mother, had told him. He only knew about the Hanrahan Pub needing 'sorting' because he'd tried to book himself a room there and found himself listening to a disconnected phone message.

So he'd taken the road out of town that brought him to Ironbark Station.

Father–son relations in the Krauss household made the Cold War look like a teddy bears' picnic; he'd half expected to be given the boot the moment he crossed the cattle grid. But he hadn't been booted off, and the days and weeks and months had gone by, and he'd repeated the whole crook/between jobs shebang to old Kev Jones, and to Mrs Grundy, and to the new policewoman in town who'd pulled him over on the Alpine Way and given him a serve about the bald tyre on his four-wheel drive.

Nobody had questioned him; Bruno had multiple sclerosis, and age *was* wearying him faster than most, and the pub *was* empty of beer, so he'd stuck with it.

His lie was so much easier to go with than the truth.

He'd been halfway to believing it himself until the time he'd darn-near collapsed in the park between Paterson and Dandaloo Streets one lunchtime. He'd had to sit for an hour on a bench seat in the sunshine beside the Great War cenotaph until he had the strength to make it back to his car. He'd passed the time reading the names of fathers and sons and brothers who'd never got the chance to return to Hanrahan and deal with whatever they'd left behind them when they'd enlisted.

If he was a better person, maybe he'd feel grateful to get his chance. Too bad he wasn't.

The bloke from the council emptying the park's bins at the time, Johnno Somebody-or-other, who'd been the groundsman at Hanrahan High back when Tom had been a student what seemed like a thousand years ago, was the one that spelled it out for him: what the lie meant; how he looked to the townsfolk of Hanrahan that he hadn't seen in seventeen years; what his current worth was as a man.

'You're old Bruno's son, aren't you? Heard you was back home with yer tail between yer legs.'

That had stung.

Johnno the bin bloke had got it in one. A fistful of commendations, a Conspicuous Service Medal and a lieutenant commander's dress uniform hanging in a garment bag at the back of his closet didn't mean diddly-squat when you were as near useless as he currently was. As he might always be.

He'd lied to the cadet in Wollongong who'd typed up his official discharge papers from the Navy, too, but that had been a different lie.

'I'm heading home to the Snowy Mountains,' he'd said. 'Stockhorses and cattle, air so clean it's like the industrial revolution never happened, and no more bridge duty on some rustbucket in the Arafura Sea.'

'But this says it's a medical discharge,' the cadet had said. 'Unfit for duty.'

Tom had stared him down. If he wasn't telling the truth to himself, he sure as sheep dung wasn't telling it to some newbie recruit who looked like his mother still buttered his toast for breakfast.

When he'd finally quit procrastinating and driven in through the old iron gates of the property where he'd grown up, he'd found his father—who he'd barely said three words to in the long years since he'd left—in a wheelchair. Mrs L hadn't mentioned *that* when she'd convinced him he was needed back at Ironbark Station ... but of course, she wasn't to know it would be a trigger.

'I was made redundant,' he said to Bruno. 'Thought I could make myself useful.' By that stage he was making up lies about himself left, right and centre, so what was one more?

Big effing mistake.

There was no welcome home. No *Hi, Tom, good to see you.* No *Thanks, mate, I could do with a hand.* No *Sorry about all that stuff I said and did and chucked in the dam.*

Mrs LaBrooy had cried and hugged him and told him to never leave again, but Bruno? He'd just added *unemployable* to the long list of adjectives he'd apparently been storing up over the years to throw at his son.

'Left arm.'

Tom snapped back into the late January morning and focused on the instructions coming from the doctor he visited at Cooma Hospital and Health Service once a week. He lifted his arm above his head, pushing it through the range-of-motion exercises his therapist in Wollongong had drilled into him before he'd been released from the rehab ward.

'Pain? Numbness? Tingling?'

'Nope.'

'Okay, right arm?'

His arms weren't the problem. Nor was his right leg. The left was where the weakness was growing, but he was ignoring that.

'How soon till I get my old life back, doc?' He always asked the same question, and she always found new and inventive ways to not answer.

Today, Dr Novak made some sighing sound that puffed out the blue mask over her face like a weather balloon. 'That's a pretty broad question, Tom. Did you read any of those pamphlets I gave you?'

'Cover to cover.'

'Really,' she said, stepping back and inspecting him with narrowed eyes. 'What are the five stages of coping after a traumatic injury?'

'Um ...' He'd have done more than chuck them in the glove box of his car if he'd known she was going to quiz him. 'Denial was one of them. Anger was another.' Been there, done that, didn't need to read it in some pamphlet.

She ticked them off on her fingers. 'Denial, anger, bargaining, depression, acceptance. Everyone's journey through those stages is different.'

Yeah, but not everyone had to *wait* the way he did. With a ticking bomb in their spine that may or may not end up with him even more immobilised than his seventy-five-year-old grump of a father.

The truth he hadn't shared with anyone was that he was back here in Hanrahan because his life had stalled. He wished he could get to the acceptance stage and start dealing with it, but he couldn't.

Maybe whoever wrote that pamphlet needed to add *apathy* to the list.

All he'd managed to work out since he'd been home was that without his arms and legs and every bit in between in top working order, he couldn't see a future. Getting involved with the family stockhorse business? He didn't have the skills to take on training even if he *could* ride, and the day Bruno welcomed his interference with his beloved horses would be the day the Snowy River broke its dam and became a major waterway again.

Un-bloody-likely.

Calling plumbers and arranging pest controllers to visit the buildings his dad owned in Hanrahan barely took an hour each day, the pub was apparently in the hands of the town solicitor, and Mrs L got all huffy and in-his-face if Tom did more than peel a carrot in the homestead kitchen.

So what else was there?

'Come on, let me see that right arm come up, Tom. Stop indulging in your pity party and concentrate.'

'Sorry.'

'You're injured. You're allowed to take time to process things. *Lots* of time.' She tapped his left thigh with an implement that looked like a drumstick. 'Now push into a slow lunge, left leg forward, let me know when it's a struggle.'

He did as she asked, cursing when the tremor started.

Dr Novak made a note on her chart. 'Yes,' she said. 'You're right, we're seeing increased left lower extremity quadriceps weakness. Strength three over five. Any tingling?'

'Some. It was four over five last time.'

She nodded. 'We'll book you in for a scan so we can see if the shrapnel's moved in the paraspinal muscles. I hope you're following orders: no work, no activity on your banned list.'

He must have made a grumbling noise, because she raised her eyebrows at him.

'You've not been horse riding, have you? Just because you're the son of a local horse-training legend doesn't mean you should put your future in jeopardy.'

'Nope.'

'Athletic sexual exploits?'

He closed his eyes. 'Nope.'

'Rock climbing the escarpment? Mountain biking the trails? Boating at high speed on the lake?'

'Could you knife me a little deeper in the chest, doc? The most exciting thing I've done in weeks is quit putting sugar in my coffee.'

'Sarcasm still sitting at five over five, I see.'

He watched her write another note on his chart. 'You have a column for that?'

She made a noise that might have been a laugh and her mask puffed out again. 'Let's get that scan done, shall we? I don't like the progression I'm seeing. We'll send the results to your specialist in Wollongong and then we may have to make some decisions.'

'Finally.' He'd just about had jack of the steel shard of ship's hull currently tucked up tight next to his spinal canal between muscles whose names he'd never heard of six months ago, but which he could now, unfortunately, spell: his psoas major and his erector spinae.

Any decision the surgeon had to make had to be better than this wait-and-see palaver.

Tom rested a hand on the wall as he felt his lunge begin to give way and the doctor—despite being five foot nothing and grasshopper thin—had to help him before he fell over. 'Useless, effing le—'

'Hey,' she said, and her voice was suspiciously gentle, like she could see he was a bee's dick away from losing it. 'You've got to trust the process, all right? I know sitting around doesn't come easy to someone who's spent their life leaping off boats into hostile oceans with knives strapped to their ankles, or whatever it is you Navy Seals do.'

'Australia doesn't have Navy Seals.' He'd said the words so often he could say them on autopilot, but that was good, because he needed a minute.

'Whatever. My point is this: maybe you're depressed, in which case we need to think about a sensible treatment plan, or maybe you're a little lost amidst all this change and lack of a normal work routine, and something simple like an action plan might help you. Come up with some things you *can* do and stop thinking about what you can't do.'

'I'm not depressed.' Oh god, he totally sounded depressed.

'Uh-huh? Really? Then prove it. Start a project, Tom. *Do* something.'

The drive home from Cooma to Ironbark Station was a bit over ninety minutes, but that wouldn't be anywhere near enough time for Tom to jam his current mood back in its box. He couldn't face another round with Bruno just yet.

*This station and the stockhorses we breed here are my life's work. You could have had it all, but you chucked it in for some bullshit career in the Navy, and how did that work out for you, son?*

Tom slewed the car through an s-bend and listened to the gravel spit out from under the tyres. Pride, that was Bruno's problem. And stubbornness. And a decades-long obsession with the stud book of the Australian Stockhorse Association, which must have encouraged him to think if he fed and watered and broke his son to bridle, he'd get a carbon copy of himself.

When Tom reached the centre of Hanrahan, he snagged one of the town's beloved reverse angle parks by the foreshore. If any of the locals noticed him take an extra-long time to get out of the driver's seat, well, he could blame that on the view. Lake Bogong was dark and moody under the patchwork sky, and a scrappy-looking pelican had found a perch on one of the pier's old wooden pylons. He felt some of his frustration ease as he pulled a long breath of air into his lungs. Smoke clung to the hill on the far side of the lake where a burn-off must be in progress and a ripple of fins, rainbow trout, perhaps, disturbed the shallows.

'You're a long way from the sea,' he said to the pelican.

The bird only had eyes for the fish, so Tom walked over to the building on the corner, where an ornate timber door was propped open by a fat brown labrador.

'Top of the morning to you, Major Tom. Just step over Jane Doe; she's nicked off from the vet clinic again and is refusing to move until she's been rewarded with a poached egg. Now, don't tell me: you want the corner table and a long black.'

So much for sliding unnoticed into The Billy Button Café. The manager, Graeme, liked to greet arrivals like he was the ringmaster at a circus and sure enough, half the café patrons had looked up to see who the newcomer was.

Tom gave them a general wave, plastered his I'm-kinda-busy face on and headed for his usual table. Because Graeme was right: he wanted the quiet corner, tucked behind the chimney, partly screened from the chatterboxes of Hanrahan by a verdant green fern.

'You know major is an army term, right?' he said, as Graeme led him past the serving counter—another of the standard responses he'd acquired over the years. 'I was in the Navy, so I was never a major.' He was certainly never addressed as Major Tom. Sounded like a tin of cat food, which, now he thought about it, would be about as helpful in the naval defence of Australia as he currently was. 'Besides, I've been a civilian a while now.'

Graeme whisked the comment away with a wave of his hand. 'Once I've seen a man in uniform, I can never unsee it.'

Tom laughed. 'You've never seen me in uniform.'

The manager winked. 'I have an excellent imagination. Now, food? We have naughty and nourishing today as always, and a batch of date scones just came out of the oven.'

'Just coffee for me, and is there a newspaper about? I better grab a bag of those butterscotch donuts too, if you have any. Mrs L has a soft spot for them.'

Graeme nodded, opened his mouth, shut it, cleared his throat, then said, 'Coming right up. I think, um, maybe you'll need a date scone with that newspaper.'

Weird. 'No, really, I—'

'I'll snaffle the *Snowy River Star* when it's free. You get yourself seated.'

Tom gave up trying to argue the point and while he waited for his coffee, he pulled a notebook and a pen out of his jacket pocket to keep himself occupied.

*Start a project*, the doctor had said.

Yeah, that was going to be tricky.

He had Buttercup, of course, the horse he'd bought (maybe rashly) when his career was destroyed, and caring for a former racehorse who was in foal was a project, wasn't it?

He did the crossword every day, he drank a ton of coffee, he'd decluttered his dad's office and put the property records into files. He'd played a lot of backgammon with Mrs L and … Oh, yes. Better not forget the happy day when he'd made Hannah Cody cry in his stables.

And he worried.

A *lot*.

All of that was doing something, wasn't it?

He took a sip of the coffee that had materialised on his table and was still trying to figure out what special something he could do to prove to the doctor (and, okay, to himself) that he wasn't totally losing it, when the local newspaper landed in front of him. Thankful for the distraction of a new crossword, he nodded up at the waitress who'd—

Crap. Not a waitress.

'Hello, Tommy,' said Marigold Jones in a honey tone that deceived him not one whit. A bigger operator he had yet to meet, and when he'd been seconded overseas he'd worked undercover with international criminals. Not that Marigold, Hanrahan's busiest and most involved woman, was a criminal; she was much, *much* more than that. A florist (retired). A celebrant: weddings, funerals and anything. Self-appointed chairwoman of every committee in town. She'd been hovering in his peripheral vision since the minute he moved home and he hadn't yet worked out what her deal was.

'It's Tom,' he said. She was standing so close that the blue fabric of her dress, if that's what such a vast, curtain-like garment was called, floated onto the table.

'Graeme said to bring you the paper when I was done with it.'

'Thanks,' he said, snapping it open and hoping she'd take the hint.

She didn't. Instead, she seemed to be taking an unseemly amount of interest in the notebook he had open on the table. He tucked it under the paper—although the page was blank, so he wasn't sure why he'd bothered—and let his lack of chit-chat do the talking for him.

Marigold sighed and a cumulus of floaty fabric sighed with her. 'Page sixteen,' she murmured. 'Look for the silver lining, my love, because there always is one. If you want my help, you know where to find me.'

And with a whoosh, she was gone.

Hmm. Ominous.

The *Snowy River Star* didn't bother itself too much with world events: the front cover was a grainy image of a python found lurking in the tap section of a hardware store over in Adaminaby. He flicked through the pages. Weather more of the same: overcast but dry, with a colder-than-average, stiff breeze that'd have leaves skittering from the trees and the countryside about Ironbark turning hard as ... well, as iron. Shops for lease, including an advert he'd placed himself for the ground floor of one of Bruno's Federation buildings near the park; tour guides and housekeeping staff wanted for the upcoming snow season; a delay on the opening of the new section of highway ...

He flicked past the remaining adverts for mattresses and big-screen televisions and there it was: page sixteen, the local gossip masquerading as a news column flagged under the misleadingly benign banner as the Hanrahan Chatter.

Is the Sun Setting on Ironbark Station? *by Maureen Plover*

Oh, crap.

A warm buttery scone, chunks of sticky date oozing from its sides, plonked down on the table in front of him and he felt the press of Graeme's hand on his shoulder.

'On the house,' murmured the manager. 'Sing out if one isn't enough.'

Bracing himself, Tom read the article.

*For twenty years, Hanrahan has played its trump card to keep the tourists coming in after the winter season, when the mountains above the town have too little snow to open the ski slopes, but are too cold for the hikers heading up to Dead Horse Gap. The town has welcomed horse floats and riders. Henderson's Ag Store on Gorge Road has sold out of rope reins and girth strap; Deanna from Clancy's Drapers has given the fibreglass horse in her front window a buff and polish and dressed up her mannequins in riding boots and chequered shirts and braided leather belts.*

*Why all this activity? What is the trump card? I'll tell you: The Ironbark Station Campdraft.*

*Families buy pies and fuel and fodder. Kids feed the ducks on the lake and spend their pocket money on ice-creams and kayak hire. The motels book out rooms and the casual hospitality workers add another weekend of good wages to their savings. Holding the annual auction of stockhorses and cattle the same weekend as a well-run, prize-rich campdraft has traditionally brought the crowds into Hanrahan in the first week of October, year in and year out.*

*But The Chatter is hearing rumours that the campdraft has been pulled from the Southern District Campdrafters' calendar this year again. That's*

*two years running. Town Mayor Barry O'Malley was asked if he'd heard*
*any news: 'Now don't quote me in your infernal article again, Maureen.*
*My blood pressure's bad enough without you adding to it. Besides, old*
*Bruno's crook. You can't pick a bloke to shreds in the bloody paper when*
*he's crook.'*

*Maybe that's true. But old Bruno's not the only Krauss living up there*
*at Ironbark Station this year, is he?*

*Seems to me it might be time his long-lost son got off his arse at the back*
*corner table of The Billy Button Café (where he hangs out all day hogging*
*the crossword, mind you!), and remembered why Hanrahan is the finest*
*country town in the Snowy Mountains. Might be time he stepped up.*

*Tradition matters here.*

*A healthy off season for our small business owners matters, too.*

Far out. He was here in Hanrahan to brood, not to get involved.
Graeme was right—he was going to need another scone.

'What's got you looking so grim?' Josh Cody swung himself into
the chair opposite.

'Hey, mate. Come to collect your slug of a dog, have you?'

Josh's face went all smiley and sappy-looking. 'Jane Doe. She
likes to keep an eye on Vera, so she nicks out through the back
office window when we're all busy.'

Tom rolled his eyes. 'You are so under the thumb.'

'And loving it.'

'If you can drag your mind off the ladies in your life for one second, have you seen this?' He turned the paper so Josh could read
the article.

His mate grimaced. 'Maureen Plover. Up to her old tricks, is
she?'

'Is it true?'

'Is what true? Give me the short version. I've got a cattle dog with a medial patella luxation coming in for a consult in ten.'

'With a what?'

'A dicky knee.'

'Riiight. Let me ask you a question instead, then. Does the local community miss out if the Ironbark Campdraft doesn't get held each year? Because Bruno's not up to it.'

'I'm the wrong guy to ask, Tom. I've not been back in Hanrahan much longer than you, and I was never into the sport the way you and your dad were.'

Tom frowned. Those days were painful to remember: the good days because they'd ended, and the bad days because they'd been spectacularly, family-breakingly bad. He'd been a kid the last time he'd helped out at an event held at Ironbark; his duties had been limited to manning the gates on the cattle chutes. He was pretty sure he'd spent the whole time flirting with girls in fringed jackets and tight-as jeans, rather than taking notes on the economic impacts of campdrafting on rural communities.

'Did he ever apologise for … you know? Stupid question, it's Bruno we're talking about. Never met a bloke so stubborn. What was the pup's name again?'

Huh. Seems Tom wasn't the only one who'd never forgotten the bad days. 'We didn't get around to names.'

'Look, I know it caused a ruckus. And I'm not condoning his actions—far from it. He'd get charged for that sort of carry on these days, and I'd report him to the police in a heartbeat. But in farming communities back in your old man's heyday, where there were no vets and neutering animals wasn't common, it was considered a quick and merciful solution to a problem.'

Tom just grunted and Josh must have clued in that it was time to change the subject. 'I can tell you where you might find an answer to your campdraft question, though.'

'Yeah?' he said, not sure whether he really wanted to know. 'Where's that?'

'Dalgety. There's an event on this coming weekend. Nothing as flash as the Ironbark one used to be, and no rodeo events or horse auctions, but it's local enough that you'd know people. Why not check it out, ask around, get a feel for what's involved?'

'I guess I could drive down and take a look.' Not that Bruno would have the least interest in entrusting his beloved campdraft to Tom's worthless hands, but still. It'd kill a day, and he'd be able to tell the doctor next week that he'd *considered* a special project, so—simple as that—he couldn't be depressed.

'Hannah'll be there, I expect,' said Josh, in the blandest voice possible. 'Her and Kev have been very secret squirrel the last few weeks, but my keen eye for detail, based on the filthy riding clothes Hannah dumps in the clinic laundry and the alarmed eyes of the steers over Kev's back fence whenever they see the clinic ute, makes me think she wasn't joking about taking campdraft up as a hobby.'

Tom blinked, kept his face equally bland, despite his surprise at Hannah's new hobby. *Say nothing. You promised.*

'Hannah Cody. My sister, remember her? Who, for some reason she will not divulge, is avoiding you.'

Far out. He took a moment to straighten the newspaper so its edges aligned neatly with the table's; an important task, and he'd done it like a boss.

'Five foot two, dark red hair, soft heart hidden—*deeply* hidden— under a cranky exterior.'

Nope, no way was he going to be drawn into whatever trap Josh was setting for him.

A deep woof at the door was a timely distraction and—

Crap.

Josh had his back to the street, so he didn't know that the person he was describing was standing right there, as though conjured up by her brother's one-sided conversation—and Tom's deeply buried thoughts.

She was here to reclaim Jane Doe, by the looks, because she had a red lead in her hand and her usual look on her face. The cranky look. Her hair was in a messy plait and it dangled over her shoulder in the way it had for as long as he'd known her. Well, other than the time when he, at Josh's urging, had cut it off with a pair of sewing scissors from Mrs Cody's sewing basket. She'd been about eight.

He hadn't been in love with her then, of course. No way, yuck, gross. The playground rules at primary school were very clear on this issue: she was covered in girl germs and he, at eleven, had been obliged to spend every minute of little lunch and big lunch playing handball, and practising saying swear words with casual ease, and maintaining his position in the school as fastest runner from the bubbler on the oval to the hot pie queue out front of the tuckshop.

Those playground girl germs had hung around for *years* until … later. Until he had stubble (true, it'd been a minuscule bit of stubble, but even minuscule counted for a lot back then) and enormous feet and Mrs L had decreed that grunting was not an adequate response to her daily questions: *How was your day at school, my lamb? Are you totally sure you understand that deodorant is meant to be used* every *day? Who ate the last of the chocolate cake* and *the lamb roast* and *the chicken coconut curry and left the empty dishes in the fridge?*

But, of course, by then he was operating under the mateship rules: Hannah was his best friend's little sister so he had to ignore the mushy knots his innards tied themselves into whenever he saw her.

And all these years later?

He tightened his grip on the tabletop. There she was, leaning in the doorway, her cranky look turned to laughter at something Graeme had said to her. She was smiling as though she'd never cried in the stables a single day of her life. As though Tom could forget about his present and return to his past and stand up, *right now*, and go over there and—

Shit.

And do nothing. Just ask his doctor: he was playing by a very different set of rules now, so there was no point sitting here with his innards all mushy again just because Hannah Cody was over there by the door looking just the way he liked her to look: sunny and capable and stroppy, all at the same time.

'Mate. The cat got your tongue or what? One of these days you're going to have to tell me what went on between you and Hannah.'

Huh. He'd forgotten all about Josh. Maybe if he tried hard enough, he'd be able to forget all about Hannah, too, and Josh would never need to know. A special project might not be the dumbest idea his doctor had ever had.

'Sorry, mate, there's nothing to tell. Thanks for the heads up about Dalgety. Now, if you wouldn't mind pissing off back to your dicky knee, I've got a crossword to hog.'

# CHAPTER

# 3

*A woman's ovaries will shrivel into prunes over time and by her thirty-second year, fertility will have plummeted to—*

'Why do you buy these, Kylie? Some of them are total junk.'

Nearly a month had passed since Hannah's epiphany, and now, everywhere she turned, were reminders.

She dropped the out-of-date chick magazine onto a table in the mechanic's workshop, where it landed next to a pile of other glossies promising an eclectic mix of articles like WIN BACK YOUR MAN WITH ROAST LAMB and OFF-ROAD ADVENTURES: SNOWY MOUNTAINS IN AUTUMN. The sun was still low in the sky and a pleasing beam of it had made its way through the open roller door and now warmed Hannah's face.

As if fertility plummeted, jeez. Although … there was nothing stopping her having a quick browse through the textbooks back at the clinic. Just to be sure. Bovine ovaries couldn't be that different from her ovaries, could they?

Kylie was on a wheelie thing tucked under the battered body of Hannah's hatchback and the only parts of her in view were hot pink socks tucked into grease-spattered boots. Her voice came out muffled. 'If we're going to talk junk, Han, we should start with your car. You're going to need a new gearbox any minute now, your main seal looks like it's about to explode—which will make your car blow up, by the way, something which even your wonder mechanic can't fix—and there's a rust patch under here that I could pass a watermelon through.'

Hannah sniffed. 'The green machine is fine.'

Wheels rumbled over the cement floor and then the face of her best friend since kindergarten was frowning at her. 'Giving your car a cutesy nickname does not disguise the fact that it has had it. I know you hate change, Hannah, but seriously. This thing is a death trap.'

Perspective was everything, wasn't it? One person's death trap was another person's safety net: having a crap car had provided Hannah with a lot of excuses over the years. Family wedding in Canberra? So sorry, I can't possibly drive that far without the radiator overheating. Vet school reunion in Wagga Wagga? Such a shame, if only I could make it, but my tyres are bald and I just spent all my money on patient-warming blankets.

'I don't hate change.' She was scared of change, which was a totally different thing.

Kylie had the bonnet up and was shaking her head at the horrors apparently on display. 'Yeah, right. And don't give me that face, Hannah.'

'You're not even looking at me.'

'I don't need to be looking at you—my bullshit radar is finely tuned. Come on, I thought this was the year for the new you. Take up hobbies; have an adventure; buy gorgeous clothes; campdrafting. Why not whack a new car on the list, too?'

Now was the moment to confide about the change Hannah really wanted in her life, but her feelings … her intentions … were all so *new*. So unexpected.

She slipped into banter because it was easier than laying bare her heart, when what was in there was still so muddled. 'I knew it was a mistake telling you my New Year's resolutions. And no way I said anything about new clothes.'

Her friend grinned. 'That was me trying to give you a little hint. But seriously, Han, you told everyone on the lakefront your resolutions. Me. Your brother. The paella bloke, the kids on the beach, even the grumpy old fart who's restoring the paddle steamer.'

'True, but you know prosecco makes me chatty and prone to oversharing.'

She had allowed herself to get carried away as the fireworks crackled overhead and she'd sat, shoulder to shoulder with friends on old driftwood. Epiphanies could do that to a person.

And despite having agreed to Kev's campdrafting suggestion as the lesser evil than being roped into Marigold's craft club, training with him and her horse Skipjack had turned out to be fun.

'Oh, heck,' she said. 'It's Thursday, isn't it?'

Kylie had hauled a dirty (yet vital-looking) piece of metal pipe from the engine and was now wiping it down with an even dirtier rag. 'Yep.'

'How soon do you think my car will be back on the road? I've got an event Saturday arvo.'

'What sort of event?' Kylie's eyes narrowed. 'Are there single men involved?'

Hannah smirked. 'Relax. I haven't been invited to some party you don't know about. It's the campdraft tournament down at Dalgety. There's a maiden event and Kev reckons me and Skipjack have learned enough in his back paddock to not completely disgrace ourselves.'

'In Dalgety. You cool about that?'

Good question.

It was such a good question, Hannah had probably made the right call not confiding in Kylie of her real goal for the year ahead. She wasn't ready to listen to good questions that might expose the weaknesses in her plan. Not yet.

As for whether she was ready for an out-of-town visit?

Of course she was. She'd driven to vet calls down the mountain, further than Dalgety to the south, past Adaminaby in the north that time the Cooma vet had been in quarantine. True, they'd been emergency trips to farm sheds or freezing paddocks, where the social interaction consisted of her, a tired farmer and a crook animal, but she'd been totally fine. No problems there, so why should a visit to the Dalgety Showgrounds be any different?

The skin on her neck itched just thinking about it.

'I'll need your car until Monday arvo, at least. You want to borrow my ute?'

'I guess I could go with Kev. One of his mates from the community hall has a horse float and loves an opportunity to get out from his missus's feet, apparently, so he's offered to take Skipjack down. They'll have room for me with them.' It would mean she'd be stuck at the showgrounds until the old blokes were ready to leave, but it wasn't as though she had any evening plans.

She sucked in a breath and let it out like she was one of the punctured tyres in Kylie's workshop. She'd be in Dalgety, away from home, for hours. It would be the first of the many tests she needed to pass.

Not the horse event. Kylie and Kev and everyone else who'd shown an interest in her new hobby might think a successful draft was her only goal for the day, but she knew better.

Saturday was when the last four weeks of soul-searching about fixing the hole in her heart would either pay off or implode. If she was really truly serious about having a baby, then she had to address her aversion to leaving the shadow of the mountains. Driving to competitions in the neighbouring towns would be a gentle way to do that.

Her friends and family might have guessed she was using camp-draft as a way to ease herself back into the rest of the world, but they were too worried about her losing the plot to push her into talking about it. Well, that wasn't totally true: Kylie was happy to push, but she generally softened her interventions with booze and those little chocolate ice-cream sandwich thingys. Also, Kylie was easy to distract with a change of subject.

Let the Hanrahan locals think she was ready for some adventure; it gave their fussing a focus. What she really wanted before the year was out was something else entirely, and there was only so much research and planning a girl could do from within the confines of a small country town hundreds of kilometres away from the nearest fertility clinic.

She needed to get cracking. Time was passing and ovaries were shrivelling into prunes.

# CHAPTER

## 4

The door to the office which housed, according to gilt lettering on its plaque, the country legal practice of BENJAMIN DORLEY BA/ LLB(HONS) was propped ajar with a box of photocopy paper when Tom made his way up the stairs on Friday morning. A harassed young man sat behind a desk telling someone at the other end of the phone that if he knew what a *caveat emptor* was, he'd be able to help, but as it was, he'd have to take a message for Mr Dorley and, yes, he knew he'd already taken half-a-dozen messages, but Mr Dorley was busy with a court matter and was out of the office.

Tom nodded a greeting, then gave the office a look-over. Files were piled everywhere, and the door to Benjamin's inner sanctum was ajar, revealing more chaos within: coffee cups; archive boxes; phone charging cords tangled and stuck like cold spaghetti. But where were the fresh flowers on the windowsill? Where was Mrs Dorley, of the red beehive hair, who ruled the reception desk like she was the reincarnation of Margaret Thatcher? What was with the overflowing bins and the sweaty look of desperation on the young man?

'Sorry about that,' said the young man, getting to his feet. 'If you're here to see Mr Dorley, he's not in.'

'So I see. I haven't met you here before. Are you new?'

'Um, yeah. I'm Alex. You're not going to ask me anything hard, I hope, because I don't know anything.'

Tom couldn't help smiling. 'Nothing hard, I promise. Where's his wife?'

A flush of red ran from the tight collar of Alex's shirt all the way up to his ears. 'She left.'

Tom had plenty of experience drilling info out of fresh naval recruits, so he dropped a little heft into his tone. 'Left work? Left Hanrahan?' He paused. 'Left her husband?'

'All of the above. Hey, do you know Mr Dorley? Because he hasn't come into work even though he said he'd be here at eight o'clock, and all these people are calling and I'm running out of things to say.'

'I haven't seen him in a few weeks. Ben looks after my father's real estate interests. I came to ask him what the hold-up is with a job he's doing for us.' Though Tom guessed he had his answer: the bloke had dropped his bundle.

'Um, I could take a message?'

'Yeah, that's not working. I've left messages and he hasn't returned them, which is why I'm here. You know where he keeps keys? He'll have the set for the Hanrahan Pub that I need to borrow.' Now Tom thought about it, if Dorley really had lost the plot, then taking on finding a publican for the town pub would make a doddle of a special project for him. With bonus points, too, because it wouldn't involve bumping into Hannah Cody or raising the contentious issue of Ironbark's campdraft with Bruno.

The young man perked up. 'Where the keys live is something I do know. Mr Dorley showed me them on my first day.'

'When did you start here?' A heavy leather binder was on the desk. Its pages held the tiny print of—Tom squinted and tipped his head so he could read the header—the Family Law Act of 1975. He ran his finger across the thin cream paper and was reminded of the hours he'd spent in the law library back when he was an undergraduate.

He'd liked the study. He'd liked reading the cases and working out why the judges had found some arguments favourable and others not. It had all seemed so very fair and objective—the polar opposite, in fact, of the way arguments had been conducted around the Krauss kitchen table.

'Um, I just started work experience here. I'm a senior over at Hanrahan High School—at least, I will be, when the term starts next week. Mum reckons working here will be, like, resumé building or something. You know, for a uni scholarship.'

'Right.' No wonder the kid looked freaked out about the boss being a no-show. Tom held out his hand. 'Tom Krauss. I went to Hanrahan High myself once upon a time.' Felt about a hundred years ago.

'Alex. Oh, I already said that, didn't I?'

'Hoping to be a lawyer one day, are you?'

'Maybe. Dunno. Mum's keen on the lawyer thing, but maybe I could be a guitarist in a band. I haven't decided.'

Tom had been undecided himself through school, but when he left home, barefoot and clueless, with three hundred and twenty bucks, one condom (aged) and a driver's licence in his wallet, the Royal Australian Navy officer's entry program had seemed like a lifesaver and law was the degree he got into. Not that he'd done much desk work in the Navy once he'd completed his law degree and basic training at HMAS Creswell; he was offered a role in naval intelligence and he'd leapt at it, which brought to an end his involvement with military administrative law and contracts for armament and bulk provisions and drydock maintenance.

That was back when he could leap, of course.

'Want me to dig out the keys for you?' said Alex.

'Sure. You let Benjamin know I've got them when he turns up.'

'What if he doesn't turn up? What if he's had a car crash on the way to work? What if I'll be here all day on my own and I should have done something, but didn't?'

Wow. If the law (or the guitar) didn't work out for this kid, he could give drama a whirl. 'I'm sure he's fine. Maybe you could put a sign on the door and go check on him.'

'But I can't drive and Mum's not picking me up until five and then I've got footy practice.'

Tom resigned himself. 'You know where he lives, mate? I can check on him. If his wife's done a runner, he's probably sitting around feeling sorry for himself.'

'I don't know his address.'

Of course he didn't. 'I'll find out. Now, can you hunt up the keys for the Hanrahan Pub for me? I'll check on your boss and you can maybe answer calls and …' What would keep the kid busy for the day? 'Tidy up a little.'

Alex seemed thrilled to have something to do. 'Yes, sir.'

Tom scrolled through the contacts in his phone. The café. Perfect. Someone there would be bound to know. He hit the dial button and Graeme picked up first ring.

'Mate, it's Tom. You happen to know where Benjamin Dorley lives? He hasn't fronted up to work this morning and there's a work experience kid here in his office who's—' he was about to say freaking out, but Alex had his eye on him and his tie was so darn tight around his neck and his shirt so ironed, and his face still red and sweaty from taking angry phone calls that he reconsidered. 'Er, the office intern is wondering if someone can go check on him.'

'Dorley. Scrawny fellow, bow ties like a professor from a seventies sitcom, double shot on lactose free?'

Tom let out a chuckle. 'If you say so.'

'I'll ask around. Want me to text you the address?'

'Yep. I'm in town for a while, about to head over to the pub for a walk around and see what state the old girl's in, so if you can find me an address I can go see where he's at.'

'No worries, mate.'

Duty done, Tom snagged the keys Alex had found and headed over to the pub.

The sandstone above the heavy wooden door said 1858. The door itself looked like it had been to battle, with more scratches than enamel paint and gouge marks around the deadlocks as though passing louts had had a crack at gaining entry.

A breeze off the lake tugged at Tom's chambray shirt while he worked his way through the cluster of keys. He pushed the door open when he heard the bolt slide back.

'Oh, good, I made it.'

He turned abruptly—too abruptly—and sucked in a breath as a lightning rod of pain shot down his leg. Marigold bloody Jones.

'What,' he managed, 'are you doing here?'

Her eyes twinkled at him beneath the green eyeshadow she must have applied with a trowel, and her greying up-do must have had a similar amount of product assisting it, because it barely shifted in the blustery wind. 'Now, don't get all stiff-lipped, Tommy. It's not my fault if I just happened to be sampling the hazelnut macarons when you rang The Billy Button Café.' She brushed a crumb from the multicoloured muumuu-thing she had draped over her formidable bosom. 'Graeme asked me if I knew where Benjamin Dorley lived. Of course I do. I asked him why, and he told me.'

'So why aren't you there, bulldozing your way through his front door?' A bit snippy, yes, but he was still not sure he could move without falling over and he sure as Sherlock did not want to collapse to the floor in front of Hanrahan's nosiest woman. He leant his shoulder against the sun-warmed stone and concentrated on breathing in and breathing out until the lightning rod dwindled to a dull ember.

'Kev volunteered to pop along. I, of course, was far too excited to pass up a chance to gain entrée into the nooks and crannies of the Hanrahan Pub. You do know I'm president of the Hanrahan and District Community Association?'

Of course he knew. Everyone this side of the Victorian border must know.

'So, here I am, giving you the benefit of my expert opinion. Now, chop chop. If we're going to look the place over, let's get it done. I've got a funeral to plan at eleven and the relatives of the dead value punctuality.'

'I'm just here to—' Too late. He was talking to himself.

A dull red carpet runner stretched from the entry foyer down a long corridor. Bar and restaurant area to the left, accommodation upstairs and a string of family rooms in the newer wing out the back. He wondered what had possessed his father to buy the place. When Tom had last lived in Hanrahan, the owners had been a middle-aged couple who'd been content with a three-star accommodation rating; a pie warmer on the bar had been as close as they'd come to employing a chef. The locals hadn't minded so much. Nor had Tom. A few cold beers with friends followed by a hot pie wasn't the worst night out a teenager barely old enough to buy booze could have.

Shutting the heavy old door acted like a muffler on the street noise. He breathed in dust and the air was stale, but there was an ambience to the place. Perhaps it was the age of it; the pub had survived generations of Hanrahan families, two world wars, bushfires and droughts.

There was something very reassuring about its solidity.

Marigold's voice boomed from the old ladies' lounge where she'd wafted in for a snoop. 'The cockroaches have been holding bush dances in here and there's some mould in the ceiling roses, but she's not derelict, Tom.'

'I hope not. Dorley's supposed to be finding a publican to lease the place.'

'In this state? I don't think so. You want to restore this grand old lady now, Tom, while it's empty. Paint the trim in heritage colours, spruce up the garden beds ... we'll get rid of those neon beer signs out front for starters and someone needs to paint out the apostrophe in "Meal's" on this sign.'

Marigold's use of the word 'we' was sweet ('bossy' might be the better word), but naive. 'Bruno's the one you need to persuade.'

'Mmm,' said Marigold. 'He and I are having a little break from each other.'

'Oh? What happened?'

'A little disagreement about the need to future-proof Hanrahan history. Nothing for you to worry about, pet. Now ... shall we start upstairs and work our way down?'

He followed her up the flight of stairs, the jangling of her bangles adding tempo to the creaking of the floorboards beneath the carpet. More dust floated up and hung in the coloured sunlight that had made its way through the leadlight surround of the front door. The place wasn't messy. No-one had broken in and torn up floorboards or ripped out fittings. Mildew stained the old wallpaper above the wooden panelling, but the ceilings upstairs were still in good shape, which boded well for the roof.

'Do you know what happened to the caretaker?' he said, opening a door and finding a bedroom complete with four-poster bed hung with some cheap lace. 'Didn't Josh cadge a room off her for a few weeks back when the vet clinic caught fire?' An ancient radiator clung to one wall and there was a small desk with a chair upturned on it.

'Gracie,' said Marigold. 'Took off a few months back to visit her daughter up in Queensland and didn't come back.' Her phone buzzed and she spent a minute pawing through a massive green handbag to find it. 'It's Kev. He's found your missing solicitor. He's—oh, dear.'

'Nothing bad, I hope?'

'He's been on a bender and the police have taken his car keys. Blew over the limit in the early hours of the morning. Kev's going to pop by his office and get the work experience boy to shut up shop for the day.'

'His wife left him, apparently.'

'Yes. Joan. She had her reasons. Now, enough of the Dorleys, where were we?'

They finished their tour of upstairs—five more bedrooms, an ancient bathroom complete with terrazzo floor and pink ceramic bathtub, and a broom closet from which a startled brushtail possum emerged, blinking with annoyance at being herded out a nearby window—and headed down to the bar.

'It's better than I expected,' said Marigold. 'The section of guttering out front hanging off the roof like an old snake skin had me worried.'

'Good news, then.'

'Mmm. Someone does need to remind Bruno he can't buy the town's most famous landmark and leave it to become a possum playground.'

He could see where this was going. 'And that someone is me, right?'

Marigold linked her arm into his and walked with him back down the corridor to the door. She opened it and the cold wind roared in, along with the noise of a truck rattling along the Esplanade and a boat engine being revved down by the pier. 'You're going to be a busy lad, Tom, what with learning how to run a campdraft and getting this old girl tarted up.'

Of course she'd seen the article in the Hanrahan Chatter. 'You're not referring to yourself, I take it.'

She chuckled. 'It's *exciting*, isn't it? No reason to be in a blue funk when there's stuff like this to be involved in. It's our heritage, Tom. Looking after it is how we pay it forward to the next generation. Makes you feel lucky to be alive.'

He frowned over the blue funk barb. Did she know something? He would have drawn his arm from hers except she was gripping him like an oyster grips a rock and he had all the strength of a wet flannel.

'I'm not in a funk, Marigold.'

'Of course not, dear. I was talking about Bruno. Why would I be talking about you?'

He cleared his throat. 'No reason at all.' And what did Marigold know of Bruno that he didn't?

She was silent for a moment, which was so out of character Tom braced himself for what was coming.

'My lamb, my pet, my sweet,' she began. 'Do you want to tell me something? A problem shared and all that.'

'There's nothing to share.'

'I'm not prying; I'm caring.'

'Yeah. Still got nothing to share.'

'Are you telling me to mind my own business?' She raised her eyebrows at him and batted her eyelashes.

He laughed. She was shameless. 'It's about time someone did.'

She smiled. 'Tom Krauss, I foresee that you and I are going to become friends. All right then, keep your secrets, but tell me this. Are you going to give this pub a makeover before you find a lessee to take it on, or what?'

'It's not my decision, but'—he couldn't believe he'd been talked into this. Where was his apathy when he needed it?—'I'll speak to Bruno. Let him know his solicitor has lost the plot.' For all the good that would do. 'That's likely where my involvement will end.'

# CHAPTER
## 5

At four o'clock on Saturday morning, the wind dropped. An omen? The leaves of the snow gum outside Hannah's bedroom window, which could usually be counted on to murmur and chatter like old friends sharing gossip, were quiet.

The bustle of downtown Hanrahan, with its population a static 760 if the painted sign on the outskirts of town was to be believed, was likewise non-existent. One of the council's fancy wrought-iron streetlights threw a golden glow onto the footpath below, but at this hideously sleepless hour, no other lights were visible.

Hannah leant into the deep windowsill and looked the other way, down Salt Creek Flats Road. No rattle of diesel engines. No scamper of possums along the powerlines. Even the summer cicadas had shut up, which would have been a blessing seven hours ago, but now she kind of missed them.

If she was asleep, of course, none of this eerie quiet would be a problem, but ... yeah. She wasn't.

Tiptoeing silently downstairs past the first floor flat where Josh was cosied up to Vera wasn't easy in the heritage-listed, Federation-era building she and her brother had inherited from their grandparents. The creaks in the floorboards squabbled almost as much as the residents.

A bit of pre-dawn sneaking into the office down on the ground floor wasn't a wise move either: it would stir up the cats (three), dogs (one snake-bite-recovery patient) and echidna (a roadside rescue) in the sleepover room. Breakfast and wee-wee time for the inmates of the Cody and Cody Vet Clinic started at six o'clock and not a second before. She'd written it on the whiteboard in large capitals, just to remind them—but, to be fair, none of the animals could read. If they heard her, they'd set up a cacophony that would wake the household.

She looked at her watch. Ten minutes had dragged themselves past since she'd last looked, which was ominous. The busy day ahead was still hours away, which sucked, because busy was good.

Busy kept the quiet at bay, and finding busywork was Hannah's special skill. In the bath? Have a book handy. Driving out to an animal-in-labour emergency? Perfect time to catch up on that true crime podcast she loved. Day off? Skipjack needed his training session and grooming and to be assured of how handsome he was, and the glass-fronted cabinetry at The Billy Button Café needed to be inspected for new treats. Graeme or Kylie or the Joneses were usually on hand to chat with.

Usually.

Hunting for Sandy's secret stash of chocolate biscuits was another excellent quiet-time-avoidance tactic, and lasted for ages, too, because the hiding spot had never yet been breached.

Hannah rested her head on the newly painted window frame and sighed. She'd known—for months now, ever since The

Incident—that lurking in the quiet were questions that she was too chicken to answer.

Trouble was, the questions were starting to get louder, and every time she saw (and then avoided) Tom Krauss, she was having a harder and harder time ignoring them.

Emotional, messed-up, troublesome questions were part of it: *Why am I never content? Why do I feel like I've sutured myself up but the scar has never stopped weeping? Why do I keep everyone at a distance?*

Well, her resolution was going to fix all that.

*Hannah Cody is going to have a baby.* Oh yes, that dimmed the messed-up stuff, all right. This was *good* emotion. *Warm* emotion. *Wrap your arms about yourself and smile* emotion. Concentrating on the good stuff had to be the right move. Making the good stuff happen had to be the right choice.

She reached over to the bedside table for her phone and called up the searches she'd bookmarked earlier. Of the fertility clinics that had popped up, three were in driving distance from Hanrahan: Albury (320 kilometres), Wagga Wagga (283 kilometres), and Canberra (120 kilometres). If she were to make a graph (which was an awesome idea and if it wasn't 4.27 am she might've) and put two of her greatest anxiety triggers on the axes—distance to travel on the x, versus population of destination on the y—which place would come out the winner?

She did the maths in her head. Wagga Wagga won out over Albury, and it had the added benefit of being the same town as where she'd attended vet school. But it was a heck of a return day trip, and while she'd driven between there and home frequently as a student, her reluctance to leave Hanrahan hadn't been as acute back then. It had grown over the years, like moss grew over stone, making all the hard bits a little more comfortable.

Canberra made the most sense, time wise.

But Canberra made the least sense, people wise.

Which was why, she thought, dropping her phone onto the bedside table, there was a lot more riding on her first draft than successfully cutting out a steer. In just a few hours from now, she'd be socialising in a strange place, with people she didn't know and with no control over when she got to depart.

She shivered and burrowed back under the doona.

She could do it.

She *had* to do it.

Saturday morning clinic usually ran late and today was no exception. Hannah had finished with her last patient, a lanky kelpie with a lump on its tail which required a blood sample to send off to the pathologist in Cooma, and was setting up a tray of used scalpels and tweezers to run through the autoclave when her phone pinged.

Hmm. Her brother was literally two metres away through a plaster wall. She'd heard him fart from this distance, so why would—

*911. Act cool.*

She frowned at her phone screen for a second until it twigged. A dog had died. No, an owner was on the rampage about their vet bill. A medical mishap! Josh had cut his finger off or was being strangled by some kid's pet python (and yet could still type out text messages) and Vera would have a conniption and—

*On my way*, she texted, wondering how on earth *act cool* was relevant to a veterinary drama, then hit the corridor at a run. She flung the door open to the second treatment room, ready for blood spatter or trashed equipment or angry faces and found—

Josh standing on one side of the waist-high stainless steel bench that had cost the best half of a grand to install. On the other side was a gangly kid whose face she couldn't quite see, but who looked vaguely familiar. Between them lay a cardboard box. A sneaker box, by the looks, in size ginormous. Holes had been gouged in its sides with a blunt object.

'Um. Hey, guys,' she said.

'Hannah,' Josh said. 'What are you doing here?'

She narrowed her eyes. He narrowed his back and gave a jerk of the head that said *come closer*.

As she moved towards the bench she could see that the kid was Braydon Fox, son of one of Josh's old flames from high school. Mid teens, spotty, blotchier than normal and his eyelashes were wet.

Okay, clearly there was drama going on, but why Josh thought she'd be any help was a mystery. He was the one who'd knocked up his science teacher at the end of Grade Twelve and fathered a daughter—who was currently a teenager. He had skills with this demographic.

Act cool, he'd said. Easy for him to say, he was the people person. 'I, er, just popped in for some—' she did a rapid room scan and spotted the bribery jar '—liver treats.'

'Sure, help yourself, but … while you're here …' Josh looked down at Braydon. 'You cool with me getting a second opinion on Peanut? Hannah is the senior partner here and she has a lot of experience with, um, unhappy guinea pigs.'

The kid sniffed and nodded his head.

Either this was an April fool's joke way too early or she did not understand what was going on.

She moved a clump of old t-shirt fabric to the side of the sneaker box and looked in at the guinea pig currently nibbling away at a carrot stick with what she would have described, if she was in the habit of dropping French phrases into her patient notes, as *joie de vivre*.

'Unhappy? That's your clinical observation, is it, Josh?'

'That's *Braydon's* observation, Hannah. He's come here for answers.' *Not judgement* was the subtext to Josh's words.

The kid lifted an arm and dragged his sleeve along the bottom of his nose.

'Right. Mind if I get him out, Braydon?'

He shrugged one shoulder, which she knew—thanks, Poppy— to interpret as approval. Huh. Perhaps being an aunt already meant she wouldn't be totally clueless when it came to her own child. Another tick in the yes-I'm-doing-the-right-thing column. Then she lifted the fat little beast from his shoebox.

'Coat's shiny. Eyes are clear. Teeth—' At the risk of losing a finger, she prised the last shard of carrot out of the guinea pig's mouth and bent down for a closer inspection, taking a cautious sniff '—are yellowed and ground down, but nothing we wouldn't expect on a guinea pig the age of Peanut. How big was this carrot? They're quite high in sugar.'

'He mainly eats grass in the backyard and veggie scraps, but he likes kale chips done in the airfryer.'

She tried not to smile. A trendy guinea pig. Maybe he had his own Insta account. 'What makes you think he's unhappy?'

Braydon cleared his throat. 'You know how I got another one to keep him company? A girl one, black and white, and all her feet are black like she's wearing boots, and her head's got these tuft things like long hair.'

Hannah pulled over the manila folder that Josh had left on the bench. She opened it up, thumbed through Sandra's colour- sticker system, and ran her eyes down the owner-patient summary page. *One guinea pig, name Peanut, male, vaccinated regularly, weight issues, possible arthritis.* There was a note scribbled in the margin dating from August last year: *Owner's mother gave Josh the shits and stormed off.* Hmm. Not sure that needed to be written up, but whatever. She tapped her finger on the next animal in the family file. 'Ah yes. A rescue guinea pig, fully vaccinated, neutered, age unknown. And you named it … Poppy.'

If the kid's face had been blotchy and pale before, now it was blotchy and red. 'Yeah.'

'Has, um …' She looked up at Josh, who was being surprisingly quiet for a bloke who was a) a chatterbox and b) totally aware, like she was, that her niece and Braydon had spent a lot of time together last time Poppy—the human Poppy, that is, not her miniature furry tribute—had come down from Sydney to visit her dad. 'Has there been some rivalry at home? Any fighting in the guinea pig pen?'

'Yeah. Well, Poppy's been ghosting me. Um, him. She was, like, all best friends, whatever, at first, but then nothing. It's like she doesn't even *like* him anymore. And now he's unhappy and I didn't know what to do, so I thought if I came here then …' His voice trickled off.

Riiiight. Life advice for a teenager. This was so not her forte.

Although this could be in her future, having to help her own child come to grips with the pitfalls of young love. She could have a crack at resolving a teen crisis using some guinea pig metaphor, couldn't she? How hard could it be?

'Well, Braydon,' she said. 'We can put your mind at ease about Peanut. He's in good health. Do you think'—she popped the little fella back in his shoebox—'it's worth giving the whole Poppy thing some time. You can't force friendship to blossom between two guinea pigs any more than you can between two people, and maybe you don't know all the facts, so you're making up trouble when it's not even there. Just be patient, and be yourself … um, encourage Peanut to be himself. You can always bring him back to see us if his mood doesn't improve. We love seeing Peanut, don't we, Josh?'

'Absolutely.'

Braydon picked up his box and started walking for the door, then turned back to them. 'Can I ask you something?' By 'you' he clearly meant Josh, so Hannah kept silent. So much for her awesome advice. 'You don't think it's lame that I've got two guinea pigs?'

'Mate, chicks love blokes with pets,' said Josh firmly.

'They do?' The kid looked cheerful for the first time. 'Well. I guess I'll get going then. Um, I just pay the lady out front?'

'No charge,' said Hannah. 'Just promise to let us know when Peanut's a bit happier, okay?'

The kid left and Hannah looked at her brother. 'Was that what I think it was?'

'The unrequited love of a fourteen-year-old country boy for an older woman who's gone back to Sydney and embroiled herself in big city life where she might meet boys who spurn ownership of guinea pigs?'

'You're referring to your sixteen-year-old daughter as an "older woman" now?'

He laughed. 'Don't tell her that.'

'I'm not sure if a 911 call was warranted. Although, I did like that part where you finally acknowledged I'm the experienced senior partner in this veterinary practice.'

'That was bribery. Totally meaningless. I'll retract it formally in an email to the human resources division.'

'Idiot,' she said fondly. 'But seriously, he only wanted to hear what you had to say.'

Josh shrugged, the exact same movement the kid had given earlier. 'It was a bit awkward. He clearly wanted to ask if there was some reason why Poppy hadn't been in touch with him, but he didn't know how to go about it.'

'Offloading his personal problems onto his guinea pig was certainly original. What did you tell him before I came in?'

'Nothing. What could I say? Poppy would have my guts if she thought I was getting involved in her personal life.'

Hearing Josh's confidence that he knew exactly what Poppy would or wouldn't want him to do or say struck Hannah as being very germane to her own thoughts of late. Her brother had had parenthood thrust upon him at an early age and he'd been single for the most part, after a few shaky months living with Poppy's mother. He'd coped.

He'd more than coped; he'd thrived.

'What was it like, looking after Poppy on your own when she was little?'

He raised his eyebrows. 'Tough. Awesome. The best years of my life, maybe, and definitely the hardest.'

'But you were a teenager. You missed out on your uni scholarship. You sacrificed a lot when you became a parent. If you had your time over, would you do things differently?'

'What's brought this on?' He frowned. 'You're not worried *Poppy's* getting up to ...'

'What? No! Bloody hell. I was just—' She paused. It was way too soon to start blabbing to Josh that she needed to know what being a single parent felt like. He'd said it was awesome. That was all she needed to hear.

Josh was in full defensive mode, like a daddy emperor penguin defending the egg on its webbed feet. 'Poppy only likes boys as friends. *Especially* Braydon. She's two years older than he is, which at that age is like being two decades older. He's just got a crush, that's all. I'll call her later and subtly suggest she might want to tag him in a funny social media post or something. You know, a friendly wave so he knows he's not being "ghosted".'

She smiled at him. 'Rightio, Dad. I wasn't trying to suggest anything, really. You okay to finish up here? I'm going out this arvo
and I need to go wash up.'

She headed upstairs to shower and switch out her scrubs for riding
boots and ancient jeans. She zipped a woolly brown vest over her
flannel shirt, and braided her hair away from her face so the tail of
her plait hung over her shoulder, just in reach of her nervous fingers. Better than worry beads, right?

Kev and his mate Lionel collected her bang on time. They headed
south on the highway and, really, it was fun.

She'd been worrying for nothing.

She'd been so freaking busy of late that sitting in the filthy back
seat of an ancient LandCruiser while Slim Dusty and hay motes
filled the air around her felt like a holiday.

When the sign for Dalgety flashed by the window fifty kilometres later, Hannah uncapped the water bottle she held and took a
long drink. Still totally fine: leaving the Hanrahan town border
didn't faze her at all! Woo! Go her!

Those paddocks looked harmless. Pasture was browning off now
the summer rains had moved north, and the wildflowers clustered
beneath crooked fenceposts looked brittle and dry and okay, damn
it, maybe she *was* feeling a little worked up now.

Crowds. People. Strangers. But she was going to deal with it,
because that's what small-town vets who wanted to have a baby did,
right?

Lionel dropped a gear and the heavy horse float behind them
clunked and rattled. Out the window, poplars marched like soldiers
along high banks that must once have marked the waterline of the

Snowy River a century ago, before the dam tamed it. Progress, she supposed. A shame, too, for the floodplains to miss out on their annual dousing with snowmelt. All that river flood which once provided water for families and irrigated the bush food and carried alluvial gold into the pans of colonial gold diggers, lost to history.

The gold had petered out a hundred and fifty years ago and the town still clinging to the river's banks was little more than a cross-roads now. Population of Dalgety? She couldn't remember, but a couple of hundred at most, and besides a café that doubled as a plant nursery, all she could see were highway signs to someplace else. A handful of old timber cottages, smoke plumes rising from their chimneys, dotted the landscape. It was charming, rural and peace-ful; nothing at all for her to be uptight about.

'You're overthinking, girl. I can feel it from here,' said Kev, twisting in his seat to look at her from under the peak of his cor-duroy cap. 'There'll be plenty of beginners today, don't you worry about that.'

Yeah, she was overthinking, just not about campdrafting.

Lionel, who so far on the trip had proved himself to be a man of few words, spoke up. 'No-one'll be having a laugh if you get disqualified.'

'You ever do campdrafting yourself, Lionel?'

'Not on horseback, but I cracked the whip a time or two at local comps if the call came out for volunteers. Weekend travel wasn't an option back when I had the feed store.'

'Yeah. Weekend travel isn't an option for me that often either. Josh—my brother—and I take it in turns to be on call.'

'Nothing wrong with sticking local,' said Kev. 'But the legends of the sport, they travel. You get good enough, you'll want to do it too. Some hard driving, sure, but then a weekend spent camping in a swag, your horse near enough so you can hear him dozing under a tree. Talk around the fire after the events are done, a bit of romance when the stars come out …'

'Sounds like something from the last century.'

'Well, that's its appeal, love. Horses and riders, not computers and wifi extenders and all that other password-hashtag rubbish.'

She smiled. 'Been having trouble with technology at home, Kev?'

He ignored her, and must have decided he was done with philosophy, because he switched into trainer mode. 'You'll want to watch the others do the cut out, Hannah. Try to avoid the cattle they're avoiding; you don't want a slug and you don't want one that's too geed up. Pick the right beast and you'll get through the gate a whole lot easier.'

He'd been drumming these rules into her head for weeks. 'Will do.'

'And pick a steer over a heifer. The steers aren't as cantankerous.'

'You know that's sexist, don't you, Kev?'

He grunted. 'Don't get uppity with me, Hannah Cody.'

The coil in her gut relaxed as she laughed and leant forward to give him a light whack to the arm. 'Flatterer. What are you two old codgers going to do while I make a fool of myself in the maiden round?'

'My prize student make a fool of herself? Not on your nelly. Besides, I reckon that horse of yours has the draft in his blood. He'll get you through.'

'Let's hope so.'

'Enough of that backchat, young lady. I know potential when I see it.'

'Kev. First up, I'm not that young.'

'When you're on the shady side of seventy, Hannah Cody, you'll know what young is and what young isn't.'

She grinned. 'Yes, sir.'

'Here's the turn. Well, look out. Someone's gone and fancied up this paddock some.'

Some? The locals who looked after the Dalgety Showgrounds had more than fancied the place up. An arch above the wide gate flew with banners advertising food trucks, fairy floss, live music. Cars were backed up ahead of them and horse floats were every-where, their licence plates not just local or Victorian but from Queensland, too.

Her gut coiled again. 'Kev, you told me this was a little event. "A school fete on horseback" were your exact words.'

'And so it was, Hannah, pet, last time I was here. When would that've been, Lionel?'

'Dunno, mate … 1970? Probably about the same year you bought that rag on your head that used to be a hat.'

'No-one would know if we did a U-turn and drove back up the mountain.'

'She's jokin', right?' said Lionel.

'Of course she's joking.'

'Ha ha,' Hannah said weakly, her eyes on the horses, the cattle pens—the *busy*. A woman strode past them and the unseasonably cold wind whipping in over the Monaro Plains had the fringed leather on her riding jacket swirling.

Goals. That's what she had to remember: her goals.

She sucked in a breath and let it out as slow as she could. It was time to find some grit or wither on the vine. If she couldn't get out of this truck and spend one afternoon of her life mingling with the actual world, then she sure as eggs wasn't ready to have a baby.

Three old cow cockies were leaning against a metal rail, their stockmen's hats pulled low over their faces, and kids in ruthlessly ironed chequered shirts were skidding about between food stalls.

People. Families. Normal things. On a larger scale than she was comfortable with, but doable.

'Hannah, my love, you've got the jitters. It's only natural. When was the last time you competed in a horse event?'

'When I was, like, ten, as you well know. Pony dressage. I don't even think I had front teeth.' And she certainly hadn't had a tremor in her hands and this desperate, desperate urge to flee. 'You don't think there'll be media here, do you, Kev?'

'What's that, love?'

'You know. The local newspaper. Instagram influencers. ABC *Landline*.'

Kev hopped out his side of the old cruiser, swung her door open and reached in to grab her hand. 'Come on, pet. Let's get your big fella out of the float and give him a look at the grounds, hey? He'll be wondering what all this smell and ruckus is about.'

'Sure.'

She knew it wasn't rational to be afraid to leave her hometown. She knew all the rules she lived by punished no-one but herself. 'Damn it,' she muttered and, pulling her wide-brimmed hat low over her head, let Kev help her out of the back seat. No-one was going to be interested in a small-town vet having a crack at the maiden run at the Dalgety Campdraft.

The weather, at least, was perfect. Scudding clouds and a wind sharper than vintage cheddar would—hopefully—keep the crowd thin.

Maybe she *could* do this.

A little grin welled up from some hidden, worry-free place she'd forgotten she had inside.

# CHAPTER
## 6

'Mrs L. Everything okay?'

'Everything is super okay. Thank you for taking Bruno with you to Dalgety.'

Tom leant against the doorjamb and raised his eyebrows at the woman who'd come to Ironbark as nanny and housekeeper when his mother had died all those years ago and become part of the family. A bossy part. 'Like you gave me a choice.'

Mrs LaBrooy smoothed his hair and tidied the collar of his shirt. He held her hands against his chest for a moment.

'I'm not six years old anymore.'

She gave his hands a squeeze. 'More's the pity. You didn't scowl as much then as you do now. Don't leave me again, you hear?'

'I'll do my best.'

'And try not to argue with your father. I know he's a grumpy old fart, but he's looking forward to this outing.'

'Did he say that? Because I've been hearing very different words come out of his mouth.'

'He's frightened, Tom, about being weak. That's why he's so angry all the time. His voice is about the only thing that's not given out on him, and he's taken to lashing it like the stockwhip he can no longer hold.'

Tom turned his head at the *clank-clank* as the wheels of his father's chair rolled down the planking on the ramp. Bruno's shoulders had caved in, but he wore a collared shirt that was clearly from the 'good clothes' section of his cupboard and the denim that bagged over his scrawny knees was starched stiff as planks. Even his hat was smart: he'd switched out the battered thing he usually wore for a new-looking black one with a leather plait circling the crown.

'Check out the buckle,' Mrs L whispered in Tom's ear. 'He was in my kitchen sniffing out the Brasso at dawn.'

A championship buckle. The old man had a few to choose from. The belt it was attached to sagged around Bruno's middle and Tom fought down the surge of pity. He didn't have room for pity where his father was concerned, he was too filled with the mash-up of bitterness he'd been carrying around with him like brass bloody buckles of his own.

'Try to have a good time. Promise me,' she said.

'I promise.'

He followed his dad down to the gravel and watched him—a bloke who'd once been a country legend—struggle to control the lever on his chair as he rumbled over the rough ground.

'Need a hand, Dad?' Not that he'd be much use, but still.

'I'm not fucking useless yet.' Bruno reached the ute's passenger side, where the door had been opened for him, and used the handles and sheer determination to pull himself onto his feet and in.

Tom turned to Mrs L. 'Here goes,' he said.

'Try to get over the cattle grid before you start arguing with each other.'

He kissed her cheek. 'You're such an optimist.'

'You gonna stand there all day or are we going?' yelled his dad.

It took a few minutes to get sorted. Thank heavens for the hoist Bruno had rigged up in the tray of his remodelled ute. Tom would have struggled to lift a toolbox off the ground, let alone his father's mechanised wheelchair.

'Staring at the bloody steering wheel won't get us to Dalgety, son.'

Tom released the handbrake and took off from the front of the homestead with—if he was honest—an unnecessary spray of gravel. It felt good.

'So,' he said, having come up with a line of conversation that might keep the peace, 'who's the local campdrafting champion in the district since you hung up your boots, Dad?'

'It sure as hell isn't you, son.'

Navigating a path for a wheelchair through an old showground crammed with country folk keen to say g'day, and where grass and mud patches outranked cement, was a challenge. To give the old man his due, Bruno didn't waste time with pleasantries. He made his way to the power brokers at the base of the officials' tower by the simple means of barking at everyone who got in his way and pointing imperiously in the direction he wanted to go. A cluster of old blokes in footy jerseys, jeans and Akubras made some room at the rail when Bruno got there, nodding their heads in greeting and saying things like 'Bugger me, it's Bruno' and 'Thought you'd popped your clogs, mate'.

'And who's this then?' said a man about Tom's own age, sporting a hi-vis vest with a walkie-talkie tucked into its top pocket. 'It's not Tom, is it?'

'You've got a long memory,' said Bruno. 'Tom, this is Roger Kettering. You might've ridden against him back in the day.'

Roger held out his hand. 'I was a couple of years ahead of you at school. Been away in the Navy, haven't you? Naval Intelligence?'

Tom shook the hand he was offered. 'Didn't know that news was doing the rounds.'

'My dad's old man was warrant officer on the HMAS *Vendetta*. He takes an interest in the local youngsters who enlist.'

'*Vendetta*. That would have meant Vietnam, right?'

'Right. So, you don't look dressed for competing. Can't tempt you to have a burl now you're back in town?'

'I'm just here as Bruno's driver.'

Roger looked over to where Bruno was giving his opinion on how the cold wind would be riling up the cattle. 'We haven't seen him since the campdraft at Ironbark two years ago. He's lost a lot of weight.'

'Yeah.'

'I hear it's been scratched off the calendar permanently. That's a real pity.'

'He didn't discuss it with me.'

Roger looked at his watch as a voice came over the loudspeakers warning people they had ten minutes to grab a sausage and find a seat in the grandstands. 'I'm needed over at the far gate. Good to see you, Tom. See if you can talk Bruno into changing his mind, why don't you? There's plenty of people who'll come up and lend a hand.'

'Thanks, mate.'

Bruno looked happier than he had in weeks, so Tom decided he could leave him to it and set off for a wander through the Dalgety Showgrounds, feeling like he was walking through some

old home movie from his childhood. Animal pens stood dis-
used in long rows, signs like GOATS and PIGS tacked to their
eaves a reminder of the agricultural shows that had been huge
when he was a kid, and probably still were this far from the
city. A long building had canteen doors flung open and its walls
were decorated with panels of plywood painted up with cattle
musters, Clydesdales pulling wagons and turn-of-the-century
fossickers sluicing river silt through gold pans. He nodded to a
group of older women seated around a plastic table—local CWA
types for sure—who'd probably put in a few hours' work on the
land already today before baking a batch of scones and prettying
themselves up in floral shirts for an afternoon of socialising at the
showgrounds.

The cattle pens were choked with two hundred head or more,
some Brahman, some Angus, but mostly Hereford, and on the field
beyond the cattle were the horse floats and tents of the families
who'd travelled a long way to get here.

He and Bruno had never camped under the stars, of course. Back
in the day when he'd been mucking about in the junior division
and Bruno had been a Snowy River legend of the draft, they'd
stayed in the Ironbark Station horse float: bunks, an aircon unit,
even a shower that was better than the ones he'd used on the Navy
boats he'd been deployed on before being seconded to the anti-
piracy taskforce in Bahrain.

He skirted a horse float and a noisy genset and—kaboom—there
she was.

Probably just as well Josh had given him the head's up; the jolt to
his heart wasn't so unexpected.

Hannah was atop the horse she'd once stabled at Ironbark, before
The Incident That Was Never To Be Discussed. Josh was beside

her, holding the horse's reins while she fussed about with a hair tie, taming that long hair of hers. Should he go over?

His boots had turned in her direction before his head could decide and pride—or something else that he had no name for, because he was pretty sure his pride was currently smashed into smithereens—kept him moving towards her just as she looked up. Her eyes locked with his.

# CHAPTER

# 7

Hannah's nerves were still on the simmer when she spied her brother and his fiancée picking their way across the paddock. Behind them, as close to her brother's ankles as the laws of physics and rough grass fields allowed, scampered an old brown dog.

'Get off, you great oaf,' she said, as Josh kissed both her cheeks and ruffled her hair. 'You'd better not let Jane Doe get anywhere near the cattle. There's a no dogs rule at campdraft. Isn't that right, Kev?'

'That's right, love.'

'You hear that, Jane, my love? Auntie Hannah doesn't want you here. What a meanie.'

She shoved her idiot brother away and turned to Vera. 'It's not too late to ditch him. I'd totally understand.'

Vera just grinned. 'We'll keep her well away, I promise.'

'What time's the maiden event starting?' said Josh.

'Soon,' Hannah said, then frowned. 'Forty minutes, maybe, but I have to be near the pen ten minutes ahead of time. Speaking of, how did you know I was competing?'

Josh slung his arm around Vera. 'How do I know anything?'

She groaned. 'That bloody coffee shop.'

Vera made a huffing noise. 'Hey, we're not the only blabber-mouths in Hanrahan.'

Josh smirked. 'You should have found a BFF who wasn't so chatty. Kylie told me, of course; she's in the queue at the coffee truck. The whole fan club's here for your debut draft.'

Great. So much for discreetly failing on her first go.

'Where's old mate?'

'If you mean Lionel, he said he was going up to sign us in, but I interpreted that to mean he was going to go gossip at the bar,' Hannah said.

'Speaking of,' said Kev. 'He might need a hand. Let's get Skip-jack out of the float and ready to rumble, then I can go supervise.'

'Have a beer, you mean,' said Josh.

Kev tapped his nose.

'I can take care of Skippy, mate. You go hang out and we'll see you before the event.'

Josh led Skipjack out of the float while Hannah pulled all her gear from the boot of the LandCruiser. Saddle, reins, helmet, gloves, thick jacket ... none of it carried the authority and famil-iarity of her vet kit, but with every piece, she felt her confidence growing.

Josh fitted the saddle over the blanket Hannah had laid over Skippy's back and she tightened the girth under the horse's belly until it pulled on his warm, rough coat. Water from a thermos into a bucket for Skip; his reins looped loosely over a bollard on the horse float so he couldn't wander off: they were ready.

'Skip's looking good,' said Josh.

The horse tossed his head and gave an affirmative whinny and she laughed. 'I had no idea he'd love all this fuss and bother.'

Josh smiled. 'You seen yourself in the mirror today, Han? Skip-jack's not the only one who's feeling chuffed with themselves, I'm guessing. I'm proud of you. It can't have been easy, deciding to enter.'

She shrugged. If leaving home and being comfortable amongst strangers was going to be her new normal, she had to stop being congratulated every time she did something that was—well, that should be—normal.

Josh opened his mouth, cleared his throat, started to say something, then turned back to fuss with the bridle the same way she fussed with her plait.

She prised it off him. 'Spit it out,' she said. If he was about to get all emotional and weepy because his maladjusted little sister had finally decided she was okay enough to rejoin society, she was going to kick him.

'Hannah—'

He was, damn it. Well, not if she could help it. 'I'm going to head over to the camp,' she said. 'Let Skippy walk his fidgets out while we figure out which steers we like the look of.'

'Looking good, girlfriend,' called a voice behind her.

'Kylie! The blabbermouth herself. Aren't you supposed to be chained to your workshop fixing my car?'

'Have a coffee, grumblebum.'

'You are so lucky you're offering me a caffeinated beverage right now, or I'd be giving you a serve for telling everyone about my event today.'

'You're welcome,' said Kylie, leaning in and giving her a hug. 'Now, just channel some of that aggro into your event and you'll have a shiny new buckle on your belt in no time.'

Winning a belt buckle wasn't why she was here. Reclaiming herself, being someone other than Hannah the sister, Hannah the vet, Hannah the small-town girl who hadn't coped in the big, bad world … that was why she was here.

She slugged down half a cup of the truly diabolical coffee Kylie had handed her, then tightened her fingers on Skipjack's reins. 'I'd better get moving.'

'You feeling as nervous as you look?' said Kylie.

'Yep.'

Vera took Hannah's half-finished cup from her and gave her a hug. 'You'll do great.'

'I'll give you a leg up,' said Josh, holding out his hands for her boot and swinging her into the saddle.

Hannah looked at her brother. He was okay when he wasn't flogging orange juice from her fridge. No-one knew her better than he did. 'Walk me to the yard?'

He rubbed her knee. 'Always. Vera, my sweet, can you keep Jane Doe with you? I'll come find you in a bit.'

'Sure.'

Jane Doe thumped her tail and Josh slipped a hand into Skipjack's bridle and led the way to the pens of temporary fencing, where steers and heifers from local farms had been trucked in to be used in the competition.

Hannah jumped as the music cut off and the master of ceremonies' voice blasted through the overhead speakers.

'And a warm Snowy River thank you to D and V Tickle of Mackenzie Plains for sponsoring the maiden A event. Des and Viv have donated a service from their champion stallion Stormy Dan. BYO mare!'

Donating a service! That was new. There'd been no prizes like that back when she did pony club.

She reached a hand down to her brother. He'd led her horse for her back then, too, if she was remembering correctly. Even braided Tubby's mane with ribbon for her when she'd asked, even though it made him look like a total wuss—his words. 'Thanks for coming, Josh. I guess I was being an idiot about not wanting anyone here.'

He rested his hand around the ankle of her boot. 'You don't have to do this alone, Han. Not if you don't want to.'

A wad of messy stuff, which felt like what she imagined a cat furball must feel like, lodged in her throat. 'You're not the worst brother a girl could have, Cody.'

He grinned at her. 'And you're not the worst boss a bloke could have, Cody.'

She frowned. 'Speaking of. Aren't you working today?'

He lifted his mobile from his pocket. 'I'm on it. Grab bag in the truck, liver treats in the glove box. Kylie will drive Vera home if I have to go lights-and-sirens back to town.'

She grinned. 'Sirens. I'd like to see that on the vet truck.'

'Why stop there? My arse would look amazeballs in a cape and tights. Mild-mannered Josh Cody by day, Supervet by night.'

'Superidiot, you mean,' she said, pulling his hair.

Her brother's ridiculous tactics were working. The nerves were settling enough for her to start taking notice of the other entrants. Men and women, some young, some middle-aged, the occasional senior citizen looking trim and wiry, all wearing what must be the unofficial uniform of campdrafting: jeans, plaid or floral shirt and a vest to keep out that vicious wind. The women's jeans had elaborate white embroidery on the back pockets and while most of the boots people wore were scuffed and utilitarian, a few of the youngsters had fancy, American cowboy–style boots on, with turquoise patches and fringing.

Heavens above. Did she have to up her clothing game, too? This personal growth stuff sucked.

'Hey, Josh,' she said. 'Check out the spurs on the boots. More people have them than don't. You reckon it matters?'

'Dunno. Why not ask some of the other entrants?'

Josh let go of her ankle to wave at someone behind her and she turned to smile. Kev must be back at last from spinning yarns. Only it wasn't Kev striding through the assembled horses looking like he'd just stepped out of an action-adventure movie billboard.

Tom Krauss. Crap. And here she was, trapped with a horse, just like … just as though … She blew out a breath.

*Just like The Incident.*

She looked at her watch. Fourteen minutes to go, which meant she should be checking out the competitors ahead of her, seeing what was working and what wasn't. She tried to drag her eyes away while Tom and Josh performed some complicated male greeting ritual which involved backslaps and insults, but her eyes wouldn't be dragged.

Tom looked better than she'd remembered, if that were possible, because she'd been remembering him plenty in between every random encounter they'd had since that day, months ago now, at Ironbark Station.

His eyes met hers. Yep. Summer-lake blue. Eyelashes that trapped the sunlight. A face that was three parts wary and one part unreadable.

'Hannah.' He said it the way a bomb defusing expert might say *Gently remove the inner screw and cut the third green wire or we all die.*

She nodded. 'Tom.'

'Since when were you into campdrafting, brat?'

The old nickname underscored how weird she'd let this whole situation get. 'Um. Just starting. And you're here, too,' she said, overcompensating with a fake jolly tone. 'Whacko.' She was embarrassing herself. He'd made a move on her, she'd made a scene, so what?

*So you haven't been able to stop obsessing about it since.*

'Dad's catching up with some old mates.'

He was looking at her as though she was going to make another scene any second. Which she absolutely wasn't. And, if she actually used her brain once in a while, she'd have remembered that Bruno Krauss was a campdrafting legend before multiple sclerosis claimed his legs. Half the horses here probably had Ironbark Station stamped in their stud book entry. It would have been odd if the Krauss family *wasn't* here.

She was scrabbling around for something normal to say when Josh leapt into the breach like the reliable bloke he was.

'Haven't seen you lately, Tom. We should grab a beer.'

'I'd like that.'

'You busy tonight? Vera's using me as a guinea pig for the autumn menu she's working on. Lamb shank pot pie and these little plum tarts for afters.'

'Boasting's not a good look on you, Cody.'

Tom was saying it to Josh, but for some reason his eyes were on her. She dug her heels into her horse and wheeled Skipjack away.

She couldn't think about Tom and The Incident, not here, not now.

*She couldn't think about Tom and The Incident.*

Damn it. *All* she could think about was Tom and that bloody Incident.

# CHAPTER

## 8

*Four and a bit months ago*

Hannah Cody buried her nose in the neck of her horse, Skipjack, and breathed in his warm smell. 'How are you, my sweet?' This was the perk of stabling her horse at a property that employed her vet services: she could pop in to spoil him between patients.

The horse shifted on his feet and dropped his head over the timber rail to snuffle at her pockets.

'What makes you think I've brought you a present?' She gave his neck a pat and relented. Skipjack knew her well; of course she'd brought sugar lumps.

'You bring anything for me?'

The deep voice came from the next stall in the quiet stable, but she didn't need to look to see who it was. The thrum that had been buzzing behind her breastbone ever since Tom Krauss moved his lean, broody self back to Hanrahan ratcheted up a notch. If only a sugar lump could cure that.

Skipjack butted her in the shoulder, nudging her away from his stall door in the direction of the neighbouring one. She frowned at him. Whose side was he on, anyway? Where Tom Krauss was concerned, she needed more space, not less. At least, she did until she'd managed to quell these funny feelings she was having every time he came within cooee.

She took a reluctant step sideways. 'Hi.'

Tom stood in the shadows at the back of the stall, looking more like a viking than a horseman. A viking in an Akubra, with a stubbie in one hand. Tall, lean in the face and with a ruthless edge to his manner that made her wonder just what he'd been doing all those years he'd been away from his family's high country horse stud. In the Navy, apparently. Doing something that had aged him.

The horse whose stall he was brooding in was just starting to swell with her unborn foal. She was a massive mare—a thoroughbred—with a white blaze streaking through her deep roan coat. 'Isn't Buttercup usually in the big stable?'

'She was fretting, so we're having some one-on-one time.'

That thrumming in Hannah's chest started up again. Yeah, Tom might have the demeanour of a Nordic warrior who burned down whole villages before breakfast, but there was a heart hiding under that don't-mess-with-me attitude—at least, there used to be, back when she was a teenager and he was her brother's best mate at high school. She ran a hand down the front of her no-nonsense navy scrubs, willing the unsettling feeling to go away. Hannah Cody didn't do feelings. Not for guys. Not since—

She dragged her thoughts away from the abyss. 'You're getting clucky, Tom. She's got a while to go yet.'

'Want to check her out for me? Since you're here?'

She tapped her finger on the stall door. 'It'll cost you.'

He waggled his empty bottle. 'Sorry, I'm all out of beer.'

'Pity.'

'I can owe you.'

'Yeah, there's the quick way to ruin for a small-town vet clinic.'

'You ever know me to default on my debts, Cody? I seem to recall promising to put a frog in your boots if you didn't quit pestering me back when you were about eight. Came through with that one, didn't I?'

She grinned, easier now they'd slipped back into insults. This was more like it. The Tom Krauss who sent a shiver frisking through her unmentionables was a new and unwelcome development, but the Tom who'd pushed her into the lake and cut off one of her pigtails and used her toys for gumnut slingshot practice with Josh? Him, she could deal with.

'Frogs don't pay the wages, but Mrs LaBrooy's apple pie just might. Put in a good word for me with your housekeeper and I'll check out your horse,' she said, moving into the stable and running her practised hands over Buttercup's impressive girth.

Tom leant back against the wall, his face relaxed for once, his grin cocky under the battered old hat he wore.

She frowned at him. 'Stop looking like that.'

'Like what, brat?'

*Hot. Charming. Flirty.* 'Irritating,' she said, and turned her back on him. 'Bloody men,' she muttered and Buttercup looked back at her and whickered. 'Yeah, you know what I'm talking about, don't you, girl?'

Tom cleared his throat. 'If you're attempting to draw some tenuous analogy between me and the champion racehorse who knocked Buttercup up ... yeah, fair call.'

She frowned at the smirk in his voice. Where had bossy Tom gone? Annoying Tom? The Tom who'd liked to argue logic with his big words and his smart brain and if that didn't work, with a headlock and a tickle to the ribs? This new hot-and-cold, broody-or-flirty version was altogether too … something.

'The Navy changed you, Tom Krauss. And not for the better.'

The pause was longer this time. 'Another fair call.'

There was no smirk in his voice now. She peered around the swell of the horse's belly. 'Did I say something?'

'Brat, you're always saying something.'

Hmm. She eyed him as she moved to Buttercup's head. What-ever she'd said, he didn't want to talk about it. And who better than her to understand that?

The horse's eyes were clear, her gums and palate a good colour. 'Your horse is fine, Tom. Calm and happy. Maybe there was too much going on up at the big stable and she couldn't relax.' Ironbark Station's big stable held upward of forty stockhorses at any given time. Bruno Krauss's reputation as a breeder and trainer—and the legend-ary skills of his long-term staff—meant the stalls were never empty.

She dug around in her pockets until she found another sugar lump. 'Don't tell Skipjack about this, Buttercup,' she said, as the mare slurped it up from the palm of her hand. 'He thinks he's the only horse in my life.'

Tom had moved away from the wall and came up behind her to rest a hand on Buttercup's neck. 'And is he?'

Jeepers. He was close—way too close—she could smell man and sunshine and soap over the ever-present smells of the stable. And why were the prickles on her neck telling her he was no longer talking about horses?

She took a step to the side, needing the sanity that a few inches of distance might provide, but the horse shifted, and oops, there she was, suddenly even closer to six-foot-something of muscle-bound male.

Her breath whooshed out.

She looked up into his face, then wished she hadn't. When had his eyes turned into the blue of the lake on a summer afternoon? And why hadn't she noticed his eyelashes before? Darker than his blond hair, tawny, almost the colour of the stable's old tabby cat snoozing in dappled sunlight—

Woah. These were cutesy man–woman thoughts. And Hannah Cody didn't do cutesy thoughts. Or man–woman thoughts. Not ever.

His mouth quirked, a quarter smile that started on his lips but ended somewhere in her rib cage where that dratted thrum had gone into overdrive. 'Not ever what?'

Crap. Had she said that out loud? She cleared her throat. 'You're crowding me, Krauss.'

'A little. Want me to step back?'

She swallowed. He plucked something from her hair. A blade of straw? A horse hair? Her last sane thought?

She tried her voice, which for some reason had forgotten how to make actual sounds and came out in a whisper. 'Um …'

He dipped his head, the brim of his scruffy old hat close enough to nudge at her hair. 'Is it so bad?'

His voice was working just fine. Better than fine. It rumbled the way thunder rumbled through the peaks of the Snowy Mountains and then got all deep and breathy in a way that sent a shiver up her spine.

'Not bad,' she said. 'Just … unexpected.'

This was Tom, for heaven's sake. She'd put snails in his bed and dobbed on him for not letting her join in hide and seek and seen him naked in the bath … admittedly, not for more than twenty years. And sure, he'd been out of town for fifteen of those years, gallivanting around doing whatever officers with law degrees did for the Royal Australian Navy when they graduated from Creswell … but still. He was firmly slotted into the brother's-best-friend category in her head.

Only here, in the stable, with his eyes sending out all sorts of searing messages, and his face so close to hers she could see a scar across the bridge of his nose, and his mouth just so, well, *close* … all that shared childhood history seemed like something she'd read in a book a long, long time ago that happened between two totally different people.

She gasped as his hand slid from the horse to her waist and grabbed a fistful of her old (and probably grubby) blue scrubs, and then—whaaat!—that firm mouth was on hers.

Oh, god. She'd forgotten what a kiss felt like.

And then he moved, just a fraction, but that fraction made her wonder if she'd ever known what a kiss was truly like, because this one seemed to be made of something a whole lot sweeter than anything she'd experienced.

A sigh escaped her and she forgot about her grubby scrubs as his lips moved to the corner of her mouth, to her cheek, to the curve of skin beneath her ear, before landing like a brand right back on her mouth again.

He tasted like everything she might once have wanted, before—

'Stop it.' She slid her hands to his chest and shoved as the first sob broke through.

'Hannah?'

His face moved from flirty to stricken in the space of a heartbeat. 'Are they—are you *crying*?'

She shook her head. If her voice had been shy before, now it had packed up and got the hell out of Hanrahan. She couldn't speak. She needed to be alone. She needed to be anywhere but here, with two horrified eyes gazing down at her like she was an object of pity.

Pity sucked.

She turned blindly for the stable door.

'Hannah. I'm so sorry. I thought— Crikey, I don't know what I thought. I'd never do anything to hurt you. You know that, right?'

'Go away, Tom,' she said, her back to him. She didn't need to see how bad she'd made him feel. He didn't deserve it, and she should tell him that, but then she'd have to tell him everything. And that wasn't happening—ever.

'I'll call Josh. Or Kylie.'

She hustled out of the stall and dropped to her knees beside her kitbag, scrabbling around in it until she'd found her sunglasses and wedged them on. She could barely see now in the dimness of the barn, but that was good. It made it easier to make the cut.

She stood up and risked a look at him. 'I'll send someone to collect Skipjack; he can find lodging in the stables in town from now on. I'll pass my patients up here over to Josh. He's had plenty of experience with horses now.'

'Is that necessary? Hannah, can we just talk—'

Dumb question; of course it was necessary. 'Please respect my wishes on this, Tom.'

He held his hands wide. 'Of course. Look, I was just … I don't know. There's no reason to be upset, I promise. I didn't mean anything by it. But Hannah …' He rubbed his head. 'What's going on?'

'Nothing. Let's both leave here and never mention this—incident—again.'

'Sure, like that's a healthy reaction. Come on, brat.'

'Promise me.'

'Shit. All right, I promise, but at least tell me how I can make amends.'

He had nothing to make amends for. She supposed he deserved some explanation so he'd understand that this was all on her, not him. She'd tell him the short version, then she was getting in her ancient green car and driving away from Ironbark Station as fast as the mountain road would allow. Maybe this stupid, hammering, idiot feeling she had would blow out the window and that would be that. Incident over.

'I don't do romance, Tom.'

# CHAPTER

# 9

A puddle of scary water leaking from the cattle troughs had Skip-jack whinnying and shaking his head and Hannah strong-armed her mind back to the present before she humiliated herself and lost control of her horse.

'The draft,' she muttered. 'That's what you're here for, Cody.'

She nudged Skip with her knee until the puddle was behind them.

'Cut a steer in the camp, demonstrate control, drive it out through the gate,' she instructed herself. That's what she needed to be thinking about. She told Skippy he was being a baby and trotted him alongside the cattle pens, where heifers and steers waited their turn for an event. So many. Campdraft was way more popular than she'd guessed.

She reached the end of the pens where a small yard about the size of the block of land the vet clinic sat on had been gated off. The organisers had announced they'd be penning eight into the cut-out yard, and at first glance the animals huddled together at the back of the yard looked much of a muchness. But—okay, yes—there were differences. Some jostled up against each other wanting to be in a pack, others stood their ground; one had a badly formed eye.

She'd have just a few seconds to make her choice when it was her turn to compete, and most probably she'd have to settle for whichever heifer or steer she could single out. It'd be luck, not skill, for her and the other newbies.

Spectators milled about wrapped in warm jackets, kids squealed, country music blared from speakers when the master of ceremonies wasn't introducing riders and events. Sitting here up high on Skipjack at the centre of it all felt alarmingly like being on stage, but so long as everyone kept their eyes on the winners with their fancy belt buckles and their dusty spurs, she was going to be okay. More than okay.

She might even start to have fun.

An official who looked vaguely familiar marched past in a hi-vis vest and Hannah checked her watch. She was up in a couple of minutes.

A showy black horse fell into step beside them, with a young owner who barely looked to be in her teens. She gave the kid a nod.

'Hi. You up soon?'

'I'm next. I like your horse. He's tall; does he have a bit of quarter-horse in him?'

'Thanks. His name's Skipjack. He's a sweetheart, but he was born on the wrong side of the saddle blanket, so there's no listing in any stud book to check his provenance.'

A whip cracked nearby, nearly taking out Hannah's eardrums.

'Disqualified,' said the girl. 'That must mean I'm up.'

'Good luck.'

'I don't need luck. I've got two other horses I'm competing on later in the draft, so practice will make perfect, hey?' the kid said, laying a hand on her horse's quivering neck. 'Ooh, he's holding the gate open for me. I'm off!'

Such confidence. Hannah had been confident too, once. Fun. Plucky. Full of ambition. She couldn't help but envy the girl.

'Today is a new day,' she told Skipjack. 'Quit worrying.'

Her horse flicked his ear at her.

'Okay, fine, I was talking to myself.'

She looked over her shoulder to the crowd perched on the old grandstands on the far side of the cut-out yard. Tom stood leaning on the metal rail, his face shadowed by his hat. All these months of avoidance hadn't dulled the confusion she felt when he was near.

If only she understood what it meant.

The stockwhip cracked.

The competitor before her—the kid—had lost control of the young Brahman heifer she'd cut from the mob and timed out before completing her figure eight, so there was no time to dally now. Hannah dragged her eyes from Tom and took a long breath.

'Let's do this, Skipjack.'

She nodded to the two men holding the gates and her first draft was underway. She clicked her tongue against her teeth and Skippy trotted forward.

For a moment all she could think about was the crowd of onlookers because a whole lot of eyes had suddenly zeroed in on her and she could have sworn she felt every one of them. But then the mob of cattle huddled at the far end of the pen began to scatter and she remembered what she was supposed to be doing.

The two brahmans were dug in like ticks down by the back rail. She ran her eye over them and discarded them as too difficult, the clock ticktocking in her head on double time now that she was actually competing. *No way* was she going to have time to cut the beast of her choosing. Kev's hours of training were forgotten as she kicked her heel into Skippy's side and drove him at the mob. Like her brother's opening move at snooker: hit and hope.

The tactic—amazingly—worked. Most of the mob cut left, but two steers tripped over each other and found themselves on the right, with her and Skippy blocking their way back to the others. They put some speed on, trying to get reunited with the mob, but she kept at them, cutting back and forth until—ha! Okay! One of them was clear!

She drove Skippy side to side across the narrow yard, finally remembering the rules Kev had drilled into her, and was able to head off the steer every time he tried to find his way back. Once, twice—

'Gate?' yelled a voice from over the rail.

Oh, hell, she was supposed to be calling that. 'Gate,' she yelled back, and the blokes at the arena end of the yard swung open the massive gates. A clicking of the tongue, a squeeze of her knee into Skippy's shoulder, and she and the steer were clear into the arena.

Their forty-second clock started now.

The posts that had been set up were bright orange and probably glowed in the dark, but the steer was rattled and bolting for the middle of the field, so the first post flashed past before she'd even caught up with the steer. She flicked a look down as she came along-side it, the braid she'd plaited into her hair that morning whipping at her cheek like a riding crop. The steer was dust-spattered and solid, all bunched shoulders and determination. His speed couldn't match Skipjack's, though.

The sheer joy of the moment bubbled up from somewhere deep in her belly and she laughed. This *was* fun. The *world* was fun and she'd been hiding away for too long.

Skipjack nudged the steer's shoulder with his own and they managed a loose arc, the steer running beside them, nudging it over in the direction of the far post when the whip crack marked the end of her time.

Disqualified, but not disgraced. She dragged in a breath and hauled on the reins. Forty seconds had never passed so quickly.

A stream of horses and riders trotted into the arena—other competitors—to help drive the runaway steer back into a pen, and she trotted out with them beyond the showground's ring of hessian-wrapped fencing as the master of ceremonies' voice blasted from the speakers.

'Hannah Cody on Skipjack is out of time. Points for the cut out, 10, horsemanship, 40, coursework, 1, giving her a total of fifty-one. Next up is Ryan Speedy-Kidd on Tabletop Tanker.'

She rubbed at the patches of sweat darkening the glossy coat of her horse's neck. 'You did so well,' she murmured and sat back in the saddle. '*I* did so well.' Pride warmed her like sunshine and she gave Skippy a nudge until they were headed for the horse float.

Josh was nowhere to be seen. She spied Kev, deep in conversation with a brown sparrow of a man she didn't recognise, and there was Vera, sitting on the tailgate of the old horse float, a smile on her face and Jane Doe lying across her boots.

Hannah started to smile back at her soon-to-be sister-in-law but paused. Vera's eyes were closed. Her face was turned up to the sun and she had her hands resting over her belly in a protective way that made all Hannah's ragingly unsatisfied hormones stand up and start shouting.

Was Vera—?

Had Josh and Vera—?

*Was there a little Cody growing underneath that corduroy skirt?*

'Hannah, my love!' Kev had seen her and broken off his conversation to come and give Skipjack a pat. 'Fifty-one points and a successful cut out! It's an excellent start.'

She tried on a grin to see if she was still feeling happy. Nope. The grin felt totally fake, but Kev was looking chuffed and she couldn't wreck his moment. 'Skipjack and your training did it mainly, Kev.'

'He'll be getting a carrot fresh out of the veggie patch. I'm gonna go grab us some food now the excitement's over. You hop off and cool him down.'

She flung a leg that was beginning to feel like jelly over the back of her saddle and was on the ground and stumbling when large hands gripped her waist.

Not Josh. Josh didn't turn her rib cage into an accordion or smell so damn fantastic. Tom.

If she could have said something when she turned to face him, she would have. Like, *Stop looking at me with those eyes, darn it.*

Tom cleared his throat. 'Josh was called out to a job.'

'Uh-huh.' That weirdness was back. Weirdness she'd caused and needed to fix. She'd known Tom since she was a preschooler, for heaven's sake, and she couldn't avoid him forever. 'Um, look.' She shot a glance over at Vera, because she didn't need an audience for this, but Vera was still oblivious to the world around her.

He raised an eyebrow.

She dropped her voice. 'About … you know.'

'The thing you made me promise never to talk about?'

Did he have to be so specific? 'Look, I'm sorry about the way I … overreacted.'

'Okay.'

'And about the way I've been acting ever since. Could we put this behind us?'

He blinked. 'No worries there. Already done.'

*Already?* 'Good, great, excellent.'

# CHAPTER
# 10

Tom forced himself to peel his hands off Hannah's hips.

What was he doing? This was like the stables all over again, forgetting about his injury just because Hannah in her braids and riding gear was reminding him of the girl he'd once known.

He tried to peel his eyes off her, too, but she'd turned to her horse and started unbuckling the saddle, and it was hard *not* to look. She was short and fine-boned, and looked more so here amidst the crowd. She wore snug-fit jeans that curved about her in a way he should not be ogling, and she was smiling at Vera who'd come over to help—a big wide grin that made her eyes twinkle and her cheeks dimple and made him feel sad and nostalgic. She didn't smile enough; if only he knew why.

Kev Jones returned with sausage sangers for everyone and Hannah put her arm around the man's scrawny shoulders and smacked a boisterous kiss into his cheek. The old bloke looked delighted.

'Extra sauce for you, Hannah, since you did so well,' said Kev. 'And I grabbed a program for you. A memento of your first draft.'

'You're an angel. Where's Kylie?'

'Saw her chatting up some bloke on a bay gelding. Didn't look like she was in a hurry to leave.'

Music ripped through the speakers, followed by an announcer's voice. 'You've got about two minutes, people, to make your way back to the arena and we'll be awarding places for the maiden A rounds. We'll be drawing today's lucky door prize, too, and don't forget the barbecue starts at six. Live music tonight will be the River Dogs.'

Hannah turned to Kev. 'Let's go see who won. I was so nervous before my race I couldn't keep track of the scores. You coming, Vera?'

'I might head home, Han,' said Vera, 'if I can pry Kylie from whoever she's chatting up. Better not push the no dogs rule too far. I'll see you later.'

'Sure. Tom?'

'I'll go find Bruno. The showground isn't the easiest place for a guy in a wheelchair to move from A to B.'

'I saw him up at the officials' tent earlier. We can go together.'

Together? That was quick. When Hannah decided she was going to put something behind her, she didn't muck around. If only it were that easy for him.

They found the officials clustered in front of the tower where the commentator sat to announce the progress of the events, Bruno— as predicted—front and centre. Someone had bought him a coffee and the harsh lines that had bracketed his face since the day Tom came home had softened.

'Hannah bloody Cody,' barked Bruno the minute he spotted them. 'Why haven't I seen you up at Ironbark, girl?'

'Josh is keen to take on our equine patients, Bruno. You're in safe hands, don't worry. He mucks up, you let me know, and I'll take him out the back and shoot him.'

'Ha! And what's all this about you getting into campdrafting? You're too timid on the turns. Come up to the homestead one day and I'll inspect that horse of yours and give you some pointers.'

'Hey,' grumbled Kev behind Tom's shoulder, 'that's my student you're poaching.'

Tom gave the old bloke a wink.

'Mmm,' said Hannah in a noncommittal tone.

'Pity Ironbark's not running its campdraft this year. We used to take real good care of our local entrants.'

'Yes, I was sorry to hear it'd been cancelled, Bruno. End of an era.'

Bruno held out a hand and she gripped it. 'End of a bloody legacy but never mind that. Now, promise me you'll bring that horse up so I can see you put him through his paces.'

A stocky young man with a wide lens camera strung about his neck interrupted them. 'Mr Krauss? Sir? I'm the social media guy for the Southern Campdrafters committee. You mind if I ask you a few questions about your glory days and get a photo?'

His dad was clearly buoyed by the request. 'Not at all. Here, Hannah, come stand in close beside me and hide these blasted wheels of mine.'

'I don't think—'

Hannah's words were drowned out by the young man, who was rabbiting on about apertures and sun from the west and how many followers the campdraft hashtag had gained on Instagram since he started adding stories about the people he met when he was covering events.

Tom stood to one side to get out of the way, his eyes on his dad's face. He'd grown so used to the frown of disappointment it was strange to see it gone. He could almost—almost—see the shadow of the man his father had once been. Before age and illness and a timid kelpie pup had soured their relationship forever.

Thoughtful, he shifted his gaze to Hannah's face and—oh. Furrows had dragged her eyebrows closer together. Her cheeks were pale, almost translucent, and she had the end of her messy braid of browny-red hair in her fingers, twirling it around and around and around. That's where Bruno's frown had gone.

A bad sign. But what was there to be annoyed by?

'Give us a smile, sweetheart,' said the social media guy, going into a semi-squat before Hannah and the wheelchair and looking through his viewfinder. 'Don't worry, I'll be sure to tag you in my media post, too. Hannah Cody, isn't it? I got your name from the program.'

Only, Hannah didn't smile. Instead, she pulled her arm back, curled her hand into a fist and let fly with a punch aimed squarely at the cameraman.

# CHAPTER
# 11

On Monday morning, when Tom headed inside The Billy Button Café for his daily quiet time—which he had no intention of giving up just because last week's Chatter had an issue with it—he discovered his corner table wasn't empty.

Which was odd, because Graeme had just assured him, like, three nanoseconds ago that it was.

Not only was it not empty, but it had extra chairs pulled around it for the crowd: Kev in his faded corduroy cap; Vera, twisting a napkin into anxious origami; Josh; someone with their back to him wearing navy workwear—ah, Kylie. Hannah Cody's BFF.

Hmm. If the nerves in his spine weren't already occupied with their own drama, they'd be on high alert.

And Marigold was there too, of course. The town matriarch was dominating the table from the far end, giving him a get-your-arse-here-stat stare. He clearly needed to mix up his routine more if the locals had known exactly where he was going to be.

'Take a seat,' said Marigold, with the confidence of a dictator planning a military coup. Only, most military dictators Tom had heard of hadn't worn feathered, dangly earrings. 'Graeme will be with us when there's a lull in customers.'

'This looks ominous.' He decided to play dumb. 'Don't tell me: the town solicitor's gone AWOL again, and you need my help tracing him down.'

'Him,' sniffed Marigold. 'Benjamin Dorley is one ibuprofen away from retirement and—frankly—is the least of our concerns.'

'Right. This must be about Ironbark not hosting a campdraft this year, then. As I told you the other day, I'll speak to Bruno about it. When the time is right.'

'Wrong again.'

Damn it. Of course they were all here about Hannah Cody losing her marbles at Dalgety. Maybe he should be making it clear that he and Hannah weren't exactly friends.

'Here's the thing, Tom. Everybody here—correct me if I'm wrong, Josh—knows that Hannah has some sort of … what's the word I want, Kevvy?'

'Agoraphobia, my love. Literally, it means fear of the market place, but that's an ancient Greek thing. Now it's a fear of leaving a place that feels comfortable.'

Not quite everyone here. He looked at Josh, but his friend was too busy looking miserable to notice.

'That's the one,' said Marigold. 'Everybody here has also seen that girl work her tail off looking after every animal in town, with no time off and no holidays and no fun. Which is why we—' Marigold looked around the table at her conscripts '—were all so thrilled when we heard she was trying to loosen up a bit. She's been to yoga—'

'Once,' interrupted Kylie. 'I had to drag her.'

'Nonetheless. She and Kev have their horse training every week.'

'She's been driving to Cooma now and then by herself for groceries and what have you,' said Josh. 'I was hoping she'd gotten over it.'

'Until yesterday,' said Kylie grimly. 'I only caught the back end of it, but you were there, Tom. Tell us what happened. I'm still trying to work out why some photographer copped a blow anyway. What's that got to do with being afraid to leave your home?'

Tom didn't want to say anything. He was trying to declutter drama from his life not add to it ... but agoraphobia? Lashing out? *Why?* And for how long had this stuff been going on?

'Don't you think you should be having this conversation with Hannah?' Tom looked at Josh again. 'And by you, I mean *you*, her brother.'

'Mate, I've been doing nothing but for the last day and a half. She's shut me out and I'm desperate. Hence ... this gathering.'

'Our concern,' said Marigold, frowning at Tom and patting Josh on the arm, 'is that Hannah will let this little setback—'

Graeme, who had shimmied into the spare chair and set a plate of macarons on the table, coughed. 'Would we describe it as "little"? Damaging third party property, running off across a manure-rich paddock and knocking over a bridle and horse-feed display by the canteen?'

Graeme was hushed by Kev. 'Hold your horses, mate.'

'—get in the way of her progress,' continued Marigold. 'That's where you come in, Tom.'

He frowned. He was in no shape to be offering advice or help to anyone. 'How do you figure that?'

'We're all doing our bit looking after her already. I'm going to give her an ultimatum: yoga or craft once a week so I can keep my eye on her. Kev is going to suggest they up their training to twice a week, and Kylie will—what is it you will do, exactly, Kylie?'

'I'm her confidante. It's a difficult job, Marigold, involving a lot of calories, and I can't take on more because I've got the workshop to worry about now, as well.'

'Understood. Josh has work hours covered, Vera is going to suggest some drives out to the neighbouring farms to see what local produce she can include in her menu, and Graeme will be grilling Hannah about her life choices over coffee and cheesecake morsels. Which leaves you, Tom.'

'She's a grown woman, Marigold. Why would she want her every minute scrutinised by you lot?'

Marigold sighed and the scarf she'd tied around her neck billowed like a bird wing. 'Because we care, Tom. You should try it some time.'

Well, that burned. Not that he could show it. 'There is no way I'm sticking my nose into Hannah's business.'

'She could be facing charges. You're a lawyer, you could help her.'

Well, technically, yes, he was a lawyer. But what he knew about police procedure in Australian country towns wouldn't fill a teaspoon. 'She'll need a town solicitor if she gets charged with anything.'

Marigold sniffed. 'Someone like Dorley, you mean? Because he's the only one we've got, and I don't see Hannah heading out of town again any time soon, do you?'

Tom thought wistfully of the crossword he could be doing. The clues to 6 down and 11 across might be cryptic but at least they could be resolved without getting personally involved. He wasn't here in Hanrahan to feel bad for the town residents that their local solicitor was useless. He wasn't here to be of use to anyone.

'We all know that Ironbark Station is hosting a campdraft this year.'

He looked up. 'What?'

'You heard me.'

'Marigold, that is the exact opposite of what is happening. Bruno is crook as a snake-bitten dog and you know it—'

'Bruno isn't going to run it, Tom. You are. With Hannah's help.'

Marigold clearly didn't understand the dynamics at play between father and son at Ironbark Station. If Tom was riding, training the stockhorses, *involved*, then yeah, maybe he'd be able to talk his dad into letting him 'take over'. But the way things stood now? Not bloody likely.

'I wish I could help,' said Tom. Which would have been true once upon a time, before the adventurous, do-anything-and-everything life he loved got shredded by a shard of steel. 'Only, I just took on another project which is going to take up all my time.'

Marigold's eyes narrowed. 'What project?'

He picked the only one that was even remotely doable. 'The pub. You said it yourself, Marigold, the old girl needs some attention.'

'What's stopping you doing both?'

He didn't have an answer for that, one that he could say out loud, anyway. He was in too deep with his lie about why he'd come home.

'Tom.' Josh didn't say anything else, just his name.

He sighed. Now he felt like a total selfish shit. What sort of a mate would he be if he ignored the worry in his friend's eyes?

This was going to end badly. 'I'll contact the Southern Camp-drafters Association,' he said wearily, 'and have the Ironbark Campdraft reinstated on the calendar.'

# CHAPTER

# 12

Hannah could have recited her third year Bachelor of Veterinary Science lecture notes on the feline reproduction system with her eyes closed, but she had them propped up on the whiteboard anyway. It paid to be careful.

It especially paid to be careful when your hands weren't the steadiest and the subject matter was making you cry.

*Speying a cat: first, an incision is made in the midline of the belly, into which a spey hook is inserted to locate the body of the uterus. The ovarian ligament can then be broken and the ovarian artery tied off. Repeat for remaining ovary, and then follow the uterine horns to the uterine body. Tie off and remove.*

So many unwanted kittens in the world. Out they popped, willy-nilly, little furry feet and pink noses for their mother cats to love and yes, sure, okay, six weeks later they were out in the wild decimating the local populations of quokkas and skinks and willy wagtails … She got it. Feral cats were a problem.

But still, there was an inherent unfairness to being obliged to sabotage the uterine horns of one animal while at the same time all you could think about was your own uterine horns.

By quarter to nine on Monday morning, however, the cat's ordeal was done, and the animal lay tucked under a little warming blanket, sleeping off her anaesthesia. Hannah bent down and listened to the snubby little muzzle breathe in and out and used the last of the clean swabs to remove the tears from her cheeks. Her own cheeks. Not the cat's, obviously.

Josh had disappeared shortly after eight to grab a coffee and then head out for a day of blood-testing cattle, for which she was mighty thankful. She was sick of looking at his long face and ashamed of herself for having put the expression there. She needed a break from thinking about herself and being busy at work was the greatest respite she knew.

By late morning she'd rescued a pet rat from a juvenile olive python and felt compelled to keep its shocked, quivering little body in the front pocket of her scrubs until it fell asleep eating a lettuce leaf. She'd wormed and vaccinated a litter of eight-week-old wire-haired terriers and had to hold all of them—all eight—to her cheek, and she'd paid so many bills and caught up on so many patient records, her desk in the back office looked positively bare.

What now?

The post-it note with her GP's phone number was stuck on the bottom of her computer screen, where Josh had left it before he cleared off.

No, nope. Not ready for that.

All she'd needed to do to prove to herself she could make it further afield on a day trip to Canberra or Wagga Wagga was survive a few hours in Dalgety, and guess what?

She'd failed. She pushed her fingers into her tear ducts until they stopped leaking. She might never get to a fertility clinic.

Her next patient wasn't due in until two, which left her ninety minutes of empty time that needed to be filled. If she wasn't busy when Josh returned he'd be on her case, again, asking her if she was either medically unsound or a bloody idiot or both and she'd better start talking or else he'd be calling their parents.

Like that threat would work. Josh was about as likely to interrupt their parents' well-earned drive around Australia to share Hannah drama with them as she was to wear a skirt to work. He knew the brother–sister code and he wouldn't break it.

Besides, it wasn't as though she had answers to his questions. She'd barely slept in the hours since she'd been driven home trapped in the shocked silence of Kev and Lionel, trying to work it out: *Was* she medically unsound? *Was* she a bloody idiot?

She'd given up trying to sleep last night somewhere about two o'clock in the morning and dug out her old journals from the last time she'd crossed the line. Reading the contents had not been fun.

She needed a coffee. And if ever there'd been a day to add a heaped teaspoon of refined sugar to a caffeinated beverage, it was today. She popped her head out the door and looked down the corridor; all was quiet, so she decided to whip upstairs and make herself something to eat while she was at it. Perhaps somewhere in the pages she hadn't yet read would be a clue to how to get back on the right side of the line she'd crossed. She'd done it once before, hadn't she?

Her flat on the top floor of the old stone building she and her brother owned was quiet. She flicked the switch on the kettle and opened the journal at the page she'd dog-eared the night before.

The entries were short and clipped. Defensive, she could see now, with the benefit of more than a decade of hindsight. Kind of like the way she'd been living ever since.

*Day thirteen*, she read. *Dr Mack is coming to see me in a few minutes. I've got nothing to say about anything.*

Day fourteen and fifteen didn't mention anything besides the dinner choices—meatloaf and mash on one day (yummy), cold pasta salad the next (repulsive)—but then came day sixteen: *The nice nurse unlocked the outside door and I sat in the sunshine with Mum when she came to visit and when she cried it was like my brain was frozen and what my eyes were seeing and my ears were hearing were muffled by snowfall.*

Day twenty. *Dr Mack said the word today: depression. I'm depressed. Me, Hannah Celine Cody. That's why I did what I did.*

She turned the page and a leaflet fell out, one of the many the staff of the clinic had given her and encouraged her to read. It didn't look familiar. Perhaps she'd been given it at the beginning, when she was too raw and wrecked to read anything. *Long-term Effects of Cyber Bullying.*

Did she really want to read this now?

Her gaze fell on the fridge door, where she had stuck crayon drawings from young pet owners. She had a framed university degree, too, but that was downstairs in her treatment room, and she had a bank loan that was ahead in repayments, and she had patients whose owners sent her Christmas cards. She was valued here. She'd worked hard and success had come her way after she earned her vet degree at the Wagga Wagga campus of Charles Sturt University.

So why, she wondered, was she still overreactive?

She wasn't a teenager anymore. She had no excuse for smacking the camera out of the hands of that photographer on Saturday. She knew she had issues and she'd thought she was finally ready to emerge from the cocoon she'd built for herself among the snow gums of Hanrahan and strive for the fulfilment she yearned for, but now she'd blown it.

A knock at the door had her ramming the journal shut and shoving it under a vet article she'd read at three o'clock that morning in the hope it would send her to sleep: IS DRENCH RESISTANCE THE EMERGING PROBLEM IN THE MANAGEMENT OF WORM INFESTATIONS IN SHEEP?

'Hannah,' said Sandy, opening the door a smidge and popping her head in. 'Sorry to disturb you—emergency downstairs. Owner thinks their dog ate one of the kids' toys when she wasn't looking. Its breathing is a little funny and it pooped out a chunk of Lego this morning.'

'How big is the dog?' When it came to dogs pooping toy chunks, size did matter.

'Pug sized.'

'Huh.' Self-reflection and her instant coffee sugar hit would have to wait. 'Send them in to Josh's treatment room. I'll be down in a tick.'

'The crate with the angry cat is in there.'

'Shoot. Okay, I'll run down and disinfect my room so give me a minute before you bring them in.'

'You got it.' But Sandy made no move to head back down to the clinic.

'Why are you lurking like that? If you're worried I've found your secret stash of biscuits and brought them up here to gobble them all up, I haven't.'

'And you never will. No, it's just—well.'

'Spit it out.'

'The police are here. One police officer, to be specific. Looks to be in full work mode and she's asking for you.'

'Full work mode? What does that mean?'

'Gadgets and guns, Hannah. And when I say she's asking for you, it's actually more like an order.'

Crap. 'Thanks, Sandy. Let me see the dog first in case it really is an emergency. Perhaps you could offer her a water or something and explain the hold-up.'

'Mrs Grundy's in early for her two o'clock, and she's been trying to pry out the reason for the sergeant's visit for the last ten minutes. Is, um, is everything all right? I can be with you if you want.'

'Sandy, you're a sweetheart. I'll be fine, but thanks for the offer.'

Half an hour later, Hannah was resting a hand on the affronted pug sprawled on the stainless steel table. The Lego hat that the dog had managed to get stuck in his trachea sat in a metal dish beside her and the owner had returned to the waiting room because he'd been grossed out by the phlegmy noises.

The door swung open and a policewoman moved into the treatment room.

'Oh, hey, I'm not quite done.'

'But I was done with waiting. I'm Sergeant King.'

Hannah cleared her throat. 'I'm not trying to avoid you, I promise. Flower here had a time-sensitive problem. I just need another couple of minutes with him.'

'I've got an hysterical Instagram influencer—his words—from Cooma emailing me pictures of the crack on his prize lens every twenty minutes. I think the crack on his ego's even bigger.'

'I'm sorry.' It was hard to hear the dog's breathing through the stethoscope with her blood rushing in her ears.

'Here's what I don't get. You're at a family event, kids everywhere, everyone's having a great old time, and then you apparently lose the common sense you were born with and ram your fist into the expensive property of a total stranger. How am I doing?'

Flower's breathing was steady, his heart rate was back to normal and he was eyeing off the liver treat in Hannah's hand as though he hadn't eaten anything in days, let alone a Lego pirate. She fed him the treat, then picked up the fat little body and held it against her chest.

'Um, Sergeant King. This isn't going to be a short conversation.'

'Okay. I've got time to listen.'

'The dalmatian out in the waiting room needs his heartworm and kennel cough shots and a liver treat, and he's my last patient for a bit. Can you wait while I do that? Ten minutes, tops.'

The sergeant looked at her watch. 'I can wait.'

Hannah gestured to the doorway. 'My place is upstairs, top floor. The door's unlocked if you want to wait there. We'll be able to talk without being interrupted.'

'I'll find it.'

She vaccinated Mrs Grundy's dog, Spot, and made some gentle commentary on his girth being on the hefty side of normal according to the dog obesity chart.

Mrs Grundy responded by giving her a rundown on every household item he'd consumed in the last month. 'And then he ate the library book I'd left on the window seat. How am I going to explain that to those dragons up there at the loans desk?'

'Dalmatians aren't known for their brains, Mrs Grundy. Was it a cookbook? Maybe it smelled like food.'

'It was one of those fabulous romances. You know, the steamy historical ones with a woman on the cover about to tear off her ballgown and command some bare-chested laird to lift his kilt.'

She laughed. 'You interested in bare-chested lairds, Mrs Grundy?'

The old lady pulled a neatly embroidered, lavender-scented handkerchief from her purse and fluttered it in front of her face. 'Those heroes have skills, Hannah. Dexterous with their sword-play, if you get my meaning. I should have slipped Mr Grundy a title or two to give him some pointers. Too late now, more's the pity.'

As Mr Grundy had been a resident of the Hanrahan cemetery on Hope Street for about two decades, the idea was almost enough to take Hannah's mind off the conversation she was about to have upstairs. 'So,' she said to the dog, 'you have no idea what's edible and what's not, but you have excellent taste in romantic literature. Spot, you've got hidden depths. Have another liver treat.'

She walked them through reception to the main door and watched them head down Dandaloo Street in the direction of the lake. Perhaps when she was making her New Year's Eve resolutions she should have thought of dalmatians and romance novels.

No-one would have tried taking a photograph of her then.

The sergeant had made herself at home at the small table by the window overlooking the park, a mug of black coffee and the newspaper set up before her.

Hannah poured herself a cup of coffee using the still-hot kettle. 'I've got biscuits.'

'No, thanks.'

'Vera made them. You know, from The Billy Button Café. She's engaged to my brother so we get treats dropped off on a regular basis.'

'In that case, yes, and don't be stingy.'

Hannah pulled a tin from the pantry and plonked it on the table. She lifted the lid to reveal a cluster of golden biscuits with chocolate and rum-soaked raisins dotted generously throughout.

Sergeant King's eyes bulged when she offered her the tin—rather like, now Hannah thought about it, Flower the pug's eyes had when Hannah shoved her blunt-nosed forceps down his throat—before snapping back into police mode.

'I'll have one in a minute,' she said. 'After we talk about the assault charge Donny Hay is hounding me to make.'

For a second Hannah wished Josh was here, so he could answer these questions for her. Cowardly, yes. Safe, also yes.

'I hit his camera, not him. My defence is that I thought he was going to take my photo.'

'He *was* going to take your photo.'

'Exactly. And I hadn't agreed to that.'

'Why didn't you just tell him that?'

'I was … well, the truth is, I kind of panicked.'

'You want to tell me why?'

'Um,' she said, hating the tremor that made it sound like she had a plastic pirate hat problem of her own.

The sergeant leant forward. 'Hannah, I'm not an idiot; I can tell when there's something else going on.'

Hannah looked at the policewoman's face and saw nothing but calm composure. God, how she envied that. She took a breath and launched into it. Like ripping a sticky bandage off a hairy paw, do it quick and all in the one go.

'I have a fear of having my photo taken because of something that happened to me. Years ago. I'm okay about it now, mostly, but only because I avoid going to places I'm not used to—you know, situations where someone might catch me by surprise. I wasn't expecting that bloke to rope me into the photo, but everyone was talking, and Bruno's, you know, not well, and anyway, I didn't speak up, and then your Cooma bloke lifted his camera and told me to smile, and … I reacted. Badly.'

The sergeant frowned. 'Tell me about this "something that happened".'

God, this was difficult. She took a swig from her coffee cup, and the heat of it was a comfort. 'Okay. Here's the short version. When

I first went away to uni I stayed at a residential college, where some girls photoshopped my face onto a picture. A rude picture. Porn, I guess you'd say. And it went viral all over college and the fallout, for me, was huge.'

'Wow. What bitches. Were they charged? What happened to them?'

Hannah frowned. 'To them? Nothing. They were the cool girls. They're probably running the Sydney financial district by now.'

'And what happened to you?' The woman's voice was becoming a little too kind. Any kinder and Hannah was going to lose it.

'The picture went up on noticeboards. People used it as a lock screen on their phones. I couldn't go to the dining room without being looked at, laughed at. There was this dumb awards night run by the college committee and I won a stupid prize. Guys would bark when I walked past.'

'*Arse*holes.'

'Yep. I was enrolled in medicine at the time—a course I'd busted eight guts to get into when I was at school—and I dropped out.'

'That's rough.'

'Yep. I came home and lay in the foetal position in my bedroom for weeks. I kept in touch, for a while, with a few people I'd known in Sydney. I had a boyfriend at the time, for instance, but it turned out he and everyone else wanted to keep in touch online, tagging each other in photos. Every time my name came up, so would that effing picture. That's when I ...'

'You what?'

No. She wasn't telling some stranger about that, no matter how well she could deliver the word 'arseholes'. 'I went into a dark place. For a while there, I wasn't sure I'd ever come out of it, but I ... healed. Well, that's not totally true.'

'The scar healed over on the surface, perhaps,' said Sergeant King.

She nodded. 'That's exactly it. I got some help. I was suffering from depression. I switched courses to one closer to home—vet school—and opened my own practice here when I was done, and here I've stayed ever since. So, you know, I've been okay. Mostly. Other than the whole afraid-to-leave-town thing.'

'You never leave Hanrahan?'

Hannah picked up a broken chunk of biscuit from the tin. Broken bits didn't have calories, did they? 'I'm working on that. Baby steps, you know?'

'Baby steps like the Dalgety Showgrounds?'

'Well. That was the plan.'

'I'm sorry about all this trauma you have to live with.'

Yeah. She was, too. 'I guess I wasn't as ready to get back out into the big bad world as I thought I was.'

'Hence the right hook to the camera.'

'Yep.'

The sergeant sighed. 'Here's my suggestion. You apologise to Donny Hay and offer to pay for any repairs to his camera. I'll let him know you had your reasons, which are too personal to go into, and maybe he'll be satisfied with that.'

'You think he will be?'

'We won't know until we try.'

'Thank you, sergeant. Really.'

'Don't thank me until you've made things right with the photographer. And Hannah? You damage someone's property again, I'll arrest you without blinking.'

'Yes, sir. I mean, sergeant.'

There was almost a smile on the woman's face. 'My name's Meg.' She stood to leave, picking up her biscuit and cradling it in her hands like it was precious cargo. 'So, what changed, Hannah? What made you step out of your safe place?'

Hannah gave in to temptation and reached into the tin for another biscuit. 'I was …' Kissed, she realised. Kissed by Tom and somehow discovered her quiet little existence was not enough. He must have woken up her hormones, damn it; wound up the cogs and set off the *tick tick tick*. She just hadn't started hearing the tick until New Year's Eve. 'I, er, decided I wanted more for myself.' No need to mention the specifics.

'And how's that going for you?'

'Not well.' She sank her teeth into the golden goodness. Tom was to blame for this mess. She should have known.

'You going to give up?'

'Nope.'

The policewoman gave her a nod. 'Good to hear.'

# CHAPTER
## 13

'You did *what*?'

For a bloke who'd shrunk into something scrawnier than a string bean and who had an oxygen canister strapped to the side of his wheelchair, Bruno could find some volume when the mood struck. Like now.

Luckily Tom had had the foresight to wait until Mrs LaBrooy was away from home before firing his first shot off the bows. She'd taken off for the giddy delights of an afternoon's shopping in town in her little SUV, then he'd tracked his father to the ramp at the back of the house, where Bruno liked to take his coffee and sit in the sun to inspect the state of the grazing paddocks.

It actually felt good to abandon the don't-poke-the-snake strategy he'd settled for since he came home. He'd been drifting along, letting Bruno say what he pleased without arcing up, and where had it got him?

Nowhere.

He'd let Hannah drift along ignoring him after she'd had a melt-down in the stables and where had that got him? A ringside seat to her having meltdown number two in Dalgety, that's where.

His doctor was right, damn it. Drifting along was not a workable solution. To anything.

Those meddlesome coffee drinkers at the café were right, too, although it irked to admit it. He'd been so busy not seeing a future for himself that he'd cut himself off from seeing what was happening in his present.

He'd spent the drive home realising his apathy was a total cop-out. He wasn't immobilised by his injury, not yet anyway, so why was he behaving like he was?

His dad's bellow felt surprisingly welcome. Pubs to open, friends to help, old family wounds to rip open … it was action.

It felt bloody good.

'You heard me,' Tom said.

Oh, sure, he could pretend he and his dad were getting into an argument about the Ironbark Campdraft, but they both knew the fracture dividing the Krauss household ran a whole lot deeper than who was running what. The confrontation had been brewing long before he got home. Since he left, in fact, over a decade and a half ago. And now the atmosphere at Ironbark was a powder keg, and the old bloke wasn't showing any sign of wanting to improve relations. Nope; Bruno was like one of the old anvils they kept down in the stables: high tensile steel and bloody near impossible to budge.

True, he'd thought their blow-up, when it came, would be about something else entirely—the reason he left home; why he wouldn't commit to learning how to train stockhorses; him being an eternal disappointment, yada yada yada—but whatever. The powder keg's fuse was about to be lit. If a few more family skeletons got blown up, so what?

'I rang Colleen McNulty, secretary of the Southern Camp-drafters Association, and put the Ironbark Station campdraft back on the calendar.'

'You're a bloody idiot.'

Tom rolled his eyes. Like that sort of insult would knock him down. 'Yeah, I know you think so.'

'I decide what goes on at this station. Not you.'

'Not this time.'

'Have you got any idea of the work that's involved penning two hundred cattle, grading the roads, manning the competition, drag-ging water troughs up fro—'

'I have no idea, no, but that doesn't mean I won't get it done. With—' he took a breath '—some help, of course.'

'*My* help? You've got a bloody nerve asking for my help.'

'Well, sure, if you're happy for me to make a pig's ear of it, then fine, lock yourself away in your study and don't be a part of it. Colleen's so thrilled we're back on the calendar she said she'll send me her notes. She's got a list of farmers in the Snowy Monaro we can approach for cattle if we don't have enough, and there's people who've put up their hands to volunteer. Roger Kettering. Kev Jones and his wife.'

'Marigold! That woman's not setting foot on Ironbark. She'll be up here, eyeing off my parents' gravesite, in my ear about bloody civic by-laws and bloody Barry O'Malley. Call Colleen. Call them all. Tell them it's off.'

'I won't do that.' He wanted to ask what on earth Hanrahan's mayor and the old station cemetery had to do with Marigold Jones, but decided that was an argument for another day.

'Are you defying me, son?'

'Yes. I am. And it's not the first time, is it, Dad?'

'I was just waiting for you to fling that in my face.'

'Talking about why this family got ripped apart is not flinging stuff in your face, Dad.'

'You shouldn't have carried on like a pork chop over a routine farm matter.'

'The way *I* carried on?' That was rich. 'I was an eighteen-year-old kid, Dad, and you had that pup in a hessian sack and in the dam with a brick so quick I hadn't a *hope* of saving it.'

He'd tried though. He'd thrashed through the brown water till his lungs burned and his eyes felt like sandpaper. The pup was found all right, but all he managed to do was swap its watery grave to a dirt one.

'A timid dog's no use as a working dog. You spoiled it. Ruined it with your petting. Your generation's too soft.'

'That's such bullshit. I could have found a home for it. You were just mad at me for wanting to go to university instead of staying here and having the future you'd picked out for me.'

'Soft, see? And you still are, by the looks. No wonder you didn't stick it out here. No wonder you didn't stick it out in the Navy, either. You can't stick when it gets tough, can you, son?'

Tom snorted. 'Well, let's see how well I stick to running this campdraft. Oh, and while we're getting some home truths sorted, here's another: your solicitor is a drunk and he's done bugger all to secure you a tenant for the pub. I'll be sticking at that, too.'

'I'll have you know Dorley's been looking out for this family while you've been gone doing god knows what and he's no drunk.'

'Tell that to the officer who picked him up on a drink-driving charge.'

Bruno looked mad enough to spit. 'Well, if that's the case, I'll—'

'You'll what? Drive to town every week and start collecting your own rents?'

'No, damn you. I'm useless. *Useless*. Can't do a fucking thing by myself these days. I can barely piss in a bottle.'

Tom fell silent.

Bruno wheeled his chair so he was facing the century-old eucalypts that marked the station's boundary with the national park. 'May as well shove *me* in a sack and be done with me.'

'Has—' Christ, it was hard to switch gears from blazing recrimination to … this. Bruno—grumpy, hard-arse *Bruno*—was looking broken. Tom had no idea what to say. 'Has your doctor given you some bad news or something?'

'Doesn't have to. Fellow's got a face longer than a wet week every time he comes up. That's why I canned the campdraft. I can't manage it and I'm damned if I'll let Ironbark Station, my legacy, put on a substandard event. I can't even be sure these damn things—' he tapped his hand to an oxygen canister '—will keep me alive until then.'

Things weren't right between them, not by a long shot, but he could see a crack in his father's determination to keep him out. He decided to test it: 'Well, if the oxygen doesn't work, telling me everything I'm doing wrong might put a bit of spark in you.'

Bruno looked up at him, surprise and suspicion written all over his face. 'Ha! Was that supposed to be a joke?'

'A bad one. Dad, I'm serious about the campdraft. I don't want to fight with you over it.'

'Suit your bloody self,' said Bruno, which Tom interpreted as grudging agreement. 'Since you've decided to lift a bloody finger, maybe you can make yourself useful and pour me a whiskey.'

'Sure.'

'Pour yourself one, too, why don't you. Then you can tell me what the hell is up with that Cody girl.'

# CHAPTER

# 14

Hannah stood at the midpoint between her two trusty evening companions: the bathtub and the fridge. The bathtub beckoned, as it always did: blissfully hot water; just enough space to rest a wine glass beside the handmade soap Sandy had given her for Christmas; and her half-read books, *Knock Yourself Up: No Man? No Problem* and *Baby Making 101*, propped on the windowsill between a vanilla candle and a long-dead fern.

The books were looking at her with disappointment, she was sure of it. They were sighing and shaking their heads, saying, *Girlfriend, what is your problem?*

They reminded her how hideous her afternoon had been. Calling Donny Hay, stumbling her way through an apology and sending him $1,199.99 for a new sigma something 85mm whatsit lens had given her a whopping headache and ratcheted her shame levels sky high. *And* he'd been sweet about her apology, which somehow made it worse.

Why couldn't she be sweet?

To the fridge, then. She could line up its contents on the counter and then hunt online for the most complicated recipe involving grated cheese and green apples and a chorizo sausage that was only a tad slimy. Or she could make her standard easy tea, a baked bean toasted sanger, but that would barely fill three seconds of her evening.

Crap.

She plucked her phone off the bench and hit dial on her most frequent contact.

'Kylie? It's Hannah.'

'Finally. I leave sixty-six messages and you decide to call me back just when I have a hot sirloin in front of me.'

'Sorry. I've been wallowing in shame.'

'Your car's been ready since mid-morning.'

'Thank you.'

'But that was only what one message was about. The others were all saying WTF.'

'I know. I behaved like a total dickhead.'

'It's a pity I was on the far side of the arena; maybe I could have done something, like, I don't know, tackle you to the ground.'

'Yeah,' Hannah said heavily.

'Come on, don't start with the sad voice.'

'I'm not sad, I promise.'

'You're a lousy liar, Cody.'

The pause blew out into a silence broken by little tinny taps and scrapes. 'Wait, are you eating while I'm having an existential crisis?'

'Maybe,' said Kylie thickly. 'Why don't you come join me? I'm at the café and tonight's special is awesome, with this mushroomy stuff on the side, and baby asparagus that squeak when you bite them. They're so delish.'

Tempting. But there'd be people there and by now the town would all know about her idiocy. She'd probably gone freaking viral again and this time she only had herself to blame. 'I don't think so.'

'You've got to face the music some time. It may as well be now, with your bestie by your side.'

'I hate it when you're right.'

'I know you do.'

Hannah flicked a glance at her watch. Quarter to six. But what if those pernicious crafters were there setting up? Marigold could be difficult to evade.

But wait, craft night was on Wednesdays. Perhaps she *could* go.

Some tourists were in the café, so was the manager of the gift shop near the vet clinic, and one of the town councillors whose name she'd forgotten, but no sign of Vera … okay. She could do this.

Kylie was tucked into a booth by the door and gave Hannah a wave.

'Take a seat. I've ordered for you.'

Graeme was refilling water at a nearby table but he looked over and blew her a kiss, which was sweet. Then he dropped a wink at Kylie, which had Hannah's radar pinging. Were those two in cahoots over something?

Her friend waited until she had a plate of food in front of her then said, 'You want to talk about it?'

'What I'd like to do is curl up under my doona until everyone has forgotten I exist.'

'Uh-huh. What's your Plan B?'

'I've apologised to the guy and paid for him to get a new lens. Apparently it was scratched and cracked when it hit the ground. I've been given a warning by Meg King. You know her?'

'The new sergeant? Sure. She and I have bonded over a shared love of a V8 engine.'

'That's so cute.'

'Hold up, you don't get to be a smartarse when you're in disgrace.'

Hannah sighed and a teensy-weensy tear plopped down her cheek before she could scare it into submission. 'True. Sorry. Being snarky seems to be my only emotional response these days.'

Kylie gave her hand a squeeze. 'It's not, Hannah, you're just holding the other ones in so tight you're going to bust. Maybe that's what happened at Dalgety—your feelings just got the better of you. Besides, losing the plot one time is not going to define you. Everybody who knows you will understand how sorry you are.'

'And embarrassed.'

'Yeah. I get it. But it's the choices you make going forward that matter.'

She sniffed. 'Did you get that from some bumper sticker?'

'Come on, I'm serious. This is *your* year, Hannah, didn't we decide that? To do stuff, and be adventurous, and think about some life goals. So you've had a small setback; are you going to give up?'

She gave a huff. 'You sound like a life coach.'

'Maybe you need a life coach.'

'I don't. I can't afford one. And no, I'm not going to give up.' Living her life in a more socially well-adjusted way wasn't just a gimmick she was trying on for a year; she *needed* to get her head straight if she was serious about becoming a mother.

'Let's set some ground rules, then. One, we use our nice words instead of our fists.'

She chuckled through her sniffles. 'Agreed.'

'Two. We have a support team around us when we're going to try something new.'

'Like who?'

'Like me, doofus. And Graeme. Your brother, the Joneses, your mum and dad if they ever finish their trip around Australia ... Tom.'

Hannah narrowed her eyes. 'Why would you include Tom? The guy's barely been here our whole adult lives.'

'Because I can recognise URST when it's six-foot-two and struts down Dandaloo Street with its eyes firmly fixed on you, Hanrahan.'

'*URST*? Do you mean—'

'Yes, I do. Unresolved sexual tension: the stuff of dreams and long-running TV series that keeps desperately horny single women like me glued to the screen.'

'That is a hundred per cent bonkers, Kylie.' Which she knew for a fact. Hadn't he told her that, in explicit words, when she'd asked if they could put The Incident behind them? *Already done.*

'I know what I know.'

'He's not interested.'

'How do you know?'

'Because he told me.'

'Wait just a freaking minute. Is there something you haven't told me? How did this topic of conversation even come up? Has something happened between you two? Don't tell me—' Kylie lowered her voice and leant in, grabbing Hannah's face between her hands and giving her the hairy eyeball '—are you having romantic feelings? You can tell me anything.'

Oh, boy, this was starting to unravel. Besides, the uncomfortable feeling she got every time Tom was in range was annoyance or irk (if that was a word) for him spinning her complacent little life out of its orbit, not *romance*. Sheesh.

Kylie's curiosity needed to get squashed.

'I don't have a romantic bone in my body, as you well know. I can't remember how it came up—' her BFF was right, she was a lousy liar '—maybe he was being a dick or something, dunno. And sure, I knew Tom pretty well when I was little, but that's because he and Josh were like two sides of the same coin back then. But now? I barely know him.'

Her phone rang, her ringtone loud and annoying because she'd forgotten to drop the volume from when she was last on call, and her and Kylie's eyes dropped to the screen just in time to see the words *Tom is calling* scroll back and forth across the screen.

Shoot. She'd have liked to ignore it, because Kylie was sitting there spooning what was left of her risotto into her very smug-looking face, but she couldn't just let it ring out and—

'Hello, Tom,' she said briskly.

'Who I barely know,' mimicked Kylie.

She raised her middle finger for her friend to inspect. 'What's up?'

'I have a proposal to put to you, and I wondered if you were free to come up to Ironbark and talk it over.'

'Well, I'm working all week, and then—'

'I was thinking this evening.'

'Oh!' She looked at her plate, which was down to a lone flat-leaf parsley stem and a few stray sprinkles of ground pepper. Did she want to talk to Tom?

Apparently the brain cells in charge of her mouth did. 'See you soon,' she heard herself saying into the phone before he rang off.

Kylie's immaculately shaped eyebrows had disappeared into her hairline. 'Well? Don't leave me sitting here wondering. What does our returned naval hero have to say for himself? Was he calling to remind you how "uninterested" he is?'

'You are so not funny. Actually … I'm not sure why he called. He wants to talk something over. Animal related, I would assume, since that's the *only* thing we have in common.' *Other than one secret kiss.*

'Or, maybe it's something that will fit into your new year, new you scheme. An adventure.'

'I doubt it.'

'But if it is … promise me you won't just give some kneejerk answer because you're anxious about change. Change can be fun, Hannah. Change can be good.'

'I promise. Whatever his reason is, me hearing it is going to require wheels. You got the workshop keys on you? Looks like I'm taking the green machine for a spin.'

'I'll walk you over. Remind me to give you the Dalgety program Kev saved for you. What with all the hoo-ha dragging you out of the showgrounds the other day, it somehow ended up in my handbag.'

# CHAPTER
## 15

Driving the winding mountain road from Hanrahan up to Ironbark Station was tricky on a dry day. On a wet late summer evening with clouds rolling down from the north and Kylie's words about URST scrolling over and over in her head … well. She'd had to concentrate.

Was her friend right? Did Tom fancy her? He'd tried to kiss her in the stable, but then he'd said it was no big deal. Why would he lie?

He wouldn't. Tom Krauss was about the most stand-up guy she'd ever known and in all those years, he'd never lied. Even to get out of trouble, which Hannah would have done in a heartbeat back when she was a kid. Not Tom. *Yes, Mrs Cody, I threw the cricket ball through your dining room window. Yes, Mr Cody, I drank six beers from your shed fridge with Josh and then we both puked behind the compost bin.*

So what could she deduce from this? The answer seemed easy: he might fancy her a little bit, but it wasn't personal. It wasn't special.

He wasn't, as he had already told her, interested, which meant Kylie's nonsense about unresolved sexual tension was just Kylie's wishful thinking.

She reached the turn where bitumen gave way to gravel track and nearly knocked her front teeth out on the steering wheel as the car hit a rut in the road. The clapped-out condition of her old car's suspension wasn't great, it had to be said. Kylie had the starter motor working a treat, which was a plus, but the back window was jammed about an inch open which made the wind flap about the back seat like Hannah had a damaged eagle stashed back there. No working heater, either, in a new and unwelcome development given the crazy cold weather the Snowies were having this summer. She tried not to think of it as an ill omen.

By the time she pulled into a park below the bullnose verandah of the Krauss homestead and killed the engine, she was shivering.

And maybe the weather wasn't the only reason.

She hadn't been back here since The Incident, and on that day she'd driven off like a wild person without stopping to think about what had upset her so much. Now she'd been invited back for 'a proposal' of some sort.

It had to be horse related. Specifically, Buttercup related. The big mare's pregnancy must be well underway now and it would be an unseasonal birth. It happened. Especially where the insemination had been done out of—

'Oh.' Hannah's thoughts stopped in their tracks. 'Oh!'

Where was that program Kylie had given her? She shoved at the pile of dressings and caramel wrappers that were littered over the passenger seat until she found it. She couldn't believe it had taken her so long to twig. The master of ceremonies had only spent most of the campdraft announcing it over the speakers strung up from tree to power pole to loo block.

She flipped the cover open. *Events … Thank you to our sponsors … Showground Rules: no dogs near the cattle pens, no smoking, no littering …* Yeah, yeah, whatever. Oh! Here it was: the list of prizes. Her eyes widened. Stallion after stallion was being offered up by local owners to service mares. And not just any old stallions, but ones with campdrafting and rodeo credentials.

A proven record.

No talk of artificial insemination, she noted, and why bother? Insemination in the equine industry wasn't outrageously expensive, but you needed equipment, a vet, expertise. Definitely more dosh needed than filling your horse float with diesel and trucking your mare to a paddock to get up close and personal with a willing, competent stallion.

No messy relationship drama, just a biological transaction with a sweet, soft-nosed little foal to show for it ten or eleven months later.

What was stopping her employing the same methodology? She'd studied biology at uni, hadn't she? She owned a zillion textbooks, she worked with animals. And—this was the clincher—she had her own ova to test her theories on. A few less every day if that dumb article in Kylie's magazine was to be believed, but she had enough to get the job done.

All she needed to do was find herself a likely candidate who'd be willing to do the servicing but who wasn't going to mess up the arrangement with a lot of relationship drama.

She stared up at the Krauss homestead. Well, well, well. Hadn't Hanrahan's recently returned bachelor spelled it out to her in unambiguous terms? *I was just messing around, brat. It's already forgotten.* All of which made him the perfect candidate to approach for the plan she'd just conceived (ha! What a pun!) inspired by the wonderful committee members who'd typed up the Dalgety Campdraft program.

But was now the time to suggest it?

She closed her eyes for a moment, trying to reassure herself that her plan wasn't dumb. Did she need to think it through more? Did she need to chicken out and drive off and come back later once she'd consulted the books waiting for her beside her bath?

The engine started its *tick tick tick* as it cooled, and she tried very hard not to think about the matching metronome of her biological clock.

Crap. Now she had gone and thought it.

She was here, wasn't she? So she should head inside and hear whatever Tom's proposal was, and then find some natural and non-awkward way to segue into a perfunctory Q and A session to gauge his willingness to contribute his gene pool to her single-mother-by-choice plan.

Hell, why not apologise to Bruno for causing a kerfuffle in front of him on Saturday while she was at it? She'd be outta here and back in her bathtub, prepping an ovulation chart before the late news came on.

'Imagine a simple linear graph,' she said, planning her explanatory speech. 'On the x-axis, we have biology and on the y-axis we have the city–country imbalance in access to technology. The x-axis tells me I need spermatozoa to create a baby, but the y-axis is telling me that the closest fertility clinics are in Wagga Wagga or Canberra or Wodonga. How do we solve this problem? Easy. You—um … your spermatozoa, to be precise—are here, available 24/7, whereas I'd be having to do multiple long distance trips to access, um … other spermatazoa.'

Maybe he'd want to hear some facts and figures about women parenting alone. Last year's tax return for the clinic would be proof enough that she could afford a cot, in case he was worried about future claims on the Krauss family fortunes.

Huh. If only she'd thought to keep her copy of *Knock Yourself Up* in the car; she could have loaned it to him. Prove the rationality of her process.

'Mrs LaBrooy,' she said brightly when the elderly housekeeper answered her knock on the front door. 'Do you ever get time off? It's past seven.'

'Little Hannah Cody. You come inside and let me give you a hug. Now, why haven't I seen you in my kitchen lately?'

Hannah wrapped her arms around Mrs L. She smelled (and felt) like a delicious clean pillowcase wrapped around a plump feather pillow. 'I'm sorry, Mrs LaBrooy. Josh has been seeing to the station horses after—' Shoot, she may as well say it. 'After I got into a bit of a snit with Tom.'

Mrs LaBrooy patted her cheek. 'You young ones. Always too blind to see what's right in front of your nose.'

'What do you mean by that?'

'Nothing, my lamb. Now—are you wanting to see Tom?'

'And Bruno, if it's not too late.'

'Oh, love, he's headed to his room. He's up with the sun and there's not too much puff left in him come nightfall. Is it important? I could go and knock on his door for you.'

'It can keep.'

'I'll tell him you popped by. Now, you go sit by the fire in the good room and warm your hands while I find Tom for you. It's been so cold these last few nights we've had a fire lit and you look chilled to the bone.'

'The heater's blown in my car.'

'You get that fixed before winter comes, you hear me? Your parents would have six fits if they could see the condition of that little car of yours.'

Hannah grinned. 'Lucky they can't see it, then. Don't worry, Kylie's just about talked me into an upgrade.' A four-wheel drive, perhaps, if her bank manager would agree to the finance. Something with room for a stroller to fit in the boot, and—heck, why not?—perhaps she should keep an eye on the patient list at the clinic for a pup from a golden retriever litter as well.

The fire in the hearth of the formal lounge room had turned to ash when she knelt before it, so she busied herself adding lengths of wood until the room flickered with golden light. Heavy bookcases and plump furniture were old fashioned but gorgeous, as was the deep, patient tick of an antique, heavily embellished cuckoo clock above the sideboard. She'd hidden under there as a child, once, listening to that very same clock, waiting for Josh and Tom to find her in a game of hide and seek. They hadn't bothered, of course. While she'd been congratulating herself on the cunning of her hiding skills, they'd been high-fiving each other at the cunning of their little sister–ditching skills and run off to play their own game of boys being dickheads in the stables.

Best not to think too much about that. Tom and her and stables were a combination that made her feel weird.

She had the ghost of schoolboy Tom in her head as the door creaked, so when she looked over, she could see that the boy was barely there in his face. The colouring, sure, that hadn't changed: the hair a wintry blond, the eyes a deepwater blue. But this Tom looked ... strong. Like hiding in a game would be a chore and he'd rather be out rock climbing or cross-country skiing. Which was kind of interesting. Tom had been a lawyer in the Navy, but he hadn't honed that muscled physique sitting behind a desk. Maybe he'd been one of those elite frogmen who swam under ships' hulls with steel blades clamped between their teeth, or—

She banished the image. Too much alone time watching action movies was her problem. She wasn't here for a play-by-play on Tom's past life. She was here to …

Darn it, she was flustered and her carefully thought-through words, which had sounded so totally ordinary and scientific in her head, were gone.

She could cut to the chase: *I'm interested in having a baby, and I believe you'd make a suitable donor. How about it?*

Too abrupt, maybe.

It crossed her mind that a woman with a baby donor proposal to make should have made an effort to dress in something a little more interesting than jeans and an old green turtleneck with holes in the elbows. Next time. There'd have to be a next time if she chickened out now. A dress might not set the right tone, but a lab coat might.

Tom regarded her from across the room with narrowed eyes.

'Relax,' she said, rising to her feet. 'I've left my right hook at home.'

'So it's a joke now, is it?'

'What? No. It's just … you're looking a little intimidating, if I'm honest. I crack jokes when I'm nervous.' *Or get sarcastic. Or punch expensive cameras.* But that last one was new and she was determined not to make a habit of it.

'I'm not intimidating.'

*Said the python to the pet rat.* She took a breath and let it out, calm and easy, the way she'd practised. A lot.

'I know you asked me here for something different, but I wanted to apologise to Bruno for messing up his outing on Saturday. I could see how much he was enjoying being the centre of attention.'

'I wouldn't worry about Bruno. He's thrown a few punches of his own in his day.'

'Really? I wouldn't have—' She broke off. She wasn't here to get distracted and she didn't know what Tom wanted to talk about, but she was going to lose her nerve if she didn't speak up. 'Look, can we talk?'

He sat on the sofa by the fire and she sat next to him, but instead of looking at her he turned to stare into the flames. 'Have you been charged? Property damage or assault? Because I've done a little reading up and—'

'No. I've apologised and paid for the damage.'

'Well, that's good news.'

'Yeah. Um, look, about wanting to talk, can you listen for a minute?'

'Sure.'

'I have a goal. I've been unsure about how to ... actuate it, and—' Jeez, was that even a word? She cleared her throat. 'Anyway, I've been considering my options and I've come up with a plan to make it happen.'

'A goal to conquer your fear of leaving Hanrahan?'

She breathed in and out. Of course he would know that now. The whole town must know it. Sheesh, this was hard. How could she phrase it scientifically so it didn't get too personal? 'Um, no, this goal is a little different, and you may be uniquely qualified to provide that help.'

'Wait. That's it? We're not even going to talk about what happened with the photographer?'

She swallowed. 'We can do, if we have to.'

He was frowning. 'We do have to. That is ... if you want my help with whatever this goal of yours is. I was *right there*, Han. It's not something I can just unsee.'

She frowned back at him. 'Look, can I just explain to you that I had my reasons, and I know I'm totally in the wrong, and I know

I'm going to have to do better from now on.' This was not going
the way she'd hoped. She'd wanted to very calmly ask him to be
a sperm donor, to which he would very calmly nod his head, and
phrases like 'nominal paternity' and 'scientific protocol' would
make up the rest of the discussion.

'Spit it out, brat. I want the actual whys and wherefores.'

She stabbed the fire poker into a blameless log. Hell. 'I suppose
you can have the short version.'

'I want the long version.'

Hannah resisted the urge to grind her teeth. Sure, she could
change her mind about the baby, about finding a donor, about how
sad and lonely the rest of her life was looking all on her ownsome.
She could buddy up with Mrs Grundy. Maybe there was someone
in the district breeding dalmatians? She'd give up campdraft, buy
herself a Spot-the-dog all of her own and renew her acquaintance
with the dragons at the library.

Or, she could talk to Tom.

She bit her lip. 'How good are you at keeping secrets?'

His hand tightened on his knee. 'Good enough.'

The smile had gone from his face and he looked like he'd take
a secret to the grave. She was grateful for the warmth of the fire.

'Okay. But I have a request, first.'

'What's that?'

'It's a weird one, but just roll with it, okay?'

His eyes crinkled. 'How weird are we talking?'

'I want you to kiss me.'

He was surprised into a sort of half-laugh, half-choke sound.
'Excuse me?'

She could feel heat on her cheeks that was not fire related. 'I have
a personal reason for wanting to know if that kiss in the stable was
a one-off.'

'It was definitely a one-off because it's not happening again.'

'That's not what I mean.' Jeepers, he was making this difficult. He'd gone all stiff and poker-faced and remote. 'Was it a casual something that might happen between two disinterested parties who happened to find themselves in the same place, or was it ...' she struggled to find the words, and he didn't race in to help her out, '... something else?'

His eyes closed and he muttered under his breath.

'Tom?' This donor sperm plan of hers was only going to work if all of that URST rubbish Kylie had been going on about wasn't true. She didn't need complications and she didn't have the skillset to navigate her way through whatever it was Kylie thought she'd imagined.

'I don't think that's a good idea.'

She narrowed her eyes. 'Why?'

'Um, how about last time I kissed you, you cried? And then barely let me apologise—for I don't even know what, exactly— and treated me like a serial killer for months. And Hannah, you were there, too. You know what went on same way I do. So what is it? Were we two disinterested parties, or were we ... something else?'

Damn, he was really riled up, and now he'd gone and got her all riled up, and she was here to ask him a favour. 'Totally disinterested!' she snapped out. 'Far out, forget I asked. Question answered.'

He rubbed his forehead. 'Jesus. I need a drink, do you want one?'

'Sure. Wine, if you've got it, but measure it out, would you? A hundred ml because I'm driving and I'm short.'

He eyed her like she was a feral cat who might scratch up the sofa if he left the room, then nodded. 'Sure. Red or white?'

'Whatever's open.'

'Expensive tastes.'

The joke was an olive branch, and she was relieved to be able to seize it and answer in kind. 'If some cheese and crackers happen to fall onto a plate while you're in the kitchen, I wouldn't complain.'

'Yes, ma'am.'

'A waiter with attitude. I like that.'

He disappeared and she stared into the flames. Ten plus years she'd had this crappy, awful thing about herself buried down deep inside, and now she was going to blab about it twice on one day?

She got off the sofa and sank to her knees in front of the fire so she could lift her hands to the warmth. Then the door creaked and Tom was back, a tray balanced in his hands. He set it on a low table and sat back down.

'Cabernet, smoked cheddar, crackers that are only a bit stale and a pear. Mrs L has retired so I had to make do with what I could find. That woman may seem sweeter than fairy floss, but you mess with her kitchen and she'll take you down.'

Hannah helped herself to the smaller glass and loaded up a few crackers, then sat on the carpet and rested her back against one of the armchairs. 'It's warm by the fire.'

'I'll stick with the sofa. I've a dicky knee from my glory days playing footy for Hanrahan High.'

Not just Hanrahan High, either, if she was remembering correctly. Tom and her brother had both played in the Schoolboys State Titles. Josh, of course, had leveraged his glory days by dating pretty much every girl at school. But Tom? Now she thought about it, she couldn't recall who Tom had been sweet on back at high school.

'Who'd you take to your school formal, Tom?'

He chuckled. 'That is quite the conversational jump.'

'You're the one who brought up high school.'

'True. Mary Frankton.'

'For real? She lives down in Cooma now. Two kids who play hockey, from memory. I didn't know you two were an item.'

'We weren't. I had my eye on someone else but was too chicken to ask.'

She snorted. 'You? Chicken? I don't believe it.'

'Who's being chicken now? It's time to stop dragging up ancient history and tell me why you assaulted some bloke at Dalgety.'

She took a swig of wine, gathered her thoughts, then launched in. 'A long time ago I had a problem as a result of a photograph taken of me.'

Tom leant back in the sofa and crossed his long legs out in front of him. His feet, in worn loafers of mahogany brown, were close enough to nudge her knee. 'Why is that?'

'When I finished school I got accepted at uni in Sydney. Medicine, a guaranteed entry spot after a science degree.'

'Really? I didn't know that.'

'Well, you were long gone by then, I suppose, learning how to bomb submarines or whatever it is naval recruits do.' She cleared her throat. 'In my first semester, some girls played a prank on me which involved a photo of me, but the body of someone else.'

'Jesus.'

'Not Jesus, no. A professional, um … person, who was engaged in skills about which I knew nothing.' Still knew nothing, if she was honest. Not that she would be telling Tom that.

'Oh, Hannah.' Tom wasn't looking so relaxed now. He'd set his glass down and was sitting forward. His face had lost that remote, forbidding look. 'What happened? What did you do?'

'I did what any inexperienced, wounded girl would do. I fell apart.'

'I'm sorry.'

'I didn't drop out of uni, not straight away. That came after.'

Tom frowned. 'After what?'

She swallowed. 'I kept falling apart. Cried a lot. Wouldn't get out of bed. Came home, eventually, to Mum and Dad, who had to drop everything and try to put the pieces of me back together.'

He reached out and for some reason her hand was in his and his thumb was doing odd things to her breathing, which was weird, because his thumb was nowhere near her diaphragm or trachea or lungs, but on her palm.

She dragged her mind off the biological conundrum. 'That's it.'

'No, it's not. The Hannah I knew would have taught those mean girls a lesson and carried on studying. What really happened?'

This was the bit she didn't want to tell. 'That's just it, Tom. I *didn't* cope. You thought I was tough—heck, *I* thought I was tough. But I wasn't, okay? I needed help. The viral photo wasn't the problem, not really. The way I reacted when a problem came up in my life—that was the problem. I was diagnosed with depression.'

Tom did that thumb thing again and let out a long sigh. 'I can't believe I didn't know all this.'

She shrugged. 'You know what Josh and my parents are like. They're protective.'

'Mmm.'

She risked a glance at him. She had an agenda, and she wasn't going to baulk now, just because Tom was looking all concerned and sad and angry and … kind.

And that thumb …

'You *sure* you're a disinterested party, Krauss?' she said suspiciously.

'For heaven's sake—'

'Kiss me and find out. It's now or never.'

He squeezed her hand and pulled her onto the sofa beside him. 'There'll be no kissing, brat. I am open to a hug, however, since I just coerced you into telling me something that I had no right to know.'

Something in her chest melted, something that had boiled itself into a hard nut. Part of her brain thought the melting might be a bad sign, not a good sign, but she told it to shut up. And then Tom pulled her in close, wrapped his arms around her and she dropped her head into his warm, broad shoulder.

This huggy nonsense was a totally unnecessary step in her plan to access his spermatozoa, of course. She'd buy a turkey baster for that, and she was pretty sure there was a whole chapter in *Baby Making 101* when it came time to learn the nitty gritty. But, gee, it felt delicious. She'd be putting a stop to it, real soon.

Well … sort of soon.

Okay, not at all soon.

# CHAPTER
# 16

Tom held Hannah against his shoulder, letting his fingers sink into the messy braid of her auburn hair.

'I'm sorry you went through that.'

'Yeah, me too.' Her breath was hot on his neck when she spoke.

This was his moment to be as honest with her. *Hannah, kissing you in the stables was not normal or ordinary.* Or maybe: *Hannah, I've loved you since you wore pigtails.* Or: *Hannah, it's too late, I've got a time bomb ticking away between two of my vertebrae. I'm no good for you.*

Instead, he let his free hand stroke her back from neck to waist—slowly down, even more slowly back up.

'Now or never,' she murmured, then lifted her head and looked at him, her clear green gaze trapping his. Her face was pale but for the freckles scattered across her nose. Her eyebrows were straight, no nonsense, determined, but there was nothing no nonsense about her mouth. On the contrary, it promised fun, laughter, life.

He shouldn't, because a kiss could go nowhere and her head was clearly a hot mess.

He wouldn't, because he was a hot mess of his own.

But his brain seemed to have lost its ability to do anything more than think wouldn'ts and couldn'ts and shouldn'ts, because she lifted herself slightly and slid one knee across his legs so she was straddling him on the sofa. Her arms were about his neck and she was so close he could see the frayed hole in the neckline of the forest-green sweater she wore, the glimmer of pale flesh below.

He shouldn't, but he was struggling to think, and the part of him that hadn't remembered sex was on Dr Novak's banned list was finding itself pressed up snug against the warm denim of Hannah's jeans.

'What are you doing?' he said.

He didn't get an answer—well, not a spoken one, anyway. He'd kissed her before, so he should have been prepared. He should have braced himself for the lightning rod that jolted deep inside where his dreams slept, woke them up and made them want.

He forgot caution. He forgot the deep ache that lived in his back; his angry, bitter father sleeping in the hospital-style bed in the homestead's main bedroom; his worry over the blankness of the future yawning out ahead of him.

All he could think about was Hannah.

Nails scraped at his nape and he grabbed her hair in his fist and bowed her back so he could kiss her mouth, her neck, the swell beneath the ragged collar of her jumper. She tasted like daffodils in spring, like pure mountain air. His hands wanted to linger, but his lust wanted to race. Her thighs, muscles taut, lifted over his. Her stomach spanned smooth and warm when his fingers lifted the hem of her jumper. The rasp of satin. The tiny metal claw of clasps. He brushed a thumb over her breast and the sound she made turned the heat into an inferno.

'Oh, yes,' she murmured, and the words acted on him quicker than a bucket of ice water. There was no 'yes' for him. He'd lost himself in the moment and now she was reading something into his response that he couldn't deliver.

He lifted his head and took a second to find his voice. 'I'm sorry, Hannah. I should have told you. I don't want this.'

She was still flushed and her eyes were bright. 'I don't understand.'

*Shit.* Could he mess this up any more? She'd been totally buying his 'disinterested party' bullshit and then he'd gone and lost his head and blown it.

He had to backtrack. But how?

'I'm not in the market for a relationship, or for a—dalliance. With anyone, and that includes you. A snog on the sofa doesn't change that.'

She turned away from him. 'That's good,' she said in a thin, low voice that he couldn't quite interpret. 'That's excellent, in fact, because I don't want any of those things from you.'

'No more bullshit, Hannah. I asked you here to talk about a town project, but no, you had something you just had to say, and—'

'I'm here for a baby.'

He coughed. 'I'm sorry, what?'

'You heard me. That's the goal I said I needed help for. I'm in my thirties, the timing is right, and I'm not in the market for a Mr Hannah Cody. So I need a sperm donor. I've chosen you on the condition that you're not interested in me romantically, and you've just confirmed that. Loud and clear. Don't worry, I'll provide the equipment and a printed set of instructions.'

Wow. And he'd thought having his hip and back sliced to the bone had hurt. Hannah Cody, the girl he'd lost his heart to what seemed like a lifetime ago, had noticed he existed at last.

But only for his chromosomes.

# CHAPTER
## 17

Hannah had seen animals in her treatment room who had swallowed something they shouldn't have, like a tennis ball or a footy sock or the neighbour's guinea pig, and they'd all had the same look of wild-eyed alarm that Tom was giving her now.

'I've thought it all through,' she said, going for an air of calm reassurance, as though her nerve endings weren't jangling like interconnected lithium-ion smoke alarms that had just worked out she was ablaze. 'It's a lot to take in, and I'm happy to prepare you a folder of information.'

'Hannah, this is—'

'I know, it's a little out of the blue, but it makes a lot of sense, Tom.'

'—absolutely nuts.'

'Excuse me?'

'I mean, what are you *thinking*?' He still looked stunned. Worse, he looked horrified. Which meant … Oh, god. His alarm wasn't about the idea of him being asked to be a donor. His alarm was about the idea of her being a mother!

Surely not. Surely Tom knew her well enough to know that deep down she was sensible and practical and caring.

'It is absolutely out of the question.' He'd turned away and was covering his eyes with one hand. The knuckles on his other hand were white as they gripped his knee. He was—she choked the hurt down—truly horrified by the idea that she thought she could be a mother.

'I've made a mistake,' she said. Her keys were somewhere, but where? On the hall table? Had she brought them in here?

He cleared his throat. 'Hey, look, it's been a wild week, I get it. I'm sorry, I—well. Emotions riding high and all that. We all blurt out stuff we don't mean from time to time.'

'Don't fucking patronise me. My emotions are fine and dandy, thank you very much, and the mistake I was referring to was me asking you. Mr *Disinterested*.' She'd have tossed her head if she'd ever bothered learning the knack of it. 'And I can blurt out whatever the hell I please when I'm talking about my own dwindling ova, thank you very much.'

She spied a glint of silver in the crease between his pants leg and the sofa. Awkward … her keys must have fallen out of her pocket when she straddled him, before her eyes had been opened to what a complete and utter dick he was.

She plucked them out, ignoring his wince. Good. Maybe he'd have a nice key-shaped bruise on his leg to remind him of what an arse he'd been. What a judgemental, patronising *arse*.

And to think she'd been going to sully her baby's gene pool with his. A nice fertility clinic with a checklist where she could tick boxes like 'kind' and 'chest hair' and 'doesn't patronise successful female veterinarians' was looking better and better.

All she had to do was change her total personality so she could drive to one.

'I'm going. No need to see me out.'

'Hannah, would you wait just a damn minute?'

She hightailed it along the corridor, opened the heavy wooden door, raced down the steps and was in her car, turning over the awesomely tuned starter motor, in about five seconds flat. She stalled on the reverse, which wasn't quite so awesome, but crunched her way into first gear and was about to floor it when Tom's hand came down on her window.

'Would you wait a damn minute?' he yelled through the glass.

'You've said plenty already,' she yelled back.

'I haven't said I'm sorry yet.'

She rolled her window down an inch, so it matched the one in the back where the cold night air was whipping in. 'I'm listening.'

He bent down so he was looking at her through the open space and his mouth was behind the glass. Blue eyes stared into hers for a long moment and she shivered. From the cold, obviously, because there was nothing in that stare to make her shiver.

Certainly no URST.

'When I said it had been an emotional week,' he said, 'I was talking about *my* emotions.'

That was unexpected. 'Go on,' she said magnanimously.

He may have done an infinitesimal eye roll—it was hard to tell with her door seal in the way.

'And when I said people blurt out stuff without thinking from time to time, I meant that I had just blurted something out without thinking. Something hurtful. I'm sorry, Hannah. You took me by surprise and ...' He sighed and her car window fogged over. 'I reacted in a bad way. For personal reasons. I'm sorry.'

She put her finger on the button and pressed it so the window went zzzzzzzh slowly down into its socket until they were looking at each other in silence but for the whip and flap of the wind lifting receipts and chocolate wrappers on the passenger seat.

'So. You don't think I'm nuts for wanting to have a baby.'

He bit his bottom lip. 'No.'

'You don't think I'll be a horrible mother.'

He closed his eyes. 'No.'

'But you're saying no to my proposal anyway.'

'I am.'

'Well.' Her fingers twisted in the keys dangling from her igni-tion and they jangled like tiny church bells. 'I guess I'll be off then.'

'You want to try not reversing over Bruno's flower bed this time?'

'Shit. Did I—?'

He smiled. 'No. Are we okay, Hannah? Because we seem to be having this fighting/not fighting dynamic going on and it's messing with my head.'

'We're okay, I guess. Bye, then.'

And she'd barely got over the cattle grid when he was on the phone reminding her that they never even got to talk about what he had invited her up to discuss, so they'd better meet for coffee the next day.

'You shouldn't have made me mad,' she said.

'It's not all about you, Hannah.'

She could hear the smile in his voice when he said it, so she answered in kind. 'Worst apology ever.'

The next morning at the clinic, Hannah was still mulling over her unsettling evening at Tom's. His behaviour towards her was just so darned confusing.

'Letter for you, Han. Looks like another of those fancy ones you keep chucking out,' said Sandy when Hannah ducked into reception to grab a patient file. The receptionist lifted it and gave it a shake. 'I'd be opening it over a waste bin if I were you. Could be one of those annoying missives that sprays glitter confetti everywhere.'

Hannah huffed out a theatrical groan. 'Pass it over.'

'I've put Toby and the guinea pigs into Room One,' said Sandy, handing her the envelope. 'There's a dog in Room Two with social issues. Knock before you go in so the owner can get her in a headlock.'

Hannah stared at the fancy cursive on the envelope. Sandy was right. This did seem like one of those annoying missives. It also looked familiar. 'Is it the doberman from Eucumbene?' she asked. 'I'll take the muzzle in with me.'

'Worse. It's a chihuahua called Teddy who identifies as a velociraptor.'

Hannah slid a finger into the thick cream envelope, broke the seal and looked gingerly inside. Sandy's instincts were correct ... confetti. She pulled out the card. *Mr & Mrs Gregory Flemington and Mr Bob Varma cordially invite Hannah Cody plus one to the wedding of Dr Karen Flemington and Raj Varma at The Shaw Winery, Lake George on February ...*

Hannah stopped reading the stiff card and turned to the loose-leaf note clipped to its back. Karen Flemington, one of the few friends she'd made in the brief and ill-fated semester she'd spent at uni in Sydney had sent her another invitation to her wedding? How many times did she have to say no?

*Hannah,* she read. *I know you've said you won't come, but please reconsider. I'd love to see you and I would love us to be friends again. Best, Karen.*

She chucked the envelope back on the receptionist's desk. 'Bin it, would you, Sandy?' she said. 'Now, let's see if I can survive an encounter with Teddy.'

The rush didn't let up for three hours, and while a lie-down before the afternoon clinic would have been welcome, she had a darned coffee date to prepare for and—even worse—Kylie had dropped in, uninvited.

Hannah slumped on her pillows while Kylie stood before her wardrobe doors, mercilessly ripping clothes from hangers.

'I don't know why you're so calm about this,' said Kylie. 'This is an emergency—your clothes are awful.'

'And I don't even know why you're here.'

'My BFF since kindy is going on her first date since Methuselah grew a front tooth and you're wondering why I came over to help you get ready? Girl, this is An Event.'

'It's not a date. It's coffee. How do you even know, again?'

'You told me.'

'Well, I do not need to change my clothes, for heaven's sake. We're meeting—to *talk*—at the café where I go pretty much every day, often in my scrubs.'

Kylie was paying no attention. 'You should have come over to my place. I at least own skirts. And lipstick. And clothing that was bought this decade.'

Hannah ignored the slight on her fashion sense and turned to her more pressing problem. Mulling all morning had brought her no answers and, let's face it, she was out of her depth. 'Can I tell you something? Without you getting all demented about what single women intuit from hours of watching television?'

Kylie threw three coat hangers to the floor and turned to face her. 'You have my undivided attention.'

'Okay. So, I haven't been totally upfront with you. Last year, shortly after Tom returned to Hanrahan, I was up at Ironbark one day in the stables after taking Skipjack for a ride and he was there.'

Kylie nodded. 'In the stables. Him. You. A sweaty horse. Go on.'

'And ... well. The long and the short of it is that he leapt on me like a hormone-crazed teenager.'

'Holy *cow*.'

'But later, and by later I mean last night, when *I* decide to kiss *him*—for purely sensible reasons, I might add, in the way of an experiment of sorts for his own protection—he puts the brakes on. Does that seem fair to you?'

'Wait. OMG, I have so many questions. You're going to have to give me a *lot* more details about the stable encounter. I cannot believe you waited months to tell me. Start with where his hands went. How they felt.'

Hannah rolled her eyes. 'Kylie.'

'What? I'm in a man drought. I need to live vicariously through you.'

'They felt good, all right? Good enough to make me wonder if it hadn't been your everyday, garden-variety snog in a stable. Also, it was a little freaky, if I'm honest.'

'You think that six-foot hunk of blond man-cake is freaky?'

'Yeah. I guess I do.'

'You've got rocks in your head.'

'Anyway,' she said, 'it was confusing, that's all, to hear him tell me straight out that he's not interested, even though it felt like he *was* interested.'

Kylie fanned her hands about her cheeks like she was trapped in a heat wave. 'Tell me more. Did he kiss your neck? I love it when they kiss your neck.'

Hannah threw a pillow at her. 'So now, even though he's definitely not interested, he wants to meet at the café—'

'The contrary rat.'

'—to discuss the "something" we didn't get around to discussing last night.'

'Because you were makin' your moves.' Kylie zipped out the words like she was the cool friend in some ditzy sitcom.

'It was a bit of a bust, anyway. But that's good. Now all that silliness is behind us, we can move forward in a sensible, friendly way with no awkwardness.'

Kylie rolled her eyes. 'Sure you can. At least let me dress you for this sensible meet-up. Green is your colour, Hannah. Or black, navy, maybe a rich plum.' She turned to the cupboard. 'Why am I only seeing denim in here?'

'I don't go out, remember?'

'Right.'

Hannah sighed. 'Come on, Kylie, do I really need to get gussied up?'

'Yes. You do. No argument.' Kylie turned back to the closet and wrestled a puffy, creased, dull pink strapless frock from its hanger. 'You've still got your formal dress? Wow. It is even more hideous than I remembered; is it my imagination, or does this thing look like a pavlova?'

'Hey. My mother made that.'

'And I thought my mum was mean.' Kylie stuffed the dress (with difficulty) back in the closet and pulled out a pair of black jeans that still had the label attached. 'Aha. Now we're on to something.'

Hannah shook her head. 'I bought them online. They're too tight.'

'Too tight to deliver a baby cow in, sure. Too tight to wear on a coffee date? I think not. Come on, try them on.'

'It's not a date,' she said but rose from the bed and stripped down to her underwear to put them on.

Kylie's mouth dropped open. 'Hannah. Seriously. Is that the best you can do?'

'What?' She looked down at her sensible beige knickers, the white cotton bra that—admittedly—had turned the colour of old dog teeth.

'I am a mechanic,' said Kylie, 'and I wear better underwear than that under my overalls.'

'But you were a beautician first, Kylie. That girl stuff sticks.'

'New underwear every year from now on, or I wash my hands of you.'

She grinned. 'Yes, mummy Kylie.'

'Okay, put the pants on while I decide if these blouses are going in the maybe pile or the over-my-dead-body pile.'

'I like the white one.'

'You've lost your vote. Here, try this,' she said, tossing over an ivory blouse. 'It's pretty warm out, but if the breeze comes up you might want this.'

A teal blue shawl landed next to Hannah as she lay back on the bed to get the zipper on the black jeans done up. 'I'm not going to be able to consume more than a macaron without busting this zip.'

Kylie ignored her and went to the oak dressing table which had come from Hannah's grandmother. 'Amber earrings! Hannah, these are lovely. See, you do have taste.'

'Josh gave me those.'

'Figures. That man has it all, doesn't he? Charm, taste and a killer arse. Broke my heart when he took up with Vera.'

'Yours and every other single heart in the Snowy Mountains.'

Kylie rubbed a hand over her chest and sighed a little. 'Yep. Still broken.'

'Oh, give over,' said Hannah, standing at the dressing table to try on the earrings. The orange crystals dangled flirtatiously from her ears. 'Hmm. These do look nice.'

Kylie put an arm around her waist and hugged her into her side. 'That's you looking nice, Hannah. You make the earrings, not the other way around, and you know what?'

'What?'

'I'm seeing a glow in your eyes. I've missed that. Don't lose that sparkle by making a dumb decision about Tom, okay? He's—gosh. How can I put this in a way you'll understand?'

'I'm not completely stupid, Kylie.'

'Quiet, I'm thinking. Oh! I've got it. Your brother, Josh. He's sweet, he'd do anything for you, but he's not dangerous, you know what I'm saying?'

'Sure.'

'If he was a dog, he'd be a golden retriever.'

'Okay, I can see that.'

'But Tom. He's a protector. Brooding, watchful eyes, deep thoughts swirling about under the surface … he's a German shepherd. He'd throw himself in front of a bullet before he'd let you get hurt.'

Huh. Hannah looked in the mirror and tried to see what sort of a dog she would be, but all she could see was a fairly short, pale-faced woman who was, deep on the inside, in the places where the mirror couldn't see, lonely.

A baby would fix that, not a pup.

And she didn't need a man for that, no matter how much of a protector he was.

'I've thought this through, Kylie, I promise.'

'Well, you know where I live when it all goes to hell and you need a shoulder to cry on. Now, perfume, show me what you've got.'

Twenty minutes later, Kylie had roared off to rescue a quadbike from bald tyres and Hannah was about to head out through the clinic's back door when it opened to reveal Tom, a white cardboard box in his hand suspiciously wrapped in ribbon.

A gift? Did he feel sorry for her? Was this *pity*?

'Apple pie from Mrs LaBrooy,' he said.

'You didn't tell her anything, did you?'

His face assumed an expression of wounded innocence. 'You're right. It's too much for me to be bringing you a dish of flaky golden pastry stuffed with stewed apple and cinnamon just because she's fond of you. Let's take it up to Josh's apartment and he can have it.'

She wrestled the box from his hands and took it into the back office to store it with the heartworm vaccines. 'I'll be the judge of who gets a share of Mrs LaBrooy's apple pie. Shall we go?'

He gave a mock bow. 'Your chariot awaits.'

'The café is less than two hundred metres away across a well-mowed park.'

'I was speaking metaphorically. Let's go, brat.'

That was more like it. She picked up the scarf Kylie had made her pinkie promise to wear, and shrugged her way into the denim jacket she'd put her foot down about. 'I'm ready.'

Tom held the door open and sniffed the air as she passed. 'Is that perfume?'

'Kylie was here earlier. She made me—you know what she's like.'

He smiled and she watched his eyes wander over her rustic braid down to the soft leather boots she wore. 'Had a tough morning being bullied into wearing nice clothes, I see.' He leant in to her neck and took another deep sniff. 'She does excellent work.'

Why did this feel suspiciously like a date? Worse, a small-town date that was about to occur in a venue where everybody would see them. She needed donor sperm, not a boyfriend. And Tom had assured her he wasn't 'on the market', so why was he jumping through hoops?

Tom was up to something, she just didn't know what. But he wasn't the only one who was up to something; the apple pie, the sniffing, the coffee meet-up … all of this niceness was giving her the incentive she needed to try and change Tom's mind.

The Billy Button Café was chock-a-block, which was no surprise. The food, the wine, the ambience … Vera had created something special when she'd taken over the lease of the old bank building last year.

Graeme, the manager, turned despairing eyes on them as they came in. 'We're out of tables, just when two of my favourite people in all the world drop in. Hannah, mwah, mwah,' he said, planting kisses on her cheeks. 'Would sir like to be kissed?' he said to Tom.

'Another time, mate,' Tom said easily. 'Good to see you.'

'There's seats left at the counter, will that do?'

'Perfectly,' said Hannah, and marched over to claim a stool. *Try making bar-counter conversation into a secret talk*, she thought a little maliciously, as Tom eased his lean self onto the stool beside her.

Kev Jones was first over, bobbing up between them, nearly buried in a home-knitted vest. 'You two know you can count on me to volunteer for the Ironbark Campdraft. I couldn't crack the whip with my bursitis, but I can judge and I pull a hell of a beer if there's kegs at the bar.'

Tom gave a groan and she raised her eyebrows at him. What was Kev on about?

'Marigold not with you today, Kev?' Tom said.

'The historical society are meeting down at the hall. I'm on stickybun collection duty.'

A small mercy. No sooner had Kev disappeared with a waxed carton of baked goods than Vera emerged from the swing doors that led to the kitchen.

'Hannah, hey,' she said. 'Those animals finally decided to give you a break, did they? Coffee, or are you …' Vera's words trailed off as she noticed Hannah wasn't alone. She looked from Hannah to Tom and back again, before her face went blank. 'Er, hi, Tom. I'll, er, let you two get back to business as soon as I've taken your order.'

'Cappuccino for me, please, Vera. What do you fancy, brat?'

'The brat usually has a latte, no sugar,' said Graeme as he moved in behind the espresso machine.

Tom was looking exasperated by all the intrusion. 'Make it a big one, will you, Graeme?' he said. 'I'm feeling caffeine deficient.'

'You got it, sweetness.'

'That's Lieutenant Commander Sweetness, retired, to you, mate.'

Vera was still hovering. 'I've got pumpkin scones. Graeme sweet-talked his granny into sharing her recipe, and they're better than Christmas.'

'Are they carb free?' Hannah's jeans were digging into her in all sorts of uncomfortable ways, and she wasn't sure how much more of her would fit before the zipper popped.

'Sure, if you ignore the flour and pumpkin and buttermilk I put in them. I'll go find you some,' said Vera, and bustled off into the kitchen.

'She is so about to text Josh,' Hannah muttered to Tom. 'Why do I feel like I've stumbled into an episode of *Fawlty Towers*?'

Graeme set their coffees down, dropping a wink at them so broadly she couldn't decide if his target was her or Tom, then they were alone. Time to get her agenda rolling.

'I've got clinic again this afternoon.' She stirred the swan pattern layered into the crema of her coffee.

Tom raised an eyebrow. 'Er … yes?'

'Just making chit-chat. Isn't that why we're here? So you can check I'm not bonkers? Because if you think I haven't seen a town intervention scheme before, you haven't factored in how long I've lived in Hanrahan. Who's behind it? Josh? Marigold?'

Tom choked gently on his drink and she resisted the urge to pat his back. She was a disinterested party and so was he.

'If you do have something you want to discuss, then you'd better make it quick; I'm removing the testicles from a one-eyed tomcat called Captain at two o'clock.'

'Poor bloke. Well, you guessed it, the busybodies have decided you need some help, um, with your social skills.'

'Ouch.'

'Yep. Anyway, they've come up with the plan that you and I organise this year's campdraft at Ironbark.'

'Was that what Kev was wittering on about?'

'Yep. Bruno is on board and I've agreed to it.'

'What, and I just do what everyone says? No thanks, Tom. I've got plans of my own. Organising a campdraft seems like a lot of work and unlike you, I already have a full-time job.'

He put his hand on hers. 'Hannah. Josh asked me to ask you. He wants this.'

Crap. Saying no to her brother was a lot harder than saying no to Tom or Marigold or Kev. She leant in a little closer, wishing now that a more private table had been available. 'Josh doesn't know how busy I'm going to be this year. I've got to find a fertility clinic, research the steps, prepare myself. I might be away a lot.' If a miracle happened and she overcame her fear of going away.

Tom stirred his coffee for an unnecessarily long time. 'What say I help you. With, you know, logistics. And you help me with the campdraft. It'd ease Josh's mind.'

'When you say logistics …'

'I'm not promising my sperm.'

'Tom.' She hated sounding so desperate. But, truth was, she *was* desperate. 'Be a mate.'

He dropped his voice to the same low-level whisper as hers. 'That's precisely what I'm trying to be, Hannah. A mate.'

She nodded, but it was really just some social reflex, because actually she didn't understand what he meant, not at all. 'Is it my parenting skills you're worried about? I know it may seem like I have a few problems but I'm working on them. The clinic's going well and I don't expect … I mean, this is a donor-only deal I'm suggesting. I'm not looking for financial input or anythi—'

'I'm sure you'll be a wonderful parent, Hannah. The same way I'm sure you'll be a wonderful life partner to some lucky bloke.'

Why was he saying that so stiffly? She'd not given him reason enough to trust her, that was it.

'I'm promising my support. Come on, Hannah, can that please be enough?'

She narrowed her eyes. 'Full truth, Tom, no half-truths: are you trying to make sure I don't do something harmful again? Because I'm not. I'm telling you straight and I need you to trust me. I don't want a babysitter; that would just piss me off. I am, however, open to the idea of having a friend. A supportive friend.'

'Full truth. I trust you when you tell me you won't do anything harmful.'

'Okay then.'

'Okay? You're sure?'

She was totally sure. Tom wanted to hang out, which meant she could still change his mind. He needed to see her facing her problems and being a calm, trustworthy, totally awesome person. Which she was, mostly.

The idea came to her in a rush. 'I think I know how we can make a headstart on this helping each other out thing. Can you wait here? I'll be five minutes, tops. Don't eat my scone when it arrives.'

'Er, sure.'

She jumped off the stool and bolted for the door. If Tom needed reassurance that she could handle herself, well she had a way to provide it. It had arrived just that morning, drenched in glitter.

She hustle-marched across the park, cursing Kylie for the fact the amber beads dangling from her ears were a great clattering annoyance when she went faster, crossed Dandaloo in the wake of a dusty old Kingswood, then ducked her head into the reception door.

'Sandy,' she hissed. 'Did you bin that invite yet, my lovely?'

'Sure, but I can fish it out.' Sandy leant into her waste basket and pulled out the wedding invite, peeling it away from a limp banana skin. 'Here you go.'

'Thanks.' Hannah shoved it into the inside pocket of her jacket, raced back to the café and threw herself, breathless, onto her stool.

'You want to tell me what that was all about?'

'I wondered if you'd be interested in accompanying me on a day trip. South. To a town that isn't Hanrahan.'

'You've not booked me into some fertility clinic, have you? Because that would be stepping well over the line.'

She frowned. 'No! Not a fertility clinic. A wedding.' She pulled the invite out of her jacket and dropped it onto the counter.

'Oh!' he said. 'Someone else's wedding. Me as your plus one.'

'What else would I mean, for crying out loud?'

His face had relaxed and he had a little grin on, giving him a dimple on one side of his face, but he was still looking at her as if she was bonkers, which was the exact look she needed to wipe off his face if he was ever going to take her seriously.

'Do you own a suit? Judging by the silver lettering on this thing, I'm guessing it's a fancy event.'

'I own a suit. Do you own a dress? That would be the bigger question, wouldn't it?'

Crap. That was certainly a flaw in her plan. No matter, Kylie could lend her something.

'And it's soon, like, two weeks on Saturday. Only, we'll have to go in your car because mine's on its last legs. Are you free?'

'I'll check my diary.'

She hadn't even considered the fact he might have plans. But with whom? To do what?

He must have interpreted her face correctly. 'I was messing with you. I'm free.' He finished his cappuccino then gave her a long look. 'A wedding, with people. You know there'll be photographers there, right?'

Of course she knew; why else had she thrown out the previous invitation she'd received? Worse ... the wedding was taking place in Lake George, which was somewhere on the wrong side of Canberra, but now it had turned into a two-bird-one-stone kind of deal: personal growth and winning Tom over to her way of thinking. It was a win-win situation. She hoped.

'I'm ready.'

'Okay, then. I'll be your plus one.'

# CHAPTER
# 18

Hannah smoothed her hand over the black dress she'd borrowed from Kylie. Her friend had insisted on doing her makeup, so she had almost as much stuff plastered to her face as she did her body: eyeshadow, eyeliner, a ridiculous quantity of matte lipstick. She'd drawn the line at fake eyelashes, despite Kylie's twenty-minute monologue on their total awesomeness. There was only so much awesome she could pack into one day.

But as she watched Tom let himself out of his dusty four-wheel drive, she realised she needed room for more, because—holy dooley—he looked amazing. A suit the colour of charcoal turned his pale hair into winter sunlight and he'd wrapped a woolly grass-green scarf around his neck, which told her the temperatures up at Ironbark must have been chilly that morning. He looked a little drawn—a long night with the colicky horse that was plaguing Josh, perhaps—or maybe that was her eyes still stinging from all the gunk Kylie had slathered on her. Any unattached female at this wedding would go weak at the knees at the sight of him, which was fine. The less attention Hannah had focused on her, the better.

His eyes met hers and stayed there as he walked up the flagstone path to the door. A rush of heat flooded her cheeks for some dicky reason, which she decided to blame on the uncomfortable bra she was wearing. Why was she just now working out that today did not have the feel of some hey-let's-be-friends outing?

Today had the feel of a date. And she'd been the one doing the inviting.

Her pie graphs and evaluation charts and scientific enquiry into the procreation of the human race seemed to have taken a back seat, so what was she actually doing?

'Hi,' Tom said. 'Wow. I'd take a photo, but this face isn't insured.'

She swatted him with the clutch Kylie had also lent her. 'Too much? Too little? What do you think?'

He sent a gaze over her that made her feel she was standing too close to a campfire, starting from her painted toenails in their (borrowed) peep-toe velvet heels to the top of her tousled updo. 'Too beautiful,' he said, a twist of a smile on his face.

She sucked in a breath and tried to ignore how the sincerity of his comment made her feel. She had planned this event, damn it. This was her strategy, not his, and if he thought she looked okay, then that was good. A two-hour drive, a wedding that she would bail from at the first polite moment after one too many glasses of champagne, and then he'd be a big step closer to having his proof that she was okay and totally fine living (and parenting) in the big bad world.

The wedding venue at the little winery outside of Lake George must have been a chapel at some point in its history, because the stone building had vaulted ceilings and stained glass windows. By the time they found a park and worked their way to the front steps it was packed with people. A lucky traffic snarl-up had added half an hour to their trip, so the pre-vow get-together had abated by the time they arrived.

Tom took her hand as they walked through the small foyer and found seats in the back row. A string quartet on a raised dais played a frivolous waltz as the guests waited for the wedding party. Hannah braced herself and looked up, straight into the eyes of a woman who had turned her head to check out the late arrivals.

Holy cow. Marci bloody Funder, one of the mean girls herself.

She pulled Tom's hand further towards her so she could clutch it on her knee, deciding she'd much rather spend the thirty-minute wedding ceremony staring at Tom's Adam's apple than checking out who else from that wretched semester at uni had been invited.

'Are you okay?' he murmured in her ear.

'I might have misjudged this,' she whispered back.

He pulled his hand away, but just for a second before his arm curled around her back and snuggled her into his side. He brought his other hand over to squeeze her knee. 'We've got this, brat. You and me against anyone who says different.'

Hannah gave Marci a nod. 'One of the mean girls is here, looking this way. Just look adoringly at me, will you, Tom? Nothing will piss her off more than me having a better-looking plus one than her.'

He did better than that. He leant over and pressed a kiss into her neck that made her toes curl up like pug tails. 'That is so shallow, Cody.'

'Yeah,' she said. 'Shallow and totally working—she just went green. Keep them coming.'

'Tell me about the bride,' Tom said.

'Karen Flemington. We shared a room at one of the residential colleges on campus. We were both from small towns, so we stuck together. Sydney was … a shock.'

'And you've kept in touch?'

'A little. Birthday cards, the odd email, that sort of thing. I was surprised when she invited me to her wedding.'

His smirk was back. 'You're not that unlikeable.'

She pinched his arm. 'Thanks. I'm okay now. Hopefully she's the only one of them here.'

The wedding passed in a blur of songs and vows and shuffling of feet as the guests rose to sing, sat to listen. Hannah found it difficult to pay attention to anything beyond the long line of Tom warming her from ankle to shoulder, and her thoughts about the upcoming reception. She'd orchestrated this, and now she was here, with him, and pretty soon the wedding photographer was going to be circling amongst the guests and it was too late for chickening out.

There'd better be champagne. Bubbles of gold to settle the bubble of nerves welling up inside.

The ceremony done, Hannah kept her eyes on the aisle as Karen walked by, her groom on her arm. The radiant bride: Karen had a smile on her face a mile wide. Hannah shuffled along the pew as the church emptied and they joined the queue to congratulate the happy couple.

'Hannah! I am so pleased you came.' Karen held her hands for a moment, then gathered her in for a hug. 'I've missed you,' she whispered in her ear, before turning to her new husband. 'This is Raj. Raj, you remember I told you about Hannah, my friend from med school?'

Hannah stiffened. What, exactly, had she told him?

But Raj's smile held nothing more than welcome. 'Pleased you could make it,' he said, shaking her hand then turning to Tom.

'Oh, this is Tom,' she said belatedly. 'My—'

She looked up at him and he raised his eyebrows at her. Yeah. Good question.

He gave up waiting for her to decide what he actually was to her and stepped forward. 'Tom Krauss,' he said, shaking hands with Karen and Raj. 'Beautiful ceremony, congratulations.' And he whisked Hannah off out of the queue before she'd had time to work out what words she would have chosen.

'You need a drink as much as I do?' he said.

'Hell yes.'

He took off and if she hadn't been wearing the dumbest shoes in the universe she might even have been able to keep up with him.

The function room of the Shaw Winery was modern, built in sleek lines of stone and glass and timber. Grape vines on criss-cross trellises stretched like neat rows of sutures over the rounded hills. Luckily Tom hadn't locked the car so she was able to retrieve the silver photo frame she'd bought in the little retro store on Hope Street back home.

He waited on the front stairs for her, then tucked her gift under his arm and held his hand out for hers. Which made it twice in one day for handholding. Or was it three times?

The clarity she'd had about what she wanted from Tom and what he had to give her was starting to get very blurry.

Inside, a large room with tables was set up for dinner and flowers were festooned everywhere. Beyond the room, a narrow sign was lit with the magic words CELLAR DOOR and, following it, they found themselves in a snug bar.

'What do you fancy?' said Tom, when they'd settled themselves into a corner table where a little candle flickered merrily against the dark. It was—awkwardly—rather romantic.

'I fancy ditching the reception. I fancy hearing you change your mind about being my sperm donor so I can have a child,' she said.

Because all this handholding stuff, and the flowers, and the candle-light, and even the silly shoes, had tapped into some very dormant part of her that liked it. If she'd called herself disinterested last week, she'd been kidding herself.

She took a breath. 'I fancy us making a plan to get the deal done. And—' she had to take another breath, because either the incy-wincy candle was making the room very, very hot or she was having some sort of weird hormonal surge '—maybe we think about trying it the old-fashioned way.'

'Hannah, I don't—'

She rushed in to speak over him. 'Or, if that idea doesn't appeal to you, then no worries. I can put a rush order in for some insemi-nation equipment from my vet supply company.'

He cleared his throat. 'That is quite an inducement. Two cham-pagnes it is,' he said, turning to a waiter who had been hovering awfully close. Please, god, not close enough to hear her spill her guts like that.

'Hey,' she said. 'I'm trying to be practical, and insemination is tried and true. I want a baby; you're single and unattached and you told me yourself you didn't see yourself as a family guy.'

'I did indeed say that.'

'Well, were you lying?'

'No. I wasn't lying. I don't see a family in my future.'

There was steel in his voice that she'd not heard before; the sort of steel she imagined he might have used in the Navy.

Well, she had steel, too.

'Yes or no,' she said. 'Will you or will you not consent to being a sperm donor for me?'

'That's not our deal. We already struck terms and committed to running a campdraft together and me supporting your solo parent-ing endeavour. Which I assume I am doing today by accompanying you on a journey out of Hanrahan.'

Two glasses arrived, tall and thin and filled with golden liquid. *Celebration drinks*, she thought bitterly. When had she ever had anything to celebrate?

She wasn't going to cry. She sure as hell wasn't going to think about another month's egg going to waste, another lonely Christmas, a lifetime of evenings sitting on the sofa, knitting orphaned possum pouches because she'd finally succumbed to Marigold's nonstop badgering to join that effing craft club.

'Why did you come with me to this, Tom?'

'Because you asked me to. Because I'm trying to be your friend. Because you seem a little vulnerable and I'm trying to look out for you and because Josh is worried about you.'

'I don't need anyone looking out for me.'

'That's not true. We all do. Since we're asking the big questions, why did you agree to help out with the campdraft?'

'So I'd have time to change your mind. I need a baby,'

'Well, today you've just got me, so suck it up, brat. Now, what about a toast? To Hannah Cody, who has successfully managed to travel a couple hundred kilometres from Hanrahan without creating a third-party-property incident.'

She sniffed. 'I guess that is something.'

He smiled at her. 'It's an amazing something. I'm proud of you.' He clinked glasses with her and threw his champers down in one go. 'Now, are we going to sit in here arguing with each other all afternoon, or are we going to go strut our stuff in front of this mean girl?'

She took a sip. The champagne was delicious, cold and dry, and hopefully Tom had put it on his credit card because she was pretty sure she couldn't afford to buy anything so French tasting. 'In the stables, Tom. I know we agreed it was nothing, but secretly I actually thought it was something.'

His smile slipped. 'Maybe I've got a thing for chicks in stables. Right place, right time.'

'Uh-huh. And how do you explain the sofa?'

'Well, a sofa is an upholstered two- or three-seat item of furniture in which one sits to relax after a day of toil.'

'Very cute. No wonder you studied law; you have a nasty way with words. Specifically, how do you explain your hand tiptoeing under my sweater while we were seated on your upholstered item of furniture?'

Tom looked into his empty champagne glass. 'Shouldn't we be finding our name cards on a table somewhere?'

'Worried you'll incriminate yourself?'

His smile faded and was gone entirely when he reached across the table and held her hand. 'Hannah. I don't know why you think having a baby with some random person—me or anyone—is a good idea.'

She swallowed. 'It's time.'

He frowned. 'Time for what?'

Oh, boy, this was way, way more difficult than she had anticipated. Time she had someone of her own to love. Someone safe. Someone sweet. Someone about eight pounds in weight who looked awesome in a onesie.

A blare of music roared into the quiet of the bar from the reception room across the lobby and she stood, grateful for the interruption. 'The wedding party has arrived,' she said. 'Let's go pretend we're enjoying ourselves.'

Three hours later, she wasn't pretending any longer. She'd made small talk with strangers and successfully avoided the photographer. She'd thrown herself into the delights of the buffet and the champagne punch. Even the sperm-denier had been fun and made her laugh.

'Let's dance,' she said to him, as they moved through the crowd by the dance floor.

'When a slow song comes on.'

She pursed her lips. 'For a guy who's apparently not interested in anything but friend stuff, you're acting weirdly romantic.'

He pulled his hand from where it had been touching her back as they eased their way between people. 'What makes you think I'm not romantic?'

'Um. You're an officer in the Navy.'

'Retired.'

'You come from a long line of ruthless horsemen.'

'That's a long line of one. Bruno bought his first horse with pocket money he earned selling eggs, and he'd be happy to tell you it was the making of him.'

'Whatever.'

'Maybe you don't know me as well as you think you do.'

'Maybe,' she said. That champagne punch had restored some of her bravado. The band struck up something schmoozy and deep, and she held out her arms. 'Is this slow enough for you?'

'Yeah. Yeah, it is.' He tugged on her hand so she slid in against him, the velvet of her borrowed dress sliding against the dark cloth of his suit. He held her close for a couple of beats while they circled the floor, then spun her out and back in a slow reverse turn.

'Tom Krauss can dance?' Hannah laughed. Okay, yes, her baby plan had taken a hit, but here she was, out in the world, happy.

The unexpected part of it all was that she'd made it here with Tom. Who currently had his hands on her, on a dance floor, making the world around all blurry and indistinct and unnecessary.

He pulled her back to him so her cheek was resting against his shirt collar. 'Stop talking,' he murmured.

She looked up and found his eyes were closed, a faint smile on his lips. He looked … softer. Like he was recording a memory that he'd like to keep. That treacherous thrum beneath her breastbone started up and she almost trod on his foot.

Maybe this plan of hers had been more dangerous than she'd realised; she'd wanted a baby and she'd chosen Tom as a necessary ingredient, but she hadn't wanted that experience to be complicated by feelings. Hers or his.

So … how to explain this thrum?

She shot another look up at his face and now he was staring down at her, his blue eyes dark as though storms gathered there.

'Hannah,' he said. 'We need to tal—'

A figure planted itself in their path and they stopped dancing. A man stood by them, and not just any man, but Charlie Homer, her boyfriend from university. From before the viral photo.

'Hannah. Excuse me. I saw you from across the room and I wondered if I could have a word.'

She looked up at Tom. 'See you in a minute?' She'd be all right with Charlie.

Tom nodded and headed for the dessert buffet while Charlie took her arm.

'You look wonderful, Hannah,' he said.

'Thanks. It's been a long time since I've seen you.'

'Yeah.' He cleared his throat. 'Listen, can we step outside? I have something to say, and it's a little loud in here.'

She bit her lip. 'I don't know, Charlie. Is this really necessary?'

'Please.'

She sighed. 'Sure. The cellar bar might still be open, let's go there.'

They found a corner table and Charlie slid into a seat opposite her. 'Tell me, Hannah. How are you? You know. After everything.'

She frowned. Her champagne buzz was threatening to turn into a headache at Charlie's ominous words. 'I don't need to relive my past, Charlie. It's done. It's over.'

He nodded. 'I'm glad. So glad. I heard about the overdose.'

'How could you know about that?' Her insides felt like they'd just been crammed full of ice chips.

He shrugged. 'Word travels.'

Yeah. So did malicious fake photos and rumours. So did her own bagful of regrets. She crossed her arms. 'That stuff's been over and done with for years. I don't know why you would bring it up.'

He took a breath. 'It's not over for me.'

What on earth could he mean? This wasn't about him, for Pete's sake; they'd broken up before it all unfolded, and he'd been the opposite of broken-hearted—he was in the arms of someone else within a week, as she recalled.

'I'm not following.'

'You know the picture.'

She dropped her head into her hands. She shouldn't have come. Karen, Charlie, Marci … no matter how far away she moved, how much time had passed, meeting up with anyone from that time in her life was a mistake. She was tired of it. Not traumatised, which, admittedly, could be the effects of champagne and having all six-foot-two of Tom cosied up against her for the last few minutes on the dance floor.

But hearing Charlie bring it up all over again wasn't making her upset. It was making her irritated.

'I've heard enough,' she said, and started to slide out of her seat.

'It was me.'

She froze. 'Excuse me?'

'I studied graphic design at high school. I was on the school newspaper, did all the photoshop work. I thought it was a joke, because, you know, we'd never ...'

'Let me get this straight. *You* made the image of my head stuck onto some porn star's body?'

He reached out to hold her hand, but she slapped him away.

'I'm not proud of it. It's a stain on my conscience and I need to apologise.'

Her breath caught in her throat then roared out. 'You wrecked my life.'

'I know it. I know you dropped out. I know about the time in the clinic. If I could take it back, I would.'

'So you just apologise, and that's done, is it? You go back to your life, your medical career, your picket fence, with a clean conscience and pick up where you left off?'

'I'm truly sorry. I was an idiot. Worse, I was an idiot with the skills to do so much damage.'

She felt the tears about to start, but she was not going to be weak before him. She was done with feeling weak. 'I don't forgive you.'

'I don't expect you to.'

She pressed her hands to her forehead and tried to tune out the inner demon that had started crying in her head.

'My wife is refusing to share a bed with me until I apologise. She—I just told her, a few months ago, when Karen told me she'd invited you. She's here, at the reception. She'd like to meet you.'

No freaking way. She was not this idiot's absolution. He could live with guilt the way she'd had to live with a shame she didn't deserve.

'We have a daughter. Lisa, my wife, asked me how I'd feel if some privileged prick put my daughter's face on a nude pic and sent it off into the internet to spread like weeds.'

She found her voice. 'You'd feel like my father felt. Like my brother. Sad, vengeful, impotent, worried.'

'I'm sorry, Hannah. You were a sweet girl, and I turned you into a joke. I was an arse.'

She stood up. 'That's where you're wrong, Charlie. I'm not a joke. And I'm not that sweet. I don't give a shit if your wife never talks to you again, but good on her for making you suffer.'

She held it together for as long as it took her to get out of the cellar bar, out of the winery and over to Tom's car, then she sank to the gutter, where an icy wind shivered through brittle red leaves, turned her face to the dust-spattered tyre and cried.

# CHAPTER
# 19

Two hundred and seven silent kilometres later—silent other than the choked sobs and shuddering shoulders in his passenger seat, which hurt worse than the steel shard giving him grief in his lower back—Tom slid his four-wheel drive into the shed out back of the homestead at Ironbark and switched off the ignition.

The tick of the cooling engine marked the time.

Hannah.

Bloody hell, she was walking a tightrope and who was there to catch her when she fell? Josh, of course, but Josh was planning a wedding and so loved up it was like he was living in a rainbow these days.

No, Hannah had hooked into Tom for her plan and he needed to tell her—straight out—that he was the one person she shouldn't have chosen, not least because he loved her. But because he was damaged goods. He'd be the last man to be saying yes to such a dumbarse proposal as she had made.

What a mess of a day. Finding Hannah in the gutter, sobbing into his tyre, persuading her to get into the car, then her refusal to talk it over for their two-hour trip, followed by her running up into her apartment and slamming her door in his face.

And the long drive twice in one day had his back aching like a goanna had just ripped him open and left him by the roadside to die. He leant over, groaning just a little, and flicked open the glove box. Painkillers, hallelujah. He popped a couple out of the blister pack and got them down without the aid of water.

Practice made perfect.

Now he needed a heat pack and a long, unmoving eight hours stretched out on the flattest surface he could find. How the mighty had fallen.

Lights flickered in the small stables as he limped from garage to house, and he paused. Buttercup was down there. She ought to be tucked up in the dark, snoozing the night away in her snug stall. So much for a heat pack and his bed.

He switched direction and made his slow way down to the stable. Bruno's station manager, Lynette, was seated on an upturned feed bin in the aisle and Josh Cody stood by Buttercup's side.

'Hey, mate,' he said. 'Lynette. What's up?'

'She was unsettled. Kept whinnying, pawing at the door. I called Josh after dinner when I couldn't settle her. She's calmer now. Think she just wanted to be the centre of attention.'

He moved into the stall and rested his head against Buttercup's. *Come on, girl. I just need one thing to go right today. Please let it be you and your little foal.*

Josh leant against the wall of the stall and looked him up and down. 'What's with the limp? Too much dancing at the winery wedding?'

'I'm tired and I've had a shitty few hours.'

Josh frowned. 'Shitty how?'

'Don't ask.'

Josh stood up. 'You've been out for the day with my sister, so I'm asking, Krauss. Shitty how?'

Tom took his hands off Buttercup. Of course. Josh would know more about the whole Hannah debacle than he did. He glanced at Lynette. 'Why don't you catch some sleep, Lynette? Dawn'll be here before we know it. I'll watch Buttercup.'

She smiled her relief. 'Thanks, Tom. I am kinda beat. I'm going to bunk down in the guest room rather than head home, so you call me if you need me.'

'Off you go. And thanks.'

'You got it.'

He waited until her booted heels crunching on gravel had faded into nothing, then faced his oldest friend. 'Hannah ran into an old boyfriend at the wedding. He told her he'd been the one to superimpose her face on the image that went viral. She'd always thought it was some bunch of girls. She was sad, we left, I drove her home.'

'Home here? Is she up at the house?'

'No. Home to her place.'

'And how sad was she? *How sad?*'

'Josh, mate. She was crying, very upset when I found her, but we had a two-hour car ride. She'd calmed down.'

Josh was pacing and barely listening. 'And you just left her there?'

'Yeah. I just left her there after she slammed the door in my face because she didn't want me to hover.'

'Christ almighty. I'm forty minutes away and she's got the keys to a goddamn drugs cabinet.'

'What the fuck are you saying?'

'She didn't tell you the whole story, did she?'

Tom's guts tensed. 'What didn't she tell me?'

'That stupid picture isn't the reason Hannah hides away here in Hanrahan. It's what happened later.'

He forced himself to ask the question. 'What happened later?'

'Sleeping tablets. A whole stack of them, followed by getting her stomach pumped and a month in the hospital while the Cody family fell apart.' The break in Josh's voice was too much.

'Mate, she's the strongest, most bloody-minded person I know. She was sad, yes, but she's not going to do anything foolish.'

'And how the fuck would you know, Tom?'

Good question. But he had a good answer. 'Because she asked me to trust her that she wouldn't.'

Josh was already on his phone. 'Vera's at my place, and I've a master key to the whole building in the fruit bowl. I'll ask her to run upstairs to Hannah's flat.'

'Let me drive you. Your hands are shaking, mate.'

'No, I … anyway, what about Buttercup? I—' Josh held his hand up as his phone connected. 'Vee, honey, can you go upstairs and check on Han? Something's upset her, just get yourself in there somehow and make her a hot water bottle or something. Oh, and socks. She loves fluffy socks. I'm on my way but I'll be forty minutes.' He was silent for a moment, his brow furrowed. 'Love you too, Vera.'

Tom caught his eye. 'I'll come with you.'

'Mate. This is family business. She won't want me dragging you into it.'

Family business. Well, that certainly put him in his place. He wasn't part of Hannah's family. He was barely part of his own.

'All right,' he said. 'Go.'

As the sound of Josh's boots faded into the night, Tom slid down the wall to the straw of the stable floor and lay very, very still. Hannah was fine—he had to believe that. No, he *did* believe that.

Hannah *was* the strongest person he knew and she could look after herself.

As for himself? Really, what did it matter?

The stable didn't smell right.

The hay had turned to ozone and the floorboards had turned to ocean and the temperature had plummeted to ice. The wind was wrong, too—it didn't have the scent of eucalypts or horses or snow in it; instead it screamed across black waves, turning the rain to salt, and within seconds he was drenched and his heart was pounding and he could barely see through his helmet.

There was a high-speed chase vessel beneath his feet and six sailors—a Turk, a couple of Glaswegians, three blokes from Bahrain—muscled in beside him as the rubber-walled attack craft cut through the ugly swell towards a fully laden Norwegian oil tanker.

Christ. It was the dream again, the one where he got to relive the bullet that struck a bulkhead next to him and drove an inch-long sliver of rusted steel so deep through his hip and back it near cut him in half. He was having it more and more often.

The guy at the helm was yelling over the engine noise: 'Starboard side's gonna have us to windward, sir. It'll be a rough connect while we get the hookup.'

The images were just flashes in Tom's head: hurtling over rough water; shooting grappling hooks up the steel hull of an oil tanker; he and his men disappearing like dark shadows over the rail and onto the deck below.

A whinny jolted Tom out of the Persian Gulf and back into the present. Those painkillers he'd taken had packed a punch. 'Easy girl,' he muttered to Buttercup. 'I'm right here.'

She dropped her head to snuffle at his hair and he gave her warm neck a scratch.

He wasn't even aware of the tears running down his face until he heard the hum of an electric motor and the *ker-thunk ker-thunk* sound of wheels struggling over the cobbled floor of the stable.

'Tom?'

It was Bruno. And he was holding out his lined, sun-damaged hand.

'Son. You want to tell me what's wrong?'

# CHAPTER

## 20

A month of hard work and dodgy sleep and training in Kev's freezing paddock flew by.

Yoga was no longer the long-running joke Hannah was trying to avoid, but something she looked forward to. She had a string of happy patients, she'd said hello to a tourist in the park and, what's more, *chatted* with them, and she'd paid off the camera lens debt that had been weighing down her credit card.

She'd even taken—with Kylie hovering nearby like a proud mumma bear—a selfie of her and Skipjack and had it printed in a frame to sit on her desk.

She'd decided an adult would go talk to their GP about a single woman with a depressive episode in her past wanting to have a baby on her own, so she'd booked herself in, talked herself ragged and then cried (again—she was blaming it on hormones) when the GP told her she was a competent young woman who could do anything she put her mind to.

She had a list of fertility clinics to try when she felt ready and there was even—seriously, who knew?—an app for choosing a donor! If she'd spent a ridiculous amount of time scrolling through for attributes like *tall, brooding, looks good in an Akubra, dances like a tall Fred Astaire*, so what? That was her little secret.

Hannah pulled the bridle over Skipjack's wide head, rubbing his ears as she slid the leather straps into the correct position. Becoming a mother was doable. She just needed to decide if she was ready, and she needed to stop hiding her dream in the shadows and be up front about it with Josh and her parents and the rest of the Hanrahan locals who liked to look out for her.

Only … her dream had shifted.

She wasn't sure how or when exactly the shift had occurred, but every time she allowed herself to think about what her future might look like, there was always another person in the hazy picture in her head.

Tom. With his arms around her. *With* her.

'I have a horrible suspicion, Skippy,' she said to her horse and confidante, 'that this might be the love thing Kylie is always going on about.'

Skipjack gently headbutted her in the shoulder.

'I know, my handsome lad, it's awful. I'm as freaked out by it as you are. Officially URSTed.'

She swung her leg over his broad back and clip-clopped out of the stables into the cold morning. Skipjack blew plumes of white mist. Autumn had arrived, and early snow lay in the hollows of the mountains shadowing the lake. She'd had to attack her windscreen with her brand-new Hanrahan Library membership card to scrape the frost off this morning.

Her phone chirruped in her jacket pocket and she sighed. Josh had been clucking about her like a mother hen for so long she was beginning to wish he and Vera would just announce they had a baby on the way so the attention would move off her and her idiocy and onto their good news.

She was fine, damn it. Fine!

To be truthful, she was the finest she'd been in a very long time. Maybe having that blowout after the wedding at Lake George had been cathartic. For her, at least. She doubted it had been fun for Tom, but he had broad shoulders. He'd get over her making a cake of herself in front of him. The bloke was like an emotionless rock.

'You hear that, Skip? I'm in love with an emotionless rock.'

She contemplated ignoring the phone message. She wasn't on call, after all. But still, for some dramas, four vet hands were better than two. She pulled her phone out and checked the screen.

*Let's talk.*

Crap. Not Josh. Tom had taken to messaging her every few days, always the same two words.

*Let's talk.*

*Let's talk.*

*Let's talk.*

*Let's talk.*

She gave up scrolling through his past messages, shoved the phone back in her pocket and nudged Skipjack out of the holding yard to where Kev was trying to haul a sack of potash.

'Let me help you with that,' she said.

'Girl, the day I can't take care of my roses is the day I cock my toes up. Go enjoy your ride. You taking the southern track?'

'I thought I'd let Skippy decide.'

'We'll do some yard work when you get back. There's a couple heifers I'm agisting you haven't scared witless yet.'

She grinned. 'I do feel as though I'm starting to get the hang of this cow-herding stuff.'

'You've been wearing me out this last month, and that's the truth.' He dragged a plaid hanky from his pocket and blew his nose on it like he was blowing on a trumpet. 'You'll be knocking their socks off at the Ironbark draft.'

That dratted campdraft. She'd committed to helping out and that was the one thing she *had* let slide over the past month. It was, what, four months away? Five?

'Go enjoy your ride, love. Watch out for fallen branches, though, won't you. Those storms that brought all that early snow would've brought some timber down for sure. The creeks'll be running, too.'

'Skippy's not too keen on creek crossings.'

'All the more reason. You'll be wanting to work on some quick turns and use your knees, not your voice.'

'Kev, today's a play day for us. We're not thinking about work.'

'Woah, was that Hannah Cody who just said that? Remind me to buy a lotto ticket when I head into town.'

She grinned. 'A girl can change, can't she?'

'She sure can, love.'

Thin frost covered the ground as she nudged Skip down the narrow track. Browned off eucalypt leaves drifted down over them every time the breeze stirred the trees, and the long grasses gleamed pale and pearly where the sun flooded through the canopy.

Skipjack picked his way along, the rumble of his breath a diesel engine out here in the quiet. She drew in a lungful of air and felt … good. Time really was a balm.

'Line in the sand, Skipjack,' she said. Hmm, a line in the snow would be easier here in the Snowy Mountains, but whatever. The metaphor worked no matter where she carved it.

She brought Skip to a halt in a clearing where gum trees bore the scars of fire. He shifted under her, keen to run, but she patted his neck until he settled down. 'Just give me a sec, my love.'

She pulled the creased paper from her pocket. *Long-term Effects of Cyber Bullying*, she read. *The psyche of the victim can sustain long-term and permanent damage from cyber bullying. Feelings of lack of self-worth can cause the victim to reject opportunities for work, educational or relationship advancement.*

Well, yeah. Check. Charlie Homer hadn't been the person who'd shoved pills down her throat, she'd done that to herself. But if she had her time over, would she still pick medicine over vet science? She wrapped her fingers in the mane on Skipjack's neck. No way. Animals had become a vocation for her. She'd found her way to work she loved.

Relationships were a different story.

*Cyberbullying in the past is a strong indicator for being a victim of dating abuse in the future, particularly where the bullying has been sexual in connotation, and targeted a female victim.*

Hannah swallowed. She'd not been a victim in the years since because she'd been cautious. Too cautious, perhaps.

She shoved the leaflet back into her pocket then pulled it out again. She didn't need it anymore. Tearing it up was a fumble at first because her fingers were cold, but then she got into it. Halves, quarters, eighths, sixteenths, what came next? Oh, to hell with doing it in an orderly way. She ripped until it was in tiny little shards, then stuffed them all into her pocket. She'd light a fire in the old grate at the vet clinic when she got home, burn the bits into smoke, and that would be it: the shadow of her past would be gone.

The hard line of her phone butted into her fingers and she pulled it out.

To put the whole episode behind her, she needed to clear the air with Tom, but now there was the whole love problem to contend with.

She needed advice. And who better to turn to than the relation-ship drama queen herself?

Luckily, Kylie must have been between oil changes because she answered on the second ring.

'Hello. What's up?'

'Nothing much. Well, actually a lot.'

'Start talking. I've got the Bridgestone rep due in about ten min-utes and he's easy on the eye. I need to find my lippy and check my butt for oil stains before he arrives.'

'Do you remember way back when you told me what URST was and I pooh-poohed it?'

'Yeeeees.'

'I may have even said I was totally disinterested in romance and men in general and one man in particular?'

'Like I fell for that pork pie.'

Hannah ducked her head as the trail took them close to a massive oak. 'Yes, it wasn't true, but I had convinced myself it was. I had just done such a great job of lying to myself that I couldn't think straight.'

'Uh-huh.'

'And then my lie to myself was like a dust bunny and it grew and grew and grew.'

'You're losing me. Let's forget about bunnies and dust and cut to the chase. You're trying to tell me in some randomly loopy way that you've finally noticed Tom Krauss is more than just your brother's best friend, right?'

'Er ... right.'

'So what are you going to do about it?'

'Well, that's where you come in. What should I do about it?'

'Just be honest. With yourself and with him.'

'He's probably pissed off with me, anyway. I was supposed to be helping him sort out his dad's event, and I haven't been returning his calls since ... Well, for a while now.'

Kylie didn't say anything for so long Hannah pulled her phone away from her ear and checked the service bars to make sure she was still connected.

'Hello? Are you there?'

'I'm here. I'm just wondering if the kindest thing I could do would be to tell you to do nothing.'

'Why would I do nothing?'

'You're rushing this.'

'Kylie. How old am I? I am so not rushing this.'

'Maybe you're rushing Tom. Not all guys are idiots without emotions, Hannah. Some guys don't want to get hurt, either. I mean, what if he does have feelings for you? And you've just been brushing him off like he's nothing?'

'I'm not rushing Tom. He's like an ice statue! He's impossible to hurt!'

'And you're the expert, are you, on what hurts or does not hurt guys? Just think about what I've said, will you?'

Kylie was right. She had no idea about what would hurt a guy.

'Don't go silent on me. I don't want *you* to get hurt, either, Hannah.'

'What happened to celebrating my year of being different? Of trying new stuff?'

'Oh, honey. I'm just worried you're out of your depth on this one. When was the last time you even had a fling?'

Hannah was so startled by the question she accidentally dug her heels into Skippy's sides and he grunted in surprise. 'Um.'

'That boy. Whatshisname. You dated him in first year uni after he wrote a poem about your hair.'

'Him,' she said darkly. 'Far out, I cannot believe you remember that poem.'

'*Oh, Hannah, woman of desire, you burn me away in great balls of fire?*'

She snorted, and then Kylie did too, and then she had to hold the phone away from her ear so she didn't get permanent damage from her friend's shrieks of laughter.

When she'd finally quietened, Kylie got thoughtful. 'Besides, that was a long time ago, Han. What about in Wagga, studying biology with all those burly guy vets. Was there anyone special there?'

'Sure, of course, heaps.'

'My lie radar is pinging.'

'I do not have to share every detail of my love life with you.' *Or lack thereof.*

'True, but I expect you to, anyway. Tell me straight, Hannah Celine Cody. How well versed are you in the whole having-a-fling department?'

She rolled her eyes. 'I'm a vet, Kylie. Procreation of the species is thirty per cent of my day job. Plus, it's science. You know how awesome I am at science.'

'Science? Holy hell, we need to workshop this.'

'We are workshopping this. I've called you, haven't I, in my hour of need?'

'Bugger, the tyre man is here. Call me later, girlfriend, and that's an order.'

Hannah was on her own again, and her thoughts circled back to Kylie's idea that Tom may not be the emotionless rock he pretended to be. He *had* tried to be her friend—would a rock do that? He'd been kind to her when she'd fallen apart at Lake George and he'd kissed her (twice!) in a very unrocklike way. He'd bought her coffee, he'd listened to her donor proposal without making fun of her; he'd even agreed to support her decision to have a baby.

What had she ever done for him in return?

Nothing. She'd carried on like it was all about her.

Yet somehow she'd worked out that she liked hanging around with him so much that now she missed him. Did he miss her? Was that what all his texts were about?

She'd assumed he was just texting to harangue her about camp-draft logistics because he'd promised the self-appointed Hanrahan intervention team he would.

Skipjack paused at the fork in the path. To the south lay the tourist trail that circled the eastern bank of Lake Bogong: an easy graded track they could plod along. To the north was the high country: gullies, snow, snags of fallen timber; weather that could whip from mild to maelstrom at will.

'What do you say, Skipjack?'

He snorted and stamped his foot, looked back at her as though to say, *Make a decision, girlfriend, I'm growing old here.*

The high country it was. She pulled out her phone and typed the message before she overthought it. *Dinner? Friday? My place at 7pm? #olivebranch*

She read it through once, squeezed her eyes shut for a moment, then hit send. A meal. An apology. And maybe she'd try to be a friend, this time, not a hot mess.

'Okay, Skip,' she said, nudging him onwards. 'Let's see what the future holds.'

# CHAPTER

# 21

The husband-and-wife handyman team Marigold had recommended spent hours on the interior of the Hanrahan Pub. The painted walls were washed down with sugar soap, the ancient carpet had been brought back to life—a thin, well-worn, slightly stained version of life—by a noisy machine that had somehow washed it, dried it and fluffed up its fibres, and the small room off the main hall with its half-wall, its boxes of accommodation ledgers and its scuffed, leather-topped desk, was beginning to look like an office again.

And Tom, much to his surprise, had fallen in love.

'Move yer arse, pet,' said Sharon, the wife half of the handyman team, and Tom stood to the side while she ran a lurid orange feather duster over a framed, sepia-hued photograph of a toothless old prospector holding a nugget the size of a deck of cards. Sharon tapped a fingernail—also bright orange and tapered like a talon—on the glass. 'Story goes, old mate here used his gold to build the pub, which might have been the start of a good business for him, but he was a little too keen on the bottle. Lost it all a couple years later.'

Tom stood beside her and took a longer look. He loved finding out about the pub's history almost as much as he'd come to love the pub itself. *Jimmy Larkins and his 7lb nugget* read the inscription on a card at the bottom of the framed photograph.

'You know a lot about the pub history, Sharon?'

'My dad worked here when I was a girl. Mind you, he was a little too keen on the bottle too, so half the stories he told me are probably made up. I've always had a fondness for the place, though. Dad was happy when he worked here. Not so much when he got the sack.'

'There'll be permanent housekeeping and barwork when we find a new lessee for the place. You think you and Darryl might be interested?'

'I dunno, love. We like the casual work. Lets us travel and that.'

'Sure. There's plenty of casual work for the moment. Darryl tells me he's bringing his high pressure hose over this afternoon to clean the exterior. I've got to head down to Cooma later; are you right to lock up if I'm not back when you leave?'

'No worries. You'll want to get a painter in to redo the upstairs windows, too. Those things are stuck tighter than a sheep's dag and just about as crusty.'

He snorted. 'That's not a phrase I'd be wanting to see in a tourist review.'

'I say it like I see it, love.'

'Painter,' he said, as he wrote it on his list, which was about ten pages long and growing by the day: liquor licence; leasing contracts; food safety certification; getting a roofer in to check gutters and downpipes; getting Mr Sooty Pty Ltd in to clear the two double chimneys. And that wasn't the half of it. He had worked up some estimates of whether it was worth doing up the accommodation rooms or just to open the bar and drafted the advert for an experienced pub manager.

Spending a month messing about on his computer tinkering with lease documents and wresting control of the Krauss family holdings working files from the mostly AWOL town solicitor had been the busywork he'd needed. It had given him some clarity. He'd stopped obsessing about the constraints that had been put on the active part of his life. Up until now he'd been so busy resenting his injury that he hadn't been dealing with it. He'd been distracting himself from it.

Standing in the old office, with the sun warm on his back and the history of Hanrahan settled about him, he was beginning to wonder if it might actually be possible to get his shit together.

'The sparky was in earlier and sorted the fuse box,' he said to Sharon. 'He reckons we can boil the kettle now without causing a blackout for the whole of Hanrahan. You and Darryl fancy a coffee?'

'We'll sort ourselves, Tom. We like to have smoko at eleven. There's a fruitcake Darryl made on the kitchen bench; you be sure to cut yourself a slice.'

She headed back out to the corridor and pretty soon he could hear the timber blinds in the restaurant area clacking and screeching as they were freed of years of dust. His phone pinged and he grabbed it, expecting it to be the roofing contractor. Or Bruno, who had dialled his grump factor down so low, father and son had been known to sit on the verandah and have a beer or two of an evening. Tom spilling his guts about his career intercepting oil tanker pirates with the task force in the Middle East had provided Bruno with plenty to think about; his injury and its high-risk prognoses Tom had kept to himself.

*Dinner? Friday? My place at 7pm? #olivebranch*

He eased into the no-frills grey office chair behind the desk and swung it around until he was looking through the narrow window. A garden bed of weeds looked back at him.

This was a development.

"'Olive branch",' he murmured. Was she wanting to make amends for ghosting him? Or was it some weird code for 'Fertility clinics are out of reach to me now so I'm going to hit you up to be a sperm donor again'.

The weeds in the garden bed didn't seem interested in giving their opinion on the subtext of Hannah's message. She'd had a meltdown at Lake George, but she'd clawed her way back from the brink on the long drive home to Hanrahan. He'd understood her need for space in the weeks that followed; she'd lost her hard-won pride, and he'd been the sole witness.

Who knew better than he how difficult it was to live without pride?

He tapped the phone's screen so it woke up and stared at the message a moment longer. She must be fine if she was sending out dinner invitations.

Hannah Cody *was* okay.

Well, that was that. All he had to do was stay away and, one day soon, she'd find some bloke who could give her what she wanted.

He put down his phone without answering.

# CHAPTER
## 22

Hannah looked at the photograph Vera had texted her, and then into her roasting pan. Both dishes had orange chunks of sweet potato, but that's where the similarities ended.

Vera's dish was an artwork of robust colour and lightly caramelised vegetables, dusted in paprika and sprinkled with sprigs of rosemary that appeared to have been cut by the dimpled hands of heavenly cherubs.

Hannah's looked like the ash from last year's vet clinic fire.

Steak, mash and carrots it would have to be—she'd used up everything else on her cordon bleu disaster. Not that it would matter, if Tom didn't show up. She still had no idea if he was coming to dinner, because he hadn't replied to her text. Perhaps it was punishment for not answering his text messages for a month?

Nearly seven pm. She'd know in five minutes, good or bad.

She hauled out the bucket of potatoes she kept in the bottom of her pantry and started peeling. Even she couldn't screw up mash.

One hour and two-thirds of a bottle of wine later, she rang Kylie. 'What are you doing?'

'It's eight o'clock on a Saturday night, and I'm a single woman with my own business and a damn fine pair of legs. What do you think I'm doing?'

Oops. 'My bad. Forget I called, get back to your date.'

'Wait!' said Kylie. 'Don't hang up, I was messing with you. I'm painting my toenails, watching martial arts movies dubbed into wacky English and I'm wondering if it's time I invested in six cats. What are you doing?'

'Getting drunk and eating mashed potatoes. On my ownsome.'

'Wow. And I thought my life was pathetic. I'm on my way over.'

Kylie breezed in ten minutes later with a waxed cardboard box under her arm.

Hannah frowned at her from the pity-nest of quilts she'd made for herself on the sofa. 'I invited you, not your devil carbohydrates. What's in that box?'

'The café door fell open as I passed so I accidentally found myself at the naughty cabinet. Graeme made me buy these. Some sort of double-deep-fried-chocolate-bliss business. I stopped saying no when he said the word bliss.'

Hannah pulled the box down to sofa level so she could lift the lid. 'I knew we were BFFs for a reason.'

'Snap. Now, where's the wine?'

Hannah pointed at the dining room table, which she'd set with her grandmother's silverware, crystal wine goblets, flowers plucked (surreptitiously because, yes, it was illegal, and she didn't need another visit from Sergeant King) from the park across the road. She was using a pewter footy trophy she'd flogged from Josh's apartment as a wine cooler.

Kylie stared at the untouched display for a long moment while Hannah let pity tears gather behind her eyelids. 'Oh, honey. You didn't follow my advice, did you?'

Hannah sucked in a shaky breath. 'Do you think you could hug me a second?'

Kylie dropped to her knees and her arms burrowed in around Hannah where she lay on the couch to hold her tight. 'For lots of seconds. You want to talk about it?'

'I think I've been an idiot, Kylie.'

'Of course you have,' her best friend in all the world told her.

Hannah opened one eye. 'Free wine and ice-cream straight from the container is the appropriate response to an emotional crisis, accompanied by unconditional support … what part of the BFF code do you not understand?'

Kylie stroked her hair. 'Sometimes tough love is the kindest a best friend can give. Where were we? You had been an idiot.'

She sighed. 'Yes.'

'And—just to check—we are talking about Tom Krispy Krauss?'

'Kylie. The man is not a donut.'

'Tell that to my hormones,' said Kylie, moving to the table and pouring a hefty glass of water. 'Now sit up, drink this, and tell me everything.'

'Okay. I might have to backtrack. My idiocy didn't really start with Tom. It started with the baby.'

Kylie's mouth dropped open so far she looked like one of those clown games you could try chucking ping-pong balls into to win a cheap and highly flammable blue tiger at a country fete. The glass of water she'd poured went *thunk* on the coffee table and Hannah realised whoever had come up with the expression 'you could have heard a pin drop' had never casually dropped a conversational bomb into a room with Kylie Owens.

'*What freaking baby?*' The shriek probably woke all the animals tucked up in the sleepover room two floors below them.

Hannah smacked at Kylie's hands, which had reefed up the blouse she'd chosen (and even ironed!) and were now podging her stomach and hip bones for evidence.

'Would you get off me,' she said. 'Potential baby, not actual baby.'

Kylie snagged the wine bottle and took a glug from it. 'Start at the beginning. Omit nothing.'

Hannah sighed. 'Okay, well—you know my New Year's resolution? Go out more, spread my wings, take up yoga, compete with Skipjack ...'

'Uh-huh, yes, on board with all that.'

'I had a secret resolution, too.'

'A freaking baby.'

'You keep saying that. I want a *nice* baby. A little one, all soft and dimpled and cute.'

'Okay. I mean, it's not okay, I cannot even begin to process what you're saying because you seem to have totally skipped the find a bloke, fall in love, date for a year and shag each other senseless part, but okay. Where I'm getting stuck in all this is—how is Tom involved?'

'He's not. He wasn't. He isn't interested at all, he's told me that, and I guess he's shown me that too, now, because he sure didn't turn up this evening even when I sent him a very nice text.'

Kylie took another sip of wine and a little rolled down her chin. 'I understand nothing. Keep talking.'

'I didn't want to get involved or anything, I just wanted some love in my life ... and what better than a baby? And I was totally planning on visiting some fertility clinics to talk it all over, but then that Dalgety episode derailed me.'

'You wanted love in your life, and for some crazy reason you think a squalling kid in a nappy is the answer, not a man. I'm still not getting the Tom connection. How does he fit into this scheme, if you didn't want to get "involved"?'

Hannah turned her face into a cushion. 'He was Plan B.'

'I'm getting a bad feeling about this. In what way?'

'Well, to be precise, his sperm was my Plan B. I asked him if he'd be a donor.'

'And to think I was filling my evening with martial arts movie drama when I had all this waiting for me here. Hannah!' Kylie seemed to feel the occasion called for more wine, but she snagged Hannah's glass this time and poured some into it.

'Hey, don't hog it.'

'You're on rations until we've talked this through. Tell me, how did Tom feel about being used like this?'

Thank god for the cushion. It made it easier to wallow a bit before admitting the awful truth. 'I didn't think to ask him.' She was a juvenile, self-absorbed nutcase. She didn't deserve friends. She didn't even deserve ice-cream. She looked at Kylie. 'I messed up.'

'Maybe. But it looks to me like you've gone to a lot of trouble over dinner, Han. Would you do that for just any old sperm donor? Would you do that for someone whose feelings you didn't care about? Or would you just do that for Tom?'

'Yeah. Well, that's the funny thing.'

'You're losing me.'

'You remember that kiss? That bloody *kiss*? Back when I truly thought I was impervious to the whole two-hearts-beating-as-one mushy stuff?'

'Remind me how it went again? The sweaty horse, the callused hands, the—'

Hannah sat up and pushed her hair out of her eyes. 'It doesn't matter, Kylie. The point is, I think it changed me.'

'Like—now you're a vampire between dusk and dawn?'

'No, you idiot. I think it woke up my hormones.'

'I don't want to argue with the girl who won the science prize at Hanrahan High, but I don't think hormones sleep.'

'You know what I mean.'

'Yes, I think I do know what you mean. It's just, you don't often talk about it. You mean it made you wonder what life would have been like if you hadn't closed yourself off to romance all these years?'

Yeah. Kylie had it a hundred per cent right. She *was* wondering. She was wondering a *lot*. She'd spent the last month wondering why she'd been so focused on the baby idea, as though it was a PhD thesis. She'd obsessed about the ova being onboarded by spermatozoa bit, she'd drawn graphs, she'd stood in the grocery aisle at the local super market and considered milk for calcium and bananas for potassium.

In among all that wondering, she'd remembered the way Tom's hands had felt, hot as brands on her shoulders. The way his stormy-lake eyes made her stomach do flip-flops. Her baby dream had grown all tangled and caught up with her frustrations with herself and her envy of the happiness of the people around her.

'I think,' she said in a low voice, 'I might have been a little rash with my New Year's resolution "have a baby" plan.'

Kylie reached over and held her hand.

'I think maybe I grabbed ahold of a baby plan as a distraction from fixing myself, when really—as much as I really, *really* want a baby—I should have been doing the fixing.'

'You don't need fixing, Han. You're wonderful. You're fun, and kind, and you're an excellent vet, and your family loves you to bits. I love you to bits. You're just carrying a lot of hurt around with you that you maybe need to learn to let go of.'

Kylie was right. But she was also wrong. Letting go sounded like an easy thing to do, like flicking a gumleaf out the window or brushing an ant off your arm. Fixing the part of her that was broken and scared of relationships and trust and vulnerability?

Hard. Very hard.

Especially when the person you'd decided all that hard work and soul-searching would be worth it for was totally cool about standing you up for dinner.

'How much of all this have you told Tom?'

'Tom? Nothing but the will-you-donate-your-sperm bit. He's been very cagey about why he's suddenly turned up in Hanrahan and will he/won't he stay. He's told me he's not interested in a family or in settling down.'

'You think that's true? He must have left the Navy for some reason.'

'His dad's dying. That's reason enough.'

'Of course.'

'But that *kiss*. I just can't put it out of my mind that it kinda knocked his socks off, too.'

'Why wouldn't he just say so if that were true?'

Hannah wrestled the glass of wine out of Kylie's hands and took a sip. 'Because he thinks I'm a nutcase? Because he thinks if he's nice to me I'll start chasing him down Salt Creek Flats Road with a turkey baster? Anyway, it doesn't matter. The kiss must have meant nothing to him. It's not as though he turned up for dinner.'

'I tried to warn you about this. Dinner for two sounds serious. It's dating language. It has subtext.'

'What warning? You said "don't rush things". That was too vague, Kylie. I needed specifics, like "start with a casual coffee and see how it goes".'

Kylie took the glass of wine back. 'I hadn't fully grasped the subtleties of the situation.'

Hannah sighed. 'I haven't fully grasped anything for years.'

Her friend gave a snort like a piglet then burst out laughing.

'Wait! I wasn't—' It was too late. Hannah had seen the funny side herself now and started to giggle. 'Oh, Kylie,' she said.

'I know, honey. Heartbreak sucks.'

She frowned at her friend. 'Is that what this is?'

Kylie shrugged. 'You're not a casual person, Hannah. If you were, you wouldn't have been so gutted by everything that's happened to you. You feel. Deeply. Humiliation, regret, affection for your brother and your animal patients and little old bestie me, loyalty for Hanrahan … and now love.'

'Huh. Who knew there was a whole emotional thesaurus out there just waiting to trip me up.'

Kylie picked up Hannah's abandoned spoon and loaded it with mashed potato. 'Maybe it's good Tom didn't turn up. You might need to spend some time understanding what it is you're feeling now.'

Just as Hannah was about to grab another spoon for herself and agree with Kylie that of course, yes, she needed time, and yes, thank heavens Tom hadn't turned up, a knock sounded on the door. A heavy knock.

Josh didn't thud like that. For one, he didn't bother knocking, he just swanned on in. Two, he'd have Jane Doe at his heels and her tail would be bashing on the wood of the landing like a wrecking ball.

Besides, this time of night, Josh and Vera would be snuggled up on their couch making gooey eyes at each other and—if her deep suspicions were correct—reading baby name books.

The door thudded again in a manly, open-me-now way.

Hannah looked at Kylie.

Kylie looked at her.

Then they turned to stare at the spuds, the mess of plates, the wine bottle and tissues and donuts littering the floor and coffee table.

'It must be Tom!' Hannah said. 'OMG!'

'There's wine left,' said Kylie. 'And potato. Let's focus on the positives, Hannah. And don't rush things! Listen to me on this, I am an expert on how to doom relationships from the get-go.'

Okay. She'd passed tipsy about half an hour ago, and dinner wasn't salvageable, and she might have just spent the last hour and a half having an existential crisis, but okay. 'I'll get the door,' she said. 'What will I say?'

'Um, crikey. I'm out of ideas,' sorry.'

'Gee, thanks. Be a pal and pretend the tissues are yours,' she said, as she swung open the door.

Tom stood there, his jaw a mess of stubble, dark shadows under his eyes, a furrow down his brow deeper than a knife cut. If she'd been sober, he may have looked worse, but tipsy, he was giving off rugged broody man-vibes that had her blood pressure sliding up into the two hundreds.

'Oh, hi,' she said, trying for casual surprise. She leant up on the doorjamb and only slightly misjudged its location.

'It's late. I wanted to see you.' There was nothing casual in his tone whatsoever and she got goosebumps hearing it.

Kylie was right. She was a hundred per cent out of her depth.

# CHAPTER
## 23

*Statistics from the 2021 study inform us that the semen quality of men with spinal cord injury (SCI) is poor. Further, the cohort in the age range 30–40 rank sexual dysfunction as a greater stressor than leg dysfunction.*

'We'll be clear to go through in a few minutes, mate.'

Tom looked over the top of the medical journal he'd picked up from the Cooma Hospital and Health Services waiting room.

'Sorry for the wait; it can get a bit crazy here on a Friday arvo.' The nurse at the counter had that blokey, sun-creased look that made Tom wonder if he spent his weekends umpiring his kids' footie games. Six kids, maybe. He and his wife drove a van with stickers of kids marching across the back window, they bought jumbo boxes of cereal daily, and his wife saved her frilly underwear for date night once a month when the teenager next door came over to babysit.

Sounded like heaven.

Sounded like the sort of outlandish scenario he'd been torturing himself with for weeks, ever since the love of his life suggested he'd like to be a sperm donor. With no frills at all. Certainly no umpiring and no date nights.

'No rush.' Tom waggled the journal in his hand. He could read about sexual dysfunction all day. Not.

He flipped his phone over to check the time and told himself not to read Hannah's text message again.

Too late. Perhaps that steel shard had messed up the nerve endings that controlled his fingers as well as his legs. *Dinner? Friday? My place at 7pm? #olivebranch*

It'd be dark by the time he got out of the hospital. Find his car, hit the highway, punch out some Teskey Brothers on the stereo ... he'd be cruising through Hanrahan right about dinner time. He could go and see for himself if Hannah had gotten over the fiasco at Lake George. Find out what exactly had led her to ghost him for the month since. He'd sure like another image of her to replace the one where she shuffled into her apartment all white-faced and puffy-eyed from crying and shut the door in his face.

'Don't be weak,' he said to himself.

'What's that, mate?' said the nurse.

'Sorry. Talking to myself.' He flipped the page and read on. As patient reading material went, it was singularly lacking in sugar-coating.

*The study broke its focus into three parts: or the three E's of SCI, as the cohort described them. Erectile dysfunction, ejaculatory failure, and "egg drive", the latter a term coined by respondents to refer to motility. The issue of reduced fertility is causally linked to motility, as both curvilinear and straight line swimming speed are less than those recorded in non-SCI test subject—*

'Here we go.' Dr Novak had appeared through two swing doors and was looking expectantly at Tom. 'You ready? A forklift driver had a head injury and we lost our spot in the queue. Come on, let's get in there before the Friday night dramas start walking in. The radiologist will be injecting contrast dye into the area around your spine, like last time, and it'll be ten or fifteen minutes in the tube.'

He stood up, the journal in his hand.

'You won't be able to take that,' she said. 'You'll need to be absolutely still.' Her eyes dropped to the article he had open and its super upbeat header: A COHORT STUDY: SEXUAL HEALTH & SPINAL CORD INJURY. 'Oh, Tom,' she said. 'We're going to have a talk about your choice of reading material. That sort of thing isn't meant to be lying around in the patient areas. Come on, let's go find you a gown.'

Dr Novak didn't quite have to strip him out of his jeans and boots and wrap him into a gown, but she stood watching on critically as he did it. 'Have you been overdoing things, Tom?'

'Physically? Nothing beyond walking, sitting, driving, typing on a keyboard.'

'And how do you think you are doing?'

'I'd be lying if I said there was no change.'

'Not your mobility. It's deteriorating, we both know it. You've some muscle wastage, too,' she said, poking a finger at his ribs. 'No, I mean how are *you* doing?' She tapped her head. 'Up here. You find anything of use in those pamphlets I gave you last time?'

'I'm not sure if your pamphlets have anything to do with it, but since my last visit, I have projects coming out my ears.'

'Really?' said Dr Novak. Her face was half-hidden by the mask she'd donned while he fought his way into the gown, but her voice and eyes and eyebrows had no difficulty conveying delight. 'Do tell!'

'I've been roped into organising a horse event that my father used to run before his health declined. I've got half-a-dozen buildings in varying states of repair that need someone to oversee their tenants, including a historic pub that needs some TLC before it can reopen, and the guy who should be doing all of that had to be sacked.'

'That all sounds fabulous. You'll be telling me you've got a job next. A life plan. Some *goals*.'

'No need to get carried away.' But she was right. It did feel good having something more to respond to her repeated questions of 'what have you been up to' with something other than 'not much'.

And that pub. There was something about seeing that pub slowly coming to life again that made him feel … contentment.

'I look forward to hearing how your plans unfold. What about everything else?' She raised her eyebrows. 'Remember we talked about those stages.'

He sidestepped answering. He was in better shape mentally than he'd been since the injury, but acceptance was so far over his horizon it was in a foreign country. Acceptance implied you knew what in hell your outcome would be.

He was just waiting, waiting, waiting.

'The pain meds are giving me bad dreams. Is there some sort of alternative?'

'None with the same oomph. Perhaps you could try taking a half-dose and if that doesn't dull the pain, take the other half. How often are you taking them?'

'Only when I have to.' Problem was, that was more and more often.

The doctor handed him a paper sack to put his clothes into and led the way into the room where the CT machine loomed like a giant white donut. 'Part of pain management is working out what's triggered it and choosing not to replicate the circumstances.'

He spent the next fifteen minutes thinking about her words. What did trigger his pain? Forget his back—he had zero expectations of that improving until the surgeon finally reckoned the time was right to cut it out, so why waste time hoping? Since he'd returned to Hanrahan he'd learned that there was another kind of pain that was even worse.

He wanted to be with Hannah, but maybe *she* wanted a van full of kids and a huge weekly cereal bill. He wanted her to be happy, but she didn't seem happy. He wanted to help, but helping Hannah always seemed to end in tears.

And if he spent too much time with her and kept on having these idiotic fantasies about families and happy ever afters and naughty red-haired children rambling over the paddocks of Ironbark Station?

Well, he'd be the one in tears.

He caved at the junction of Hope and Quarry Streets. Straight along Hope to skim the outskirts of town, a merge right into Gorge Road, and he'd be at the gates of Ironbark before the evening news finished. A whiskey. An ibuprofen. With luck, Mrs L had covered some leftovers in foil and left them warming in the oven for him and …

But here he was, parking round the side of the clinic and climbing out of the car into the chill of an early autumn evening. Fairy lights lit the trees in the park across the road and light spilled from The Billy Button Café on its far side. A couple walked arm in arm down Dandaloo Street with a little poodle thing dancing along ahead of them on its lead. An everyday evening for everyday people.

It made him want what he couldn't have.

He felt the bitterness rising and clamped it down. No way did he want to become like Bruno: angrier and more bitter as the years passed. No-one needed to be subjected to that.

The back door was unlocked, so he let himself into the clinic then made his way up the two flights of stairs to Hannah's place. Lucky he didn't have an audience; he had to take a breather on the landing before thumping on the door.

She opened it a scarce few seconds later. 'Oh, hi.' Her hair was escaping its braid and she looked rumpled, but she didn't sound mad that he'd turned up after ignoring her text message.

'It's late. I wanted to see you.'

Her face split into a grin and he reached out to touch her messy braid (why, Tom? Why! Because he was a sucker for punishment, that's why) and—

Too late, he realised they weren't alone. Kylie was standing by the couch wrapping herself in scarves and a woollen cap and a hot pink fleece-lined jacket that a lumberjack would have been proud to own.

'I'm just leaving,' she said.

'No need,' he said. Kylie being there was perfect. Three friends, just hanging out, no thorny unrequited love drama lounging around like an elephant in the room with them.

'*Definitely* leaving.'

'Kylie, it's late,' said Hannah. 'You can't walk home alone.'

'I'm barely two minutes away and I have a six-inch spanner in my handbag. I'll be fine.' And with two kisses aimed loosely into the air either side of Hannah's face, and a long, cool, raised-eyebrow look at him, she was gone.

Tom moved further into the flat. The dining table was set up for dinner with fancy glasses and napkins. The coffee table looked like a bomb had exploded on it. He cocked his head. 'Is that Carly Simon playing?'

She sniffed. 'You don't get to arrive nine hours late for dinner and criticise my music.'

'Two hours.'

She looked at her watch and it seemed to take quite a while for her to perform the calculation. 'I'll agree to three.'

'Three it is. You seem to have a fair bit of wine on board, brat.'

She frowned. 'More criticism?'

'Not at all. Just an observation.'

She took a deep breath and stared at him and the silence lengthened long enough for him to remember that he had promised himself he wouldn't come here tonight.

'I guess now you're here I can tell you that I'm sorry I didn't answer all your text messages,' she said at last.

'I figured you needed some time. How are you doing?'

'Good. Mostly. Good enough to know you were very nice to me at that effing wedding and I never thanked you.'

'I don't need thanks.'

'But still. Up until the last ten minutes, I was actually having a nice time. That's … kind of a big deal. So thank you.'

He shrugged. 'You're welcome. Since we're being so adult and all and using our nice words, I'm sorry I didn't answer your dinner invite.'

She looked across to the kitchen counter which, now he stopped to notice the dripping pans and scattered utensils and slight aroma of scorch in the air, was in an even worse state than the coffee table. 'Calling it dinner might have been a stretch.'

'Hannah,' he said, moving towards her until his hands gripped her shoulders. 'It's been a long month. I've been worrying about you.'

She pulled away. 'Not you, too. I get enough of that from Josh. I'm fine. I was embarrassed, all right? That's why I needed to crawl into my cave for a while. I've been regrouping. I actually think travelling away and then getting the opportunity to tell dickwad that he was a … a … total *dickwad* was a good thing.'

'Well, that's good then. I'm pleased. Really pleased.' He'd got what he came for, he'd assured himself she was truly okay, and now he needed to go before everything got sticky again. 'I'll, er, say goodnight.'

'Not so fast. We had a deal, remember? I know I've been a little AWOL, but we agreed. My help with the campdraft for your support on out-of-town adventures.'

'The campdraft is coming together. I know you're busy; don't worry about Marigold and her minions. I'll tell them you've got too much on.'

'Over my dead body. I'm helping.'

He frowned. 'What?'

'You have no idea how useful I can be; I own my own business, remember? That makes me awesome at everything. I can make posters and put them up at the vet clinic. I can do an animal talk on the day: when does a hoof need trimming, that sort of thing. All the horsey people there will love an opportunity to tell me why their method is better. I can do a spreadsheet for the entries, ask my vet supply contacts if they want to sponsor a prize. Besides, I'm looking forward to some of those drives you promised me.'

She said it so matter-of-factly. Like that's really all it was: a trade. Her help with logistics or promo or whatever, and his help with company and bravado on a few sorties out of town.

Saying no, the deal was over, would be the prudent thing to do. 'Okay,' he said.

She grinned. 'Let's both keep an eye out for some market days or festivals we could visit within a couple hours' drive and I can ask Josh to cover for me if I'm on call. I can make sandwiches.'

He risked a look at the destroyed kitchen. 'Better leave the sandwiches to me.'

# CHAPTER

## 24

Lights were blazing and a photocopier machine was shooting out pages of text when Tom turned up at the solicitor's office to check on the last of the Krauss records. The pub's office had room for all records, old and new, and the more files he opened, the more expired leases and unattended to requests for maintenance and repair he found.

He was hoping Benjamin's personal issues were over and he'd be at work so he and Tom could have a frank discussion about what might have been left to slide and might need an urgent review. Like property insurance bills being paid, for instance. Like rental payment balances lurking in Dorley's trust fund that ought to have been paid out.

Or not. An old bloke in hi-vis workwear and muddy boots walked out of the inner office as Tom arrived. 'Don't waste your time, mate,' he said. 'There's a lawyer down in Cooma who won't take your money but then do—' he craned his head back towards Dorley's office and raised his voice to shout, '—diddly-effing-squat.'

Tom walked past the outer desk piled with so much junk, the school kid, if he'd been there, would have been buried alive, then stood in the doorway.

'Having a bad one, mate?' he said.

Benjamin Dorley did not look well. His hair was a mess—grey and wiry and oily looking. The cardigan he wore over a button-down shirt had something that looked like egg yolk dripped down its buttons and he was muttering under his breath.

'Hello? Benjamin?'

The solicitor barely made eye contact with him. 'Look, I don't know what I've promised you, and I probably haven't prepared it, but maybe I have and it's printing now. Maybe you could come back next week?'

'Tom Krauss. Bruno's son. We met a couple of months back.' About a dozen times, did the guy not remember? 'The kid you had here on work experience was organising our archived files to be pulled out of storage.'

'Good old Bruno,' said Benjamin in a vague way that sounded like he'd used too many vowels and not enough consonants. 'Control P, that's the shortcut for printing.'

'Um … yes it is. Did the boxes turn up yet?' Tom was on the clock this morning. He had an interview with a potential pub manager. There was a stack of boxes in the room, packed on a removalist's trolley. Hopefully they were all neatly labelled in the kid's handwriting: *For Tom Krauss To Collect. Have an Awesome Day With Your Boxes.*

'Control P. That's what she said. If in doubt: control P.' Dorley made no move to get up.

'Benjamin? Are these boxes mine?'

'She said, she said, she said.'

Was Tom imagining it, or was one side of the solicitor's mouth drooping? He stepped forward. 'Can you lift your arms, mate?'

'Whaaaat?'

'Your arms,' he said loudly. 'Lift them now.'

Still nothing. Shit. He grabbed the phone on the desk and hit 000. 'Hello? Yes, I'm at the corner of Ballarat Street and Hope Street, Hanrahan. A legal office, Benjamin Dorley on the name-plate. There's a man here with a suspected stroke.'

He answered the questions. 'Yes. No. Late sixties, I'd say. The paramedics will need to come up one flight of stairs. Okay.'

He set down the phone. 'Benjamin? I've called an ambulance because I think you might need to see a doctor. Is there anyone I can call for you? Mrs Dorley? Anyone?'

'If in doubt, control—'

'Uh-huh. How about your keys? I can lock up the office for you.'

There was nothing of sense coming out of the solicitor, but he looked comfortable enough in his chair. Please god he didn't try to stand and stumble, because no way Tom could catch him. They'd both need to be stretchered out.

He gave the guy as reassuring a look as he could muster, then opened the lid of the top archive box on the removalist's trolley and took a gander. *Krauss—63 Dandaloo Street, Krauss—46–48 The Esplanade, Krauss—Last Will and Testament.* Definitely the right boxes, so that was one step forward at least.

He put the lid down as two paramedics in the dark green uni-form of the NSW Ambulance appeared at the door.

'This the patient?' said one.

'Yep. He seems confused, and he couldn't lift his arms.'

'Come on then, mate. Let's have a look at you. Can you tell me your name?'

'Benjamin Dorley. I'm a lawyer. Love the law more than my wife. At least, that's what Joan said when she left.'

'Speech is fine,' said the older paramedic. 'A little rambling.' He squatted so he was at eye level with Benjamin. 'Face asymmetry. Let's get your arms up, Mr Dorley. That's right, up they come.'

The paramedic nodded at his colleague. 'Two out of three stroke signs. Good call on your part, mate. Not everyone knows the signs.'

'Seventeen years in the Navy. I've sat in on a lot of first aid refreshers.'

'You called his family?'

'Sorry, I don't have those details.'

'Let's make sure we take his phone and ID with us. The hospital will get onto it,' the younger paramedic said. The two of them had Dorley out the door and down the stairs with a minimum of fuss.

After they left, Tom stood for a moment in the quiet of the office. Beneath the clutter he could see that the room had once held more than a little charm. Deep-silled windows, panelled walls, a brass pot with an almost-dead ficus. He filled an old mug with water from a dispenser in the reception area and tipped it into the soil, then hunted around for the office keys, which he found still in the door.

Dorley had cared about this place once.

'Look at you, Tom Krauss,' he said to himself. 'Being neighbourly and everything.' He spent a minute looking through drawers to see if Dorley had his wife's number written anywhere, but he just found the work experience kid's. He debated calling, but school would be in session, and he didn't want to alarm the boy.

*Hi, Alex, Mr Dorley's taken a leave of absence, so work experience won't be happening anytime soon*, he typed into a text message. *This is Tom Krauss. I've got the office keys.* He thought for a second. *If you fancy making twenty bucks, there's a stack of boxes loaded up on a trolley in his office that need to come to me at the Hanrahan Pub. Let me know and I can meet you here to unlock.*

He fixed the sticky note he'd scribbled onto the opaque glass before starting a careful descent to the ground floor: *Closed for Personal Reasons. Office keys can be collected from the Hanrahan Pub—ask for Tom.*

Poor old bugger … wheeled out of his place of business by paramedics. Tom knew how that felt, although he hadn't been wheeled so much as bundled on a gurney, dropped into a waiting high-speed vessel, and roared off over a nasty swell to the medical facility aboard a naval frigate.

But that was in his past. Lucky for him, he had stuff to look forward to. Now … why was that phrase ringing a bell?

He set off for the pub by way of the lake, and it came to him as The Billy Button Café came into sight.

*Makes you feel lucky to be alive.*

Marigold. She'd been talking about how lucky he was to have the Hanrahan Pub to restore, and he'd brushed her words off as just grandiose prattling. Maybe she wasn't totally wrong.

Now he had her in his thoughts, he pulled out his phone and called her. 'Marigold? It's Tom. The pub's not officially open but we're test running the keg lines this week in the public bar. Pick a day that suits you and I'll put the word out: it's time for a meeting of the Ironbark Campdraft volunteers.'

# CHAPTER
## 25

*The Laird of Finchmore waited—alone, rugged and windswept—at the cliff's edge. He could hear waves crashing on the rocky shore below, but the weather, no matter how bone chilling, how tempestuous, would not deter him now.*

*His kilt swirled about his burly thighs as he paced.*

*A yellow flicker lit the sea mist and his fists clenched. 'At last,' he growled. He pulled back the shroud which covered his own lantern and held it aloft. One long flash … two short … one long …*

A muffled sound came from the corridor outside her treatment room, but Hannah was so focused on fumbling with the well-thumbed corner of her library book (thank you, Mrs Grundy!) to turn the page that she paid no attention. The thin paper flicked over and she carried on reading. It was naughty, true, to be reading fiction at work, but she'd done about six hours' hard labour already and it was barely morning tea time. Besides, the cat due to have three teeth removed must have seen its travel crate come out of the cupboard at home and scarpered, because her ten o'clock was late.

*He found the hidden path on the cliff face and hurtled down it. The oarsmen would struggle to beach the dory in this weather; he'd wade out to them if he had to. He'd wade to hell and back if he had to.*

*The time had come to reclaim his stolen bride and the bairn that she carried.*

Crap, not again. Why did bloody fertility signs have to be everywhere she looked? She was having a break from obsessing about a baby. Trying to, at any rate. She'd made a decision the other night after crying all over Kylie that she was doing things the right way from now on.

What was Kylie's definition of the right way? Something about meeting and time passing, and a lot of senseless shagging before the nitty gritty of family was brought up. So that's what Hannah's decision had been: stop. Take stock. Pretend she and Tom were two people who happened to bump into each other a lot and liked each other, and see what flared from there.

When he'd reminded her she'd said she'd work with him on his campdraft committee, she'd seen the lightbulb of opportunity flicker on. They'd just be two people who liked each other, getting along, talking about low drama stuff ... and at the end of all those meetings and when all those driving adventures they'd agreed to were done and dusted, maybe he'd see the truth: she was absolutely positively perfect for him.

*If he had to hang, draw and quarter a dozen Spaniards to get her safely home and in his arms ... well. He'd done worse.*

*The difference this time would be that he'd be doing it for that noblest of motives: love.*

*Love.* Aww. A voice at the door had Hannah looking up into a face that was not rugged or windswept.

But those arms ... oh, yes, she thought dreamily, they could clasp a woman as manfully as a vengeful Scotsman, she was sure they could. Her eyes dropped to the snug, well-filled denim before she could remind them she was in her place of work. She was a professional woman with a successful small business. She certainly shouldn't be scanning Tom's thighs to see if they qualified for the adjective burly.

Huh.

Turns out, they certainly did.

Remembering where she was, she slammed shut the large-print edition of *The Laird's Legacy* that she'd borrowed with her new library card, and shoved it under a pile of histology reports.

'Tom. Sorry, I didn't hear you, this—um—fatty lymphoma specimen had my attention one hundred per cent.' She dropped her face to the microscope and had a quick look so her words weren't totally a lie. Then she picked up a pen and made a tick on some random piece of paper (probably a pizza receipt) on the desk. When she was done she turned to face him.

'Couple of things. We're having a volunteers meeting for the campdraft in the pub next week. Five o'clockish on Thursday, can you make it?'

'If I'm not out on an emergency call, I can. Do I need to bring anything?'

'Pen and paper. Ideas. I've asked Roger Kettering, one of the blokes who ran the Dalgety one, to come and speak, and I'll try to take notes of what he says, but best to have a second set in case I miss anything.'

'Sure. Your popping in is actually perfect timing.'

'Really. What for?'

She had it here somewhere. She turned to the counter and rifled through the mess. Not the histology book, not the blister pack of worming tablets, not the— 'Aha. Here it is.' She flipped open the *Snowy River Star* and turned through the pages until she reached the community section at the back.

'Don't tell me Maureen Plover's been including the Krauss family in the Chatter again.'

'No, next page, here we go: the Adaminaby Picnic Races are on, and guess who's running?'

'Um … I don't know?'

'You're slipping, Tom. I thought you bossy, aloof types knew everything. There's a mare running that has the same sire as Buttercup! We should go. Make a day of it.'

He grinned. 'For real? How on earth did you find that out?'

'There's a write-up about the trainer because he's having a successful year so far, and they mentioned the provenance of the horses he has running and one of the names rang a bell. I looked up Buttercup's file and spotted the connection.'

'What time's the race?'

'Sunday. Ten am. Adaminaby is ninety-six kilometres north of here, population 301.'

He cocked his head. 'Did you look that up?'

She could feel herself flushing, so frowned to cover it. 'Maybe. Can we go in your car?'

'Sure. I'll pick you up at nine.'

'Don't forget the sandwiches,' she called as he disappeared.

*And that's how it's done*, she congratulated herself as she peeled off her rubber gloves. One non-date but date-like day with Tom coming up. Two, if she counted the committee meeting. Perhaps she should celebrate with a biscuit!

She wandered down the hallway to the reception area. 'Morning, Sandy.'

'Hi, Hannah. Early start?'

'Too early. A dog fell off the back of an interstate truck taking gravel out to Crackenback and we were the only local vet who answered the owner's phone call.'

'Ouch. How was the dog?'

'Battered and bruised, but nothing broken. Fattest kelpie I've ever seen. Wouldn't be surprised if she'd bounced. She's doing the rest of the trip in the passenger seat and probably getting hand fed Chiko rolls every time they pass a servo. Any word from Sally Rees? Her cat was due in.'

'You say cat, I say demon. But no, I haven't heard from her. I'll give her a call.'

'It's not urgent if she has to reschedule. I've got biopsy samples to keep me busy, anyway. You got the bookings page open?'

Sandy turned to the computer and clacked about on the keyboard for a second. 'Yep. What do you need?'

'Who's on call on Sunday?'

'You are.'

'Can you give that to Josh? I've ... got something on.'

Sandy pulled her glasses off and looked her over. 'Does this something revolve around the six-foot-two of eye candy that just disappeared out the side door?'

Hannah felt her cheeks burning. 'It's not like that, Sandy,' she said. Unfortunately.

'You sure? You look kind of flustered and red in the face.'

'That'll be the book I was reading on the sly in the back room. Mrs Grundy recommended it.' As an excuse it wasn't her finest, but she'd said it now. She motored on before Sandy could start making any more deductions—or worse, ask to borrow the book before she'd finished, because no-one was getting between her and the Laird of Finchmore before she'd made it to the last chapter.

'Picnic races. To look at a horse.'

'Because you're an expert on racehorses?'

'Was that sarcasm?' Sandy was so dry it was hard to tell.

Sandy grinned. 'Make me a cup of tea and I'll remind Josh that you covered for him when Poppy got suspended from school and he had to hightail it to Sydney.'

'I'd forgotten about that. You've got an excellent brain, Sandy. One cup of tea coming up. I can't remember: is sugar a yes or a no this week?'

'It's a hell yes. Parent meetings are on at school this week and I'm carbo loading to get through it.'

'Oh no. Which son is giving you grief this time? Oh, hang on, tell me all about it later. I think I can hear yowling from the bowels of hell on the footpath. My ten o'clock just arrived.'

# CHAPTER
# 26

On Thursday, only fifteen minutes late on account of a talkative spaniel owner, Hannah pushed open the door to the Hanrahan Pub and let herself into the corridor.

Everything gleamed: the paint, the banister and newell post of the wide timber stairs, the glass on the old photographs lining the walls. Furniture polish hung heavy in the air as did the smell of something delicious.

Beer.

The public bar wasn't crowded—far from it—but she took a moment to check out the faces to see who she knew and who she didn't. The only stranger was still vaguely familiar … he must be the guy from Dalgety.

'Hannah, my lamb, pass these around and drag some chairs into a circle, will you, pet?' Marigold thrust a bundle of papers in her hands and roared off to a table in the corner where Kev was laying out cups and saucers and ripping open packets of Arnott's Assorted. Beside him was the big silver urn that followed the Joneses around from function to function: craft, weddings, community hall, anything.

'Kylie,' she said, spying her friend sliding in from the direction of the beer garden. 'Here, have a flyer. Marigold wants me to hand them around. Why are you dripping wet?'

'Small incident with one of the tap handles. Tom had to call for aid and Hanrahan's finest mechanic was on hand to save the day.'

Hannah leant in for a sniff. 'I hope that's Kosciuszko Pale Ale.'

'It is. Go hand out your flyers and I'll pour you a schooner. I'm on double duty as finest mechanic and bar wench this evening.'

Hannah said hello around the room to Kev and Lionel and the guy from Dalgety, who introduced himself as Roger Kettering. Of Tom there was no sign, but her brother rocked up with Jane Doe at his heels. When she raised her eyebrows at him he lifted his phone and rolled his eyes.

One on-call Cody at a time. Thankfully it wasn't her.

'I'll need a flyer,' said a chilly voice.

Maureen Plover! Hannah didn't see Maureen out and about very often. She'd assumed she spent all her spare time drafting tidbits of meanness for the Chatter or cackling over a cauldron.

'Hello, Mrs Plover. I didn't know you were helping out.' She'd have bet the glass of lager she was hoping to soon be given that Marigold didn't know either. Two matriarchs on one committee? Bosoms would be heaving before the first agenda item was read out.

'I thought, since I'd championed the need for the Ironbark Station campdraft in the Hanrahan Chatter, that I should volunteer some of my expertise to see it done.'

'That's very civic minded of you.'

Making her escape, Hannah took a seat next to Kylie and thanked her for the beer. 'What?' she said, because her friend was looking her over critically.

'You're wearing a blouse.'

'I couldn't come in my scrubs. By 5 pm the only place for them to go is the soaking bucket or the incinerator.'

'But a blouse. I love it. Tidy hair, mascara, you even smell pretty. I'm getting some subliminal messaging here.'

'Relax, Kylie. You're not my type. The subliminal messaging is for our host, who doesn't appear to be at his own meeting.'

'He's outside, waiting for— Oh. Here they all are.'

The buzz in the room died down as Bruno Krauss, Hanrahan's living legend, wheeled himself into the public bar. He was flanked by Mrs LaBrooy, who had lived up at Ironbark, taking care of the family, for as long as Hannah could remember, and none other than Barry O'Malley, the town mayor. Behind them, carrying a collection of belts draped over one arm, was Tom.

'Bruno looks terrible,' whispered Kylie into her ear.

It was true. His cheeks had a grey cast to them, and thin was too plain a word to describe the angle and bone he'd become.

'You're all here,' Bruno said, in a voice that had lost none of its bark. 'Well. That's saying something.'

Hannah couldn't quite tell if he was happy about it or angry about it.

'Welcome to the meeting,' said Marigold smoothly. 'Why don't we get started? There's a flyer going around for everyone to nominate their inter—'

Bruno cut her off. 'I'll be running this meeting, Marigold Jones.'

Hannah sucked in her breath. Seemed like they now had three of Hanrahan's fiercest citizens to deal with.

Marigold took a seat. 'Of course.'

Bruno settled himself in his chair and took a look around. 'Well, you all know each other, I expect. I'm here to say my bit and then I'll butt out and leave you lot to see it done. Ironbark Station has produced some of the finest campdraft horses this country's ever seen. That's the way we do things up at Ironbark. We expect the best. So that's what I'm expecting come October when the draft is on. I've got enough cattle to stock the camp, and my manager Lynette will see to the cattle chutes and arrange paddocks where the entrants can park their floats and water their horses. You'll be doing the rest. But you'd better be ready. When you open the draft up to competitors on the tournament circuit, you're going to sell out real quick. Every campdrafter in the country wants a chance to win what we're offering. Tom? Where's my … oh.'

The belts were old and their buckles were polished. 'I'm offering as prizes my championship belts. They're no use to me anymore, and Tom's agreed. It'll be a campdrafter that'll value them more than the wall on my study, where they've been hanging twenty years or more.'

'That's a generous prize, Bruno,' said Roger. 'You can bet your backside I'll be competing for one.'

'Good lad. Right. Now, who's getting me a beer?'

The mayor and Bruno went into a huddle after the meeting came to an end. Marigold kept herself very low key, other than to ask people to use her form to nominate themselves to any roles that she and Tom had cooked up, and Tom ran the meeting in a no-nonsense manner that had Hannah reflecting on how little he ever talked about his old job.

Her moment came when he sat down next to her, a beer in his hand, with the air of a man who'd done enough for one day and just wanted to sit and chat.

Suited her. Chatting was a totally date-like thing to do.

'How did Bruno react to seeing all you've done here at the pub?'

Tom grinned. 'Dad's not one to mess about with fulsome praise. I don't think he hated it, put it that way.'

'He must love having you here to take on these jobs. He doesn't look up to it, does he?'

'He's not up to it, but he's not of a mind to let go, either. Don't think for a minute he wasn't micromanaging this pub reno. There's nothing wrong with his mind, it's just his energy that's failed him.'

'Oh. I thought he'd maybe handed it over.'

'Nope. You know the Krauss family has a lot of real estate, right?'

'Sure. Everyone in Hanrahan knows you own half the town.'

'Yeah, but here's the thing about family empires. I don't own half the town, my dad does. And he likes me to remember that.'

'Because he's a control freak?'

'I think it's more than that. You know his parents were immigrants?'

'I don't think I did know that, no.'

'Germans. Came here after the war for a new life because their home was destroyed. They kept to themselves, as you can imagine. Anti-German sentiment must have run strong in the 1950s … I mean, you've seen the cenotaph in the park. There wouldn't be a farming family in the area who hadn't lost a son or brother in the war. Bruno was born on the ship coming out. I think being an immigrant drove his need to start a legacy here in Australia because his parents had to leave theirs behind.'

'He's certainly created one.'

'It's not the buildings he cares about, though. It's the breeding he's done. The stockhorses. Ironbark Station is the legacy he cares about most.'

'You're sounding very "past tense" in this conversation, Tom. Are you worried about your dad?'

'You've seen him. He's in trouble.'

'Yeah. Multiple sclerosis is a tough sentence.'

'And the rest. Emphysema is his biggest worry. He's on oxygen bottles pretty much every day now.'

'I'm sorry, Tom. That's rough.' She rested her hand on his for a moment, but wondered if she'd overstepped the non-dating rules when he shifted away.

'Bruno's legacy means a lot to him. He's always been a proud man, but he's also a hard man. Like his pride and anger are all wrapped up together, and if he lets go of it, he'll be back to being an ordinary bloke, not legend of Ironbark Bruno Krauss. He's also shitty about me not wanting to take over the stockhorse business. But we've reached a sort of armistice where I look after the property holdings and he trains up his head ringer, Lynette, to take on the sales part of the horse business as well as the training. He's not the man he was and Mrs LaBrooy is getting pretty long in the tooth herself; too old to be minding Dad, at any rate. So, if I'm going to stay here in Hanrahan—'

'Tom! Have you decided? Are you going to make Hanrahan your home?'

He shrugged. 'If I do, I need to find my own way.' He took a sip of his beer. 'I haven't told anyone else that, so keep it quiet, will you?'

'You can trust me.'

'I do trust you.'

Hmm. Well, that was very nice to hear. Perhaps there was something to Kylie's method after all. Bring on Sunday … she was starting to get the hang of this non-dating palaver.

# CHAPTER
## 27

A traffic jam greeted them at the turn-off to the Adaminaby race track.

Utes were parked three abreast in the carpark, with picnic rugs and deck chairs and eskies spilling out of their trays onto the parched grass below. A few of the women were teetering about on crazy-high heels, the blokes were in the bloke uniform—jeans, plaid shorts, boots, fancy belt—and food trucks had queues stretching in loose snakes waiting for their coffee or their loaded wedges or their banh mi.

Tom turned to look at Hannah. It had taken him months to work out that when she'd hung up her scrubs and stethoscope for the day, she pulled up a barrier between her and the big bad world, but now he was clued in, the signs were everywhere.

When tourists had walked past them in Hanrahan because the only park he'd found was on a back street? Hannah busied herself on her phone, looked down at the pavement, hugged her arms about herself. When they'd driven through Berridale, had Hannah looked in the window of the car pulled up next to them at the crossing? Nope. Eyes fixed straight ahead. No wave, no engagement.

Was it habit? Or did she need to distance herself like that?

Today's beanie and oversized sunglasses were another example, perhaps, of her disinclination to be noticed.

But she'd invited him out, remember?

'You ready?'

'Yes,' she said brightly. Her knuckles looked a little white where they held her handbag in a death grip, but he took her at her word.

He got out of the car and walked around to her side. 'Need a distraction? I can give you a monologue on any subject. Let's see, I've got topics aplenty: useful knots for seafaring, how to clear brushtail possums from an abandoned building, ultimate payback strategies involving frogs in boots ...'

She smiled and bumped her head into his shoulder. 'I know what you're doing and it's very sweet. Also: it's working. Tell me about racehorses. When did you develop an interest in them? I thought stockhorses were the Krauss family bread and butter.'

'That's Bruno's thing. And Buttercup's more of a hobby than the start of a racing empire. I bought her when I was—' He broke off. Damn it. He couldn't make slips like that.

'Tom?'

He flicked Hannah a glance. 'I was missing my old life in the Navy when I bought Buttercup.' Which was true. 'She was already in foal and her owners were a syndicate who had had some sort of personality blow-up, so co-owning a horse had become a problem. I was missing the adrenalin rush of my career and owning a racehorse seemed a good alternative.'

Hannah made an indistinct noise.

He grinned. 'What?'

'It's just … it's peacetime. I thought all you Navy types did was patrol the Torres Strait for illegal fishermen, play cards and make awesome recruitment ads.'

He rolled his eyes. 'Wow. That's like saying all vets do is shove thermometers up cat bums. Us Navy types see plenty of action, even in peacetime, especially when we're seconded out to the Middle—' The tug in his lower back reminded him his role overseas was not up for conversation because a) it was unethical to blab about military operations even when you'd hung up your sea boots and b) he'd signed about six hundred non-disclosure agreements and wasn't keen on a prison term for breaking said agreements.

He backtracked to the cover story he'd used ever since he left his operational role in the Royal Australian Navy and switched to covert naval support. 'I was an analyst with a desk job. Biggest threat in my nine-to-five was from a paper cut.'

'Really? But you just said you missed the adrenalin rush.'

He put on a wounded face. 'Paper cuts can be extreme.'

'Right. I guess that would explain the scar on the back of your hand.'

A barnacle from a hull had torn through his neoprene glove. He'd been at a depth of twenty feet, attaching a listening device to a merchant vessel in the Persian Gulf, a vessel reputed to be running crystal methamphetamine from Bandar Abbas to Istanbul. The blood loss would have worried him if he'd been in the Atlantic, but the Persian Gulf's biggest predator had been swimming alongside of him, a Special Ops diver from the Turkish government in a joint mission anchored by the US Navy. Good times.

'Not quite a paper cut,' he said at last. He could make up some bullshit reason but he didn't have the heart for it.

'Uh-huh.'

'What do you mean, uh-huh?'

'It's just … you always sound a little glib when you talk about yourself. Like you're giving some presentation to a group of strangers and any minute now you're going to click through to the next slide in your presentation and change topics.'

'I'm sorry. I don't mean to sound glib. I guess life here in the country is so far removed from anything I worked on in the Navy, it's hard to reconcile them.'

They'd cleared the carpark and reached the people queueing at the gate for entry. Families had brought eskies with them, some even had marquees, and the row of small, red-tin-roof grandstands already looked crowded. 'There'll be journos here covering the races for the local paper. Are you going to be okay with that?'

Her hands were busy winding her scarf about her face so she was covered throat to nose. Between the dark glasses and green woolly cap she was now mostly hidden.

'Yes,' she said.

He smiled. 'Because you're unrecognisable?'

'Because I'm not a total narcissist. And, since you know all my secrets anyway, I can tell you that I've been going through some of my old therapy journals and revisiting the behavioral therapy exercises. What does it matter if my photo winds up on someone's social media page and all that tagging nonsense identifies me? There's a zillion trillion more images out there in the world now than there were all those years ago, and nobody cares.'

'I care,' he said. 'But in a good way.'

She sighed. 'I care in a bad way, but not so much as I used to. I've worked out that I'm a lot more than one dumb photo image—be it real or fake.'

A strand of her auburn hair had curled forward out of her cap and clung to her cheek. He tucked it back into place and smiled at her. 'I'm proud of you.'

She blushed, and it took a moment for him to recall that they were here standing in the sunshine for any reason other than for him to stare at her.

'Er … right. I'll get us some tickets,' he said.

He was an idiot. Hannah needed him to be a good sport about squiring her to out-of-town events, that's all this was. That's all this could be.

He tried to buy their entry only to be told it was free, then fell into step beside her.

'Okay then.' He pulled out his phone to check the screen. 'Manson Rous is competing in the Picnic Maiden Plate. It's eleven hundred metres, starting in an hour. You want to look around the stalls first?'

She looped a hand into his arm. 'Only if they're serving snag sangers.'

He grinned. 'I'll buy you as many as you can eat.'

# CHAPTER
## 28

Telling herself back in Hanrahan that she was all grown up and totally sorted was one thing. But Hannah was discovering that actually being relaxed so far from home was another thing entirely. At the Dalgety Showgrounds, she'd had Skipjack. She'd had an event to think about, a riding helmet to wear, a mob of steers and heifers to concentrate on. And she'd still lost it.

She found herself covertly scanning the crowd—not an easy habit to break. Keeping up the banter at the same time, slipping her hand into Tom's arm and acting all casual, joking about sausages in bread while people were looking and snapping selfies all around them … yeah, that was crazy hard. She'd be knackered by the end of the day.

She decided she'd split the anxiety up. Go full science and observe the crowd. Take the kid in the stroller for example. He was staring at her with wide dark eyes, but he also looked like he was more concerned with filling his nappy than outing her as a woman who'd once starred in a viral porn pic. So, she could quit worrying about everyone in nappies. It was a start.

The officials and the canteen workers were too busy to be bothered with anything but their jobs, so she could quit worrying about them, too.

Kids eating hamburgers? Not a threat.

If she had been tracking all this on a pie graph, with green for safe and red for unsafe, the green pieces of pie were growing.

'I can smell sausages this way,' said Tom. 'Or shall we lay a bet first? What do you say? Two bucks each way?'

'I can just about afford to lose four bucks.'

They stood in the queue to make a bet then headed around the track to where the local CWA members were running a food stall with marvellous efficiency.

'One for you?' said Hannah, moving into the queue behind a kid being towed by a dalmatian.

'I'm good. I'll get us both a coffee in a bit.'

'That'll be three bucks, love,' said the plump woman behind the trestle table, handing her a snag in bread wrapped in a paper napkin. 'Help yourself to sauce.'

Hannah handed over a bunch of coins, loaded the snag up with barbecue sauce and they headed over to the marshalling yard, where jockeys in coloured shirts were milling about, gossiping and carrying saddles.

This was better than hanging out with the spectators. The air smelled like horse and manure and sweat; it smelled like most of her vet callouts to the farms around Hanrahan. She had this. Keep calm, chat with Tom, get home and chalk up the day as progress; a step towards the next day out being easier and the one after that easier still.

'Did you read the form book on the mare?' she asked between bites.

'Mmm. Not quite two years old. Only been racing a couple of months and no wins or places yet.'

'Is that a bad sign?'

'Maybe her trainer's easing her in.'

'Maybe she's a stay-at-home kind of horse, not interested in making a splash out in the big world.'

Tom stopped walking and looked at her. 'Wait, are we talking about the horse now or you?'

Good question. 'The horse, of course.'

'Are you sure you're okay being here, Hannah?'

She shrugged, a whole heap of lying words forming in her head, before stumbling out with the truth. 'I want to be okay with being here.'

They'd walked to the furthest end of the track, to an old-fashioned grandstand with lacy ironwork. The seating was maybe a quarter full, and the crowd had migrated to the northern end, where the sun was slanting in and lighting up everyone's faces.

'Let's go join them,' she said.

She picked a fullish row and they excused their way past knees and boots and handbags until they found a gap and Hannah plonked her bum on the planked seating.

Tom pulled off his jacket and laid it along the bench next to her. 'You want to share my cushion?'

'What, your pants are too precious to sit on timber?'

He tweaked her ponytail then sat down next to her. 'It's my buns I'm looking out for. When your arse is as good looking as mine, you don't want to risk a splinter.' He shook out the program and held it on his knee so they could both read it.

Tom had lost his summer tan and his cheeks were pale above the stubble he hadn't shaved that morning. It was an effort to drag her thoughts away from how comforting it felt to be shoulder to shoulder. A race was about to start. Horses, their bright-silked jockeys perched hunched and focused above them, milled behind the gates.

She checked her watch then looked at the program. 'Which one's this, do you reckon?'

'Two thousand metre handicap. Endurance will count, but a little pace at the start will count more. The maiden race should be next.'

The blare of the starting horn sounded and it was a wrench to drag her eyes away from him. *The horses*, she reminded herself. *The races.*

They should have brought binoculars with them.

'Welcome to the third race at the Adaminaby Picnic Races! They're lined up at the gate, and they're off! Jumping to the lead is Parlay and Coco Loco—'

'Nice stride on the lead,' she said, ignoring the announcer and concentrating on the horse with the rider in a butter-yellow shirt. 'Maybe we should have put money down on all the races.'

'It's beyond nice. Long, measured.'

'Falling off the back is Pandemonium, and here's the turn, here's the back stretch, Parlay's lost the lead to—'

'That last one looks like a slug compared with the rest of them.'

'Got spooked at the starting line, maybe? This race isn't a maiden.'

'—and challenging for the lead in the home stretch it's Mackadaddy tearing up the field from the outside, it's Mackadaddy and Coco Loco neck and neck, it's down to the wire and it's … Coco Loco.'

Whoever in the crowd had bet on Coco Loco let out a roar, but mostly there was just a lot of tickets being torn up. 'Winner must have had long odds,' she said.

'It's nice when the unexpected one wins, don't you think?'

'Sure.' It depended on your interpretation of the word 'win'. For people like Tom and her brother, who had always been great at everything they tried in life, winning meant competition and coming out ahead of other people and having their already healthy egos swell up even more.

For her, winning meant something totally different. It meant being safe, being competent, being sure.

The woman in the officials' tower calling the races announced the first maiden race. 'They're moving in now for the Adaminaby Maiden Plate, Red Calliope giving her handler some grief ... there they go, and Fuller Cross the last to go in.'

'The jockey in the fluoro green is on Manson Rous,' Tom said. 'Hemi Markell, who I've never heard of, have you?'

'Tom, the only horse racing I watch is the Melbourne Cup, and it's pretty much tradition at the clinic that we'll get an emergency callout at three pm on the first Tuesday of every November. That's what me, Josh and Sandy make bets on, not the Cup.'

'They're all set ... and they're racing! Red Calliope bolted out and took the early lead, Fuller Cross close behind—'

'She looks good, doesn't she? Steady pace, she's not shy about getting in with the pack. Look! The jockey's trying to move her into the rail ... will she make that gap?'

Tom's hand had found hers and Hannah didn't think he'd noticed he'd grabbed her.

'Manson's doing great. Look, she's on the inside rail now, and there's clear space in front of her! Go! Go!'

A toddler in the row in front of them was staring over his father's shoulder at Tom, who was caught up in the moment and urging Manson Rous on to greatness. The kid had chocolate smeared over his cheeks and his thumb was jammed into his mouth like a snorkel while his other fat little arm was wrapped tight about his father's neck. He had big blue eyes and pale, silky baby hair. The toddler's colouring was so like Tom's, he could have been his son.

'At the four hundred it's Fuller Cross then Purple Prose, then Red Calliope and Faramar Lady swooping up from the outside.'

Or—the realisation landed like a fist in her ribs—he could have been their son. Hers and Tom's. That could be Tom's neck being gripped by a chubby little arm. They could be out at a picnic race day in the country together. A family of three.

She took in a long breath and held Tom's hand a little more firmly. Just because she could.

Now that she'd opened her mind to one image, a billion others popped up: visions of children with straw-coloured hair asking her if they could help out at the vet clinic after school. If they could have pancakes if they helped Dad muck out Buttercup's stable. A vision of Tom, on the surface a calm, serious bloke who didn't wear his heart on his sleeve and who grumbled about attending family dinners, but who arrived early and stayed late and actually loved every noisy second.

'We're seeing a shake-up at the two hundred. Manson Rous is making up ground, and Turn The Tail is dropping back. Purple Prose has lost her lead and Red Calliope is neck and neck with Fuller Cross.'

She sighed. She was getting ahead of herself. Again.

'And out of nowhere, sprinting down the outside, it's Love Yer Guts, and Love Yer Guts has snatched the win from Red Calliope, and Fuller Cross over the line in third.'

Tom had let go of her hand. 'What do you think?'

'She looked awesome.' Hopefully, because Hannah had grown a little distracted at the end there. 'How do you feel about finding that coffee?'

'Let's go. If you don't punch anyone, I could even be persuaded to buy you a lamington.'

She laughed and linked her arm into his. Okay, he wasn't on the same page as her as to what their relationship could be, but that didn't mean this wasn't a good day. This was fun. This was jokey, and sweet, and nice. This was more dates—well, technically they were non-dates—in one week than she'd had in a decade, so there was nothing to be sighing about.

Anyway, she was supposed to be proving what fun company she was. 'Have you been to many race days, Tom?'

'Not many. My dad took me and Josh out to the country races at Echuca once when we were kids. I remember being near the rails when the winner thundered past us at the finish and I think that's what stirred my interest. That gallop, the power of it travelled down the horse's legs, through that turf and up into my chest. I'll never forget it.'

Hannah rubbed her hand over her own breastbone. She understood that sort of power all right. 'I don't remember getting invited along.'

'Brat, your brother and I invested a lot of time and ingenuity working out ways to ditch you.'

She grinned. 'Nice.'

'Well, you know, girl germs being what they are.'

He really was adorable. How had she not noticed that when she was younger? 'Now you remind me, I do recall you both ditching me at the Hanrahan Show.'

Tom turned to her and raised an eyebrow. 'Did we? I can't remember Hanrahan ever having its own show.'

'Maybe it was a church fete or one of Marigold's events. I was … seven? Eight? Whoever was running it had built a temporary fence so only ticketholders could get in. You idiots decided we should climb the fence behind the portaloos so no-one would see us and save ourselves the dollar coin entry fee. I got stuck because one of my arms was in a plaster cast and then some angry bloke showed up and you two ran away like the brave heroes you are.'

He chuckled. 'I'd forgotten about that.'

'My backside didn't forget about it for weeks. Wire mesh and the humiliation of getting stuck leaves its mark. *And* I was grounded. Mum threatened me with ballet classes if I didn't learn how to behave like a young lady.'

'Ballet. Ouch.'

'I know, right?'

Tom grinned at her, and her heart went pitter-pat.

It felt great.

It felt like something that might happen in one of Mrs Grundy's excellent novels.

# CHAPTER
# 29

As Tom drove the last winding curve of road into Hanrahan, Hannah's phone trilled.

'I hope that's not a vet emergency. I swapped my on call with Josh, but every now and then we get two dramas at once. I was hoping to slide upstairs unnoticed, but you know Josh: he'll charm me into mucking out the overnight cages if he sees me looking idle and I'll have said yes before I remember that it's his job today.'

She worked hard, his girl. Driving that clapped-out little car of hers through farm paddocks and up mountains, saving the animals of the district, on duty more often than not.

'Oh, it's Vera. Maybe she's run out of space in the café fridge and needs to store a cheesecake or three at my place. Hi, Vera,' she said into the phone.

Vera's voice was a bubble of chatter that he couldn't distinguish. Hannah's words were almost as incomprehensible.

'I do answer my phone, Vera. I'm talking to you right now … no, I was out … with Tom … uh-huh … uh-huh … Oh! An announcement? Well, sure, I guess. Tonight at six? I'll be there.'

Hannah's cheeks had bloomed redder than Kev's roses.

'You okay?' he said, taking a hand off the wheel to touch her arm.

Hannah cleared her throat as she slid the phone back into her bag. 'Yes,' she said.

He narrowed his eyes, but before he could call her on it, his own phone rang. *Vera De Rossi* ran the text over his in-dash screen. The plot thickened. He killed the call before it could play through his car speakers; he could call her back later. He pulled into the kerb beside the vet clinic then slipped from the car and moved around to open Hannah's door.

'I can open it myself, you know. This is a brave new millennium, where women can go to the moon and rule the universe.'

He shrugged. It was a courtesy and one he felt privileged to still be able to perform. If he lost the use of his legs, walking a girl to her door would be a thing of the past. 'Consider it an apology for leaving you stuck on a wire fence.'

She tugged her jacket around her as the afternoon breeze coming up from Lake Bogong swirled around them. 'I had a nice day. Incident free, in fact.'

He smiled. 'So you did. Come on, you better get inside before you freeze to death. Smells like snow's coming to the high country tonight.'

'It's barely April. That's about a month too early.'

'The stable heating bill would agree with you.'

'You … er … fancy coming in?'

Was that a blush or just the wind colouring her cheeks? And why was she asking?

'I can't.' He was abrupt, and he was sorry for it, but he'd said it now.

'Of course. Well. Thanks again.'

He gave her a wave and headed off. It was as he slid down a gear and turned his car up the steeply winding Gorge Road that he remembered the phone call he'd declined. He hit the phone controls on the dashboard and scrolled until the number he wanted came on screen.

'Vera?' he said. 'Tom Krauss. I missed your call earlier.'

The stable yard was quiet when he drove in the gates. Sunday afternoon, so the ringers would all be at their homes, the horses fed and watered and tucked up in their heated stalls.

He could see Lynette seated on a rail by the training yard, busy on a phone call. If the woman ever stopped working, he'd never seen it.

He paused on the front steps a moment. Wouldn't hurt to check his emails before he went in to find his dad. A miracle might have happened, and a halfway decent publican might have been in touch.

He scrolled through the emails on his phone. Nothing from the employment agency. A few from his old team on the Combined Maritime Taskforce: how are you, hope you're getting better, yada yada whatever.

One from his specialist in Wollongong.

*I've reviewed the CT scans ordered by Dr Novak and the news is good and bad. The good news is that the shrapnel's been encapsulated. This means the scar tissue is forming a cushion around it. The bad news is that it has moved deeper into the spinal sheath. You're next scheduled to see me in September but I think we need to bring that forward. Call my receptionist and tell her to find you an appointment by end of July at the latest.*

*Regards, Jackie Tse.*

Shit.

He tracked his father down in the room that had once been Bruno's study but was now decked out like an aged care facility. It housed a wheeled trolley that doubled as a place to put meals, an oxygen system, and a hospital bed with a lifting mechanism so Bruno could get himself into and out of his chair without assistance.

'Dad. You got a minute?'

'Depends. What for?'

Tom ordered himself to keep his cool. 'For some plain speaking.' His back and mobility problem was not on the table for discussion, but he'd learned over the last few months that the injury wasn't the only thing going on in his life. And he wanted to make sure those other things weren't under threat as well.

Bruno looked at him for a moment, then grunted. 'Pass me that rug, will you? If we're going to do some plain speaking, I'd like to do it outside.'

'Sure.' Tom handed the blanket over and watched in silence as his dad's hands tried—and failed—to tuck the heavy fabric down. There was no manual or pamphlet he'd found that gave a son life advice on how to care for an elderly parent who'd once drowned the pup he'd loved and then watched and done nothing as his only son ran away from home.

Bugger it. He stepped forward and tucked the bloody thing in. 'It's cold out, maybe snow coming above the treeline tonight. You want me to get a hot water bottle?'

'Truth be told, Tom, it's not the cold that bothers me, it's the sitting on my bony arse all day. Bit of a jaunt outside in numbing weather might be just the thing.'

He followed his dad down the hall to the back door where a ramp had been installed a couple of years ago. A crushed gravel path led between huge pots of hydrangeas, sparse and pinched looking with autumn, to the paddocks stretched out beyond the fence.

Bruno seemed oddly chatty, so Tom let him run on.

'*Rosa Rugosa Grootendorst*.' His dad patted a faded red bloom on a rose bush. 'Planted this one the year you left. Been a reliable flowerer every year, keeps going well past autumn … I like to think it's reminding me a fella can make a mistake or two and still have roses in his life so long as he learns from it.'

Tom frowned. 'I didn't think you owned up to mistakes, Dad.'

'I've made plenty. As we both know, son. Your pup was just one of many and I'm sorry for it. Real sorry. Can you forgive me?'

His dad's leathery hand was shaky, but it had some strength in it yet when he gripped it.

'It's in the past,' Tom said. Just where he wished all his mistakes were. He took a breath and said what was on his mind. 'I'm thinking I might sell my place on the coast and make Hanrahan my permanent home.'

'What? I thought you had no interest in the stockhorses.'

'I said I've got no skill with the stockhorses. What I'm saying, Dad, is do you want me here? At Ironbark? Because I can live in town if you don't.'

'You're a Krauss, son. Ironbark Station will be yours one day. Pretty darn soon, maybe.'

'Will it? You keep telling me I don't deserve it.'

'Well, why don't you get on a fucking horse once in a while, son? I can't bloody do it, can I? Did you think about that? Did you think about how it burns my gut to see you, all fit and strong, and you won't even give your old man the pleasure of seeing you taking on the family business?'

He could tell Bruno about the steel shrapnel in his spine. But then he'd have to tell him about the operation he was one day—and quite soon, if that prophetic email from his specialist was any indication—to have. The operation with the risk factor that not even a bookie would issue odds on.

Nope, he couldn't do it. Losing his ability to train his beloved horses had just about done his father in. He'd not bounce back from hearing his son was facing the same future. Better to think Tom didn't ride by choice. Better the old bugger was angry about it than sad.

'I hope you've put something aside for Mrs L in that will of yours. She loves it here, and we both know we couldn't stop her turning up in the kitchen to cook for us even if we drove her off with a pitchfork. Be easier all round if she could lay claim to a little part of Ironbark Station that could be all hers.'

'Of course I have. She's got a life interest in her cottage.'

'Good idea. Add in a clause that we maintain it, we get a cleaner through it once a week, organise help for her if and when she needs it, and Mrs L gets to retire as much or as little as she wants to.'

'What, are you my bloody lawyer now?'

That was the first time ever—*ever*—that he had heard his father mention his university degree. And he hadn't said it like a swear word either.

'Would—' Tom kept his tone very calm and very even '—that be a bad thing?' He was already manning the property portfolio. But horse sale contracts needed to be written up, lease agreements renewed, employee disputes resolved … he could do it.

He *needed* to do it. It would give him a focus if the worst came to pass.

Bruno scowled. 'That one in town turned out to be as useful as a fart in a henhouse.'

'He was having a crisis, Dad. Divorce, drinking, medical problems.'

'Don't correct me, son. If I want to poke a stick at someone, I'll poke a bloody stick, understood?'

That sounded like a yes. 'So it's agreed. I'll officially handle the Krauss legal matters, on the condition that you can be as surly as you like to anyone you like.'

'Ha!' said Bruno. 'Maybe you've got a bit of me in you after all.'

'It's a deal, then.'

'You'll work from home.'

Bruno always had to be the boss, didn't he? Tom prevaricated with a non-answer: 'The files are all at the pub.'

His dad grunted and wheeled his way forward to the next garden bed. 'Ah. *Rosa Bonica*. Put this beauty in a few years ago, maybe the last time I could get on my hands and knees and dig in the garden the way god intended. Pinch that stem off for me, would you, son? There's something growing on it. I'll get the magnifying glass onto it in my study.'

Tom fiddled with the stem his father was looking at, trying to work out how to snap it off without snapping off half the bush; that'd be a sure way to set back this new accord he and his father had found.

'When I'm gone, I want these roses looked after.'

Today was a day for firsts. His dad was being franker than he'd expected and Tom wasn't sure how to respond. Not with pity, Bruno would hate that.

'I'm no gardener, Dad. You want these roses babied, you're going to have to pass that job on to a gardener. Maybe Kev can come from town every now and then and tend to them.'

'My legs and arms may be useless, Tom, but my brain's working just fine. Of course I meant get an expert in; only a moron would leave their prize roses to you. Now, it's time for a little plain speaking of my own. I'm gonna need you to wheel me over to that snow gum if you want to hear it.'

The station's small cemetery lay under a stand of old gums. Wrought iron railings, weathered to rust, guarded the ragged patch of ground, and the small headstones within had tilted askew. He'd had to whipper-snip in there as a kid: tough dry paddock grass and tiny yellow dandelions had kept his grandparents and his mother company over the years.

He had no memories of any of them.

'What do you see?'

He could see the Snowy Mountains, of course. They filled the horizon to the west, purple with shadow now the sun had fallen behind them. The paddocks, the stables where his father had spent most of his working life.

The homestead.

'Do you love it, Tom? Do you love Ironbark? Or did I wreck it for you all those years ago?'

He sighed. 'Dad.'

Bruno's pale hand clutched his. 'I worry ...' Now his dad's voice was becoming creaky and weak. 'I wanted this place to be ours. The Krauss family. I wanted it to be a place people loved. And then I drove you away.'

Tom wasn't about to argue that point. Bruno had driven him away and it had taken him close on twenty years to erase the bitterness.

'I never stopped loving Ironbark Station, Dad.'

'Then promise me something.'

'What?'

'Promise me you're going to stop messing things up with that girl you've been mooning over all these years and tell her you love her.'

Tom's thumbnail tore a strip of bark from the gum tree's shredding trunk when he jerked. 'Hell, Dad,' he said.

'My rose garden would make a lovely spot for a wedding. Be a blessing to see it used by my own son. That Hannah of yours … she's a keeper. Sweetest thing to get born in Hanrahan in my lifetime.'

Hannah was sweet. And sarcastic, and strong, and fun, and gorgeous … Tom didn't need his dad to list her virtues, he had them all figured out, had done for years.

'What's stopping you, Tom?'

The wind was carrying ice chips with it, flurries of cold that couldn't quite decide if they were rain or snow. 'Let's go back inside before we freeze,' Tom said.

'All right, don't listen to me. You never have, so I don't know why this would be any different.'

Bruno didn't want to let it go. Truth was, Tom didn't want to let it go either, but what choice did he have? He hadn't known he'd been so obvious that even his housebound father was wondering what his intentions were.

Luckily he'd made it clear to Hannah he was a no-go zone.

Although … he thought back to the blush on her cheeks that afternoon when she'd invited him in, the smile in her eyes at the picnic races when she'd laughed at his monologue nonsense.

Oh. Crap.

# CHAPTER
## 30

Everything was perfect.

The Billy Button Café was closed for the night, but you wouldn't have known it from the crowd there. Kev and Graeme's partner, Alex, were bickering over whether soup spoons took precedence over dessert spoons as they set the large table in the back room where the craft group did their stitching or flouncing or whatever it was they did in there on Wednesday nights.

Marigold was tucking flowers into vases, Kylie was zhoozhing the cushions on the bench seating by the window, and Graeme, dressed in an eye-watering blue plaid suit, was filling glasses with champagne and chattering like a kookaburra.

Hannah squealed as a hug nearly took out her diaphragm.

'Auntie Hannah! Hey, is that a new frock?'

'Poppy! When did you arrive? And the dress is Kylie's, of course,' she said. 'I borrowed it from her a while back and never got around to returning it.' Or washing it, either, probably. But it had been a month since she'd worn it, and that was like wearing a clean dress, wasn't it? She gave her niece a return hug then stood back and inspected her. 'Hmm. You do *look* like the same Poptart I last saw at Christmas.'

'Why wouldn't I look the same?'

'I don't know. I thought maybe a sixteen-year-old who'd been suspended from school would look different. Like, maybe you'd have an ankle monitor or something.'

'Don't be like Dad, Hannah.'

The disapproval was so weary and the eye roll so dramatic Hannah couldn't help but grin. 'Come on, spill the beans. He wouldn't tell me why you were suspended. Not even when I offered him a slice of cold pizza out of my fridge that was only two days old.'

'That must have taken remarkable restraint.'

'That's what I thought.'

'But he does have Vera in his life now. I mean, have you seen inside their fridge?'

'You're trying to distract me by making my taste buds jealous. It won't work.'

'It was all a misunderstanding.'

'By you?'

'No. By the geriatric dinosaur who calls herself principal of the school Mum and Dad force me to attend. She has no understanding of modern youth.'

'Is that so?'

'Yep.'

'But ... I'm still in the dark. What happened?'

Poppy kicked her monster-sized boot into a chair leg. 'I prom-ised I wouldn't say.'

'Well, you are no fun. Hey—are you still ghosting Braydon Fox? I think he's missing you.'

'Yeah, Dad said the same. I sense a conspiracy: why are the two of you so invested in how often me and Braydon talk?'

Hmm. Hannah wondered what the vet to guinea pig owner confidentiality requirements were. She pleaded out: 'I promised I wouldn't say.'

Poppy stuck out her tongue. 'Now you're the one not being fun.'

'Something which I am about to remedy. I'm going to find champagne.'

'You can't have any. I heard Dad tell Vera that you were on call for the rest of the night since this was their party.'

'Huh. Now I know why you were suspended. You're a spoilsport and a killjoy, Poppy Cody.'

Her niece giggled. 'I know how to make you an epic coffee on Graeme's machine,' she said winningly.

'Fine. A latte. But I'm a vet, not a botanist or a romantic, which means I want a swan pattern on it, none of that heart or fern crap.'

Hannah turned to check out who else was there and spied a fat brown lump with a waggy tail disappearing under one of the tables with a sausage roll. Excellent. Hannah loved Vera's sausage rolls almost as much as Jane Doe did. All she had to do was track down whichever Hanrahan local was handing them around.

And there the local was. Hannah helped herself to an especially tasty-looking sausage roll and dipped it in sauce. 'Did you know this was planned, Sandy?'

The vet receptionist was almost unrecognisable in her going-out gear. She'd swapped her navy Cody and Cody Vet Clinic polo shirt for a shimmery bronze blouse and she wore heels so high she towered over Hannah.

'Got the phone call this arvo. Luckily the boys had been invited to a campout in the neighbour's backyard, so I was free for once. First night out I've had in yonks.'

Hannah bumped her half-eaten sausage roll up against Sandy's champagne glass. 'Woo hoo! Are we both thinking the same thing about why we're here?'

'The bump? The flowy dresses? The daft look on your brother's face? Oh, yes, I am totally expecting an announcement.'

'You know, you really are the smartest woman in Hanrahan.'

'You bet I am.'

A cold breeze made the serviette on the plate Sandy was carrying whiffle up and down as the door opened. Hannah looked over to see who the new arrival was.

Tom.

*Pitter-pat, pitter-pat, pitter-pat* went her heart before she could shush it.

He'd changed into a collared shirt and a dark jacket, and mole-skin jeans so tight they looked like they'd been painted on with a butter knife. His hair was a little mussed, like he'd driven down the mountain with the car windows open. His eyes were pensive, like he'd been wrestling with heavy thoughts.

'You know,' said Sandy in her ear, 'Josh isn't the only Cody who's been wandering around the vet clinic with a daft expression on their face lately.'

Hannah stopped gawking at the new arrival. 'Shut up, Sandy,' she said weakly. 'I'm on call, and you know what that means.'

'No sense of humour? High degree of bitchy commentary? Sorry for all of it the next morning?'

'You know me so well.'

Sandy gave her a wink and wafted away in her silky blouse.

Hannah tried to rearrange her expression so it didn't look daft. Maybe she could swing it so she could sit next to Tom when they had dinner, because if he smelled as delicious as he looked, she didn't want to miss out.

She watched him move through the room, saying hello to Kev and to Graeme, who must have said something funny, because Tom's face lost its brooding look. He said hello to—who was that, sitting in the corner?

Holy moly, *was that her mum and dad?*

But they were on the other side of the country!

She tossed the uneaten half of her sausage roll to the dog that had emerged from the shadows to sniff for fallen bounty and raced over to throw herself on her parents.

'Hannah Banana!' said her dad.

'I cannot believe you're here. When did you arrive? Where are you staying? How long are you here for?'

Her mother, who was looking very, *very* dressed up, in a cream and gold jacket and with her hair looking like she'd just had it trimmed and streaked and blow dried, took her hands. 'We're here for two nights. The campervan's in Broome, so we had a decent airport nearby, so when Josh rang and asked us to come, we thought, why not?'

'You can stay with me if you like. I've probably even got clean sheets for the spare bed.'

'We booked ourselves in at the motel on the highway for tonight, but we'd love to spend tomorrow with you. Josh wanted us being here to be a surprise, so ...'

'Surprise!' her parents cried.

'You're looking lovely, darling one,' said her mother. 'Everything okay?'

'Yes. Why wouldn't it be?'

'No reason. We just don't see you looking so dolled up very often, do we, Bert?'

'Who's the lucky fella?' her dad said with a wink.

'Now, Bert,' her mum said.

If only the fella in question thought he was lucky. If only the fella in question wasn't still giving the world's best impression of an emotionless rock. He'd smiled at her—a neighbourly, 'hey you' smile—as she'd rushed past him to her parents and now he was at the counter chatting with Graeme, who was passing him a beer. What did the smile mean? What did him spending time with her mean?

Why did his actions, and his expressions, seem so at odds with his assertion that he wasn't interested in altering his single status?

A ting-a-ling of spoon on glass brought the roomful of chattering to an expectant hush. Josh stood in the centre of the café.

'Thank you all for coming. We have news,' he announced.

Vera was beside him, looking flushed and pretty and ... just a teensy bit plump.

'In about five months from now, Vera and I—'

Bless. Josh was getting all choked up and was having to hold onto his fiancée for support. Hannah could rib him about it later when she stopped feeling choked up herself.

'—will be welcoming a baby into the world.'

'Called it,' muttered a voice behind Hannah.

She turned and gave Sandy a wink.

'A little Cody, brother or sister to Poppy, niece or nephew to Hannah, grandchild to Bert and Amy.'

It was sweet. It was really, really sweet. It was also exactly what she would like to be announcing, only she'd do it with a little less style than her charming brother. *Mum, Dad, I'm having a baby. Some time. Probably solo. Get over it and for the love of god, don't let Marigold badger me into knitting booties.*

Although ... everything would be a whole lot easier if Tom would get off his high horse and rethink his stance. Cody-Krauss would make a heck of a surname to fill out on school excursion forms. If they had a girl, they could name her Annabel, or Laura, or Sarah. If it was a boy … She looked up from Vera's smiling face and found Tom was staring straight at her.

Yowza. She felt her cheeks get warm, and … she wasn't imagining the blistering heat in that look, was she? Had he read her thoughts?

She could have looked away, but didn't. She wanted a baby. But she also wanted Tom. Only, he didn't seem totally on board—or at all on board—with any of her wants, despite the looks and the hot hands.

Josh was still talking and Tom had turned his attention back to his friend.

Her brother. Whose night it actually was, so she should stop thinking all about herself and start celebrating a wonderful, happy moment.

'To a new Cody,' Josh said and held his drink up for a toast.

'A new Cody,' everybody chorused. Hannah held an imaginary drink up in the air because that swan-topped latte she'd been promised had not yet materialised.

'Now, don't chug all your champers down at once,' said Josh. 'Because that's not the only reason we're here. Poppy? Cue the music.'

An orchestral recording of the wedding march rang out from the café's speakers and Hannah gasped along with pretty much everyone in the room.

No way. No freaking way!

But yes way, because there was Poppy, in her humungous boots and her fifties-style dress going up to stand beside Vera with a bouquet of wildflowers in her hands and there was Marigold, puffed up like a giant, self-important mushroom in a silvery-grey caftan, looking officious and regal, joining them.

'We didn't want any fuss,' said Josh. 'We just wanted everyone we love to be here. And that's you guys. We hope you'll all stay to witness us taking our vows.'

Bloody hell, now Hannah really was crying, and so was her mother.

'Did you have any idea this was going to happen?' she whispered to her parents.

'Your mother suspected. That's why she had her hair done and spent two hundred dollars on a new top,' Bert said.

Her mother shushed him. 'I didn't want to look a fright in case there were photographs,' she said.

Of course people would take photographs. In fact—Hannah looked about the room—there were phones in everyone's hands. But she could be cool about it. She had to be cool about it. Despite the fact no-one had given her even a teensy hint to wear a scarf, or a low-slung beret, or a balaclava.

This was not about her.

'We are gathered here today,' began Marigold, 'to celebrate a marriage between two of our favourite people: Josh Cody, who I have known since he was a young menace who loved to ride his BMX down Dandaloo Street and do wheelies to show off in front of the tourists, and Vera De Rossi, who has become a dear friend to me and Kev, and to all of us here this evening.'

Hannah let the words wash over her. Josh was getting married. Right this very minute.

His world was bounding forward just the way he wanted it to.

So why couldn't it be her turn next?

# CHAPTER
## 31

What came after weddings?

Dancing, that's what, and the dance she'd been enjoying at the Shaw Winery had been cut rudely short by that idiot ex-boyfriend who had gone on to wreck her evening. Well—he wasn't here in The Billy Button Café, and if he turned up, she was pretty sure Graeme was buff enough to chuck him out.

Luckily, she knew the DJ and could put in requests, and even luckier, she knew what Tom liked to dance to.

'Poppy. We need a slowish song so people don't get exhausted too soon.'

'No way! I have a whole playlist of sick beats, Auntie Hannah.'

'That's fine for you sixteen-year-old rebels, but we're—' what was the phrase Poppy had used? '—geriatric dinosaurs. We need a slow one from time to time. Give us some Michael Bublé.'

'That's gonna cost you.'

'Chocolate? Money? One of my kidneys?'

Poppy grinned. 'You take me to visit Maximus while I'm here.'

'You drive a hard bargain.' And a totally sweet one! Max was from Jane Doe's litter and he'd gone to live with a young family on a farm on the outskirts of Cooma. 'I accept. Make it that "Feeling Good" one.'

By the time the first line about birds and sun and feelings was oozing out of the speaker, she had Tom's arm under her hand. 'Dance?' she said.

Sandy, who had been talking to Tom, took one look at Hannah's face and melted away.

'Um … I'm not really a—'

'Don't bullshit me, Krauss. I know you can dance, and this one is slow and waltzy.'

It was bloodwarming and hot as, too, she thought, as he quit arguing and put his hand in the small of her back.

'A new life,' she said.

He leant his head down a little closer. 'Excuse me?'

'I was quoting the lyrics,' she said. 'Feeling good, a new life … it's making me think.'

His hand tightened momentarily around hers as they weaved their way past Kev and Marigold, who were sliding a few spins and fancy turns into their dance routine.

'Show-offs.'

She felt more than heard Tom's laugh. 'Marigold was probably a dance instructor in a former life. You know, somewhere in between the yoga and the florist shop and the celebrant and the town busybody.'

'They're an unlikely couple, aren't they?' she said.

'How do you mean?'

'Well, Marigold is like a power station, all noise and energy, whereas Kev is more of a quiet thinker.'

'I guess.'

'What would you say—' she took a breath '—if we decided to become a couple?'

The music hadn't stopped but Tom's feet had.

'Well?' she said. She could hear an insistent buzz, like one of the speakers had a wire loose.

'We talked about this. I told you I wasn't interested in a relationship.'

'But that was before, when I was hung up on a baby, and I hadn't understood what I was feeling …' she tapped her chest, '… in here.'

'This was a mistake,' he said.

'No, you don't mean that. You—' Shoot, that wasn't a wire loose. It was her phone, buzzing away via the watch she wore on her wrist. As much as she didn't want to check the words flashing on the screen, she couldn't not check.

'It's the clinic's after hours number,' she said. 'I have to take this.'

The calf didn't make it.

No fault of the farmer. Breeding out of season happened, bad births happened and sometimes the calf just wasn't strong enough, no matter how much Hannah hoped they would be. No matter how many hours the mother cow laboured and bellowed and pushed.

She covered the small animal with a hessian sack and returned her attention to the cow. 'I know, darling one, it's awful for you. All that time growing your little one and now you have nothing. I'm sorry.'

The farmer, a big burly brute with an oilskin coat over bright red flannel pyjamas, had wet eyes. 'Poor little bugger,' he said. 'I've a special place where I put the ones who don't make it. Snow in winter and wildflowers in summer make a pretty headstone, I reckon.'

She had to swallow, hard, at that lovely image. She was the professional here and professionals didn't get weepy over farmers with a turn for the poetic.

'It's your cow we need to think about now, Phil. I can give her an injection to dry up the milk since she's not dairy stock, but we need to wait until the placenta arrives and make sure there's no prolapse. If she's been in labour since nightfall, she's going to be exhausted, so let's keep her calm and quiet. I can sit with her if you need to get some sleep.'

'We'll sit together, love,' he said. 'You want a stool or something?'

Kylie's dress was never going to be the same now, no matter what she sat on. 'This hay is good enough for me, Phil,' she said, sitting on the floor and putting her back to the wall. Thank heavens she'd stopped long enough to switch out her idiot heels for her boots and grab an anorak. The temperature wasn't quite low enough to have frost on the ground, but when she'd got out of her hatchback, her breath had hung white in the air.

'The wife'll be over soon with a cuppa for us, I expect.'

'That'd be mighty welcome, Phil.'

It wasn't quite dawn when Hannah judged the cow to be out of danger, but to the east, a grey cast lightened the night sky. She was very, very cold and as she coaxed her car's reluctant engine into life and stabbed uselessly at the buttons that had once worked the heater, she looked in the rear-vision mirror. The farmer and his stout, steely-haired wife had their arms around each other, lifting their hands in a joint farewell.

That's what she wanted. Arms that would go around her because they wanted her there, not because she'd persuaded them into it.

Arms that would still be there when she was old and stout and wore red flannel pyjamas.

She'd spent all these years thinking 'for keeps' wasn't for her, because that would make her vulnerable, and she couldn't risk the crash that would come if it all failed. The last time she'd discovered what risk led to she'd curled into a dark corner and forced a bottle's worth of sleeping pills down her throat. But now?

Now she felt strong. Now, she felt like all she had to do was give herself permission to release the handbrake.

It had been a stable very like Phil's where Tom had kissed her and it had felt as though he'd woken her from a deep sleep. Everything that had happened afterwards—training Skipjack, getting involved with campdraft, even punching the camera out of that poor man's hand—had been the New Hannah finally waking up.

Hannah didn't stop at the clinic when she drove back to Hanrahan. Instead, she turned up Gorge Road and willed her decrepit little car to make it another forty minutes up the mountain to Ironbark Station.

She killed her headlights before approaching the house and parked to the side, out of the way, so none of the ringers up for the dawn shift would see her car and wonder why the vet was here.

She'd finally worked it out. The catalyst for change was not about forgiving the dickheads in her past. The change had come when she worked out she needed to forgive herself. She'd made some mistakes along the way. The overdose when she was eighteen. The half-baked plan to acquire donor sperm from Tom. The idea that a baby would salve her lonely heart.

That had been a cop-out. Worse, it had sent Tom very weird messages. He may not even know what she felt for him. She certainly didn't know what he felt for her.

She just knew she wanted to find out.

Right now, while the memories of that cup of tea and the waving, flannel-pyjamaed, loved-up farmers were showing her what was really important.

# CHAPTER

## 32

Of course, the front door was shut. But was it locked? The station was miles from anywhere and its value was in the animals in the stables, not anything tucked away in the homestead.

She tried the handle, and the door creaked its way open.

The corridor was dark, but god had invented the torch app for just this occasion, surely, so she flicked it on, hauled off her stinking boots and headed in. She knew where Tom's room was—at least, she knew where it had been twenty years or so ago when she short-sheeted his bed as retaliation for the frog-in-boot incident—so she made her way there, socks sliding silently on the polished hoop pine planks.

'Tom?' She whispered his name, scratching at the door with her fingernails. 'Tom? It's Hannah.'

No sound, no movement. Crap, she couldn't just barge on in—could she? Sure, she'd barged into the house uninvited, but—

Was that a noise?

'Tom,' she whispered again, only a little louder. She went for a soft *rat-a-tat-tat* this time.

A light flickered on under the door.

She waited and, a moment later, the door swung open. There he was, not—disappointingly—in red flannel pyjamas, but in grey tracksuit pants and a dark blue t-shirt that hugged ribs and abs and pecs. His feet were bare and his hair rumpled, and he had stubble on his face that glinted in the soft glow of the lamp.

Yellow vials littered his bedside table and a paperback lay on the floor and—

'Hannah? What on earth? Is everything okay?'

She swallowed. Now or never. 'We didn't finish our conversation. Tell me, if I was out in the stable at three am, would you bring me a cup of tea?'

'You want a cup of freaking *tea*? What time is it, anyway?'

'It's—look, I can't conduct this conversation at a shouty-whisper in your hallway. Can I come into your room?'

He stepped back with obvious reluctance.

She waited until the door was shut before continuing, 'My question is not meant to be taken literally, but symbolically, and I would like an answer.'

He rubbed his hands over his head and turned back to his bed, but he must have thought better of getting back into it, because he pulled the doona up, knocking over the contents of his bedside table in the process, and picked up his watch. 'Five o'clock. Holy shit.'

'Well?'

He dropped into a wingback chair with a groan. 'If it means I can go back to bed, then yes, Hannah, if you were in my stable at three am, I guess I'd make you a cup of tea.'

She smiled. 'That, Tom, is the correct answer.'

He was looking wary and wide awake now. 'Have you been on call all night?'

'Yes, and the second I was done, I headed here. Tom … I want to talk about being a couple.' With matching pyjamas, but that part could come later.

'Hannah, we already talked about this.'

'But all of our previous conversations have had a shadow looming over them because I clued you in on the fact that I want to have a baby. I've been thinking, what about if I shelve my baby plan for a time? You and I could—you know—have a crack at the sort of relationship other people have. And you don't need to be frightened off by thinking I'm expecting babies and weddings and all that fluffy guff, because I'm prepared to put my dream aside.'

*For you*, she wanted to say. She'd put anything and everything aside for Tom.

He was staring at her, and he'd gone full broody. 'I'm not frightened of fluffy guff, whatever that means. But I'm not relationship material, Hannah.'

'What does that even *mean*? I know we have something together, Tom. I feel it every time you touch me.'

'You're mistaken.'

'I bloody well am not. URST, Kylie calls it. And you and me, Krauss, have it.'

'URST?'

'Unresolved sexual tension.'

'Jesus,' he muttered and the adrenalin that had been humming in Hannah's veins since she drove away from Phil's farm with a heart full of love spiked. Kylie was right. This URST stuff was unmissable when you knew what to look for. The room practically buzzed with it.

'So,' she said breathlessly. 'What say we resolve some of it? See where it takes us. No commitments or anything scary like that, just you, Tom. And me.' She took a step closer to him and started undoing the buttons of her borrowed dress with a shaking hand.

# CHAPTER

# 33

Scotch was a bad idea for breakfast, but Tom needed one.

Badly.

Crisis number one: Hannah Cody had arrived at his bedroom door, at dawn, and made a pass at him.

And he'd sent her away. She'd shuffled off down the corridor in her ridiculous socks and her borrowed black dress that had been covered in hay and something that smelled really, really bad, and her shoulders had been drooped so low he'd wanted to throw himself at her feet and have her stomp him into little pieces on the way out.

Hannah Cody wanted him.

He let that thought swill about in his head for a moment.

Life sucked.

His, in particular. Especially now, when he had a team of neurosurgeons warning him that the use of his legs was hanging by a thread—literally. So, yeah, when the woman he'd been in love with for more than half of his life finally worked out he could be The One? That was a reason for scotch if ever he'd heard one.

He opted for milk instead, and sploshed it onto muesli which he pretty much expected would taste like dirt, because why would anything good ever happen in his life now?

He pressed a finger to the crease between his eyebrows that he would have sworn wasn't there yesterday. He needed to burn the memory of today out of his brain.

He sucked in a breath. Okay, maybe he didn't want to forget the whole memory. That moment when Hannah had said she wanted him … yeah, that he was happy to remember, even if the ache was as sweet as it was bitter.

But her look of desolation when he'd turned her down.

That was a memory that could burn.

# CHAPTER
## 34

Monday morning at the Cody and Cody Vet Clinic began quietly, for which Hannah was beyond grateful. She was wrecked.

No sleep, a calf fatality and a broken heart could do that to a girl.

Sandy had dragged herself in the door five minutes late, heavy-eyed and full of apologies, but also bearing takeaway coffee and a batch of pinwheel sticky buns from the bakery near her home.

The two of them were collapsed on chairs in the back office when the elephant tread of Josh on the stairwell announced his arrival. He had a hangover, for which he was unapologetic.

'I'm drinking for two now,' he said, as he chugged down two paracetamol, a rehydration tablet that dissolved into fizzy water the colour of one of the urine samples sitting in their bloods fridge, and two sticky buns.

'How many patients are booked in, does anyone know?' said Hannah. 'I'd look myself, but I'm too tired to boot up the computer.'

'Why are you tired?' said Josh. 'You didn't get married last night and dance until dawn. Remind me to schedule a day off afterwards next time I decide to get hitched.'

'I'll be sure to let Vera know you're already planning your next one.'

'Now, now, sourpuss. Did you get called out? Is that why you disappeared?'

'The Waterhouse place. Calving. Took hours and didn't go well. I haven't written it up yet.' She could add that to the list of jobs she felt too tired to deal with.

'Oh, Han, I'm sorry.'

'We've a cat due in to have stitches removed, a few vaccinations and then a busy window with both of you booked between two and four,' said Sandy, who'd pulled the keyboard in her direction and logged into their system.

'Why don't you go get some sleep?' Josh said to Hannah. 'I'll cover us until two. I can probably do all day if Sandy can juggle the afternoon bookings around a bit.'

'What about Mum and Dad? They're coming over today.'

'They can hang out with me. You'll just frighten them away if they see you now.'

'Gee, thanks. I thought you were the charming one.'

'Not anymore. I've bagged my bride and now I can settle down into a life of tactless misogyny and rampant ball scratching.'

Hannah snorted and Sandy gave a giggle. Josh was an idiot, but he knew how to cheer her up.

'Okay. Thanks. I'll hit the doona for a bit and then maybe we could do lunch with the oldies at noon.'

'It's a plan.' Josh got to his feet as the bell on the front door sent a melodious dong through the ground floor. 'Look alive, Sandy; it's you and me this morning, and that sounds like our first customer of the day.'

Hannah didn't think she'd sleep.

She lay on the doona with an ancient, marshmallow-soft quilt dragged over her and indulged in miserable thoughts about herself.

What specifically had been the problem between her and Tom?

What specifically had been the thing about her that put him off?

She was snippety a lot. She didn't wear fancy clothes, or brush her hair as often as she should, and she worked pretty much seven days a week. And of course she wasn't without her complications: she wanted a baby, desperately, and she had that difficulty-with-new-places problem she was working on. And the being photographed thing, let's not forget that one.

Okay, she was a lot to take on.

She huffed and smacked her pillow a bit and lay down again, but still, no sleep. She eyed the stack of library and fertility books on her bedside table, but even the burly thighs of the Laird of Finch-more held no appeal.

She must have drifted off, because the next thing she knew, she was waking up with her face smooshed into her pillow and a heavy lump of brown fur snoring on her feet.

'Is that you, Jane Doe?'

A tail wag shook the bed, assuring her that it was, indeed, her brother's ancient labrador. How she'd made it up to the top floor was a mystery. Determination and an appreciation for a good feather doona, probably.

Hannah opened a bleary eye and examined her watch until the face swam into focus. Eleven thirty! She'd better get up and at 'em if she was going to make it to lunch with the oldies.

She was halfway into an ancient pair of jeans when she caught sight of herself in her bedroom mirror. The underwear she'd thrown on was clean but tatty and one of her bra straps had lost its elastic-ity so her boobs were lopsided. Her knickers were probably even older than the jeans and they sagged at the back in a spectacularly unattractive fashion.

Maybe this was part of the problem. If she didn't value herself, why would other people—not just Tom! There were other people besides Tom!—value her? All they saw was some chick in scrubs who had a way with animals and some demented social habits.

The underwear situation could be remedied by a visit to the Big W in Cooma. No biggie, she'd been there plenty in the quiet last hour of late night shopping. And it would be no biggie if the place was buzzing when she visited, she reminded herself. She had wider horizons now. She was practically an adventuress.

She did own better clothes than the ones she habitually wore. They weren't new, of course, they just weren't often worn. Kylie had shaken them out and hung them closer to reach and all Hannah had to do was choose them.

Okay, then. A navy dress with white polka dots. It was swirly and possibly a little summery for the late autumn day outside, but she had thick navy tights and a pair of boots, didn't she?

A denim jacket. Her amber earrings again (thank you, Josh) and— what the hell—she found a lipstick in her top drawer that, when she put it on, looked awesome. Some of Kylie's magic to hide the vicious black rings under her eyes would have been useful, but alas.

She brushed her hair out and left it loose for the first time in about a year, to distract from how wrecked she looked. It had grown down to nearly waist level and the edges were a little uneven, but a quick snip with her nail scissors sorted that out.

The Billy Button Café had the usual lunchtime crowd, and Graeme and two waitstaff had the place humming.

Her parents were seated in one of the booths with a view through the windows over the lake, and they looked to have been there a while. Newspapers, latte glasses with the remains of chocolate powder clinging to their rims and maps lay spread out in front of them.

She slid into the booth opposite them and gave them each a kiss. 'Sorry to ditch you this morning. I didn't get much sleep last night.'

'No problem, darling. We've had a lovely time catching up with everyone. This place has become the hub of town—we haven't had to leave our booth and we've heard everything and talked to everyone.'

'Graeme's been looking after you, I see,' she said, inspecting an empty plate that held suspicious-looking remnants that might have been from the plum crumble tart. Her favourite.

'That man,' her mum said, blushing girlishly.

Hannah chuckled. 'Look out, Dad. Mum's got a crush on the barista.'

Her dad grunted, unfazed. 'What's this Maureen's writing about you taking up campdraft?'

'What?'

'Here.'

He pulled a sheet of newsprint out from the clutter of stuff on the table and spun it around so she could see it. Of course. The Hanrahan Chatter.

THERE'S MOVEMENT AT IRONBARK STATION (FINALLY) *by Maureen Plover*
*You're reading it here first, folks … the Hanrahan Pub is having its dust sheets ripped off, its garden beds replanted and its fridges restocked. A van belonging to handyman team Sharon and Darryl Rodgers has been spotted outside every day for two weeks, so this is not rumour. This is fact! I have seen it with my own eyes!*

*It's wonderful what a little community pressure can do: The Chatter asked why the heir to the Krauss family was spending all his time sitting on his arse drinking coffee when he could be helping this town out and whackadoo! Not only is the Ironbark Campdraft back on, but the pub with no beer looks like it's on track to be open again before the big event.*

*Roger Kettering from the Snowy Monaro Campdraft Association tells The Chatter that the prizes on offer at Ironbark include not only service fees and horse feed, but the real drawcard will be the legend himself, Bruno Krauss, judging the Open 1 and Open 2 rounds, for which he has donated his campdraft championship belt buckles, to be awarded to the winners.*

*Hanrahan and the surrounding region has plenty of talent in camp-drafting: Fraser Oxley and Dana Baxter are regulars on the circuit, as is Coralie Moon. We expect Hanrahan local and newbie campdrafter, Hannah Cody, will be competing and maybe the heir of Ironbark Station himself might throw his leg over a saddle and see if he's inherited any of his father's legendary skills.*

Huh. As though she'd be competing now. As though she'd go within ten kilometres of Ironbark Station now.

'Is it true, Hannah? Have you been doing campdrafting?' Her mother's eyes were shining like Hannah had just solved the world's methane problem.

She shrugged. 'I've done one competition down in Dalgety. There was another one I was booked in for, but it was cancelled due to rain. Skippy's a natural, and he loves the training. It's … something to do.'

Her dad was looking ridiculously pleased, too. 'It's great, Hannah. Just great.'

'Dad, it's just a hobby. Nothing to get emotional about.'

'We can come back for Ironbark's campdraft and see you in action.'

'What a great idea,' said her mother. 'I could get team t-shirts made!'

This had to be nipped in the bud. Hannah was just about to let them know she had no intention of riding in the campdraft when her mother plucked a tissue out of her purse and started dabbing at her eyeliner.

'Mum. Don't get like this.'

'I'm sorry, darling. Don't worry, these are happy tears. We just love to see you involved, and getting out and about, and—'

'Don't read too much into it, Mum, please. It's a hobby. I'm not that serious about it.'

'But, darling, you're mentioned in the paper and everything—'

Her dad must have nudged her mother's foot under the table, because she broke off and frowned at him.

'We're happy if you're happy,' her dad said firmly. 'Isn't that right, Amy?'

Her mother gave her eyes a last dab and pushed the crumpled tissue up the sleeve of her cardigan. 'Yes, dear. Why don't you text that son of yours and his lovely wife and see if they're ready for some lunch.'

'Good idea,' said Hannah. She'd had just about enough of the lunchtime conversation being about her. 'I'm going to the bathroom.'

She was in the stall, regretting the amount of chiffony fabric she was having to deal with, when she realised that she wasn't quite done with having to listen to conversations about her.

'Is it true?' said a voice.

Kylie! Oh, goody, hopefully she could join them for lunch. Her parents were as fond of Kylie as Hannah was. She was about to call out when she heard another voice.

'I'm not sure, but we might not be able to count on Tom helping us with our Hannah intervention any longer.'

Oh, right. She'd forgotten the only reason Tom had asked her to get involved with the campdraft was because the Hanrahan locals had asked him to. Maybe that's why he'd said yes when she invited him to the races.

Maybe that's all she'd been to him: a duty. A favour to others.

And who was that out there with Kylie anyway? Marigold?

She had to decide whether to piddle quietly and eavesdrop or slam out the door noisily and confront them. She opted for the slam.

Two pairs of eyes looked at her like wallabies frozen by headlights.

'Little Hannah,' said Marigold, recovering first.

Kylie looked like she was about to do a runner.

'Your intervention is officially at an end. I'm no longer volunteering at the campdraft.'

'Shoot. What happened?'

She frowned at Marigold. 'You know everything around here, Marigold. Why don't you tell Kylie what happened.'

'Now, pet,' said Marigold majestically. 'All I know is that Tom called me to say we should delay the volunteer meeting scheduled for Thursday. He said you and he had some stuff to clear up first.'

'Huh.'

'But, of course, I saw Valerie LaBrooy at the IGA, and she told me she'd seen you coming out of Tom's room before dawn this morni—'

'What!' breathed Kylie.

'—ing, and she felt that the mood was, um, grim. Tom didn't appear for breakfast.'

Bloody hell. Hannah had thought she'd got in and out undetected.

'So, my love, when I saw you come into the café looking sad, I put two and two together and called Kylie into my office here so we could have a little confab.'

Hannah closed her eyes. 'I am an adult. I can deal with my own shit.'

Silence.

She opened her eyes and they were both looking at her, Kylie with what seemed awfully like pity, and Marigold with understanding. Ha! As though Marigold had ever had her actions gossiped about and workshopped and confabbed!

'Okay, fine, I do not have a wonderful track record of dealing with my own shit. But you know what? If you lot keep stepping in and saving me from myself, when am I going to learn?'

Marigold wrapped her in a leopard-print embrace. 'When you put it like that, it makes a lot of sense, my lamb.'

'It does?' She pushed her way through the folds of caftan until she could see again. 'And yes, so you can all stop wondering, I laid my heart bare to Tom and he turned me down. He's not interested, so I told him to go screw himself and that is that.'

'I'm so sorry, Han,' said Kylie, coming in for a hug too, but Hannah took a step back. 'What? Don't you forgive us?'

Hannah looked in the mirror and adjusted her polka-dotted blue dress. Her hair looked awesome, reddish and neat and wavy like a freaking movie star's. Her lipstick was only slightly smudged and she fixed that with a fingernail that was also awesome, and clean, and smelled nothing like animal innards. She hauled up her knickers so they didn't sag, fiddled with her bra strap so her boobs were even, then smiled at herself in the mirror.

'You two, I forgive. Josh and Vera and Kev, I forgive. I may forgive Graeme if he crawls over broken glass and sobs at my feet and ensures I never have to wait in a line of tourists for a latte ever again.'

'And Tom?' said Kylie, her eyebrows raised nearly to her hairline.

'Tom is dead to me from this day forward.' Actually he'd been dead to her since dawn, but she couldn't work out how to get that into her sentence without it losing its punch.

And with a dramatic swish of her skirts (which was also awesome) she marched off.

# CHAPTER
# 35

Tom let himself in through the side door of the pub, hoping for a quiet hour or two in the office. The café he was avoiding, but there were teabags in the pub kitchen and that would do.

He was looking forward to reading through the latest applications for pub manager; it would be a welcome respite from thinking about his dawn visitor. So would starting up a file for each of his dad's properties and making a checklist of insurance policies and bank accounts.

Unexciting but totally safe, unemotional busywork. He'd just about had enough of emotions for one week.

The day was too chilly to open a window and there was no kindling on the premises yet so he couldn't light a fire in either of the pub's fireplaces, so he left his jacket on. The sky he could see through the office window had all the warmth and colour of mortician's putty, which matched his mood precisely.

'I think we need some distance,' he'd said to Hannah after he told the biggest bloody lie of his life: that he had no interest in her suggestion that they become a couple. 'I've got a lot on my plate. Dad, his business interests. The campdraft.'

She hadn't believed him so he'd added the clincher: 'I don't really have time for babysitting my best friend's little sister at social engagements.'

That was when she'd stormed off. Crying.

He'd spent the time since fighting the urge to text her to see if she was okay. She would be okay. She'd be better than okay. As soon as she moved on and got him out of her life.

And now it was time for him to move on. He had to focus on building a life to come back to after his surgery: one that he could live no matter how the surgery ended.

He lifted the lid on his laptop and scrolled through his emails, pausing at one that had come through late last night.

*I am interested in applying for the position of General Manager at the Hanrahan Pub.*

❧

He was two mugs of tea into the morning when a hammering at the front door of the pub disturbed him. Sharon and Darryl had their own key; perhaps it was the new commercial oven being delivered.

It wasn't.

It was Benjamin Dorley. Thinner, but with clear eyes. His mouth still had a faint downturn on one side, but he was standing on his own two feet and carrying a small briefcase.

'Hello. You're looking better than I saw you last.'

'I wondered if it was you who found me. I'm afraid I have zero memory of that day.'

'So it was a stroke, then?'

'Yeah. The doctors reckon the quicker you get to a hospital, the better the outcome, so I have you to thank for that.'

'No worries, mate. I've got your keys here; let me go find them.'

'Actually—there's something I wanted to talk over with you. Can I come in?'

'Er, sure. There's no heating. I've cleared some space in the office so we can talk in there.'

Benjamin sat in the chair on the opposite side of the desk and didn't say anything for a moment or two, so Tom decided to kick things off.

'That kid you had doing office experience. He was keen to get a reference from you.'

'Alex,' said Benjamin with a faint smile. 'He came to see me in the hospital. His mother's a distant cousin of mine somewhere on the family tree. He'll get his reference.'

Tom pulled open his desk drawer and took out the keys to Dorley's office. 'I haven't been back since I collected those archive boxes. Alex lugged them round here for me.'

'That's what I wanted to talk to you about.'

'Your office?'

'I—well. The thing is, Tom, I didn't know you were a lawyer.'

'That's because I'm not a practising one. I have a law degree and I've done the minimum post-admission legal experience, but that was all through the Navy. I haven't worked in a legal office for years.'

'I've got something for you. Had to get the ladies at the library to print it up for me. Technology isn't really my forte—the wife did all that sort of stuff at the office and when she left, well, that's when things became difficult.'

'Control P,' Tom murmured.

'Excuse me?'

'Nothing, sorry.' He accepted the folded piece of paper Benjamin had taken from his attaché case. 'What's this?'

'It's an application form for the course you need to get an unrestricted practising certificate. Maybe three days, something like that? That's what us lawyers need in New South Wales to run our own business.'

'No, wait, I'm not—' He paused. He wasn't what? Looking for a future? Capable of attending a three-day sit-down course that involved zero physical capability beyond wielding a pen and a computer keyboard? 'Three days? Is that all it takes?'

'The form has some options. You can do it at the University of New South Wales in thirty hours, mostly online, just one day has to be there in person.'

He'd had no idea. 'Wait. Aren't *you* the local solicitor? Why are you telling me this?'

'I'm retiring. I should have retired when Joan took off, but I didn't and I've been providing terrible service for every client since then. I can pass my clients over to one of the solicitors in Cooma or I could pass them to you. Of course, if you wanted to take over my lease, I'd be thrilled. It has another six months to run, but since you know the owner of the building, you could probably get it extended.'

'Krauss Holdings, huh?'

'Yep.'

It was a lot to think about. Was now the right time? What if his surgery, whenever it happened, was a disaster?

'There's no lift in your building, is there?'

'No. It's on the heritage register, too, so retrofitting one would be troublesome. Why? Is that a problem?'

Quite possibly, yes, but he wasn't admitting that to anyone. 'When do you need an answer?'

'I'm going to spend a few hours in at the office tidying stuff up, calling clients, shutting down accounts, that sort of thing. Shall we say a week?'

He held out his hand and shook Benjamin's. 'A week it is.'

'And if you do decide to take over, I'd like to be your first client. Turns out I have a property settlement to attend to now that my wife has left me; ignoring it has just pissed her off and I have a hall table covered in vicious letters from some legal turkey in Brisbane.'

'Ouch.'

'Yeah.'

He walked Benjamin to the front of the building and then went and sat in the office chair again, swinging it from side to side while he inspected the weeds in the planter box. One of them had a little yellow flower on it, a bright speck in the otherwise drab box.

*Tom Krauss, Publican and Lawyer.*

Huh. Maybe that wouldn't look totally awful engraved on a brass plaque by the front door of the pub.

# CHAPTER
# 36

May began with storms that growled through the Snowies in the dark of night, leaving snowfall in their wake. Tonight's storm felt like it had begun in the Old Testament. Thunder drummed through the valleys like an avenging army on the march and forks of lightning speared the mountain peaks.

It matched Tom's mood. So did the rain, which had brought a false dusk with it. He was supposed to be down in town, holding the postponed meeting for the Ironbark Campdraft volunteers, but Bruno had told him to cancel it.

'That sky's turned ugly, son. It's not a night to be on the road.'

No matter. He could email the volunteers just as easily, and it saved him the regret of staring at Hannah's empty chair for the duration of the meeting. Two weeks had passed since he'd listened to her hurt intake of breath and they were back to being strangers who gave one another remote nods as they passed.

Tom flicked the heater switch on in the main stables, then made his way through the rain to Buttercup. Lynette's second-in-command stood by the mare, running a brush over her broad sides so she gleamed in the low light.

'Bill. You get along home before this storm gets any worse. Anything else needs doing, I can manage.'

'Don't mind if I do, Tom. Lynette's sent the others home and she's off mountain tonight. Some graduation thing for her kid down in Melbourne, so I'm the last one. Those clouds have been building up something fierce. Hope it rolls around us and not through.'

'Weather bureau wasn't too bad, but Bruno's forecasting a doozy.'

Bill nodded. 'My money's on your old man. He knows these mountains better than anyone.'

'True enough.'

'Mate, the heating will need to go on in the stables tonight, I'm thinking. Temperature's dropped about ten degrees the last hour.'

'I just switched it on.'

'Harper's poultice hasn't been changed yet.'

'I can do that.'

'Feed's done, water's done, paddock gates are locked.'

Tom clapped Bill on the back. 'Go home, mother hen. I know I've not been around much, but I was shovelling shit in these stables when I was three.'

Bill handed him the brush. 'Yes, boss.'

Boss. Huh. That was the first time any of the ringers had called him that. It felt a little odd after all those years being addressed as sir or lieutenant commander. It also felt like acceptance.

He was heating the poultice when his phone buzzed.

'Boss? It's Bill.'

'You still here? I thought I told you to go home.'

'I'm trying. Got to the turn-off from the mountain and there's a lot of debris on the road. Dead wood's come down and the wind's blowing it every which way.'

'We'll get a crew out in the morning.'

'Yeah, but that ain't the worst of it.'

'Yes?'

'There's an oak down over the main gate out to Gorge Road. It'll need a tractor and chainsaw to clear it, so I went cross country aways to Barker Road, but the stream's up. I got through, but I shouldn't have tried. Even in the big Ford I slid sideways so bad I was wondering what my wife would be telling everyone about me in her eulogy. Road musta been washed out beneath the water. There's no-one getting through that until this rain's done.'

'Bill, are you okay? Is your truck okay?'

'I'm fine, but the road up to Ironbark is blocked every which way.'

Hell. Please, god, don't let Buttercup go into an early labour tonight.

'Thanks, Bill. You get home safe before anything else goes wrong. Call me when you get there, all right?'

'You got it, boss.'

Tucking up the horses took longer than Tom had expected; the wind had unsettled them, so he lingered, stroked a few ears, gave a few reassuring words as he tidied everything away. By the time he made his way out of the stables, the trees beyond the home paddock were being whipped by the wind and leaf fall scudded over the gravel paths. The horses would be restless, but they'd be safe.

The wind carried the first bullets of rain with it, which stung his face. When he got back, he'd do some work then sit by the fire and think through the mad idea of setting up a legal practice. A small-town country practice: wills and conveyances and estate planning. He'd need to do a lot of reading, maybe some courses to bring his knowledge up to date, and that sounded the opposite of exciting. Which, actually, made it just about perfect. Excitement was overrated.

A flicker and a crack like automatic gunfire made his heart nearly leap out of his chest when he was halfway between the stables and the house. What the hell? He spun awkwardly on his bad leg just as sheet lightning flickered, showing him the old gum tree in the home paddock alight. If it had been dry, the lightning strike could have set off a bushfire that would threaten the whole mountain, but there was no chance of that tonight.

He kept his eyes on the paddock as he went up the homestead steps. The fire was doused already by the rain that was icy and sharp and almost, but not quite, snow. He shook off his oilskin and hung it on the hooks by the door, but before he could get his hand on the latch, the door opened.

'Tom? Honey?'

Mrs L must have been on the watch for him, and her voice had a quaver in it that wasn't just age, but also alarm. The housekeeper's face was in shadow against the light of the hall and she was clutching her cardigan close against the wind that was whipping past him down the hall.

'Everything's fine, Mrs L. Lightning took out a tree, that's all. Let's get this door closed,' he said.

'I've messed up,' she said. 'I'm so sorry.'

Now he'd shut the wind out and his eyes were no longer stinging from the whip of ice and leaf litter, he could see she was crying. He held her plump hand in his. 'Mrs L! You could never mess up. What's wrong?'

'It's your father.'

'Is he all right?'

She dragged her hand out of his and wiped the tears from her cheeks. 'For now. But he's been using his mask a lot the last few days, and I just went to the storeroom to bring out a new oxygen bottle, because the one he's got will be empty in an hour or so … but, oh, Tom! There's two in there, but they're both empty. I always have a spare, always—the MediGas crew deliver them once a week—but I must have messed up my order.'

No oxygen. And a long night ahead with a power outage likely and a frail man with emphysema totally reliant on him and Mrs L. 'I'll go now,' Tom said. 'If the clinic in Hanrahan is out, I'll stop by the Ambulance Depot.'

Mrs LaBrooy clutched his arm. 'I hate to see you driving in this weather. The roads will be treacherous.'

'It's fine, I'll be care—' *Fuck.* The road was cut. By a tree and flash flooding and god knew what else.

'What is it, Tom?'

He rubbed his hands through his hair. 'Bill had trouble getting out of here. The road's cut.'

'Oh, god. Oh, Tom. Bruno's going to die without oxygen and it will be my fault.' Her face crumpled and she slumped into the wall.

'Mrs L, this is not your fault. I'm here, aren't I? There was nothing stopping me checking we had plenty of oxygen and I didn't do it either, did I?'

'But I'm the one here to look after you.'

He hugged her. 'And that's what you're doing right now, looking after us. Let's go into the kitchen and put the kettle on and get a plan going. We're isolated up here, but we're not on the moon. We'll find a way.'

Mrs LaBrooy gave a gasp. 'We could call a medevac helicopter.'

'In this wind?' Tom knew Navy helicopter pilots who'd flown through gunfire and tornadoes, and even they wouldn't be able to land on his back paddock in this storm. In the dark, no landing lights, no windsocks? 'No, helicopters are out.'

'We call the ambulance,' she said. 'You can ride down to where the road's cut and meet them.'

Yeah. That was an excellent idea. Too bad he couldn't get on a horse without running the risk of severing his spinal column. That plan had to be the last resort. 'Does Dad know there's a problem?'

'Not yet. He's been very sleepy today. I've set him up by the television in his room, but he's not in a good way.'

Christ. 'Okay. Let me make a few calls. You want to make a pot of tea for us while I'm on the phone?'

'Of course.'

He watched her bustle off through the house. Though he'd be grateful for the tea, keeping Mrs L busy was the real benefit. Busy got in the way of worrying. He'd learned that lesson right here in Hanrahan.

He pulled his phone out of his pocket and realised he knew exactly who to call.

Josh picked up on the third ring. 'Tom. Hello, mate. What's up?'

'I need help.'

'Anything. What can I do?'

'You still know how to ride a horse?'

'Last time I checked. Bit late for trail rides, isn't it?'

'We're in trouble.'

'What, now? Tom, I'm—'

'Dad's going to be out of oxygen in a few hours and the road's shut. We need a bottle brought up the mountain and it's horseback or nothing.'

His friend's breath made a whoosh through his earpiece. 'Tom, I'm in Sydney.'

'What?'

'Poppy's won a prize at a student art exhibition. Vera and I were making a long weekend of it, treating it as a mini honeymoon. Can't you get the old man medevacced out?'

Tom closed his eyes. 'There's a storm here, Josh. No-one's lifting off in this weather.'

'There's a guy I know works for the Air Ambulance out of Canberra, they service the Snowies. Bill Hooper. He's a good guy.'

'It doesn't matter how ace your flyboy is, Josh. There's a storm overhead feels like hell's just upended its dirty laundry over us. Road's flooded and the gate's been crushed by a giant oak. There's branches and debris blowing all over the paddocks. There's no helicopter getting in here at the moment.'

'Hell, man.'

'Yeah. I was thinking you could pick me up some oxygen and tow a horse float as far as the floodwater, then take a horse up the bridle trail to the east of the road. Drink a well-earned beer by the fire, then lose your shirt in a poker game.'

'You've got a stable full of excellent horses up there at the stud. Why don't you ride down? Get an ambulance to meet you where the tree's over the road?'

Yeah. That's what a real man would do. Too bad he wasn't a real man anymore.

'Tom? You still there?'

'I'm here.' He huffed out a breath. Really, if he couldn't tell his best mate since primary school, now, in a goddamn emergency that might just kill his father, who could he tell? 'I can't ride.'

'What do you mean?'

'I've got an injury.' He rattled it off like he was giving a report to his commanding officer. 'Shrapnel, lodged up next to my lumbar vertebrae, between the psoas major and the erector spinae. Certain activities are on the no-go list while the surgeons work out which direction it's going to travel in. It goes the wrong way, my chances of paraplegia become high.'

'Tom, my god.'

'I know.'

'Tom, we should have been having this conversation over a beer, man. In person. I'm sorry. How long are the surgeons going to leave you wondering?'

'I'm having weekly check-ups with Dr Novak down in Cooma. But no time frame. No promises. Just this damn waiting.' He caught his hand wandering to the scar the shrapnel had left as it tore its way through him. Could he put his own future ahead of his father's if the oxygen ran out?

He couldn't. He only had one option left.

'Suppose I find a rider,' he said. 'Here's the question: if the ambulance is on a callout, who do we know who could drive up the mountain with a bottle of oxygen in this weather?'

'Hannah will do it,' said Josh.

Tom caught his breath. No, he couldn't ask it of her, not after everything. Especially not in her beat-up old car.

The sergeant. Meg King had a police cruiser equipped for all-weather mountain terrain and she'd track down an oxygen bottle in a heartbeat. The difficult part would be meeting her at the flooded crossing. What if the shrapnel were to shift mid-ride and sever his spinal column? Meg would be having a long wait in rough conditions for him to crawl his way down a mountain and through a flooded stream.

'Hannah can ride the bridle trail,' said Josh when Tom remained silent.

Tom's heart quickened, just for a second. Long enough to remind him that a broken heart could still hope. 'No, Josh.'

'She's a better rider than me and you're not going to be a damn fool and risk your back by doing it. Besides, Skipjack's a hell of a horse.'

'You don't understand.'

'Sure I do. You need help and there's a Cody on hand to help you. I'm calling her now.'

The phone went dead in his hand.

# CHAPTER
# 37

'You have got to be kidding.'

'Nope.'

Hannah frowned at her toenails poking up through the suds at the far end of the bathtub. Chipped nail polish and riding boot blisters … it was quite a look. 'Did Tom ring you to ask me to help him?'

'He rang me for help. I'm in Sydney, therefore you are the one who must help. Follow the dots, Hannah.'

'You don't understand.'

'Funny, that's what he said. I'll tell you what I told him: Codys help their friends when they're in trouble. You going to make a liar of me, Hannah, just because you're in a snit?'

A snit? She'd had her freaking *heart* broken. 'Josh Cody, if you weren't five hours' drive away, you wouldn't dare say that to me.'

He chuckled. 'Come on, Han. Can you get off your high horse? I know there's some stuff happening between the two of you, and never feel you have to tell me the icky details, but if Bruno needs another bottle of oxygen before this storm burns itself out, he's going to be in deep trouble.'

Why did Josh always have to be right, darn it?

She pulled the lowered blind away from the window. Rain threw itself at the glass and the black branches of the snow gum were thrashing about like airborne spaghetti. 'The storm's certainly wild. It'll be wilder still up the mountain.'

'You call Kev's mate Lionel and see if he'll drive you and Skipjack out in the float to where the sealed road's gone under. It's twenty minutes up the trail from the crossing in good conditions. Better get Lionel to wait for you in case you have to turn around. I'll call Meg King and see if she can get a weather report off the SES.'

Hannah sighed and gazed at the paperback and glass of wine she had sitting on a stool next to the bath, the tealight candles she'd lit on the counter. 'I suppose I'd better get out of the bath, then.'

'Up and at 'em, Hannah Banana. Keep your phone clear so I can call you back.'

Her brother had done a lot better than call her back. Hannah looked through the windscreen of Lionel's truck to the lights-ablaze police cruiser heading up the mountain ahead of them. The sergeant had come through with an escort, a police-issue hi-vis waterproof jacket for Hannah and handheld radios because there'd been no calls in or out of Ironbark Station since Josh had spoken to Tom an hour ago.

'Phone tower on the ridge back off Gorge Road is down,' said the sergeant, when they pulled over at the start of the bridle trail. 'None of our phones will be working out here until it's back up, and emergency services will be waiting for this storm to blow through before they send a team up there. This handheld radio will keep you connected to me for a while, but the range will be rubbish once you get into the treeline.'

'Okay, I'll—'

'I'm not done. The oxygen tank weighs in about five kilos. It's too long for a backpack, but the dispatch officer at the Ambulance Depot suggested you lash it to your saddle like a blanket roll.'

Hannah eyed the silver steel tube. 'Sure, that'll work.'

'I'll do that,' said Lionel. 'I'll saddle up Skip in the float and tie this down. Best keep the lad in the warm until you're done planning.'

The sergeant nodded. 'Here's three flares. You ever lit one?'

'No.'

'Unscrew the cap. See this trigger? Haul it down, hold the flare away from your face. Aim for a clear patch of ground so the light clears the treeline. You get in trouble, you fire one. Do not move more than a yard from the trail. No matter what. You go off piste, we won't find you quickly, and it's cold enough to freeze a bunyip up here.'

Hannah stuffed the flares into the oversized pockets of the anorak. Her fingers were starting to numb with cold, despite the leather gloves she wore. 'Got it.'

'Lionel and I will stay here until you let us know you've cleared the treeline and reached the homestead. When you're there, you fire the red flare, got it? Red for Romeo. That means you're safe and we can go home to our beds.'

'Red for Romeo when I'm safe at the homestead, got it. Thank you, Meg.'

The sergeant looked out into the blackness, where giant trees were groaning under the wind. They could all hear the cracks of splitting timber. 'We've got the easy job. Make this a quick twenty-minute joyride, will you? There'll be trees coming down up there. Branches big as logs. You got a helmet?'

'Yeah.' A clatter of hooves against steel told her Lionel was done saddling up. Hannah held the walkie-talkie to her mouth and depressed the button. 'Hannah to sergeant.'

An answering crackle came from the unit clipped to Meg's jacket.

'Okay then,' Meg said. 'Looks like we're ready.'

Skipjack put the brakes on when Lionel tried to lead him off the ramp onto the snow-covered blacktop, but an assurance that he was the handsomest, bravest horse in all the world lured him on. Hannah shoved her boot in his stirrup and swung herself into the saddle the second he cleared the ramp. Freezing conditions in the middle of the night—up a mountain—were no good for a horse; he'd need to keep moving.

'Here,' said Meg. 'Take this.'

Hannah took a head torch from the sergeant. Excellent. It would be way more useful than the baton torch she had stuffed in her pocket. She slipped it over her helmet and fumbled the switch with her gloved hands until it shot out a thin white beam.

'Okay, Skippy,' she said, clicking her tongue and giving him a nudge with her heels. 'Let's go be heroes.'

The bridle trail up the mountain was wide enough to still be visible despite the leaf litter blown all over it, and within a few seconds the flickering lights from the sergeant's patrol truck had disappeared.

Her head torch threw a thin, chalky beam ahead of her and the deeper they went into the forest, the louder the growl of wind and rain became. 'Not creeped out at all,' she said.

She'd ridden this trail a hundred times back when Skipjack was stabled at Ironbark Station, but never in the dark. Never in the rain.

Never when the wind howling through the forest sounded like the souls of the damned clawing their way out of the earth.

Skipjack tossed his head and gave a loud snort as she nudged him into a quicker trot.

'We are totally fine,' she told him.

He blew a plume of frosty breath back at her.

'Yes, I know I'm overlooking the hazards of falling trees and getting lost and hypothermia, but if I don't reassure myself that this mad ride isn't one headless ghost away from a horror movie, I'll freak out. And where would that get us?'

Static burst from the radio in her pocket and she pulled it out. 'Sergeant?'

Words were crackling from the speaker, but the wind ripped them away before Hannah could hear them. She pressed the buzzer and spoke. 'I can't hear you, but we're okay. I'll check in again in five minutes.' She shoved the radio halfway into her pocket then reconsidered. 'Over,' she said into the mouthpiece. That's what the movie cops said, right?

A limb of a forest giant lay across the path in front of her and she edged Skipjack over it. 'Third of the way,' she told the horse. And when she got the whole way, Tom bloody Krauss better have a fire waiting. And a glass of wine big enough to have a bath in. An apology and an admission of being a heartless moron wouldn't hurt, either.

She huffed out a frosty breath of her own. The weather must have shoved her brain cells into cold storage. Nothing was going to change Tom's mind about her, he'd made that as crystal clear as his icy, cut-glass eyes.

Skipjack shied on a curve in the track and she felt her backside slip on the rain-soaked saddle. 'Whoa, pal. What's up?'

Not a bunyip, please, god. Not in this weather. Not this close to winter.

'Don't be a scaredy-cat, Skip,' she told her horse. 'Bunyips aren't real.' She hoped.

She cast a look over her shoulder and her mind revisited every scary movie she'd ever watched on those sleepover parties she'd had with her girlfriends in high school. Red eyes blinking, chainsaws whirring, tree roots growing long clawed hands that stretched up to wrap arou—

'Stop it, Hannah Cody.'

Skip tossed his head at the sound of her voice and came to a standstill. She nudged, but he wouldn't budge.

'What is it? What can you see that I can't?'

She pulled her baton torch from her pocket and shone it ahead up the track. Oh, crap. Water, a whole river of it by the looks, cut the path. One of the streams that ran down from the mountain must have broken its banks.

She reached a hand back to the ice-cold steel of the oxygen tube they carried. There was no turning around. There was only forward. Thank god she'd remembered to put sugar lumps in her pocket. Skipjack hated water, but he loved sugar lumps.

'Together, Skip. You and me.'

She eased a boot from its stirrup and swung to the ground, keeping the reins wrapped twice about her fist. Skippy had never run away from her before but she'd never asked him to face his greatest fear in a raging storm. Now wasn't the time to be taking a chance on trust.

Using both torches, she mapped the amount of water crossing the path. Stay high, she thought. The lower edge of the track would be more likely to have washed away and have hidden holes. Water over her boots? Horrid, but nothing she hadn't coped with a thousand

times before. A thigh-high pothole with floodwater strong enough
to wash her down the mountain? No, thank you.

'One step at a time, buddy,' she said, planting her foot squarely in
the onrush of water. The cold was so fierce it felt like it was bruising
the bones in her feet.

'Now it's your turn. Come on.' She gave the reins a tug and the
massive horse whinnied in as clear a tone as though he'd actually
said *Not a chance in hell, lady.*

She took another step and put her weight into it, hauling on his
bridle like a tug-of-war rope. 'Come on, Skip.'

He didn't budge.

'Flipping heck.' Both her feet were in the water now, the chill
making her teeth chatter. She burrowed one hand in beneath the
layers of jackets and jumpers and scarf to the top pocket of her
shirt. The sugar in there was probably a sodden mess by now, but
it was all she had. Her gloved fingers were clumsy, but she found
a cube.

'Now, Skip. How about this, hey?'

The horse shook his head.

'It's delicious.'

She took a step backwards, deeper into the water, and let the
horse taste the sugar lump before pulling it just out of reach.

He took a step.

'That's my brave, handsome boy. Come on. Another couple of
steps and it's all yours, buddy.'

Two steps, three, and then Skippy seemed to realise how totally
unfun the temperature of the water around his hooves was, and he
trotted the rest of the way so abruptly he yanked her off her feet and
she fell. Freezing water engulfed her, sliding under the protection
of her jacket. She shuddered with the shock of it and leapt up. She
was colder than cold now, and saturated.

She'd lived in the mountains long enough to know that this was when the bad stuff happened: hikers lost their way, got exposed to the elements and were found dead ten yards from their tents; skiers, off piste and underdressed, lost their toes after a night on the slopes. People who were too cold made dumb decisions.

Her teeth chattering, she swung her frozen limbs back into the saddle and pulled the walkie-talkie from her pocket. 'Sergeant, it's Hannah. Do you copy?'

A crackle of sound, then, thankfully, the clear words of Sergeant King. 'We copy. Are you there yet?'

'Halfway, maybe a little more. I've fallen in floodwater and I'm very wet. We're going to speed up. If you see a white flare in the next little while, it's me, and it means I'm in deep trouble.'

Silence. Then, 'Copy that.'

Okay, then. She shoved the radio back in the pocket and drove her heels into Skipjack's sides. Her midnight rescue run had just turned into a race.

A figure, shrouded in oilskins and carrying a hurricane lantern, stood in the centre of the sweep of gravel. As mad as she was with the idiot she'd fallen in love with who'd flicked her off like she was a fly on his sausage sanger, she'd never been happier to see him.

She was cold. Deeply cold. The sort of cold that killed lovesick Snowy Mountains veterinarians who didn't find their way into dry clothes by a fireside, stat.

'Hannah?'

Tom's voice was all but ripped from his mouth by the scream of wind and rain. She didn't bother responding. Skipjack was as cold as she was and twice as valuable. She nudged his side as soon as they cleared the treeline and headed for the main stable at a gallop. Horse, oxygen, Hannah, that was the order of events that needed to unfold. And once her teeth had stopped chattering, she was going to use them to take a bite out of Tom Krauss's idiot self.

Tom hurried over as she reached the stable and dragged back the huge sliding door. Dull lighting strips flickered at knee height and a gust of warmth formed a cloud about her as she trotted Skipjack inside. The horse came to a halt, his sides heaving, water and steam streaming from his neck. She tried to pull her boot from the stirrups, but there was no strength in her legs. The rumble of stable doors closing brought her head up, and there was Tom, throwing off his oilskins, hoisting the hurricane lantern onto a mounting block so a yellow glow filled the barn.

'Hannah,' he said. 'My god, you're soaking.'

'A little help here,' she managed through the tremor that had her in its grip.

He came forward and removed her feet from the stirrups, then bent her knee to get her leg over the horn of the saddle.

'Slide between me and the horse,' he said, and she literally did just that, because none of her muscles remembered how to work. She waited for his arms to grip her and they sort of did, but then she kept sliding and landed butt-first in the straw of the stable.

Tom hovered above her, his face pale. 'Christ, I'm sorry. Are you okay?'

She gave him the look she usually reserved for Josh when she caught him pinching food from her fridge. 'I'll worry about me. If you want to be helpful, get that oxygen up to the house. I need to dry Skipjack.'

He handed her a blanket and heaven-oh-heaven, a hot water bottle, then wrestled the silver canister out from under the saddle straps. 'Tuck the hot water bottle somewhere in your … somewhere. I'll be right back to help.'

'Wait!'

Tom turned to face her.

'I've got to send up the flare so the sergeant and Lionel know I've made it. The walkie-talkie she gave me has lost its signal so I can't radio down.'

'Where's the flare?'

She dug into the huge inner pockets of her police-issue jacket. 'Here. The red one means I'm here safely. You know how to light it?'

He almost flashed his quarter grin. 'You're asking a retired naval officer if he knows how to light a flare?'

She shrugged. 'How am I to know what you can and can't do? You can't catch a girl who's falling off a horse.' Bitchy, sure. But crossing that creek in snowmelt conditions entitled a girl to the odd vicious swipe.

Tom headed out into the rain.

Alone again, Hannah stripped off her soaking gloves to start work on the buckles of Skipjack's saddle. The saddle was saturated and would weigh a ton. Her horse needed drying, then walking until his temperature stabilised, and he needed a torrent of grateful words from her for keeping her safe through that hideous journey up the mountain, and then he needed a treat of hot, mashed-up bran.

'You're my hero, Skip,' she said and rested her hand against the thudding of his heart. 'Not that idiot Krauss. Did you see how he let me fall to the floor? Huh?'

Her horse whinnied and stamped his foot, and she moved her tired arms over him with a scrap of blanket. 'I know, makes no sense to me either.'

# CHAPTER
## 38

Tom lit the flare with wet hands then held it high so the red glare soared above the treeline. She'd fallen to the floor. Actually fallen, because the son of the old man she'd risked her life for in a hard ride up the mountain hadn't caught her. Instead, his stance had just … buckled. From cold? Or because his shrapnel had shifted? That was the shitty question he didn't have time to consider.

An answering flare from down the mountain shone a green glow through the mist. *Message received.* He tossed the flare into a puddle and headed for the house. They had oxygen, so that was one disaster averted. The next step was to make sure Hannah and her horse didn't suffer from exposure.

By the time he returned to the stables, Skipjack was tucked into a stall, mowing through a feedbag, a blanket draped over his back. Rake marks from the brushing Hannah had given him still furrowed his coat. Hannah was wrapped in a blanket and stood looking over the stall door at Buttercup, who was in her last month and moody as all hell.

A bit like him, now he came to think about it.

The big mare was snoozing and her heavy breathing was loud enough to be heard over the roar of the rain.

'The fire's on up at the house.'

She turned to him and her face was pale. 'Listen, Krauss, I almost don't need a fire. You know why?'

Huh. This was one of those rhetorical questions that it was best not to answer. He did anyway. 'Why?'

'Because I have *rage* filling my veins. You blow me off, you decide I'm not good enough for whatever life plan you have for yourself, but suddenly it's okay for you to stay warm and dry and cosy while I risk *my* life to get *your* father some oxygen?'

Josh hadn't told her.

Which was good, because Tom's worry was for him to shoulder, not Hannah, but bad, because now she thought he was even more of a louse than before.

'My riding's not up to it.' It was a pathetic excuse and she knew it.

'I don't get you at all, Tom. I don't understand what makes you tick.'

'I'm sorry. I wish I could be … more.'

'Yeah,' she said, and like that, her anger disappeared. In its place was resignation, which cut twice as deep. 'So do I.'

'Will you come inside? Mrs L wants to make sure you're okay.'

'In a minute.' She turned back to Buttercup. 'She's carrying heavy.'

'Josh said that, too.'

'How's her appetite?'

He liked this version of Hannah the best, with her dirty overalls, her soaked boots covered in horse manure and a plaid bandanna keeping her hair from her eyes. This was the Hannah he found it

hard to say no to. The perfumed, dressed-up version was like meeting a person he didn't quite know.

'She took a bite out of one of the stable hands this morning.'

'She may not make it to term. You should rig a camera in here
and she should be checked every six hours. When she goes into
labour, she's going to need help getting that great heffalump out.
Josh's help.'

'Okay.'

She turned to him and gave him a flat-eyed stare. 'You can't
cop out on her the way you copped out tonight on your dad. Do
you understand me, Tom? She can't tell you what she needs, so
you'd better make damn sure she's got someone here who can
help her.'

Fuck. 'I won't let my horse down.'

'Good. What, are you just going to stand there? I'm dead on my
feet. Let's go. I hope your hot water system's not out in the storm,
because I need a bath to warm up.'

'It's fine. Power's not out yet, and if it goes down, we have a
backup generator. Come on, it's still pouring out there, I'll hold an
umbrella over you. There's curry on the stove.'

Mrs LaBrooy met them at the front steps, still crying, but now
there was a smile as well as worry on her face.

'Hannah Cody, bless you, my sweet. You come on in now and
I'll take you to a guest room. I've put towels on the heated rack and
there's a bathrobe of mine and some thick socks.'

'Thanks, Mrs LaBrooy.'

'Tom, go ahead and get the bath water running. Hannah, you
give me those wet clothes you're wearing, and I'll get them washed
and dried for you.'

He led the way to the back of the house to the spare room beside
his. A lamp was on, a fluffy pink bathrobe lay over a chair and the

bed looked as though Mrs L had spent the last half hour plumping up its pillows.

'Boots first,' said Mrs L, and Hannah sat on the stool by the dresser and yanked off her boots.

Tom walked into the bathroom and turned the taps on, letting his hand run under the flow of water until he was sure the temperature was just a couple of degrees short of scalding. The voices from the next room filtered into him over the sound of rushing water.

'I'm so sorry to have dragged you out into this weather, Hannah. I should never have let the oxygen supply get so low, and Bruno, I'm so worried about him. He's got his heart set on this campdraft. He feels it's going to be—how did he describe it?—his last ride, and I have a horrid suspicion that once it's done he's going to cock up his toes. He's so determined. If he decides he's done, he just won't wake up and that will be that. What will I do then? I just couldn't bear it if ...'

He heard Hannah's voice murmuring to the housekeeper. She'd know what to say to ease Mrs L's mind. Unlike him. He had no idea what he would say to Hannah once the housekeeper had taken herself off to bed and it was just him and the woman he was trying his darnedest to let go.

He headed back into the bedroom just as Mrs L was attempting to wrestle Hannah out of her wet shirt. His eyes met Hannah's and the blush across her cheeks sent an arrow of regret through him.

'I think I can take it from here, Mrs LaBrooy,' Hannah said, holding the front of her shirt together.

Tom gestured behind him. 'Bath will be full in a minute. See you in the front room when you're done.' He gathered up the blanket, rain jacket and boots currently forming a pool on the floorboards. 'Take your time.'

He followed Mrs L out of the room, concentrating on his gait. He wasn't going to limp, not now. Instead, he was going to think about what he'd just overheard the housekeeper say to Hannah. Bruno's last ride. Not literally—that day was long gone. But the campdraft meant a lot to his dad and sure, he and Lynette had had their heads together, but maybe it was time to think bigger.

They could turn it into an occasion that the locals of Hanrahan would talk about for years. Have a band, get a dance floor set up on the home paddock. Hell, get a track set up across the paddock that an electric wheelchair could navigate, lay on kegs from the pub. Party lights and portaloos and pigs on the spit, and he could invite some of the old campdrafting champions to stay in the house for the weekend. Let the old legends tell their stories by the fire.

Bruno would love a chance to dust off his hat.

The sight of Hannah in the housekeeper's fluffy bathrobe when she found him half an hour later was quite something. 'Well, well,' he said. 'The human marshmallow walks amongst us.'

Hannah frowned at him. 'Don't think for a minute that we are friends and you can joke with me. I rode up here for Bruno, not for you. And because Josh guilt-tripped me into it.'

He gestured to the tray he'd set on the card table near the fire, where a covered plate waited and a glass of merlot shimmered in the firelight. 'Shout at me after you've eaten something.'

She sniffed. 'Don't mind if I do.'

He let her settle into a chair, then sat in the one opposite.

She ate a forkful of curry then coughed. 'Holy moly.'

'What?'

'How much chilli is in this?'

He shrugged. 'A bit, I guess. When you grow up with a Sri Lankan housekeeper as your adopted mother like I did, you don't even notice chilli anymore.'

Hannah lifted her water glass and took a sip before returning to the curry. She finished the bowl, scraping the spoon around until she'd eaten every last scrap, then set it down on her tray.

'You know,' she said conversationally. 'I hate you.'

'What?'

'It's true. You made me feel small, Tom, and I'm done with feeling small.'

She had a determined look on her face that had his intuition tingling worse than the compromised nerves running down his left leg. 'And, actually, I'm a hero now. Sergeant King told me so, just this evening, so you don't get to tell me what I want, or what's good for me, or how I feel or don't feel.'

'I never—'

'I'm not finished.'

He rested his fingers on the glass of wine he'd poured for himself, ran them along the ridge of cut crystal.

'Riding up that mountain was bloody difficult.'

'I'm sure it was.'

'It was dark and scary and I nearly lost my nerve when I had to get off and drag Skipjack through a foot-deep torrent of water.'

The cut crystal felt warm suddenly, soft and smooth, and when he looked down he realised his hand had moved from the glass and found her fingers. *No touching*, he reminded himself. No future, no hope, no Hannah. He dragged his hand back to the glass and lifted it to take a deep, numbing sip.

'You know what else is bloody difficult?'

He knew plenty about difficult, but Hannah was on a roll. 'What?'

'Feelings. They are messy and complicated, and one day you think you know what you feel and then suddenly it's totally different. Like when I was happy spending time with you, but then you decided to ditch our friendship and it hurt. And then, when I tried to be honest with you about my feelings, you brushed me off again. That hurt even worse. You know why?'

Tom swallowed. He knew, all right.

'Because my heart was broken, Tom.'

Maybe she'd tell him that now she thought he was a coward—a cop-out—that hate was all she felt for him now. She'd tell him she was over him. She was moving on.

This was good. This was what he wanted for her. He looked into the fire and wished it didn't tear him up into incy-wincy pieces to hear it.

'But the thing I've learned about feelings is that they are resilient. Which is why,' she said, 'not only do I hate you ...'

He looked up. Oh, heck. Hannah's eyes were watering and he'd have put it down to the heat of the curry if it weren't for the light shining in them. The tremble to her mouth. The wide-eyed look of hope and longing and vulnerability, all of which he understood, because wasn't that the secret he was hiding in his own heart?

Oh, god. Not now, not to him.

'... I love you, Tom.'

# CHAPTER

# 39

There, she'd said it.

She'd heard that adrenalin did weird things to people and now she knew that was true.

It had made her brave.

She was a warrior princess from history who'd never had to bother with pesky trivialities like social media trolls, she'd ridden up a mountain through the blackest, stormiest of nights and she was claiming her man.

But then she saw the look on Tom's face, and her thoughts stumbled. Or had adrenalin just made her stupid?

Why was he looking so horrified? Why was he so *surprised*, damn it? She looked at the pool of wine spreading across the table. Oh, he'd snapped the stem of his glass—why wasn't he picking the two-inch splinter of glass from his palm?

'Um … Tom?'

'Hannah.'

Oh, god. She'd misjudged this, again. What was wrong with her? Why did she keep thinking she was seeing more in Tom's eyes when he looked at her than was truly there?

She pushed the glass of merlot—her glass, the one that hadn't spilled because she wasn't the one who'd been horrified by some pesky declaration of love—and the ridiculousness of her sleeves distracted her for a moment. Were they her arms, wrapped in hot pink velour, the hands at the end of them shaking?

They were. And she realised it had been a long time since they'd shaken that way. A long time since she'd opened her heart up and let herself really feel stuff.

And Tom wasn't taking that away from her.

He pulled the shard from his hand and wrapped a serviette around the gash. If she'd been a better person she'd have offered to stitch it.

'Hannah, I haven't changed my mind. I can't be what you want me to be.' His voice was remote, his face even more so.

'Tell me straight: do you think I'm trying to get you to help me have a baby? Because, yes, sure, there was a time when that was all I was thinking. That's not what this is about now. I want more. I want you now.' Should she be on her knees? A pink marshmallow begging on the Krauss front room floor? Was that what it would take for him to believe her?

'Even so.' He hesitated. 'Perhaps I need to explain something to you, why you may have felt I've been sending'—he shrugged—'mixed messages your way.'

'Please. Explain away.'

'Do you remember, ages ago, you asked me who I took to my school formal?'

'Mary Frankton.'

'Uh-huh. You remember why I said I took her?'

She frowned at him. 'You were—how did you describe it?—too chicken to ask the person you really wanted to go to prom with.'

He nodded. 'The person I wanted to ask was you.'

'You wanted to ask me, Hannah Cody, to your school formal?'

'You were a high school crush of mine but, you know, I was—am—Josh's mate. You don't go out with your mate's sister. At least, not in high school you don't. That's why I kissed you that day in the stables—for old times' sake. I haven't felt that way about you for years. I'm sorry if I misled you. I'm a guy. Guys are jerks; you of all people should know that.'

The rush in her heart flashed from wonder to hurt. She pushed back from the table. 'Me of all people ... I cannot believe you could be so cruel.'

'Hannah.'

'Yes?'

The silence stretched long enough for her heart to crack.

'Goodnight,' he said at last. 'And thank you for the oxygen. My father's life is safe because of you.'

Yeah. It was. Too bad her own life was only just being held together by one hideously pink fluffy bathrobe.

Four hours later, Hannah still wasn't asleep. Her brain was the first problem. It kept swirling thoughts up at her, waiting to file them away in piles labelled *To Do*, or *Regret Forever*, or *OK, You Can Keep This One*.

Thoughts like: she no longer cared about that dumb photo. It was a memory from childhood that had no bearing on her current life. Her adult life.

Thoughts like: she'd forgiven herself for falling apart afterwards.

But what was still swirling about unresolved and misunderstood was why was she getting it so wrong, trying to interpret what Tom was thinking.

She had always had a theory—and maybe this was because she was addicted to that show about the dog whisperer with the warm, trusting, brown eyes—that being in tune with animals gave her an advantage about being in tune with humans.

Well, her theory sucked.

She was clueless when it came to being in tune with Tom, because she could not work out how to make herself understand why he felt so right to her, but she was nothing to him.

She rubbed a hand over her heart. This love stuff was raw, and messy, and it hurt. It hurt a whole lot more than humiliation.

Despite what she'd believed Tom's eyes had said, or how she'd interpreted the touch of his hands, the quiver in that quarter grin of his when he turned it in her direction, she should have listened. His actions hadn't mattered, because the words he'd said had made it clear, time and time again. She wasn't the future he was looking for. She was nothing but a boy's long-ago crush that had not lasted.

A noise interrupted her planning. A groan? The fumble of a hand hitting a wall, perhaps? It sounded as though it had come from about a foot behind her head. She sat up, listened. There it was again. She turned and stared at the blank section of wall.

Could Bruno be in trouble? Or was Tom getting up to check the horses? Maybe a stable alarm had gone off.

She got out of bed and padded to the door in the thick socks Mrs LaBrooy had loaned her. A floorboard creaked outside and she opened the door and looked out. Definitely Tom—fully dressed still, walking down the corridor away from her.

She went to call his name, then spied a pile of clothing on the floor outside the room. Her jeans, shirt, jacket and boots, all mud free and crisply dry. Even her underwear, tucked and folded as neatly as … she frowned. Yes, as neatly as though they'd been folded by someone who'd had military training.

Had Tom stayed up late to launder and fold her clothes? Hmm, maybe god really was a woman. And, double plus, now she'd be able to get the hell out of here in the morning without having to make any awkward conversation.

She looked down the length of the dark corridor. Where was he going at this hour of the night? Had something happened to Bruno? If he was having a medical crisis, she might be able to assist. One year pre-med and a veterinarian degree equated to zero knowledge about multiple sclerosis, but still.

Tying the robe more firmly about her waist, she set off down the hall. The kitchen was empty. So was the good room, the bathroom and the laundry. She stood by the front room's windows and checked the stables. Security lights shone on the stable door, which was firmly shut. The rain had eased, but leaf litter still swirled in the strong wind.

Not outside then. She turned to survey the house she'd run wild through as a kid. Where hadn't she checked?

The door to the old sleepout, when she found it, was open, with enough dim lamplight spilling out to let her see it had been set up with a desk and a computer. The horse stud's office, perhaps.

She should leave. She was being nosy, pure and simple. A busybody, a sneak, a stickybeak.

Or she could inch her way in, pop her nose through the gap in the door to see what was so important that Tom had got up from his bed at this godawful time of the morning.

At first, all she saw was some odd sort of foam. A patch of carpet underlay perhaps? No, an exercise mat. And on it, stretched out like a man on some medieval rack, was Tom, his arms crossed over his eyes to drown out the light.

Why would a grown man leave a soft, comfortable, warm bed for a cold, hard floor?

She headed back to her room.

Because he had a cold, hard heart, of course. He was, after all, an emotionless rock.

# CHAPTER
## 40

Tom set his glass of whiskey down on the counter just as the smooth purr of rubber on carpet and the hiss of an oxygen bottle announced the arrival of his father.

'Son.'

'Hey, Dad.'

'If I'd known you were uncapping the good stuff, I'd have joined you.'

Bruno Krauss was becoming a shadow of his former self. His white hair had thinned, his cheeks had sunk into gaunt hollows and his knees poked through his blanket like coat hangers through a too-thin shirt.

'Sorry, Dad. I was in a bit of a mood and didn't want to inflict it on anyone.'

'Something on your mind, son?'

*Too much.*

But he shook his head. His dad's determination to see his legacy carry on after his death was all he talked about. Some days it felt like that was all that was keeping him alive: the stockhorses; the breeding and training program; the campdraft scheduled for the offseason when the snow had receded.

The last thing his dad needed to know was that his heir might not be able to do any of that.

'I've been thinking about the campdraft, Dad.'

'Yes?'

'I'm thinking we go big.'

'What do you mean? The plans are up and running; if you mess with Lynette's system she'll have your guts for garters.'

'I mean the off-paddock entertainment. We've got food stalls and market stalls sorted already … but I'm talking about stepping that up.'

'The riding's the entertainment, son.'

'What about a band for when the drafting's done? Country music. Coloured lights strung up above the barbecue area and the bar. Maybe a dance floor. A real, old-fashioned country party with a campfire cook-up.'

'Sounds like a bloody circus.'

'It'll be as great as anything they've ever run up north at Paradise Lagoons. It'll be the stuff of legend.'

Bruno's eyes sparked, as he'd known they would. The brothers who ran the campdrafts out of Rockhampton were legendary.

'A band? You reckon we could get one?'

'Sure. And we organise a couple of minibuses to do the run from Hanrahan out here, so the locals who want a beer can join in.'

'Have Mrs LaBrooy bake some sweets. No-one bakes as good as her, not even that new woman at the café in town.'

Tom chose his words carefully. 'True, but maybe we could send Mrs L an invitation so she knows she's a guest and can relax. I can call The Billy Button Café and ask them to cater. Salads, trays of potato bake, apple pie.'

'We've enough beef to supply the barbecue. I want the Ironbark Station brand on every carcass. Get us a few of those spits, son, the ones they do pigs on.'

'That's a great idea.' He didn't bother telling Bruno he'd already asked Kylie if she could rig up a few in her workshop.

Tom took the hand his father held up to him. Twenty years ago, they'd had plenty of chats like this. Easy conversations about school, about footy, about horses and girls and the epic stack he'd taken off his BMX. They'd have walked the paddocks in summer, checking on the horses, with a dog snuffling along beside them. In winter they'd have crunched through the frost and talked about whether they had enough hay baled up to get through the winter.

So much had changed. His dad's health, for one, and the only sign of the kelpies that had once ruled the paddocks was a row of graves beneath the hydrangeas.

'Why did you come home, Tom? It can't have been easy. Not after the way we left things.'

Wow. That was as close to an apology as he'd ever heard. And he was ready to accept it, which meant this would be the moment to come clean to his father about his injury, but ... he didn't have the heart.

The burden was bad enough for him to carry. His father needed to be preserving his strength for himself.

'I came home to Ironbark because I wanted to be here, Dad,' he lied gently. The fact that he'd come to realise this was exactly where he wanted to be was just a bonus.

# CHAPTER
# 41

Hannah worked the next few days with only half her head on the job. She dragged herself around, cried in the shower a bit—well, a lot, but who was counting? Then she'd come up with a new plan to celebrate her newfound adult way of looking at the world.

It was going to require Kylie's expert assistance.

'Earth to Hannah.'

She frowned at her brother. 'That's earth to Boss Hannah to you, handsome.'

'Vera's doing a roast beef special tonight up at The Billy Button. Fancy having dinner out? My treat.'

It was tempting: Vera's cooking versus her usual weekday dinner of a glass of wine in the bath followed by a tin of warmed-up soup.

'Will you and Vera be blowing kisses at each other over the roast potatoes?'

'I'll try and restrain myself.'

A thought struck her: Josh wasn't in the habit of treating her to anything fancier than a cold slice of leftover pizza. She cast her eye

over him. Now she really looked, she could see he'd turned on the
Cody charm that had led many a netballer to swish her skirt in his
direction back in high school. Too much charm, darn it.

'What do you know?'

He was wide-eyed like a baby owl. 'Me? I know nothing.'

'Don't think I'm fooled by that face.'

He rolled his eyes. 'Okay, Sandy said she saw you crying in the
office yesterday.'

'Maybe I stapled my finger by accident.'

'And Graeme said you ate three donuts in one session.'

'That dobber.'

'Kev asked me why you had a long face. Barb Smart out at
Crackenback nabbed me this morning when I was pulling a
chunk of barbed wire out of a cow's hind leg and said you'd
called to ask her about her next litter of dalmations and could
you have one.'

'What of it? You have a dog, why can't I have a dog?'

'A *dalmation*? Come on, Han, we're vets. We both know they've
got zero brains and they're only good for appearing in movies,
looking cute with a hundred siblings.'

'Brains aren't everything.'

'And about half an hour ago, Marigold cornered me when I
was getting out of my ute to tell me that knitting pouches for
injured wildlife was excellent therapy for crisis management, just
in case I knew anyone who needed to come along and start knitting.' His voice had a note of finality to it as though this was the
clincher.

Hannah's brain zeroed in on the one name he hadn't mentioned.
'You spoken to Tom lately?'

'I was up at Ironbark Station yesterday. One of the breeding
mares has a colic problem.'

'Pepper? You've not had her on mineral oil, have you? She doesn't respond to that.'

Josh smirked at her. 'I'm the equine expert now, Hannah.'

Huh. Still, if Tom hadn't blabbed about her latest humiliation, how did the whole town know about it?

'So ... you're inviting me to dinner because you think I'm sad, right? Not because anyone's said anything specific or Marigold's having another of her dumb intervention sessions?'

'Maybe Vera and I love your smiling, unsuspicious company while we eat.'

'Funny. You should have been a comedian, Josh. I can't make dinner tonight, as it happens. I have plans.' Her decision to enlist Kylie's help couldn't have come at a better time.

'What sort of plans?'

'The sort that don't need your permission or input, Dr Cody.' Okay, that had come out a little snippy. He was being kind; why couldn't she learn how to be kind back?

Josh didn't appear to be wounded. 'Fine with me, Dr Cranky-pants. Now I get to blow kisses at Vera over the roast potatoes to my heart's content.'

She gave him a poke in his annoyingly firm gut. Considering the amount of gourmet food Vera shovelled down his neck, he ought to have a total dad bod by now. Just another example of the unfairness of life. 'Since you asked so nicely, I guess I can share.' A bit, anyway. 'I'm setting up an online profile.'

'For the clinic? We already have a website.'

'No, dumbo. For *me*.'

'OMG. Wait—crying in the shower, dalmations and now online dating? I don't know, Han. It's a lot.'

'It's *my* lot.'

He gripped her shoulder. 'I don't want to worry about you.'

Now he sounded sincere, not judgemental, which was territory she found a lot harder to navigate.

'Is there some Tom-related angle to this?' He said it like he didn't want to know the answer.

'Why would there be?'

'Because you are acting weird and he is acting weird, and Vera keeps asking me if there's something going on with you and Tom that I need to tell her about.'

Hannah tried for blasé and patted him on the cheek. 'I'm not weird, you are. And you can tell all the other busybodies to mind their own beeswax, including Vera, who you have my permission to blow kisses at. I've got this.'

She so did not have this.

'I have to input *what?*'

Kylie took a sip of the wine Hannah had brought. She'd also brought a frozen pizza, a tub of low-fat ice-cream and a packet of jelly snakes. Bribery, for when things got vicious.

'Likes. Dislikes.'

*Dislikes typing her likes and dislikes into a computer program*, Hannah typed.

Kylie sighed. 'Maybe this would be easier if we swapped places. I'll just type in everything I know about you and you sit behind me to supervise and drink wine.'

'Okay, okay,' she grumbled. 'I like horses and brooding men with lake-blue eyes. I dislike cities and brooding men with lake-blue eyes. How about that?'

'Hannah, we are here because you want to forget about Tom, remember?'

'I can take my wine and my pizza home. And my snakes. And my ice-cream.'

'Fine, whatever,' Kylie huffed. 'Okay, back to the screen. Maybe lay off the details about brooding men so you don't sound like a bunny boiler. For "likes", people say romantic, broad brush statements, like long walks on the beach, dancing like nobody's watching.'

'Ugh. You can't be serious.'

'Fine, we'll leave what you've typed. Now, you need to pick a demographic.'

'How do you mean?'

'Well, I assume you're going to tick the male box, but what about the age range?'

'Mid thirties.'

'That's too narrow. This is Hanrahan, Hannah. I mean, seriously, the chances of there being an eligible single bloke within a hundred clicks that you don't already know is negligible.'

'How do you know that?'

Kylie touched her hands to her beautifully blow dried and orderly hair, then ran them down her highly coordinated outfit down to her thighs and back up to her immaculately made-up face. 'Hello, *look* at me: I'm a winsome single woman, I own smokin' hot underwear, but I can't get a date for love or money. And guess what? I have my own profile on this very same dating app and I have had no joy. Zip, zero, diddly-squat. And can I say I was a lot chattier than you when I did my profile.'

'Wow. It's really that hard to find a date?'

'When you live in a small town it is.'

'So my revenge plan is doomed to failure.'

'Oh, honey,' said Kylie. 'If only you'd told me that's what we were doing, I'd have made a playlist with a lot of Tina Turner. And

Air Supply. And K-Pop! Is this … do you … now, don't get angry again, but maybe it's time that we *did* talk about what happened when you …'

'Accosted Tom in his bedroom?'

Kylie opened the jelly snakes and shoved three in her mouth. 'I'm ready to listen. Any detail you've got, no matter how insignificant it may seem.'

Hannah closed her eyes. She just wasn't ready to make a joke about it. About any of it. Her doomed life as a woman. Her even more doomed life as a mother. Her unrequited love.

'Do you mind if we just watch *The Notebook* again?' That way she could bawl her eyes out like nobody was watching.

# CHAPTER
# 42

By the time her hangover from her night with Kylie had gone, Hannah was feeling slightly less grim, so when Kev rang her and suggested they take Skippy and the new horse he was stabling out for a gentle trail ride, she was keen. Fresh air and horses could cure pretty much anything, couldn't they?

At least, that's what it felt like once they'd saddled up and the horses had picked their way through the scrub out the back of Kev's place.

'Snow's coming down lower each night.' Kev had brought a battered set of binoculars with him and was scanning the mountains in the distance.

She'd smelled the snow during the night. Had spent a few precious hours when she should have been sleeping curled up on the chair by her window, watching the inky blackness of the night sky, knowing that every missing star had been replaced by heavy, leaden cloud.

'Yep,' said Hannah. 'Saw the forecast. We seem to have jumped straight from summer to winter and missed out on autumn.'

There was nothing fun about getting called out by an anxious farmer in the dead of winter. The backroads had precious little in the way of lights and railguards. The animals she was called out to were often kept in barns with no heating, and the shock of getting out of her warm bed and her warm pyjamas in the dead hour before dawn was something she wouldn't miss if winter never came again.

'Winter's the season I love best in the mountains,' Kev said.

'Really? I'd've thought you'd have loved spring and summer, when you can work outdoors with your roses.'

Skipjack's hoof crunched through a decaying log and she took in a big breath of clean, lovely mountain. Okay. She loved it too, who was she kidding? She wouldn't give up Hanrahan for any amount of sunshine.

'We might see some pockets of snow if we can get some altitude. Where's the new horse from? He seen snow before?'

'The banker in town just brought him from Queensland, so I'm guessing no. His daughter's keen to get into dressage and such, but this fella may be a little long in the tooth for learning.'

Kev gave the horse under discussion a nudge and they headed up a narrow track. His green corduroy cap got caught on a branch and Hannah retrieved it for him as she passed through.

'You know, a helmet wouldn't get snagged, Kev. Maybe you should think about wearing one.'

'This old codger's not going to throw me. Besides, Marigold bought me this cap. She says it makes me look dapper.'

'Really? Dapper? There's a word you don't hear much.'

'I hope that's not your smart mouth telling me I'm old, pet.'

She giggled. 'Never.'

'It's true though. If I was younger I'd still be able to go for a gallop, but I know my limits. My glory days racing up and down these mountains are over.'

'Sometimes the glory isn't in the gallop. It's in just showing up, Kev.' At least, it was for her.

'True enough, love.'

That's what she'd determined to do. Disappointment could only provide so much motivation. Hope … that was the real motivator. She'd lived without it long enough to know.

But somehow, and despite the disappointments of the past month, she had a little hope burning in her breast, and she figured the best way to keep it burning was to show up every day in her own life. Live every day like she deserved to be in the here and now. Mistakes would happen and she'd deal with them. Mistakes and setbacks weren't going to send her into a dark place, not anymore. Mistakes and setbacks were going to make her invincible.

Especially a setback called Tom.

Kev grunted. 'Don't tell Skippy that.'

'Er, sure.' She'd drifted so far along in her own thoughts that she couldn't remember what they'd been talking about.

'I've been telling him for weeks he won't be getting any more sugar lumps from me until he's scored a sixty-pointer at the Ironbark Campdraft.'

She smiled. Glory: that was what Kev was talking about. And she was in a mood to want a bit of it for herself, no matter that there might be some (a lot!) of awkwardness involved. Besides, campdrafts within an easy drive of Hanrahan didn't happen all that often, and being on call every second weekend left her free to go even less often.

'Don't worry, Kev. No need to bribe my horse to convince me; I'm going to enter the Ironbark Station campdraft.'

'Of course you'll bloody enter it. Aren't your oldies coming back for it and all?'

Shoot, she'd managed to conveniently forget that. 'They are.'

Kev turned his head to look at her and grinned. 'Go get 'em, girl.'

She laughed. 'If I don't get more than sixty, you're buying me a beer.'

'You're on.'

# CHAPTER
# 43

Tom spent the afternoon interviewing the third candidate for the position of pub manager and within a handful of minutes he knew he'd found the right one.

Greg Badgery was forty something and his family had been in the pub game for three generations. He'd run country pubs, the last one successfully for a decade.

'Why are you looking to change?' Tom said. 'Moving to Hanrahan from southern Queensland will be a big shock, and I don't just mean the weather.'

'Marriage breakdown,' said Greg. 'The further I can get away from southern Queensland the better.'

'No chance of reconciliation? Sorry to be personal, I'm just wondering what happens if we put you on and then you pack your bags in two months' time and clear off.'

'Not gonna happen,' the guy said. 'Mrs Badgery has taken up residence with someone else.'

'Right. Look, I'll be checking your references, but I'm feeling real good about this, Greg. Question: would it bother you to have me on the premises more often than not? I wouldn't be looking over your shoulder—I don't know the first thing about running pubs. But I've got the liquor licence under my name and I've had a business offer and I'm thinking of running it out of this room.'

Greg shrugged. 'Wouldn't bother me at all, mate, so long as there's another room where I can set up some space. Some pub transactions are best done out of sight of the bar, if you get my drift. Hiring and firing, rep visits, that sort of thing.'

'There's plenty of space. I appreciate you coming all the way down here for the interview, Greg. I'll get back to you soon, okay? Feel free to have a look around before you leave; you'll want to know what you're up for if you get the job.'

'Thanks, mate. Appreciate it.'

Tom took a minute to heat up the wheatpack he'd taken to carting around with him. It smelled chokingly of lavender but, man, oh, man, when he propped it behind him in his office chair and leant back on it … it was good.

He thought about Greg while he flicked through a few more files on his computer. Sensible-looking bloke, imposing enough to be able to discourage the young ones who'd had a few from remaining on the premises, but approachable enough for the Hanrahan Pub to be a family venue.

Tom liked him. If his references checked out, he'd be offering him the job.

He hadn't planned to talk about being on the premises, but the idea of being a country solicitor was growing on him. Close enough to Ironbark that he could drive down every day, but a space of his own. A career choice of his own.

He opened the drawer and pulled out the application Dorley had left him. He could fit in a visit to Sydney for the mandatory hours of the course with his trip to see the specialist in Wollongong.

The phone interrupted him before he could do more than look in his diary. Lynette, his dad's head ringer, was on the line.

'Hey, Tom.'

'What's up?'

'It's Buttercup. Not sure if she's in labour, but she's pacing.'

'Okay.'

'She was fine an hour ago. I've had Bill up here off and on this afternoon because she was a little unsettled, but nothing out of the ordinary. I just came up now to see her and she's definitely edgy. It could be the weather—we can all smell the snow coming—but I think this might be it, Tom.'

'I'm on my way.'

Holy heck. He wondered if this was what prospective fathers felt when their partners might be in labour. Excited, worried, useless.

By the time he made it up the mountain to Ironbark, the afternoon had deepened into evening. The stable lights were still on and he hurried over to the smaller one where Buttercup was housed.

The mare was down on her knees, blowing hard, making a noise like a foghorn with every breath out. He'd seen horses have foals before—hundreds of them—and maybe Buttercup was fine, but still. That sound of distress was giving him a bad feeling.

Lynette came round the corner with a bucket of water. 'Oh, Tom, I was just about to call you. She's been breathing funny the last five minutes. I was going to call the vet if I couldn't reach you.'

He moved into the stall and laid his hand on the mare's head. 'Buttercup, hey, girl. Let's get you some help, hey?'

He took his phone from his jacket pocket and punched in the quick dial number for Josh, who answered second ring.

'Josh, I need you, man. Buttercup's gone into labour and she's taking it hard.'

'I'm delivering a litter of pups down south of Crackenback. I've another hour here at least, then it'd take me over an hour to get to you.'

'Shit.'

'Have you called the clinic? I'm on call, but I'm busy. The service will switch through to Hannah. She was riding earlier with Kev but she'll be home by now.'

'No.' There was a silence where all he could hear was Buttercup's laboured breathing and the blood rushing in his ears.

Josh sighed. 'You've got to call her, man. She's an expert in foal delivery.'

'I can send a helicopter for you.' Could he? He was grasping at straws, that's what he was doing. Who even owned a helicopter that they'd rent out with three seconds' notice, anyway?

Josh's snort carried all the derision his offer deserved. 'Just because you've got a lot of money doesn't mean the rest of us have to help you be a proud, insufferable jerk. I don't care how many helicopters you send for me, I'm not leaving this dog—or her eleven-year-old owner—until I've got a row of pups snoozing in this whelping box I'm currently sitting in. Buttercup's foal means a hell of a lot more than your fragile ego, mate, so call Hannah, damn it.'

Tom's phone beeped as Josh ended the call.

If only it were his ego that had a piece of shrapnel about to sever it in two.

He started keying in Hannah's mobile, then paused. If she saw his number come up, she'd dodge his call. No, this had to be official. He found Cody and Cody Vet Clinic in his contacts and waited while the call clicked through its answering service and on to Hannah's mobile.

'Cody and Cody, Hannah speaking.'

'Buttercup's in labour. She doesn't sound good, Hannah. I'm worried.'

He knew her well enough to envisage her kicking something and swearing at Josh for having the gall to be busy so she was the one who had to deal with him.

'I'm on my way. Is she on her feet?'

'She's on her knees.'

'She may lie down and get up a few times, that's normal, don't try to stop it. I'm leaving now.'

'Hannah?' he said, but the phone had gone dead. 'Drive safe,' he muttered, then turned to his horse. 'Did you hear that, Buttercup, my love? The vet's on her way.'

# CHAPTER
## 44

Why her? Why now? A thousand weekends on call, delivering labradors by C-section, rescuing piglets from bore pumps, even pulling a pissed-off cat from the depths of an old galvo water tank. She'd have traded a thousand more nights of disturbed sleep and poor pay for this one callout to Ironbark Station.

To top it off, Josh was already out on a job, so she'd have to take her car, which still had no freaking working heater. Why, oh why, had she not bought herself a new car when Kylie had told her to?

Hannah put on her old sheepskin jacket and gloves and pulled a knitted cap over her hair. It was freezing here in Hanrahan. Up in the mountain at Ironbark Station, it would feel like the depths of winter—and that would just be the climate between her and Tom.

Sliding into her green bomb, she crunched the gears into first and took off from the gravelled drive with a spin of wheels. She had a foal to deliver. That's all. Tom Krauss and his hot hands and cold words could go hang for all she cared. Buttercup and the baby horse were all that mattered today.

She went through all she knew about horses as she drove up the mountain. She'd had flash cards for this sort of stuff back when she was at vet school in Wagga Wagga, and it was amazing what the brain recalled.

*A mare is, in general terms, receptive to breeding in autumn with the majority of foals born eleven months later, in spring. Out-of-season breeding season can occur. The term of pregnancy can vary wildly.*

Not overly helpful, but it was soothing, snippets of knowledge popping into her head as she drove.

*A thoroughbred may only be the product of a live cover: a witnessed 'natural' mating of stallion to mare. Thoroughbreds in Australia are given the birthdate August 1 for the purposes of racing.*

August 1 was a couple of months away, which meant Buttercup's foal would be young for her year. In racing, that was not a positive. It meant she or he would be competing against animals that might have ten months more development. Probably why Buttercup had been sold to Tom at a discount price.

*1.4 per cent of foals die within two days of birth in Australia.*

Okay, that snippet wasn't so soothing. Tugging her beanie down a little more over her freezing ears, Hannah took a corner in her little green car and flicked on the windscreen wipers as a blast of moisture hit her windscreen. Rain? Hopefully not snow, although there was that special something in the air that smelled like it was coming. Hopefully not tonight. If she had to spend another night in the guest room of Ironbark Station in Mrs L's dressing gown, she'd be adding a special service fee to the bill. A 'Just Because' fee. And it'd be hefty.

The foal was breach. That was the first problem. The second was that Buttercup was a massive horse and Hannah was a short woman. She dried her hand off on a towel and called Josh.

'Hey,' he said.

'You done at the Winfrey farm yet?'

'Complication. The mama dog has hyperplasia and we're in the truck now hightailing it into the surgery for a C-section. Pup in the birth canal isn't going to make it, but I'm hoping we'll save the others. How's Buttercup?'

'Breach.'

'Hmm. Foal must have turned during the week.'

'Yeah. I was hoping you and your long brawny arms might be nearby.'

'Sorry, Hannah. I can come the second I'm done here.'

That would be too late, by the look of Buttercup. The mare was exhausted. This foal had to come out and quickly.

'I'll keep you posted.'

'Han? You've got this.'

She swallowed. She'd better. She dropped her phone into her kit bag and turned to Tom.

'Buttercup's foal isn't in the right position. It could be worse, but it's not ideal: the tail is presenting to the birth canal and the hind legs are tucked up under, pointing forward. Problem is, to get the foal out, we need to turn it.'

'What can I do?'

'I'm short. My arms are short. I don't have the power of a guy. When I'm turning the foal, I need you to wedge yourself in behind me to keep me close to the horse. If I have to brace myself, I'm not going to have enough reach.'

'I can get Lynette.'

'Are you crazy? This is no time to get skittish, mate. I need *you*, Tom. Now. You promised me no more cop-outs. Not with this horse's life on the line.'

He looked at her for a long moment, then he nodded. 'All right.'

Hannah sized up the horse, who was lying on her side, her ribs heaving with the effort of labour. 'We need to get her up first. The act of walking will slow down the contractions and give us a chance to manipulate the foal in the uterus.'

'She doesn't look like she's getting up any time soon.'

'So we make her. You pull on her bridle and I'll encourage her from this end.'

'And walking is okay? This far into it?'

'Walking is good. Out in the wild, a mare will get up and down and walk around during labour; it helps position the foal. Buttercup's been stabled indoors a lot with this poor weather; it may have contributed to the foal not getting itself in the right position. Usually mares foal in spring. Buttercup's just a little out of season and a little out of sorts, aren't you, darling?' Hannah slapped the mare on the rump and gave Tom a look as the mare began to scrabble her hind legs in the hay. 'Now, Tom. Urge her up.'

The huge mare lumbered to her feet and Tom led her in a circle around the stall. 'There's my girl,' he muttered.

'Okay, let's do this.' Hannah had peeled off down to her singlet before the first examination, but she had hay stuck to her arms so she sluiced it off with antiseptic. 'Head her into a corner so she can't move away from me. I'll come up behind her and then you stand behind me. When I say, you lean in against me, okay?'

Tom did as she asked, crowding Buttercup towards the wooden wall. Hannah slipped in behind, felt the loosened muscles below the horse's tail.

'When the foal's turned, it's going to be real quick. We've got to be alert, okay? Ready for anything. You ready?'

His eyes met hers and he looked worried and deathly pale. The professional mask she'd been forcing herself to wear slipped for a second. Then she shoved her concern for him away, hoping it would land in a pile of manure, where it belonged. She was here for Buttercup and her foal, not for Tom.

'I'm ready,' he said.

She turned her back on him and began the long plunge into the birth canal of the horse. 'Up against me now,' she said as her cheek brushed the stiff coat of the horse's rump. Tom moved in behind her, a solid mass bracing her from thigh to shoulder.

'I've got my hand on the foal's rump, I can feel the tail. I'm breaking the sac now, then I'm going to try to roll the foal.' Man, this was tough. She'd rolled foals before, but on stockhorses, never on such a huge and pampered beast like Buttercup. Her hand found a hoof, and she shoved it forward, wincing when it jabbed back and kicked her.

'Foal's alive,' she said.

Tom's breath was hot against her neck.

'Lift me a little, can you?' she grunted. 'I can't quite ...'

Her shoulder was screaming as she rotated her arm within the horse's cervical canal and she heard a muttered curse behind her as Tom hefted her so she was wedged beneath Buttercup's tail. A rush of hot fluid gushed about her arm and she felt a great, sucking whoosh as the foal began to tumble.

'My god,' she breathed. 'I think we've done it.'

She eased her way free of the horse, ignoring the mess of amniotic fluid dripping down her front. 'Walk her, Tom, just around in a slow little circle. With a bit of luck it'll jiggle the foal into the right position. If she wants to lie down, let—'

Hannah broke off as Buttercup dropped to her knees and rolled in the hay. The mare's sides gave a great heave and a tiny hoof slithered free from beneath her tail.

She laughed. 'Spoke too soon.'

She squatted next to the mare, content to let nature take its proper course. Another hoof, a soft nose, and then a small, perfect horse, the colour of autumn leaves on a bright sunny day, plopped onto the hay beside her.

'Well, hello to you too, my sweet,' she murmured. She glanced up at Tom, who stood braced against the wall. 'I think you can break out the cigars.'

He let out a breath. 'Yeah. How's the foal?'

The foal was snuffling in the hay and Hannah eased a hand beneath it until it had see-sawed its way to its feet. 'Just fine. Perfect, in fact. Let's see if Buttercup wants to stand up and check out her new daughter.'

'A girl.' Tom's voice was quiet.

'Mmm.' It was hard to remember how much she disliked him in a moment so profound. She gave Buttercup a gentle slap to the rump. 'Up you get, lovely.'

The horse rose to her feet. When Buttercup's muzzle reached down and whickered softly over the ears of her new foal, Hannah felt tears choke her throat. She had the best job in the world and this was one of the moments that proved that.

She slipped Buttercup a sugar lump from the pile she kept in her kit bag and laughed as the foal nuzzled her fingers. 'Not for you, little princess. You're on a milk-only diet for a few days yet.'

'Sugarplum,' said Tom behind her.

'Excuse me?'

'Her name. Sugarplum.'

She stroked her hand over the foal's soft ears. 'A pretty name for a pretty girl.' She cleared her throat. 'Right. I'll make sure the placenta's out in one piece then I'll be on my way. You'll need to check on them every couple of hours during the night, make sure Buttercup's okay. Any sign of excessive bleeding or fever, call the clinic. Josh will be out first thing tomorrow to check on them.'

'Hannah, thank you.'

She looked at him, quickly, dragging her eyes away before they could linger. 'Just doing my job, Tom.'

She spent the next forty minutes ignoring him while she eased Buttercup through the third stage of labour, cleaned herself up as much as was possible given the muck covering her overalls, then left.

# CHAPTER
# 45

Tom waited until the sweep of Hannah's headlights had headed down the mountain, then relaxed his death grip on the stable wall and slid to the floor. His phone, thank god, was still in his pocket.

The first call was to the naval base at Wollongong, to call in the favour he'd been promised as part of his separation package.

The second was to Lynette, who needed to mind Buttercup and the foal in his absence, then find the hurricane lanterns, then come up with whatever cover story she could think of to satisfy Bruno and Mrs L who, in about fifty minutes' time, were going to hear a helicopter land beside the stables.

The next was to Dr Novak.

'It's Tom Krauss. Sorry to call so late, but I might have a problem.'

The doctor's exhalation hummed through the phone line. 'Define problem.'

'I can't move my left leg.'

'Oh, Tom. Call an ambulance. You need to get here straight away.'

'I've got a different plan. How free are you tonight and tomorrow?'

'Consultations booked tomorrow, but no surgical list. I can reschedule. What do you need?'

'I've called in a favour. A defence helicopter will be collecting you in about forty minutes from the helipad at Cooma Airport. Bring anything you think we might need for the run down to Wollongong. Once you're in, the chopper will come here and collect me.'

'Forty minutes! I'll be ready. Tom—stay still until I get there, will you? Very, very still.'

Tom dropped the phone and considered his position, sprawled on the hay-strewn floor of Buttercup's stable, the huge mare and her tender young foal breathing gently into the cold evening air beside him. 'I'm not going anywhere,' he muttered.

He closed his eyes to wait.

The chopper ride was a blur of noise and movement. Two medicos built like tanks had lifted him onto a gurney and strapped him into place while Lynette manned the hurricane lanterns.

Once he was secured straight as a board on the stretcher and they were in the air, Dr Novak sat by his side, her cool hand holding his, which he felt absurdly grateful for. She'd ditched her mask, he noticed. She had a kind face and worry was written all over it.

Fifty minutes, give or take, of airtime, then a flurry of wheels and white coats and gloved fingers as he was wheeled from room to room while scans probed and photographed their way through his flesh to uncover the drama within.

Dr Novak came to say her goodbyes and he felt a tug of regret as she left the room. She'd been a link, if a tenuous one, to home.

Now here he was, again, in the place he'd spent so many weeks when the injury was fresh and the ceiling hadn't grown any more interesting since he last stared up at it.

A cough sounded in the doorway. One of the flag officers from the naval base had come to see him, her service cap tucked under her arm.

'Lieutenant Commander Krauss.'

'Retired,' he said. 'At least, I'm trying to retire and stay that way. This blasted shrapnel keeps bringing me back. I'd salute, but they've trussed me up like a pot roast. Nil movement, nil food. I'm surprised they let you in here.'

She moved closer to the bed. 'I used my nice words. I'm sorry to see you back here, Tom.'

'Yeah,' he said on a sigh. 'Me too, commodore.'

'They going to operate?'

'Three surgeons are arguing about it as we speak. Two of them say it's too risky—I should wait here in traction and hope the shrapnel shifts.'

'And the other one?'

'Wants to operate. She stuffs it, I'm a paraplegic.'

'Risky now or risky later.'

'Yep.'

'Your thoughts?'

'We're in the risk business, commodore. You know that.'

'Yes, I do. So, you're going to push for the operation now?'

Yes. Yes, he was. He was done with waiting.

The commodore sat in the chair by the bed. 'You want a little company?'

'Wouldn't mind. The thoughts in your head'll be way more interesting than the ones in mine. Any news from the Combined Task Force?'

'Leadership passes from Turkey to Japan soon. Australia's role won't change too much, we expect. Oil tanker piracy seems to be getting more about politics than ransom these days. Iran just seized two Greek tankers in the Gulf and that's causing a lot of grief.'

'Yeah, I heard that on the radio.'

'You have radio out there in the Snowies?'

'Funny,' he said. 'You know, when I was in Bahrain, up to my neck in it, it was all I thought about. But having this time away … it makes you think.'

'Like what?'

'Like … I've done my bit. Let someone else have their turn defending the oceans. I didn't think I'd ever say it, but I'm ready to start defending things on a smaller scale.' Like Benjamin Dorley's property settlement. Small on the world scale, but important to the bloke whose life it would affect.

'That's good. I mean, *I'd* hate it. If I had to sit in the suburbs and write grocery lists and battle for a carpark space at the newsagent, I'd blow my stack, but I'm pleased you've found some contentment, Tom.'

Well, not quite. Contentment was not something he could claim to ever have with this thing lurking in his back.

'How's life at Creswell treating you, commodore? Any gossip?'

He let her words fill his head; they helped block out the fear that was dug in like a tick.

# CHAPTER
## 46

Hannah scrambled backwards as the two-hundred kilogram sow lunged for her leg.

'Jeepers,' she said, as her heart rate shot into the stratosphere. 'She always so stroppy?'

'Marilyn?' The farmer scratched his nose. 'Precious girl's a peach. Usually. That's why I've called you out. Poor lass has been snapping at everyone for near on a week.'

'Hmm. She off her food?'

'Nope. She gets a mash cook-up done special, same as always.'

'She been scratching herself against posts? Frothing at the mouth? Sleeping more than normal?'

'Not so as I've noticed.'

'Could she be in the family way, Eddie?'

'Marilyn Monroe? Oh, no, she's retired from all that nonsense.'

Hannah grinned. 'You named a pet pig after a movie star?'

Eddie Gunther puffed out his chest and rocked a little on the balls of his feet. 'She's beautiful, ain't she? And you look real close, her hair's golder'n sunlight.'

She eyed the pig, whose eyes were slit like a demon's and whose yellowed teeth were currently displayed in an impressive snarl. The beauty, she didn't get. The decision to retire from the nonsense of hanky-panky? That, she got. Unfortunately.

Josh leant on his forearms over the rail from the safety of the shed's aisle. 'Complicated set of symptoms, Eddie. Now you see why I needed my expert sister here for a second opinion.'

Hannah eyed the malevolent expression of Marilyn the Devil Pig. 'Yeah, you keep telling yourself that, you big coward.' She eased as far away as the narrow confines of the pen allowed. 'Unexplained mood change. Okay, I suggest we get a blood sample, see if there's an indicator of disease. Look at her feet, see if there's a cut or infection. Look in her mouth. At her age, a rotten tooth is a real possibility. That'd make anyone—any pig—a little tetchy.'

'She's a little old for an anaesthetic,' said Josh.

'Time to put those muscles of yours into action, handsome.'

'You'll be meaning me, I expect, Miss Hannah,' said Eddie, rolling up his sleeves.

She grinned at Josh. Eddie was eighty if he was a day. 'Absolutely. And we've got Josh here as backup just in case we need him.'

'Gotcha.'

'Okay. Blood sample, hoof check, teeth check, in that order. We ready, team?' Hannah pulled a syringe from her kit and eyed the cranky pig. 'Let the fun begin.'

One hour and a palette of bruises later, Hannah hauled her muddy self through the pen rails and headed out of the sty, leaving Eddie holding a blackened pig tooth as a souvenir in the palm of his hand. Josh was ahead of her, hosing the worst of the mud from his boots with one hand while he held his phone to his ear. Her brother couldn't go an hour without ringing his new bride. Please, god, whatever Vera was cooking up for breakfast, let there be enough for her, too. She was beat. Dragging a huge pig around after the physical demand of a horse's breech birth, plus a string of sleepless nights, was hard work. As strong as the lure of crawling into her apartment and collapsing onto the sofa was, there was no way she was missing out on one of Vera's breakfasts.

Besides. She was due a comfort eat. Bacon, eggs, chocolate and ice-cream, all at once if need be, until she got Tom Krauss one hundred per cent out of her system.

'Why the hell would you not have told me this earlier?' she heard her brother explode into his phone.

What the heck? Whoever her brother was talking to, it wasn't Vera.

'Nope,' said Josh, the hose water running, forgotten, over the cracked ground. 'Of course … shit, man …'

Hannah bent over to lever off her mud-caked boots.

'Which vertebrae? Uh-huh … you need me to——? Does Hannah know about this yet?'

'Does Hannah know what?' she asked across the wide, rusted tray of his work truck.

Josh spun around, the look on his face telling her he hadn't known he had an audience. 'Too late, Tom,' he said into his phone. 'Hannah's right here.'

Tom? She opened her mouth to tell her brother she didn't give a flying fruitbat what news Tom had to share, then paused. Were those …?

Holy hell, her strong, sensible, easy-going brother was crying.

She gripped the tray of the truck with both hands. 'You're scaring me, Josh Cody. What's going on?'

Her brother held up his hand. 'Tom,' he said into his phone. 'You need me, you just call, all right? … Okay, of course … Uh-huh. Yep, bye.'

She waited while her brother dropped his phone into the tray then looked up at her. 'Is it Bruno? Buttercup? The foal?' she said.

Josh came around to her side of the truck and stood next to her, his shoulder warm against hers. 'No. They're all fine.'

'What, then?'

'It's Tom.'

Fear turned her innards to stone. 'For god's sake, Josh. Just tell me.'

'You noticed his limp lately?'

'No. Well, I guess I have, now you ask. And he was a bit off the other night when Buttercup had her foal, but I was trying not to, um … things got complicated.'

'You were avoiding him for days before Buttercup had her foal.'

She bit her lip. 'Yes. Wait—he told me a month or so ago he had a bad knee. Blamed it on footy or skiing or something. I wasn't really paying attention.'

Josh picked up her hand and held it in his. His voice came out low. 'Hannah, Tom has a piece of metal lodged in the muscles next to his spine from an injury which occurred some months ago. It has been immobile to now, but something has happened and if it causes any more swelling in his spinal sheath, he'll lose function in his legs. Unfortunately, one of his legs has gone numb. This means they have to operate. Urgently.'

She drew in a ragged breath, 'Oh my god. How did it get there? And where is he? In Cooma? Let's drive there now.'

'He's not in Cooma. He was evacuated by helicopter to Wollongong.'

'Wollongong! Wait …' Her voice had a quaver in it that she couldn't control. 'How long have you known?'

'About the injury? For a while, since I asked him why he couldn't ride down the mountain himself to get Bruno's oxygen. About the shrapnel moving and the high-risk surgery he's having later today? Since just then, when he rang to ask me if I'd help Mrs LaBrooy with Bruno while he's gone.'

'When did all this happen?'

'He was medevacced out the night Buttercup had her foal. That's why I've only seen Lynette when I've been up at Ironbark. It seems he swore her to secrecy.'

Hannah leant forward until her head rested on her hands. How could Tom have kept this a secret?

'He couldn't ride,' she said. 'I called him a cop-out.'

'Uh-huh.'

She frowned at her brother. 'What else aren't you telling me?'

He frowned right back. 'You've really got to have this out with Tom.'

'I made him help. With the foal.'

'Help how?'

'Well, you've seen how huge Buttercup is. I had to turn the foal, so I got Tom to help keep me up close so I could reach in.'

Josh pursed his lips. 'I'm sure that wouldn't have been—'

'I made him lift me. I couldn't get the foal to tumble forward, so I made him lift me and I didn't ask him I just sort of shouted. You know what I'm like, Josh. I'm awful. I'm *awful.*' The last few words didn't really come out right because she was sobbing while she said them.

Her brother pulled her in for a hug. 'Hannah, there's no blame on you in this. And you're not awful. You're a wonderful vet and you put animals first. That makes you admirable, not awful.'

Josh was just being Josh. Kind. He always said kind things. But her? She remembered the times she'd pushed at Tom, sniped at him. Added to the burden he'd been carrying alone.

She faced her brother. 'Did he tell you how he ended up with shrapnel in his back? I mean, he's been out of the Navy for ages. And he told me he worked a desk job.'

'He didn't say, but does Tom seem like the guy who would work a desk job?'

No. He didn't. Which maybe she'd have picked up on if she'd spent less time being a shouty, snappy person and more time being quiet and nice and thoughtful.

'Now, Han, Bruno doesn't know about any of this. Nobody knows but me and Lynette. And you.'

'Some things,' she said slowly, 'are starting to make sense.'

'Like what?'

'Like when I was up at the homestead one evening, he wouldn't sit on the floor. Maybe it was his back that was the problem.' A thought struck her, a great, gnarly, monster of a thought. Was this why he'd kept turning her away? Was this why his eyes kept saying *love me*, but his words kept saying *leave*? He didn't want her to know his secret?

'Oh my god,' she breathed.

'What is it?'

'I've just realised—' She broke off. This was her brother she was talking to. There was only one person she needed to be having this particular conversation with, and that person was Tom. 'I've got to go to him.'

Josh raised an eyebrow. 'To Wollongong? Hannah, are you sure?'

'I'm sure.' She patted his arm. 'Let's get back to town. You right to cover for me while I'm gone?'

'Of course. But Han—I don't want to talk you out of this. If you need to go and be with Tom, I am one hundred per cent supporting you. But will you be okay? Let's not forget how the Dalgety Show-grounds turned out.'

She shook her head. 'I went to the Adaminaby Picnic Races and it was a doddle.'

'What about the wedding in Lake George?'

'That was Charlie who upset me, not being in a new place.'

She walked around to the driver's side and turned the key in the ignition until the diesel engine rattled into life.

'But it upset you a *lot*.'

True, she thought, as she crunched the gearstick into first and roared out of the farmyard. Okay, so there'd been some crying in the gutter. Some misery and shame and heartache. She blew out a breath. She could barely recognise that poor, deluded Hannah who'd fallen apart by the roadside.

She was different now. And it was time for the secrets to be over and the truth to be lived, no matter what. Her secrets *and* Tom's.

# CHAPTER
# 47

She'd make the midday plane if she hurried. She barely knew what she was throwing in her duffle bag. Underwear, check. T-shirt, jeans, boots … she had all those on her body currently, so maybe a spare t-shirt. Socks? A veterinary journal to read on the plane would be both educational and an excellent reason to make eye contact with exactly zero people. Eye mask, another winning idea. She spun on her heel and checked the surfaces of her bedroom, looking for inspiration. What did one take on a mad dash to hold the hand of the man one loved through the darkest hours of his life?

Her gaze fell on the open door of her closet, where all the clothes Kylie had rummaged through the other week bulged from the hanging space. Her breath quickened. Oh, yes. That would be *perfect*. A grand gesture that would say it all.

Five minutes later, she was running out the back of the vet clinic to her car. The engine caught, fired, then cut out.

'Come on, car. You know you want to,' she muttered, turning the key again and pounding on the accelerator. The motor under the faded hood whined in a half-hearted complaint then fell into silence. 'Crap,' she whispered. 'Crap, crap, crap.'

The fear and turmoil she'd been covering with action since she'd learned what Tom was facing broke through and a sob escaped her. She leant her head on the wheel and gripped it while the tears flowed. *Think*, she urged herself. *Think*.

Josh had rounds to do, so she couldn't steal his truck. Sandy had kids who needed her to drive them to karate. Kylie! She dived for her phone and hit the speed dial.

'Come on,' she said as the phone rang and rang.

'Hanrahan Mechanics. We can't come to the phone right now because we're busy fixing cars. Leave a message, and we'll get ba—'

She stabbed the phone silent. An answering machine was no darn use at all. Who, then?

A thought struck her and she grabbed her duffle from the passenger seat and took off across the square. The Billy Button Café was usually filled with customers sitting around stuffing their mouths with cake. Most of them were usually super keen to stick their nose into her business. Today one of them could give her a ride.

She shot through the doors and Graeme looked up from his treasured machine.

'What's up, honeypie?'

'Graeme. I've got to get to the airport at Cooma but my car broke down.'

'Not the green machine?'

'I don't have time to laugh. Not today.'

'Okay, honey. Let me get Vera. One of us can take you, for sure.'

'Thanks.'

He gave her arm a squeeze then hurried into the kitchen and came out with Vera on his heels.

'Hannah? Is everything okay?'

'Can I tell you on the way to Cooma? I don't want to miss my plane.'

'Sure.' Vera pulled a set of keys from under the till. 'Let's go.'

Graeme shoved a box of tissues and a cupcake into her hands. Now that was a man who understood a crisis. 'You need me, you call me, Hannah. Any time.'

She blew him a kiss over her shoulder as she raced out the door after Vera. She loved this town.

But she loved Tom more. Strapping herself into the front seat of Vera's tidy little car, she gave herself a moment to think. She had money. Correction … she had credit cards that weren't totally blown out, and that counted as money, didn't it? She had a plane ticket barcode saved in a photo file on her phone. And she had a great, welling lump of fear settled around her heart that wasn't going to ease until she saw Tom for herself.

Vera shot over the cattle grid at the bottom of the mountain and made the turn at the airport sign. 'You ready to tell me what's going on?'

'I've been a fool, Vera.'

A hand gave hers a pat. 'Been there, done that, honey. How have you been a fool?'

'You know I've been running around making a great moonling of myself over Tom Krauss?'

Vera winced. 'I try to tune out all the gossip I hear at the café, Hannah. I try really hard. But yes. Me and everyone else in town knows that.'

'Thing is, Vera, I've been getting these mixed signals.'

'From Tom?'

'Yep.'

'Seemed like the green light from my side of the counter. The guy looks at you like you're icing on a cake.'

Hannah nodded. 'That's what I thought, but he kept pushing me away.'

'Men. What idiots.'

'Well, that's a given, but I just found out he had a reason for pushing me away.'

'You're saying that in a way that's scaring me,' said Vera. 'Is that why we're racing to the airport?'

'Yeah. He's in hospital. And it's bad, Vera.' Her voice broke. 'It's really bad.'

The carpark at the airport was half empty, but Hannah directed Vera to the drop-off zone. 'I've got to run if I'm going to make the boarding call.'

'You want me to wait in case you miss it?'

'No, it's fine.'

She buried her head in Vera's neck for a moment as the woman brought her in for a hug. She smelled like vanilla and plums and growing baby. 'Thanks for the ride.'

'Any time. Go be with your man.'

The airport was quiet but for the departure queue lined up at gate two. Incoming travellers were streaming through the gate as she ran up, and her duffle slapped into a woman and a man and nearly knocked over a stroller.

'Sorry,' she called out to all the eyes that turned her way. 'Sorry!'

She raced around to the check-in counter, held up her phone so the barcode could be scanned and was waved through.

It wasn't until she sank into her seat at the back of the plane that she realised she'd not given a thought to drawing attention to herself. She just hadn't cared.

# CHAPTER

# 48

Tom returned his gaze to the ceiling after the surgeon left the room. Eighty-one punch holes in each ceiling tile, forty ceiling tiles, that made—crap, now his maths skills were packing up too— three thousand two hundred and something?

The surgeon had been in for the final talk. The anaesthetist had visited with questions about allergies and medical histories and risk. Both of them had spoken in that upbeat, jocular tone medical staff liked to use, which was both patronising and comforting in equal measure.

Kind of like his and Josh's kindy teacher, now he thought of it. Mrs Howdy-Doody, they'd called her, but that couldn't possibly have been her real name.

He returned to his brooding. He had a will, of course. Bruno and Mrs L to inherit.

Regrets … he had a few. Oh, man, did he just *sing* that? Perhaps the anaesthetist had slipped a little something into the drip attached to his arm—a little pre-surgery pickling fluid.

He went back to counting the dots in the ceiling tiles.

He was somewhere in the six thousands when he heard raised voices in the corridor, then a laugh cut short. It had to be the big nurse, Samuel. He was always bursting in and out of rooms spreading his personal brand of cheer. Like Santa in scrubs.

A scratch at the door, then it was being pushed open and he braced himself. The orderly, come to wheel him into the operating room where his future would be decided.

Only ... it wasn't the orderly who poked a nose around his door. It was Hannah.

'I'm coming in,' she announced. 'I don't care what you say.'

He really must have some sort of drug percolating through his system, because he found his will to resist had entirely deserted him. He held out his hand and she sobbed and ran to him.

He blinked. 'Am I hallucinating or are you wearing something really ... er ... I mean ...' Words failed him.

'My high school formal dress. Yes, I am.'

His eyes skittered over the dull pink bodice, the straining seams at the waist, the huge marshmallow skirt, all of it fashioned out of some sort of waxy fabric the colour of ... he gave up. 'What do you call that colour? Looks like putty.'

She did a little twirl. 'My mother made it for me over a decade ago. I thought you might like to see what I'd've looked like if you'd worked up the courage to ask the girl you *wanted* to take to your formal.'

He leant his head back on the pillow and closed his eyes against the sting. 'Dodged that bullet.'

She brought his hand up to her mouth and held it there, so he felt her lips move against his skin. 'You can stop lying to me, Tom.'

He breathed in, then out, then thought of absolutely nothing he could say.

'I think you are a mighty fine liar and I think you've been lying to me six ways from Sunday about all the reasons why you're not interested in me.'

She had him. She'd called his bluff.

'You can ask me now.'

'To be my date to the formal?'

She squeezed his fingers. 'I'm waiting.'

He opened his eyes and looked at her. Problem was, he wasn't eighteen anymore. He was a man who knew what deep regret felt like. Who knew what injury or illness could do to a man who felt robbed of his life's dreams.

No way could he do that to Hannah. He was Bruno's son, after all. Who was to say he wouldn't become just as much of a bitter, angry man as his father had when his legs failed him?

'I want to,' he said at last. 'But I don't know what my future holds. I'm not in a position to be inviting anyone to a formal. Even you.'

She pressed a kiss onto his hand. 'That's not true. I know about your injury. I know about the risk. And I make my own decisions about who I let invite me out.'

The door opened and this time it really was the orderly.

'Tom, we're ready to rumble. Oh! Sorry, I didn't know you had a guest. That's quite an outfit.'

Tom looked over Hannah's shoulder at the orderly. 'Can you give us a minute?'

'Surgical team's prepped.'

'Come back in five.'

He met Hannah's gaze and swallowed. He had to tell her, regardless of the gesture she was making here in her hideous dress. 'There's no guarantee of a happy ending, Hannah.'

'I don't care. You don't get to decide what makes me happy, Tom Krauss. I do. And I've decided it's you.'

He shook his head. 'It can't be, Hannah. If this surgery doesn't work, I won't …' Shit. He really did not want to say the words out loud. 'I won't be the man you want me to be. Ever.'

'You're exactly the man I want you to be. Strong. Kind. Loyal. Brave. You're the one I'm having, Tom, no matter what. For a while there I was thinking I wasn't good enough for you, on account of how I can be fairly stroppy most of the time, but then I discovered what a liar you are. So that cancels out my stroppiness.'

'Your logic is … alarming.' But adorable. And he wished it was enough.

The orderly was back, the big nurse behind him. 'It's roll out time, Tom. Sorry, love.'

Tom had to get it said. 'If this surgery goes badly, my ability to give you or anyone a baby might be gone. I'm not going to be the bloke who stands between you and your greatest wish.'

'You're not hearing me, Krauss,' she said. 'I'll be waiting for you. No matter what.'

Her hand closed tight on his for a moment, then he was moved beyond her reach.

# CHAPTER

# 49

She spent the first three hours in a horrid grey chair by a fake pot plant in the waiting room. She spent another hour over a pot of tea in the cafeteria, staring out the window at the security lights shining down on the carpark, then she spent an hour hiding in the ladies restroom on the ground floor, crying.

She was wiping her face when a tall woman in blue scrubs found her.

'Hannah Cody?'

'Yes?'

'I'm Dr Tse.'

Hannah gripped the hand dryer and took in a shaky breath. 'Is it over?'

The doctor smiled and the fist around Hannah's heart eased, just a fraction. 'The steel fragment is out. The spinal cord is intact. We're expecting the swelling to go down and for Tom to be just fine.'

'Oh my god.'

'You okay?'

'Yeah.' She sniffed. 'Relieved, happy, a little crazy all at the same time.'

The surgeon put a hand on her shoulder and gave it a squeeze. 'You can be as happy and crazy as you like.'

'Can I see him?'

'He's in recovery and he'll be there all night. Well, what's left of the night,' said the doctor, glancing at her watch. 'I'll clear you to see him tomorrow, but we'll be needing some time with him first. Rehab starts early with this sort of injury and we'll not be calling you until he's managed a walking lap of the ward, so get some sleep.'

'Thank you.'

'Are you planning on spending the whole night in here?'

Hannah stared at herself in the mirror: tired eyes, tear-tracks of mascara, a crumpled daggy dress puffing out around her hips. 'Not anymore, I'm not.'

She stayed in the cheap motel the hospital doorman had recommended. Warm sunlight floated across her when she woke to the sound of her phone. It chirruped again and she lunged for it, pulling it off the charger so wildly the bedside lamp tottered to the floor with a crash.

A number she didn't know.

'Miss Cody?'

'Yes?'

'This is Samuel from the hospital. There's a certain patient in Room 308 who's wondering where you are.'

'He's awake?'

'Awake and filled with attitude.'

A muffled voice came through the receiver. 'Hang on a sec, Miss Cody. He's snapping out orders from his bed again.'

She put the phone on speaker then ripped open her duffle bag and started pulling on clean jeans, listening to the half-heard conversation.

'Everything okay?' she said when Samuel came back on the line.

'Tom wants me to tell you to get your arse over here and bring decent coffee, or you can look forward to finding a frog in your boot some day real soon.'

She grinned. Tom really was feeling okay. 'Tell him I'll put it on his tab.'

He was standing in that same sunlight, a square shaft of it that turned his hair into pale flame. The hospital issue gown of yesterday was gone, replaced with jeans older than hers, a navy sweater that looked homemade. Mrs LaBrooy's work, she thought fondly. Taking care of her boy, as always.

She stood in the crack of the door for a moment and rested her eyes on him.

Tom.

She hadn't known she was running away from fate that day all those months ago, when he'd kissed her in Buttercup's stable and she'd panicked. She'd been damaged, still. Raw where it mattered, down deep where her emotions lived. Tom had helped soothe the wound.

Being loved—even in his sneaky, I-don't-love-you way—had helped to do that.

Because that's what he'd been doing, even when he was saying differently, even when he was driving her nuts. It was love he'd shown her when he dragged her off the guy she walloped. Love when he came calling with an apple pie in a box. It had been love when he'd held her in the gutter so she could cry away her humiliation. Love when he'd gently suggested her baby plan was bonkers.

And now it was her turn to show him how good she could be at loving someone.

She stepped into the sunlight. 'Looking good, sailor. Although, I'm not sure who let you get out of bed.'

He turned to face her and all the worry and rush and heartache of the last few days—well, months and bloody *years*, really, but who was counting—blinked out.

'Hannah.'

'I managed to get my arse here, as you can see. Coffee, too,' she said.

'Come closer so I can check it out.'

'Milk, no sugar, right?'

'I wasn't talking about the coffee,' he said, and that grin that he so rarely wore was there, just how she liked to see it, aimed right at her.

She felt heat swamping her cheeks. Flirty Tom was not the Tom she'd fallen in love with. Grumpy Tom, aloof Tom, teasing and let's-just-be-friends Tom … she was totally cool with all of those. Flirty Tom sent goosebumps chasing over her skin.

She moved into the room and handed him a cup. 'Seriously, should you be standing?'

'Day one: four fifty-metre walks. Every day a little more.'

'Okay then.'

The silence lengthened and she felt shy, suddenly, which was silly, because hadn't she known Tom her whole life? Hadn't she seen him naked in a tub?

She lifted her coffee cup. 'So. You're all good then,' she mumbled, thinking what she really wanted to do was set her coffee down on the windowsill and just hold him. She'd rushed all this way, she loved him, but now the idea of just stepping forward and *hugging* seemed very, very difficult.

'I'm all good.'

'And … no more secrets?'

'None,' he replied. 'How about you?'

'I'm an open book.' At least, she'd like to be an open book. A *Laird's Legacy* type book, where burly-thighed heroes swept up lusty maidens and wickedly delicious things happened in chapter fourteen. And chapter twenty-one. And chapter thirty-two.

She choked on an overly hot gulp of coffee when he hooked a finger into the neckline of her t-shirt and pulled her closer to him. 'And I'm an open book. At least, I will be, when I 'fess up and tell you that yes, I was lying the whole time.'

She shivered. 'I want an apology for every lie.'

He drew her in a little closer. 'I apologise for lying to you when I said I was a disinterested party.'

'Um, I accept your apology.'

He was barely a breath away now, and one hand was sliding along her rib cage. 'I apologise for lying to you when I said kissing you in the stables wasn't much of a snog.'

'It wasn't? I mean, it was? I mean …'

'Let's go for a re-enactment so I can show you what *I* mean.' He shifted, and the sun-bright window was on one side of her, with six foot of muscle-bound male on the other. She'd been as close to him before, but never like this. Not with this awareness that she *knew* that he wanted her and he *knew* that she wanted him.

Her breath juddered out and she looked up into his eyes. It was like looking into a deep, deep lake. The worry that had framed his face had smoothed itself away and been replaced with … she chuckled, and tried to think of a more manly, appropriate word for his expression than 'horny'.

His mouth quirked. 'What's so funny?'

'You're crowding me, Krauss.'

'I know.'

She swallowed. His hands had slid up her back and his thumbs were finding ridges of scapula and rib to rub against and it was playing havoc with her ability to think. 'Are we really ready for this?'

He kissed her cheek, just a fleeting press of lips, and his breath was soft in her ear. 'We are so ready, Hannah Cody. For this and everything. For this and *anything*.'

He was right. She was ready. She rose onto her tiptoes, wrapped her arms around his neck and touched her lips to his.

This wasn't their first kiss, but it felt like it. He moved around, swivelling her until her back was to the wall, and his arms wrapped around her so she was tight within his embrace. She ran her hands up his sides, hesitating for just a second as they encountered the crepe bandage on his back, then ran them up his chest, which felt just as warm, just as good.

A sigh escaped her, and she felt herself melting as his lips moved to the corner of her mouth, to her cheek, to the curve of skin beneath her ear.

After a searing moment that all but made her forget her own name, he rested his forehead against hers. 'Hospital room. Maybe not the most private of places.'

She willed her heartbeat to settle. 'True. But I don't think you've reached the end of your apologies.'

He laughed and it was lovely to feel it as well as hear it.

'I apologise for lying to you when I said guys are jerks. Clearly that wasn't true and I'm totally awesome.'

She snorted. 'I think you must still be drugged.'

'Maybe.'

They stood there looking at each other, her hands pressed against his heart.

Tom spoke first. 'You know, when they woke me in recovery, I was still so woozy from the anaesthetic all I could think was *So, that's it. Legs gone.* I couldn't feel anything and I had never allowed myself to hope. The whole time, all the waiting ... to me, it felt like I was just pushing out the inevitable paraplegia. The medical staff were speaking to me, saying the surgery was a success, but I couldn't get it, at first. I thought success meant: you're alive, Tom. I couldn't believe it when I understood they meant the removal had been a success.'

'You'd worried about it so long, it had become the only reality your brain would accept.'

'That actually sounds quite smart.'

'Hey, I've got plenty of practice in the worry department.'

'I know you do. Which is why I couldn't let you worry about me, too. I'm sorry I wasn't honest with you.'

The door slammed open and Samuel stood there, filling the space. 'Physiotherapist is ready for you, Tom. We need to head down to the rehab centre, and since your chart says sedate walking for brief periods is the only activity allowed, I'm gonna pretend I haven't seen you snogging your lady friend in the corner. On the bed. Sir.'

Tom muttered under his breath and Hannah smoothed his jumper then let go.

'Wait for me?'

'Always.'

# CHAPTER

# 50

***Four and a bit months later***

*FirstLook© tests alert you to the presence of a hormone (human chorionic gonadotropin [hCG]) in your urine; for best results, use the test first thing in the morning.*

Hannah stuffed the instruction leaflet back in her pocket and looked at the stick for what felt like the eighty-sixth time. Two stripes. *Two.* That first one was the control line so, okay, the kit was working. But that other line!

She felt a little scream on the inside.

She knew biology, and she could science the shiitake out of anything she put her mind to, but for some reason she was having a lot of trouble interpreting these results.

It seemed … it could be … it was, in fact, highly likely … that she was pregnant.

An impatient hand, which she was guessing was liver-spotted and sinewy and belonged to Kev Jones, banged on the door. 'How long can one chick spend in one portaloo?' he yelled.

*Maybe it wasn't just one chick in here*, she thought. *Maybe it was two chicks! Or one chick and one pale-haired, blue-eyed little horseman.*

'Your event is on in ten,' Kev said, and he must have had his face mushed up right into the crack of the portaloo door, so she took pity on him, shoved the stick down the front of her bra and opened the door.

'I'm coming,' she said. 'Hold your horses, mate.'

'Like I've not heard that before. Come on, Skippy's raring to go and your mum and dad have elbowed their way onto the platform closest to the cutting yard, so make sure you give them a smile, all right?'

'Yes, Kev,' she said.

She was good at smiling these days. She smiled every morning when she woke up in Tom's arms, and every night when he stroked her hair and told her she was beautiful and embarked upon wickedly delicious things that—hello—even the burly Laird of Finchmore hadn't mastered.

Skippy was saddled and ready to go, with Josh holding his bridle.

'Where's Vera?' she said.

'Sitting with Mum and Dad. We'll see you after the maiden event.'

'Where's Tom?'

'Am I your secretary? I can't keep track of everyone.'

'But you're taller than I am. You're my lookout.'

He gave her a leg up. 'Not anymore I'm not. Your boyfriend and I have engaged in a secret men's ritual whereby I passed my mantle of duty to him.'

She snorted. 'Did this ritual involve beer breath and back slapping?'

'All the finest rituals do. Now, get your head in the game, Hannah Banana. I've bet Dad two dollars you won't get through the cut out, so go prove me wrong.'

'No worries.'

She ruffled his hair in thanks for his help and nudged Skip towards the competition arena. The cut-out yard was set up just to the side of Ironbark Station's training paddock and portable fences had been brought in to pen the groups of cattle. Ironbark Station's campdraft had been up, up and away since shortly after nine and the day could not be more perfect.

Bruno gave her a nod from the officials' area, a raised platform made accessible with a wide steel ramp. He wouldn't be judging her event—oh, no, she was way too insignificant a contender for Bruno's expertise—but it was sweet of him to be taking an interest. Especially since she'd had to sidestep all his offers of help. Kev would have had his heart broken and she was too aware of how that felt to be disloyal. Bruno had taken it on the chin, so that was fine.

In fact, *everything* was fine.

The rider ahead of her on the program charged through the open gates and into the cutting yard and Hannah watched as the steers and heifers splintered into two groups. A tough one. Ride at them and hope one got separated? Or pick one and try to nudge it free without trapping it up against the fence?

The rider caught a break when two steers bolted across the yard and like a flash, horse and rider had one of them cut off. Back and forth they went, side to side, and the rider called, 'Gate!' and the first part of the event was done.

The crowd all turned to the main arena and watched the steer put some speed on. The first post was made, the second post was a bust and then—*whip crack*—the rider was done.

Not bad. Hannah would be thrilled to do half as well.

Nobody had ever said the draft was easy, but by heck it had taught her a thing or two about tenacity. And patience. Both qualities she'd had to learn the hard way.

She looked at the officials' stage as she and Skippy entered the cut-out yard for their turn, and there he was.

Her Tom.

He wore a dusty old hat low over his forehead and denim jeans that clung like oil, and she'd probably fall off her horse and embarrass herself in front of every campdrafter for a thousand kilometres if she didn't stop ogling him and concentrate.

Pick a steer, that was Kev's constant advice, but there was a heifer on the edge of the group who was looking right at her.

'You are mine, my precious,' she muttered, and drove Skippy in with her knees. The heifer turned to bolt, but Skippy's shoulder was there, blocking her way.

Another turn.

Another shoulder.

'Gate!' she called—like a boss!—and the ringers manning the wide stock gate swung it open and the heifer bolted like the hounds of hell were after it.

Hannah and Skippy weren't quite hounds, but they were riding hell for leather now. They drove the heifer round one post, and this, Hannah knew, was officially the best they'd ever done. The second post, yes! Around they went!

She had no idea where they were for time, but they were on that heifer's tail, and driving her to the gate, when *whip crack*! They were out of time, but only just.

It'd be a good score.

'Skippy, you're my wonderful boy,' she told her horse, patting him on the neck.

He gave a little head toss and they trotted out of the field.

Her event was done.

Now all she had to do was bide her time, chat with the locals and catch Tom on his own.

Because, boy, oh boy, did she have news for him.

# EPILOGUE

*Bruno Krauss was born on the SS* Partizanka, *a ship that left Malta on 15 December 1947, carrying 808 immigrants bound for Australia. He was the first and only child of Rudi and Marlene Krauss.*

*Rudi and Marlene—my grandparents—were married on Marlene's eighteenth birthday a month after the Second World War came to an end. The cost of passage to a country far from depressed and war-torn Germany was promised to them as a wedding present by a relative whose name has been lost to history, and the young couple hoped to turn this windfall into a new life as farmers. Upon disembarkation in Sydney on 15 January 1948, they found work and accommodation here in the Snowy Mountains on a cattle property, where Marlene supplemented the family income as a seamstress for local families.*

*By 1956, they'd tucked away enough savings to convince the bank manager down in Cooma to lend them the money to buy two hundred acres of poorly cleared scrub country on Gorge Road. Bruno, who was eight at the time, took one look at the property that was to be his new home and fell in love.*

*The story goes he gave his mother the run around when she tried to interest him in reading and writing, until he learned the local school had a paddock and the kids were welcome to arrive on horseback. Of course, this meant he needed a horse, which cost money his parents didn't have, but Bruno was nothing if not enterprising, stubborn and determined. He chopped wood, he sold eggs, he convinced Marlene that he deserved a hefty commission when he talked the neighbour into paying his mum to sew school clothes for his eight children.*

*Bruno was saddled up and attending school in no time, but he's been happy to tell anyone who'd listen in the years since that the real lessons he learned there, until he left school for good at the age of fifteen, all happened riding down and back up the mountain on horseback.*

*Bruno loved to ride.*

*He was soon getting odd jobs in the district as a ringer, and at sixteen he took off mustering for two years, returning home only when the news of his mother's untimely death reached him. He told his father that Ironbark Station's cattle were not enough to keep him home; Bruno saw his future in the breeding and training of stockhorses. Rudi—perhaps grieving or perhaps just glad to have his son home again—put his savings into Bruno's hands and the rest, as the cliché goes, is history.*

*Bruno has not been shy about telling all of us that grit and determination are the two qualities that a man—or a woman—needs most. I suspect that is because these are the qualities he learned from his parents and from his years pursuing his dream.*

*Ironbark Station stockhorses can be found in the studbook record of any number of champion horses—campdraft, rodeo, polo—the list goes on. Where Ironbark's true success lies, however, is in the working horses it has bred, trained and sold over the years. The stayers, who do the work, day in, day out.*

*Bruno's philosophy on life was one of endurance. Of overcoming setbacks. Of cracking on until he met with success. Was he a stubborn old goat? Often. Did he have a softer side? Sometimes. Am I proud of him? Yes.*

*He lies now at rest in the family plot along with his wife, my mother, and his parents Rudi and Marlene. We are grateful to Marigold Jones for her hard work in negotiating with the authorities so he could be buried here on the station rather than in the cemetery in Hanrahan. Bruno had little patience for regulations that didn't suit him, and he gave Marigold more than her share of grief when she informed him, some years back, that he might want to be commencing negotiations with Barry O'Malley.*

*Hannah and I hope to carry on with the stockhorse breeding program at Ironbark. We have Lynette and her offsider Bill here to guide us, and pretty soon—any day now, if Hannah's girth is any indication—we're hoping to have an enterprising, stubborn and determined kid of our own who we can pass all our chores to.*

*Wait, no, Hannah made me cross that last bit out.*

*We're hoping the newest member of the Krauss family will feel as much love for Ironbark Station as Bruno did, and as we do.*

*Dad, if you're lurking somewhere in the snow gums making sure I'm getting this speech right, I just want to say: I'm sorry it took us so long to sort ourselves out. I guess maybe some of that stubbornness you're famous for might run in my veins, too.*

*Mrs L, I can see you, and there's no need to nod in agreement with quite such enthusiasm.*

*Here's to you, Dad. And to your legacy, which I am proud to say encompasses not just fifty years of stockhorse breeding, but extends also to the custodianship of some of Hanrahan's fine old buildings, to a lifetime spent here in the Snowy Mountains among friends and family and, most importantly, to the next generation of the Krauss family.*

Eulogy reprinted with permission of the writer, Tom Krauss
The Hanrahan Chatter, April Edition
The *Snowy River Star*, p.16

# ACKNOWLEDGEMENTS

I spent a fabulous day at the Allora Campdraft in 2022, taking photos, inspecting the artwork, conducting 'research' at the coffee van (where I stood nervously in the queue with a *horse*), and generally soaking in the sights and sounds with the many families who were there spectating and encouraging friends and family in their rides. I also watched a stack of videos online where legends of the draft demonstrate skills for the benefit of newcomers to the sport. My friend Maryann helped me out with some questions I had; her cousin Julie from Boonah, a campdraft committee regular, was able to help me out as well.

I'd like to send a shout-out to Robyn and Helen, who I often run into at my local café. They always have a smile and a word of encouragement when they come across me lurking in the dark corner pecking away at my keyboard, and Robyn was the inspiration for the idea that knitting could be a random act of kindness. In her case it was a fluffy pink jacket for a baby who visits the same coffee shop, and in my case it was the idea that Marigold could see that Hannah needed some focus outside of work, and knitting possum pouches could be just the thing.

I downloaded a pattern from www.wires.org.au and began my own pouch which hopefully I will have finished and sent in before this book is released.

I'd like to thank the many women, young and old, who were happy to chat with me about their experiences with fertility. By the time I was 32, I had 4 children, so having an unresolved urge to be a mother was not my experience. But times have changed since my own slapdash approach to progeny. Careers, relationship mishaps, issues with endometriosis and familial breast cancer genes, two-mum and two-dad families, cost-of-living pressures, even enforced separations due to worldwide epidemics(!) are all part of the wider conversations taking place now about the how, and the when, and the why of parenthood. I was delighted to discover that there really is a book available with the title *Knock Yourself Up*.

My son, who is ex-Navy, reviewed the naval ocean chase scene for me (which was originally much longer in the first draft, when I thought I was embodying the spirit of Clive Cussler for a while there until my publisher questioned its relevance for a rural Aussie drama LOL) and deemed it not totally inconceivable.

I'm thankful as always to have had the support of the Harper-Collins Harlequin crew to see this manuscript from scribbled idea through to finished book: Rachael Donovan, my publisher, Julia Knapman and Kylie Mason for their editorial prowess, Annabel Adair for the final proofing, and Louisa Maggio, the cover fairy.

Finally, thank you to all the readers who got in contact with me after they read *The Vet from Snowy River* to ask why there was so much URST between Hannah and Tom, and when would Hannah's story be told. (I know I don't have to explain URST to you: Kylie the BFF did a much greater job of that within these pages.) I was able to pass many of these messages on to the publisher and now you hold the proof in your hands: readers have power in publishing. Without you, this book may not have been written.